THE
BURNING
ISLE

WILL PANZO

ACE
NEW YORK

ACE
Published by Berkley
An imprint of Penguin Random House LLC
375 Hudson Street, New York, New York 10014

Copyright © 2016 by Will Panzo

Library of Congress Cataloging-in-Publication Data

Names: Panzo, Will, author.
Title: The burning isle / Will Panzo.
Description: New York : Ace, 2016.
Identifiers: LCCN 2015049581 | ISBN 9781101988107 (paperback)
Subjects: LCSH: Magicians—Fiction. | Imaginary places—Fiction. | Imaginary wars and battles—Fiction. | BISAC: FICTION / Fantasy / Epic. | FICTION / Action & Adventure. | FICTION / Fantasy / General. | GSAFD: Fantasy fiction.
Classification: LCC PS3616.A395 B87 2016 | DDC 813/.6—dc23
LC record available at http://lccn.loc.gov/2015049581

First Edition: November 2016

Printed in the United States of America
1 3 5 7 9 10 8 6 4 2

Cover art © Alejandro Colucci
Book design by Tiffany Estreicher

To my mom.
For all the books she gave me.

THE
BURNING
ISLE

1

—◦◦◦—

"I don't want any trouble."

The barkeep had accepted the coin without thought, but he saw now its worth, saw too that it was caked in dried blood. He held it up in the dim light of the bar and squinted at it, then at the young man in the corner, as though appraising each by the other.

The young man suffered from the comparison. The coin was gold, and the embossed spear on its back marked it as the product of a mint in Curicum, a mining settlement on the mainland. A good, honest mint and known for making coins worth their weight. The barkeep had not seen one of their pieces in years, not a real one anyway.

The young man looked neither good nor honest. He did not weigh much, and his worth was suspect.

He sat with his back to the wall and his hands beneath the table. He was twenty or so, beardless and thin. The folds of his ash-gray cloak swallowed his small frame, a burial shroud draped over a skeleton. He had stooped shoulders and skin the color of whiskey, mud-brown eyes set deep in his head. His dark hair hung just past his ears. At a glance, he could pass for a girl.

"You think it's fake," the young man said.

The barkeep rubbed the coin between the pads of his thumb and forefinger. He chipped away the dried blood with his nail. He bit the coin, and his face grew slack, incredulous, as though he had tasted something unexpected.

"It's good all right. Better than any gold piece I've seen in a long while." The barkeep shuffled back to the table, walking with one hand on his lower back so that his belly seemed to lead him. He flipped the coin onto the table. It landed faceup, displaying the Antiochi eagle. "But I don't have change for it."

"I'll buy a meal, then. A meal for both of us. And drinks. What's left is yours to keep."

"You trying to make a friend, boy?" The barkeep was a heavy man, balding and with olive-hued skin. He had a fleshy face, not fat exactly, but full.

"Consider it a gift." The young man picked up the coin and again offered it to the barkeep. His hand was small and clean. It practically shone in the dim light of the bar. "No good deed goes unrewarded, right?"

"No good deed goes unpunished. That's the saying."

"You don't believe that." The young man held out the coin, insistent.

"We've got fish," the barkeep mumbled. He snatched the coin and tucked it into the pouch at his hip. "Bread from yesterday, too. It's probably stale."

"That'll do."

The barkeep fetched a bottle of wine and a pitcher of water. He set out earthenware plates and cups and retired to the kitchen.

The main room of the bar was lit by candles set at each table and by a tall candelabrum near the entrance. A stone hearth was set in one wall, warm embers smoldering where there used to be a fire. A narrow staircase led to the second floor. Past the bar, a door opened into a room that served as pantry and kitchen. The wall behind the young man bore a mural of a wolf cub suckling at the breast of a sleeping woman.

The barkeep returned from the kitchen with a platter of bread and steaming fish. They began to eat.

"My name is Cassius," the young man said.

The barkeep grunted, his face low over his plate, eyes down.

"I don't make a habit of eating with strangers." Cassius sipped from his cup and watched the barkeep as he ate.

"Is that your coy way of asking my name?" the barkeep snapped, without raising his head.

"I didn't think it was so coy."

"A word of advice, boy." The barkeep gripped his fork as though prepared to defend himself with it. "Around here, you mind your fucking business, and others will do the same. That may seem strange to a mainlander like you, but it's our way."

"Is that language necessary?"

The barkeep smiled. "My apologies."

"Why do you assume I'm from the mainland?"

"Your delicate fucking sensibilities for a start. And your carelessness. No one from this island would walk into a bar and throw gold around the way you did. Not if he wanted to live long."

"I can take care of myself," Cassius said.

The barkeep laughed and began to choke from laughing. He sipped his wine.

"I've seen a hundred like you, boy. I know how your story ends."

"Enlighten me."

"Here for a bit of adventure, aren't you? If you're lucky, this ends with you penniless, begging on the docks for passage off this stinking, rotting island. And if you're not lucky . . ." The barkeep waved his fork absently.

"I'm here to work," Cassius said.

"Here to work? Hands me a coin worth more than I make in a month, then tells me he's here to work. Ha! You are a strange one, boy."

"I'm serious."

"This island is five miles of slum dug into fifty miles of jungle. It's a refuge for people who can't live elsewhere in the Republic. Debtors and criminals and exiles. There's no work here. No work for you anyway."

"Why so eager to warn me off?" A wry smile played at the edges of Cassius's lips.

"What's your angle, boy?" The barkeep held his cup with both hands and stared over its rim. His eyes were small and gray. "Come in here, throw gold at me, then ask after work. I'd think you were a thief, but you're too goddamn soft. Are you a whore?"

Cassius glared at the barkeep. He set down his cup. The barkeep laughed.

"Is that it? I have no problem with your kind. It's not my way, but I know a good business opportunity when I see one. You can have the upstairs room for a cut of your take. We'll make a fortune."

Cassius lifted a pair of worn iron gauntlets from his lap and dropped them onto the table. The gauntlets were lined with supple leather and had thirty jewels dusted over each finger and the dorsum of each hand. The jewels were multicolored, big as pebbles, and when they caught the candlelight, they gleamed like sunrays on the edge of an eclipse.

"I've come for different work."

The barkeep sat back in his chair. He pulled himself up to his full height, as someone might who has come across a bear in the woods and wishes to appear formidable before the beast.

"So you're a killer?"

"That's an unfortunate term," Cassius said.

"Is it accurate?"

Cassius did not answer.

"At least tell me you're good," the barkeep said.

"Good enough to earn that coin in your purse."

The barkeep looked the young man over, then looked back to the gauntlets.

"My name is Lucian," he said, extending his hand.

The street was unpaved, the ground moist from an early-morning rain. Cassius's boots sank a half inch with each step, and below this loose mud, the earth was hard-packed and slick.

A sprawl of sagging houses loomed on either side of the street, squat shacks built of fleshy jungle wood. Roofs were a hodgepodge of thatch and tile and weaves of enormous leaves that dripped continuously. Everything wet and rotted. It seemed a stiff wind could flatten it all.

At each doorway they passed, Cassius caught sight of furtive eyes appraising him from the dark. He raised his hood, pulled his cloak tight to hide the gauntlets dangling from a thin chain hooked to his belt.

"We don't see many new faces in this part of town," Lucian said.

"Should I be worried?"

"In Scipio?" Lucian smiled. "Always."

Ahead in the road, two hogs had settled in the deep mud. They rolled and splashed one another, squealed at passersby and stray dogs.

"I'm a trueborn citizen of the Republic," Cassius said. "I won't be intimidated by savages."

"Don't call them savages."

"Why?"

"Because I don't like it." The barkeep spun on Cassius. "This is a province of Antioch. These people are citizens of the Republic, same as me or you. So you call them Natives or Scipians when you're around me. Or you learn their word and use that. All right?"

Cassius did not respond.

"All right?"

"What's their word?"

"The Natives call this place Kambuja or the Khimir Kingdom. They call themselves the Khimir." Lucian spat. "Why don't the young ever know their history?"

"Do you know every outland province and border town on the mainland?"

"I don't live on the mainland. I live here. And I respect my home enough to learn about it."

"I'm sure you'll be quite the teacher."

"Scipio has been part of the Republic for sixty years." Lucian stomped through a dirty puddle, splashing muck and rainwater with each heavy step. "Took the legion ten years to subdue the Natives here. When they finally got a proper city built, those tribes that escaped the early wars returned and burned it to ash. City has a history of that. Rising from ash."

"Are the Natives still a problem?"

"Those in the city are peaceful. Overindulged and complacent, like the rest of us good citizens. We haven't seen the jungle tribes in years. Town's mostly quiet now."

They rounded a corner and continued past the remnants of a burned hut, a charred husk supported by neighboring homes. In the entranceway sat a stiff body, its mouth a bleeding rictus stretched over a swollen tongue. Both its hands had been sawed off and the stumps cauterized. A block of wood hung draped from its neck and on the wood this warning: A THIEF'S DEATH.

"Is that written in blood?" Cassius asked.

"Mind your business."

"Quiet town, you say?"

They made their way down soot-stained alleys and cramped lanes, wading through refuse piles calf high, foul with the scent of piss and offal. Here and there, the barkeep called out the names of roadways or neighborhoods, but to Cassius, everything bled together into one unending slum.

They emerged onto a wide avenue that led to the Grand Market. Here the wild otherness of the native-built shacks and the crushing immensity of tenements gave way to a more structured plan. Common insulae, large buildings of apartment-style housing, familiar from any Antiochi city, fronted paved roads. Made of wood and mud-brick, with a few having poured-concrete facades, they rose four or five stories tall, regulation height for the Republic and much shorter than the rickety tenement buildings Cassius had seen earlier.

They were modest structures although some had flourishes. Arched entranceways, iron-gated gardens, covered terraces, murals of Antiochi gods in bright oils, whose painted eyes followed Cassius as he walked. Two-head Iaunus guarding doorways, the grandfather Taranus with his plow, beautiful Vinalia on her throne of roses.

The market square was a hundred yards across, paved with concrete, and littered with scores of merchant stalls and collapsible tents. Large storefronts bordered the periphery, bearing the names of famous mainland merchants or signs written in Native script. Some bore no signs at all, their goods known only to those who needed to know.

"Impressive, isn't it?" Lucian approached the fountain at the center of the square and seated himself on a low, stone bench. Stagnant rainwater filled the fountain, a drowned rat floating in the muck.

Smoke hung thick in the air, a pungent cloud gathered from ovens and hissing grilles and candles burned to deter mosquitoes.

"It's bigger than I expected." Cassius had seen markets before, bigger markets in cities so large that all of Scipio would fit in a single neighborhood. But the bustle of this market, the number of shops and traders, the sheer magnitude of wealth changing hands stood in contrast to the squalor he had witnessed earlier. "Who are these people?"

Hundreds milled about the square. Most were Antiochi, like Lucian. Short, swarthy people, with dark hair, the men garbed mostly in tunics, the women in dresses that had been fashionable in mainland cities years ago.

The native Khimir were generally taller and had broader faces and straight black hair, their skin the tan of aged paper. Most affected Antiochi dress, but some still wore traditional garb, bleached shirts and long shorts for men, bright, simple dresses for women.

Traders from distant lands were common as well, bronze-skinned Fathalan merchants, their ships laden with jewels and spices, ruddy Jutlund sellswords, with great red beards and bottomless appetites for drink and violence, pale Murondian reavers, with waxed mustaches who spoke of chivalry and fancied themselves noble corsairs in service to their kingdom instead of the common pirates they truly were.

"Smugglers mostly," Lucian said. "And not just small operators. The huge mainland crime syndicates trade here, the unions and collegia of the Republic, Fathalan flesh merchants, the junk fleets of the Silk Sea. Anyone and everyone in pursuit of dishonest coin."

"Why here?" Cassius wiped his damp brow with a damp hand.

"Scipio is close to the mainland, so it's convenient for trade. And the people in charge here welcome the business. There's no threat of getting caught or punished. You can sell illegal goods in the open. Hashish, opium, goods without tariffs, magical texts. It's all fair game."

"With that sort of money changing hands, why is Scipio such . . ."

"A goddamned pit?" Lucian offered. "These people don't leave their money here unless they lose it at dice. Or to wine or whores. They take their money home. And Scipio is home to none of them."

Two main avenues fed the marketplace, one from the north and one from the south. At the south avenue entrance rose an open-air temple to the Antiochi god of commerce Mirqurios, set on a low podium atop a flight of steps. As Cassius watched, priests in ceremonial togas of deep orange dragged an ox into the portico. Supported by four stone columns coated in stucco, the portico would have seemed natural in any Antiochi city but stood out here. The creature, already bleeding from a neck wound, staggered drunkenly and lowed and stomped and snorted at its tormentors to no avail.

In the west end of the square, a large statue of a nude Khimir woman loomed over the marketplace, most likely a representation of some Native goddess that early Antiochi settlers had tried to appropriate into their own pantheon. Behind this rose the council hall, atop which perched a massive, gold-plated eagle. Twoscore legionnaires stood watch at the base of its steps under the eagle's gaze, geared in crimson tunics, burnished-steel cuirasses, and wide-brimmed helmets.

"Is that where the legion is stationed?" Cassius nodded toward the hall.

"Their fort is a mile outside the city walls," Lucian said. "But they guard the hall still."

A squat figure emerged from the hall and began to bark orders. He was dressed in an ornamented steel muscle cuirass, with acid-etched scrollwork inlaid with gold. He wore a sword on each hip after the fashion of a centurion, each a short, stabbing gladius, although clearly this man was no common centurion. Two tall white eagle feathers decorated his wide-brimmed helmet.

"That's Vorenicus." Lucian produced a small pouch of powdered tobacco from his tunic pocket. He sprinkled some into the small divot between the base of his thumb and wrist and then snorted it. He coughed, wiped his eyes.

"The legion commander?"

"General Quintus's son, and his second-in-command. Good officer from what I hear. Fair with his men and the Natives. About as honest as they come in this damn place."

"Do his legions patrol the streets?"

"Did you run into a bit of trouble on the mainland?" Lucian smiled. "Is that what this is about?"

"What was it you said about people here not asking questions?"

Cassius stared at the council hall. His face was impassive, but it seemed to Lucian a kind of forced calm, like a gambler trying to hide a favorable position. His eyes though, deep-set and dark, belied something fierce, something the boy struggled but failed to contain.

"Unless you make a terror of yourself, the legion won't notice," Lucian said. "This town is a den of thieves. The legion's presence is a show of force, nothing more."

"What about the council?"

"They're puppets." Lucian waved a hand dismissively. "They hold no real power. The city is split in half. Metellus Cinna's gang runs Hightown, where my bar is. Gnaeus Piso runs Lowtown."

"A city with two bosses?"

"This town has one boss, boy. Him that lives in that jungle"—the barkeep hooked a finger north—"surrounded by his personal army. Piso and Cinna are powerful. But they both serve at the pleasure of General Quintus."

"These two bosses—Piso and Cinna—they're enemies, right?" Cassius looked off into the middle distance, his eyes unfocused.

"Why do you think that?"

"You said Quintus is the power here, yet he lives in the jungle. That far from the action, it only makes sense that he'd set up two bosses, have them both kick up a share of their earnings. They'd fight each other for position, and neither would grow strong enough to challenge him."

"You've got a devious mind," Lucian said.

"Am I right?"

"The bosses are enemies."

"Why?"

"That's old business."

"Maybe that could be an opportunity for work."

"You don't want to mix with them." Lucian stood. He looked around to see who was nearby, who might have overheard their talk.

He leaned in close to Cassius. "And, anyway, I told you we're here to meet a connection of mine. You two can head to Lowtown and arrange prizefights. It's not glamorous work, but it pays. There's no coliseum on this island. No spellcaster guilds and no schools of magic. A killer's options are limited."

"Why such strict rules about magic?"

"The bosses maintain a stranglehold on killers. They don't want independent operators on the island. Especially those who practice other than Antiochi magic. The Murondians and Fathalans are forbidden from building their churches here. Without churches, their magic users can't contact the beings beyond the veil from which they draw their powers. We had a Blood-magic cult a few years back, came up from the Southern Kingdoms, but the bosses rooted them out. Burned them alive and tossed their ashes in the sea for fear their corruption would spread throughout the island. Some Native tribes had shaman callers, but they were all killed in the early days of conquest. Killed or shipped off to Antioch City, so the runemasters could study their secrets."

"So only Antiochi magic is tolerated here?"

"And only if you work for one of the bosses. Remember that when you head to Lowtown, boy. Make your money, but do it quietly. Don't draw attention to yourself."

"You're not coming with us?" Cassius asked.

Lucian shook his head. "I'm not welcome in Lowtown."

"Why not?"

"Old business."

The bar smelled of smoke, and smoke hung thick in the air. Tobacco smoke, heavy and pungent. Awanu dream root, darker and redolent of fruit. Wisps of blue opium that streaked overhead like shot darts. Strong hashish that left Cassius's throat oily and raw.

"Have a drink," Sulla said. "It's not every day I offer to buy a round."

She was pale for an Antiochi, slender and tall, with chestnut hair. She had sharp eyes, light brown and locked in a permanent squint, and had also a pinched face, a receding chin. She seemed always to be tasting something unpleasant. Cassius put her age at twenty-five, but she wore her makeup thick, as was popular on the mainland, heavy powder for her cheeks and forehead, charcoal for her lashes, her lips covered with beeswax and flower extract the red of a fresh wound. In truth, she might have been much older or much younger.

"You don't have to buy me a drink," Cassius said. His eyes had started to water from the smoke. He wiped them and scanned the room.

All the windows were shuttered, and on the far side of the bar, a door opened into a long hall, where Cassius glimpsed scores of men huddled over gaming tables.

The front room itself was small, with a dozen customers sitting alone, drinking watered wine or mugs of beer, a few with bowls of vegetable porridge or stew set before them. Hard men. Old beyond their years and worn, some with ruined limbs, mangled arms, or stumps for legs. They might have been laborers' injuries, suffered in a quarry pit or timber yard. But Cassius knew at first glance not a man of them had ever worked an honest day. The other wounds told that story. The missing eyes and missing fingers, the shorn ears, the brands on their faces and foreheads that read the same judgments in a dozen languages: cutpurse, horse thief, rapist, murderer. He fixed his cloak so that it hid his hands and dropped his hands to hover near his gauntlets.

"You don't want a drink?" Sulla asked.

"I can buy my own," Cassius said.

"A man who asks nothing of others, is that it?" She smiled. "A man who settles his own scores?"

"Something like that."

"You've never had a girl offer to buy you a drink before, have you?"

It was true. He hadn't. And although there might have been circumstances where Sulla's question could be read as flirtatious challenge, it was clear, even to someone of his inexperience, that this was not one of those times. She was not being playful. She was appraising him, sizing him up. And after only a few minutes of conversation, and one offered drink, she had read him expertly.

He flushed, despite himself. Thankful, at least, that no one would notice in the darkened bar.

"I'll have tea with whiskey," Cassius said.

"How cosmopolitan." Sulla slapped the bar top, called for the tender.

"What's yours?" the barkeep asked. He was a young man, broad-shouldered, with heavy brows and jet-black hair slicked with lard.

"Salvē, brother." Sulla reached inside the sleeve of her slate-colored dress and produced a few coins, more than enough for two drinks. She palmed them into the bartender's grip, the gesture swift, discreet. She leaned in close. "Who's handling the fights today?"

"Master Dio."

"Any decent action?"

"Slow day," the barkeep said. "Junius showed up. Everyone is too scared to fight him. The oddsmakers are furious. But he won't leave till he gets his match."

Sulla released the barkeep. When he returned with their drinks, she nodded her thanks and offered Cassius his mug.

"Are you a half-breed?" she asked offhandedly.

"What?" Cassius seemed taken aback by the bluntness of her words, offended that she would make such an assertion so directly.

"Don't be sensitive," Sulla said. "Only mainlanders care about that sort of thing. Everyone's a mongrel out here. You just don't look full Antiochi. Your skin tone is a bit strange. And there's something about your face I can't place. Are you part Fathalan?"

"No," Cassius said flatly, not rising to her taunt as he had the first time.

"Don't get offended. I'm an eighth Murondian on my mother's side if that makes you feel better."

"It doesn't."

In the long hall, the men at the tables gamed by torchlight. They shot dice and rolled knucklebones and flipped coins and at one table, two men moved pieces around a semmet board brought up from the rich deltas of Awanu, the Sun Empire, whose kings were gods and monsters both, with the bodies of men and the heads of animals.

"How long have you known Lucian?" she asked.

"A day. And you?"

"Longer than that."

"Was he right to send me to you?"

"Better me than one of the bosses," Sulla said. "See, I work for myself. I'm an independent. That's rare in this city. But I make it worthwhile for everyone to let me operate on my own."

"Doing what?" Cassius glanced at each table as they moved toward the back of the room. Huge piles of coins and banknotes sat stacked before the players, sums that could ransom kings.

"I'm the best fence on this island. Ask anyone, and they'll tell you Sulla can sell water to a well. I don't like killers, though." Sulla sneered. "Arrogant bastards."

"I'm just here for the work, same as you."

"There's a ring for sparring outside. I'll introduce you to the gaming master."

They passed through a doorway hung with a gossamer weave, into a quiet back room peopled with men in conversation over drinks. Here, away from the raucous noise of the gaming tables, deals were being made, conspiracies plotted. With whispers so soft they might go unnoticed in church, men arranged heists, masterminded kidnappings, said words that would set in motion events to end another's life, irrevocable proclamations. They might have been Blood-magic cultists uttering death curses instead of the common criminals they truly were.

"I was thinking about doing other things," Cassius said.

"There's not much honest work for killers here. Maybe you could be a bodyguard. But you'd have to be good. And my commission changes if you land a contract with the bosses."

"Your commission?" Cassius stopped.

Sulla drained the rest of her mug and set it on a nearby table. "Standard ten percent."

"Five." Cassius placed his cup on a windowsill. "Plus a guarantee that I'll fence any unwanted spells I earn in the ring through you, subject to your standard commission."

"Never had a girl buy you a drink," she said, "but something tells me this isn't your first negotiation."

"I'm good at what I do, too."

She stood silent. He could feel her studying him.

He had seen a bull-baiting once, in a small town near the Muron-dian border, the bull set upon by six Rhuiss war hounds, the most vicious dogs in creation. It was an unpleasant show, but he had forced himself to watch. There were lessons to be learned from it, certain truths regarding the struggle of one against many that could not be gleaned from tactical texts, truths that could only be explicated in blood.

An unpleasant show but still he remembered it, could recall viv-idly the look of the hounds as they made their approaches, searching for a weakness in the bull. It was the same look he saw now on Sulla's face.

"Deal." Sulla forced a smile, then lifted Cassius's cup from the windowsill and glanced inside. "You know, it's bad luck not to finish a drink bought for you."

"Bad luck for me or bad luck for you?"

"Maybe both." She offered him the cup. "So finish, damn it."

A mudbrick wall, crumbling and covered in charcoal graffiti, en-circled the courtyard. The yard itself was roughly a hundred feet across, an arid slab of hard-packed earth barren except for patches of scrub grass, streaked with dried blood and black grime. The lifelessness of the place struck Cassius as odd.

The rest of the island had seemed wet and alive to him, aggressively fertile. Even where the city sought to tame the land, he witnessed the endurance of the jungle. Stunted banana trees grew amidst refuse heaps. Strangling vines scaled the walls of tenements. Snakes and small lizards stalked the corners of the Market. But here, that same resilient life had been extinguished, snuffed by fire and magic.

Two men stood on opposite sides of the clearing, both Antiochi, one dressed in a blue tunic, the other in purple. A pair of jeweled gauntlets hung from each man's hip. A crowd of fifty men gathered behind them, near the crumbling wall. They smoked and shouted, eager for a show. It was early afternoon, but all were drinking, some even drunk. Four oddsmakers serviced those who wanted action, arguing gaming spreads and exchanging clay tokens for coins. A greasy fat man in a black tunic moved through their ranks. He held a small writing slate and a nub of chalk, and with these, he noted the bets placed within the crowd so he could collect the house's take.

Coins from every corner of the known world changed hands. Coppers that bore images of hooded cobras, pillaged from eastern temples perched atop mountain ranges so large and so ancient, they formed the backbone of the world itself. Lion-headed silvers from Murondia, whose armorers knew secrets of fire and metal handed down from the age of heroes. And everywhere, on coins of all weights and worths, from rude half-coppers to newly minted gold pieces, shone the Antiochi eagle.

As Cassius watched, a man in the crowd fainted, either from excess drink or heat. Fellow revelers dragged him to the shade of the bar before unburdening him of purse and blade and rings and sandals and anything else of worth. A bearded man staggered up to the prone figure, lifted his tunic, and prepared to relieve himself on the unconscious man, to the cheers of those nearby.

Cassius looked away. Sulla fixed him with her gaze.

"We don't have to do this," she said. "I can take you back to Lucian."

The savagery of the island was no surprise to Cassius. He had prepared himself for that as best a man could, knowing he was journeying to a place that no longer abided the rule of law. Nor was he a stranger to violence or cruelty or vice. He had traveled much in his short life. Had learned the art of Antiochi spellcasting at the knees of brutal men on the Island of the Twelve.

But still something here unsettled him. Something he had not prepared himself for, could not prepare himself for, because it was alien to him even now, a thing he could not name. For the first time since arriving on the island, he wondered if he was equal to the task at hand, if he could do what needed to be done here.

"Just get me in the ring," he whispered. There, at least, he would feel at home. There he could master his doubts and his fears, bend them to his will. There, amidst the blood and fire, he always felt in control.

"That's Junius in blue," Sulla said. "One of Piso's lieutenants. A first-rate killer. The barkeep said he's been looking for a match all day, but no one wants to face him."

"Why not?"

"Afraid he'd paint the courtyard with their brains is my guess."

"Seems they found someone to accommodate him."

"Not sure who that is in purple. But I can tell you he doesn't have a chance against Junius. I'm going to get some action. This is guaranteed money."

Sulla elbowed her way into the crowd, calling to see which chiseling bastard had the best odds.

Cassius eased back against the outside wall of the gambling den. The fat man announced the last round of bets, and the crowd fell silent just as Sulla emerged from the press.

"Guaranteed money." She was grinning.

The fat man lifted a hand, and at his signal, each fighter unhitched his gauntlets and donned them. Cassius felt a tug in his chest, a sign the men were drawing on the energy used to power their spells. It was part of his gift, shared by all spellcasters who practiced Antiochi magic, or Rune magic, as other practitioners referred to it.

"Junius," the fat man yelled, and pointed to the fighter in blue, his other hand still held aloft. A smattering of applause rose from the crowd.

"Appius," the fat man yelled, and pointed to the fighter in purple. Mumbles, then silence.

The fat man held his hands high for a count of five, then let fall his hands, and both men leapt forward. The fighters circled. Junius, the spellcaster in blue, thrust his gauntleted hand before him, and a cloud of smoke blossomed in the center of the ring. The courtyard filled with the smell of hot sand, and as the smoke cleared, the shape of a massive lion limned in the haze.

The crowd sighed.

The lion tossed its thick black mane. It scanned the lot, then, as if seized by an outside force, its muscles grew taut. It roared at Appius and leapt forward.

Appius waved his hand, as though shooing a fly. A streak of silver dust floated into the center of the lot and hung, sparkling with reflected sunlight. The lion crossed through the cloud and slowed.

Cassius closed his eyes.

He did not see the blinding flash, but he felt the series of staccato explosions that followed. The smell of burned hair singed his nostrils. When he opened his eyes, he saw the lion collapsed on its side, convulsing, its mane streaked with blood and flecks of gore.

"Son of a bitch." Sulla was bent at the waist, hands cupped over her eyes.

"A rare spell." Cassius leaned forward, tensed, as though prepared to leap into the fray himself.

"You could have warned me." She wiped tears from her face.

"Your man in blue saw it coming. Must be well-read in spellcraft." Cassius pointed. "Look. He's regrouping already."

Junius raised his hands, palms up like a penitent invoking some wrathful god. The air grew heavy, and a smell like manure drifted over the courtyard. A jet of liquid fire streaked down from the sky and enveloped Appius.

The crowd gasped.

"He's going to kill him," Sulla said.

The flame vanished to reveal Appius kneeling in the ring, unburned.

"Fire ward," Cassius said.

A smattering of applause carried through the crowd, a few boos. Appius staggered to his feet.

Cassius felt a stirring in his chest, stronger this time. Junius pointed his fist, and a flash of lightning lit the sky. Cassius averted his gaze as screams erupted from the crowd. The report of thunder struck with physical force, like a punch to the chest. When Cassius opened his eyes, he saw Appius still kneeling.

"Yield," Appius shouted.

Junius continued to advance.

"I yield! I yield!"

Junius raised his hands.

Cassius started to scream for the man to defend himself, but another flash of lightning tore overhead, and his words were lost beneath a thunderclap. When his vision cleared, he saw the corpse lying facedown, wisps of smoke rising from its charred short cloak.

"Match." The bald man waved his hands above his head. "Your winner, Junius!"

Sulla led Cassius through the crowd and collected her winnings from a crook-backed oddsmaker. The gambling men eyed Cassius as he passed. He knew they thought him an easy mark. He was young, still a boy to them. Thin, almost frail. His face smooth and soft. No scars or burns to speak his struggles for him, at least none they could see. The world's meanness not yet writ in deep lines on his skin. But when he let his cloak hang open to reveal his gauntlets, every man gave him a wide berth.

Sulla approached the fat man who had served as fight master.

"Salvē, Master Dio," she said.

"Salvē," Dio said. It was clear he recognized Sulla but did not know her name.

"This is my associate Cassius. He's a spellcaster."

"Is that so?" The fat man wiped the sweat from his neck with the back of his hand. He marked his writing slate.

"He's interested in prizefights."

"A dangerous pursuit," Dio said, without lifting his gaze.

Cassius started to speak, but Sulla silenced him with a hand on his shoulder.

"Any chance you could add his name to the fight rosters this evening?" Sulla asked.

"Absolutely not." Dio shook his head. "Every fool who can steal five jewels and a pair of gauntlets fancies himself a killer. But that doesn't make it so. I'll need to see him in a test of skill first. How else can we calculate odds?"

"I can fight now if you'd like," Cassius said.

"Fight who? Junius?" Dio snorted. "I've no time to dispose of two corpses today, boy. Come back at the end of the week. I've got a kid from Trajean you can spar with."

"Thank you, Dio." Sulla headed for the hall.

Cassius did not follow, intent on pressing the point with Dio, but Sulla shot him a grim look, and he fell in behind her.

"Is that the best you can do?" he asked.

"Don't be so impatient," she said. "You don't want to anger these people."

"What about selling water to a well?"

"I'm not here to sell you. I'm here to make an introduction."

Cassius glanced over his shoulder and saw Junius standing with his second, a thick young man with a head covered in black stubble. In the center of the lot lay the lion, twitching in the sun.

Cassius turned and headed toward the beast.

"Where are you going?" Sulla called.

"To make my own introduction."

He stared down at the lion, its face hidden under a mane soaked with blood black as pitch. It was breathing wet and loud, and its tail writhed in the dust, jerking like the body of a snake with a pinned head.

"Step away from that," Junius's second called to Cassius from across the ring.

"Aren't you going to put it down?" Cassius said. "It's cruel to leave it this way."

"Only fighters are allowed here," Junius said, his voice low but full of menace. He stepped in front of his second. "Leave before you get hurt."

"By it or by you?" Cassius asked.

No one spoke.

Cassius lifted the edge of his cloak, and at the sight of his gauntlets, a tense murmur spread through the crowd. Behind him, he heard Sulla curse.

He unhooked the gauntlets attached to his belt and slipped them on slowly, deliberately. A rush of hot pinpricks warmed his arms. He kneeled by the lion's side and placed a hand on its chest. Through his gauntlets, he could feel the beat of a massive heart.

His eyes were open but unfocused, and he pictured a colorless canvas on which were drawn eight shining lines, intersecting at precise angles. Rune magic was unique among the arcane arts. Whereas other cultures had rich magical traditions that involved complex sorceries and rituals, sacrifices and incantations, Antiochi magic eschewed such ceremony. Antiochi magic was stolen magic. Its highest practitioners learned to disassemble other magics, distill them to their simplest forms, then encode these secrets into runes. A select few, gifted at birth with the ability to channel mystical energies, could then be taught to power these runes and reproduce these spells.

The resulting imitations were generally weaker than the original spells. But what Antiochi mages lacked in raw power and arcane knowledge, they made up for in speed and adaptability. What had once been a complicated sorcery known to Kell Shaman of the Stormcaller Clan, a spell produced by lengthy incantation in the ancient tongue of the Primal Ones, was now reduced to eight imaginary lines in Cassius's head.

As he completed the rune, his palms grew hot.

He did not see the spark jump from his hand. There was no flash, only a sound like a twig snapping. The lion's body jerked, stiffened, then fell still. The beat of the heart under his hand grew faint; and then he could no longer feel a beat.

He stood and dusted his hands.

"Standing there with gauntlets on," Junius said. "Are you threatening me?"

"Fighting amateurs is beneath me." Cassius waved his hand dismissively.

Junius stared silently, stunned by the boldness of this boy. The courtyard was quiet.

And then an oddsmaker called out for bets on Junius.

Cassius glanced over his shoulder and saw that Sulla stood by herself, between the crowd and the clearing. Almost imperceptibly, she shook her head, a warning, quick and discreet, like her palming of the coins at the bar.

"Whose man are you?" Junius called. "What business do you have in my master's house?"

"I came to see a fight, nothing—"

Cassius felt a faint tug in his chest. The air rippled and a wave of heat sped outward from the center of the lot. A whip of liquid fire, wire thin, arced toward him.

Cassius's palms tingled. He drew with his mind's eye a simple shape, a figure comprised of three lines, all of equal length. The glowing whip lashed downward, and when it reached his body, it broke on his shoulder. He felt no heat, and his wrap did not ignite. There was only a faint hiss, then the wire snapped as it touched Cassius's invisible fire ward. Where it fell, the scrub grass ignited in a strip of white flame.

Cassius circled to Junius's flank. He pointed to a spot between himself and Junius, the pointing to help direct his spell. Out of the ground rose a mound of clay that quickly took the shape of two slavering hyenas.

With his mind linked to the summoned beasts, Cassius felt a sudden gnawing hunger in his belly. He smelled the rich lion blood, and his heartbeat quickened. He breathed deep and cleared his thoughts. He focused on his anger, on a wordless urge for violence, then he focused on Junius. The hyenas sat stunned, ears folded down. Then, as one, they tensed. They dipped their noses and slunk across the ring, fanning as they moved.

Junius raised his hands, fingers splayed. A coil of green light spiraled up from the ground, and when it faded, a giant snake lay in the ring. It was fifteen feet long, with a wide, stiff hood and a blunt muzzle. It curled its body into two loose coils and then reared, hissing. It darted for the lead hyena but missed, its jaws snapping air.

In a flash, the snake twisted back on itself, seized the second hyena by its neck, and shook. Something inside the hyena broke with a wet crunch.

Just then, a large rock appeared overhead, trailing smoke and fire as it sailed toward Cassius.

He watched its approach, measuring speed and trajectory. He closed his eyes, and when he opened them again, a cube of translucent green gel hung before him. Staring through it, he saw the fireball grow larger as it neared.

When the fireball struck the cube, a hiss of steam wafted through the air. The fireball slowed as it sank into the gel, then it stopped completely, hanging motionless in midair, wrapped in a skin of sputtering green ooze.

Junius advanced through the center of the ring, where his snake had subdued both hyenas. Leaning down, he touched a fingertip to one, then the other of the prone beasts. Their bodies swelled and burst, and a swarm of spiders, each the size of a fist, spilled forth on a tide of blood.

The spiders spotted Cassius and scampered toward him, their fangs dripping with yellow venom that smoked as it hit the ground. He retreated, raising a wall of ice that grew six feet tall and four feet wide. The air cooled. Fog rose from the earth, settled ankle-high.

The spiders moved to circle the wall. Behind them, Junius approached the floating green blob that had been his fireball, and as he passed the fireball exploded, liquid flames washing over the ring. The blast bowed his body, and he hit the ground facedown.

No one heard him collapse. The sound of rushing flames drowned out the impact. Some of the crowd had recoiled from the blast of heat or the sudden burst of light. They opened their eyes to see Junius struck down, but the act of it had happened too fast for them to process.

"A reversal," someone called.

"Killed him with his own damn fireball."

The crowd fell silent, awestruck. Who among them had ever seen such a finish? Who would believe them when told that they had seen one today? This wasn't a duel of champions fought in the grand coliseum of Antioch City. This was a prizefight outside a gaming house.

Yet they had just witnessed a reversal worthy of a master spellcaster, there was no denying that. The proof of it lay smoldering in the ring.

Small fires blazed along the ground. Flames licked at the ice wall and at the side of the gambling hall. The spiders hissed and steamed as they burned.

Cassius stepped carefully through the clearing, bits of flaming rock crunching underfoot. The body lay on its stomach, its hair afire. He rolled it with his foot and reached for the gauntlets.

"I'll not let you take those." Junius's second stood just outside the ring, his hands balled into fists. He had seemed a man before, but at this distance, Cassius could see he was maybe seventeen. He was sobbing and trying to contain the sobs.

"Will you stop me?" Cassius asked.

"I'll kill you," the boy said.

"You'll have to."

The boy looked to the body, then to Cassius.

"He was my brother." The boy's voice broke. He tore at his tunic in rage. "Murderer." His hands dipped toward his belt, where his gauntlets hung.

"Go on," Cassius shouted. He turned to face the boy, stared him down, his large eyes manic and wrathful.

The boy checked himself.

"Go on." Cassius pointed at the boy. "Reach. I'll bury you together. You'll be reunited beyond the veil."

The boy's hand trembled and dipped lower. And then, in one swift move, he unbuckled his belt and let the belt and the gauntlets fall. He sighed, as though relieved of a heavy burden.

Cassius looked down at the discarded gauntlets and then up into the pained face of the boy.

"You did nothing wrong here." Cassius spoke softly. The boy was close enough to hear, but the crowd, driven back from the clearing by the explosion, was too far away to discern his words.

"What?" The boy looked like he might retch.

"Remember that. None of this was your fault. It was out of your hands today. Out of your hands from the start."

A tremor passed over the boy. His eyes rolled up into his head; and then he fainted.

Cassius crossed the courtyard and kneeled over him. He heard frantic whispers in the crowd. Probably they thought he was going to murder the defenseless boy, but if they were outraged, none raised a hand to stop him. They had come for a fight but had lucked into a bloodbath. And now they waited, almost panting, for this inevitable conclusion.

Cassius checked the boy's airway to see that he was breathing, then fixed him so that he lay comfortably, arms at his sides, head straight.

Just a boy, he thought, and as the guilt rose in him, he shook his head and pushed those thoughts aside. He was not done here.

"Any man who touches this boy's purse will answer to me," he shouted to the crowd.

Probably they would pick the boy clean anyway.

Standing, he collected the boy's gauntlets. He was doing the boy a favor in some small way, he thought. No one who wore the gauntlets met a good end.

He returned to the corpse and bent to take hold of its gauntlets and stepped on the corpse's chest and pulled, and the corpse made to sit up and he stomped it down and the gauntlets slipped free. Skin and burned flesh sloughed off.

He tucked away the gauntlets inside his cloak and turned to scan the crowd. He saw no sign of Sulla, and the faces that stared back at him were mostly gape-mouthed, but some were smiling, some even laughing.

He closed his eyes, and his shadow reached up from the ground to embrace him. When it sank back to the floor, he was gone.

It was dark when Cassius returned to the bar. The sun had set hours before, and it was too late even for drinking. He tested the door and found it unlocked. The front room was dark but for a table where the barkeep lay with his head on his arm, next to a small candle.

As Cassius made his way to the steps, the barkeep snapped awake.

"Who's that?" he called.

"It's me," Cassius said.

"Who?" The barkeep reached into the dark for something Cassius could not see, a table knife, probably.

"Cassius."

"Yes, Cassius." The barkeep snorted and coughed. His hand returned from the dark. "I remember."

"Do you?"

"What?" The barkeep's eyes began to clear. He squinted into the gloom.

"Nothing."

"You should announce yourself at this hour, boy. I keep a crossbow under the bar. Next time I hear a noise in the dark, I'm shooting at it."

"Is your aim any good?"

"I can shoot the balls off a bedbug." The barkeep reached for a nearby cup. He drank and grimaced. "How did the fights go?"

Cassius shrugged. "I'm still here."

"A good finish, then."

Cassius considered the fight and its finish. He thought about the boy. "I suppose," he said.

"You'll have to forgive my slovenly appearance." The barkeep's face in the candlelight shone with a film of sweat. "Been a while since I had a boarder. I'll keep my drinking to my room in the future."

"No need to inconvenience yourself over me."

"Leaving then?"

"No, I think I'll be staying, actually."

The barkeep nodded, resigned. "There's money to be made here, for those who can survive."

"What makes you think I'm only here for money?"

"Why else come to Scipio?" the barkeep said.

"Tellium had a saying."

"Who's Tellium?"

"You scolded me for not knowing my history," Cassius said, "and yet you don't know the great champions of Antioch. Tellium is second only to Attus in the heroic cycle."

"A bunch of stinking horseshit, the lot of it." The barkeep belched.

"Heroes and monsters and maidens in distress. I've been alive a long time, and I've never known a hero. Or a maiden, come to think of it. Where have they all gone?"

"Do you want to hear the saying or not?" Cassius asked.

"What is the saying?"

Cassius lowered his head, and shadows covered his eyes. He began to recite.

"A man has only three reasons for being anywhere: to right a wrong, to earn a coin, or because he got lost."

"I don't believe that," the barkeep said.

"You don't?" Cassius smiled, amused by Lucian's naked obtuseness. His teeth shone with reflected candlelight.

"I don't know. I've never thought about it." The barkeep rubbed his eyes and looked at Cassius as though seeing him for the first time. "You aren't lost, are you?"

It did not sound like a question to Cassius, and he did not answer but climbed the stairs to his room instead.

Cassius woke in the dark, his body slick with sweat. The fear of the dream still lingered. He recalled running without direction while the thing that gave chase gained on him. He might have been moving through a forest or through the streets of a city. He dared not turn to glimpse the monster behind him.

He sat up in bed, his face aching from the pressure behind his eyes. The room was hot, the air heavy with a moist, oppressive heat.

Thoughts of the dream faded quickly, replaced by an image of Junius's burned corpse, the raging tears of the boy. Cassius's hands trembled. He tried to ignore the trembling, but ignoring it was a kind of acknowledgment.

He rose from bed and felt his way to the window set in the far wall. He opened the shutters and leaned out. A waning smoke-white moon hung in the sky, and the city visible under its glow was mostly shadow, with here and there a section lit by pitch-fueled streetlamps. Beyond the roofline, the dark shape of the jungle grew steadily in all directions.

The air outside was charged with a rich, wet smell that hinted at the fecund jungle life beyond the city, an earth matted with things overripe and rotted, where nothing stayed buried.

He crossed the room to his bed and picked up his gauntlets and donned them, and, finally, the trembling stopped. He held up a cupped hand and pictured the rune for the Ghostfire spell. A small flame appeared in midair, as if balanced on his fingertips. The flame was cornflower blue and smokeless.

He thought about leaving this place. He thought about the distance he had traveled to be here and about the time it would take to return home; and then he realized he had no place from which to return.

He thought about the barkeep. He thought about sleep and about the nightmare. And when he pushed aside these thoughts, there was still the matter of the trembling hands and returning to somewhere. After a while, he decided to burn down the house.

It seemed the only choice. Burn the house, flee the island, and leave the nightmare behind. He was not safe here. He knew that now. For a while, he had thought the island would be a refuge. It accepted all those who washed up on its shores. But he was different. He was bringing fire and death with him.

The island knew this. It wanted him gone, and the nightmare had been its warning.

He gathered his large rucksack and turned to face the bed. He tilted his hand, and the blue flame slid toward the edge of his palm like mercury. Suddenly, he noticed a glint of light in his periphery.

He carried the flame to the edge of the nightstand, and there he saw a spider's web stretched from the lip of the table to the wall, a spider the size of a grape perched in the upper corner.

The sight of the spider stunned him. There was a time he had been a spider. He was Cassius now, but he had not been Cassius for long. Spider. The name made his back ache. The scars there were healed, the ruined flesh nearly insensate, but the sight of the spider made them throb with fresh pain.

As a boy, he had nearly died. To survive, he had pretended to be a spider and had lived as a spider for years, until the day he decided to become a man.

Or maybe that was all wrong. Maybe he had never been a man pretending to be a spider. Maybe he had always just been a bug dreaming himself a man.

Then, in the dark, a memory came to him. A vision from years ago. Before spiders and before the scars and before even the dream. A place where he had been safe. Safe in the dark.

He extinguished the Ghostfire. He removed his gauntlets, and his hands began to tremble again. He moved to the end of the bed and lifted it by the wooden frame and dragged it to the middle of the room. With the bed clear, he returned to the corner and felt along the floor. He searched with shaking hands until his fingertips brushed against a hole the size of an acorn. He worked his finger into the hole and pulled. Something gave, and he peeled back a section of loose floorboards.

The hole in the floor was small. When he crawled inside, there was room enough for him to lie with his knees to his chest. He pulled the removable segment of floor into place above him.

Safe in the dark, he began to recite the first verse of the Attus epic.

He breathed the air from under the floor, and his hands were still again.

KNOW YOURSELF,
KNOW VICTORY

—◦◦◦—

On the Isle of Twelve, they called him Spider. He was one of four initiates in his class, one of eight classes on the Isle, and when the Masters of the Isle had need to distinguish one boy from another, a rare event, they referred to each as a creature. He was Spider, a young man of twenty-two.

The Masters gave many reasons for his name, but the Masters were unrivaled in mystery, as they were in cruelty, and he never believed their answers. They told him he had a methodical disposition on the battlefield. That he waited with unrelenting patience for his opponents to commit mistakes, spinning webs to trap them at every turn. That when he struck, he struck without mercy.

They said these words through smug half smiles, as the twelve-headed lashes with which they taught discipline dangled from their hips. He knew the truth, though.

They called him Spider because his name mattered nothing to them.

He had trained for eight years on the Isle, long enough to be considered a peer, to have left behind his initiate robes, his shaved pate, the sting of the lash. If he survived eight more years in service, he would become a master in his own right, and he would teach boys like himself, teach them humility at first, then discipline, teach them runes and the eight laws of victory, teach them to endure pain and to dispense it.

Every day spent on the Isle, he had studied these lessons. But it was only on his last day that he truly learned the first law.

He had met the red-haired man at the foot of the mountain that day. The red-haired man had ridden his spotted charger off the beach, riding through surf and spray to the appointed place at the bottom of the four thousand steps that led to the Temple of War. It was Spider's job to escort this man but also Spider's job to appraise him. The red-haired man was here to make a purchase, after all, and only those deemed worthy would be allowed to bid. In the eyes of the Masters, gold made any man worthy, and the red-haired man had such in plenty.

"What is your name, boy?" The red-haired man had offered his hand in greeting, and Spider saw his large fingers covered in jeweled rings. He smiled, and Spider saw his every tooth capped with gold. Gold rings bound up his great red mane, and heavy bands of gold circled each of his upper arms. Gold rings hung from his nose and from each ear, and the bit of his horse was gold and gold his spurs as well.

"I am Spider," he replied. "A former initiate."

"A former initiate but now a true weapon of the Twelve." The red-haired man was huge, near to six and a half feet tall, and his hand swallowed Spider's completely when they shook.

"A weapon of the Masters and of any they deem worthy."

"I have heard of you, boy." The red-haired man stared down at Spider with eyes wide and unblinking.

Spider held his gaze for a time. As an initiate, he was forbidden to raise his eyes to a Master, an act punishable by five lashes, but he was no longer an initiate. He looked in the eyes of whomever he pleased now and in so doing had learned a strange truth. People hid their weakness in their eyes, plain enough for any man to see if he knew how to look. After eight years on the Isle, Spider knew how to look.

But the eyes of the red-haired man showed no weakness. They were the color of flint chips, as hard and as sharp. They met Spider's stare openly, and a cold chill swept Spider's body. He began to sweat, then he looked away.

"Are you all right, boy?"

"A queer sensation has come over me." Spider suppressed a gag. He wiped at his damp brow and fixed his robes and straightened himself. "It seems you have me at a disadvantage. How have you heard of me?"

THE BURNING ISLE   31

"The Masters speak highly of you. I wonder if you'll live up to their praise."

Pleasing the Masters sometimes spared an initiate from a beating, but rarely did it lead to praise. Spider was a peer now, though. His circumstance had changed. The Masters had a vested interest in praising him. As a peer, he would be contracted out to the highest bidders, to serve them in council and in war, to enhance their prestige and to cow their enemies. Buyers would pay the price of an entire mercenary company for his services alone. And it would be money well spent, for no spellcasters could rival those trained on the Isle of Twelve.

"There will be a demonstration of our skills tonight," Spider said. "You can judge my worth then."

After the mock battle and the sparring, after each peer had given a long discourse on military tactics and lectured on the use of spellcasters in historic campaigns, after demonstrations of their skill in language and their knowledge of the current political landscape, the peers commenced a grand feast. Thirty guests attended, men from every corner of the known world. The lords of Antiochi mercenary companies, Fathalan satraps, warlords from the foreboding Hulun Steppe, Sharrupuran magi, breathstealers from the witchlands in the dark heart of the Southern Kingdoms. There were others in attendance as well, men who served blasphemous gods, conspirators who sought to place deposed kings on contested thrones, researchers who toiled away at arcane studies long since outlawed in civilized lands.

After the feast, when the other guests had excused themselves and returned to their quarters to discuss what they had seen and to debate the prices of the contracts on offer from the Masters, the red-haired man alone remained at his table. He sat, eating hunks of seal meat with his bare hands and drinking honeyed wine from an ox horn, all the while calling for more music and more dancing from the women in veils and more opium for his ebon pipe. He called for more of everything, throwing back his head and laughing openmouthed, his maw so wide and dark it seemed capable of swallowing the known world.

The Masters, in their wisdom, denied him nothing. His personal revelry continued for hours and at the end, when he had exhausted the larder and the last of the dancers had collapsed from exhaustion, finally, he called for Spider.

The boy sat across from him at a table where only a single candle remained lit.

"Are you tired, boy?" the red-haired man asked.

"The hour is late," Spider said, eyeing the man curiously. He had seen Northmen in his travels, red-haired savages who drank from horns, as this man did. But this was no Northman. He seemed unlike any man Spider had ever met, with a strange accent and honey-colored skin that could be a mix of any race of men or of no known race at all. Staring at him over the smoking light of the candle, Spider wondered if he were not a demon from beyond the veil, some trickster djinn from a fabled kingdom of fire and air.

"I did not ask the time. I asked if you were tired. Are you?"

"A bit," Spider said.

"I never tire." The red-haired man smiled over the rim of his horn. "I never sleep. Do you believe me?"

"I have no reason not to believe you."

"Answer me true."

"You are a guest in the house of my Masters," Spider said. He lifted his eyes, tried to match the red-haired man's gaze once again, but in the near dark, the man's eyes seemed almost to glow, and Spider looked away. "I don't wish to give offense."

"Your pleasantries offend me," the red-haired man said pointedly.

Spider hated pleasantries, too. It was one of many things on the Isle he had learned to tolerate and obey without fully accepting. All that stooping and scraping and kneeling. It turned his stomach. Had the red-haired man noticed this while observing Spider tonight? Or did he have some special insight?

"I can leave if you wish," Spider said.

"Then I would have no one to talk with." When the red-haired man spoke, he seemed to address his words not to the young man sitting before him but to the inner voice in Spider's own head. It was at once unsettling but also cordial, inviting.

"There are other guests, others peers. The Masters themselves, even."

"And yet you're the only man I wish to speak with." The red-haired man drank from his horn, all the while staring at Spider with a fierce, unblinking gaze.

Spider did not think the man drunk despite the wine he had consumed. Nor did he seem lost in an opium haze. He looked alert and focused, searching for something, although Spider knew not what. He feared what would happen if the red-haired man did not find the object of his search, feared also that he would find it here.

"What do you wish to speak of?" Spider asked.

"Dungeons."

"I know little of dungeons."

"What do you know of yourself?"

Spider held his tongue. The Masters had similar tactics, often asking enigmatic questions during training. Incorrect answers brought beatings, and Spider could not recall a time he had answered correctly. He knew enough of rhetoric to know the question itself had no true answer, only false answers that would serve to deepen the question. After eight years on the Isle, he had grown weary of such displays. Resentful, even.

"You do not wish to answer my question?" the red-haired man asked.

"How can I answer such a question?"

"What is the first law of victory?"

Spider shifted in his seat. If before the red-haired man had made him uneasy, now he was fearful.

The laws of victory were the sacred teachings of the Masters, the framework with which they taught the art of conquest. None but a peer or a Master himself knew all eight laws. Initiates studied one law a year for eight years, and only then did they learn the full scope of their art. To teach an outsider the laws was a transgression punishable by death.

Spider glanced around the room to see if anyone had taken notice of their conversation. Several of the Masters had convened on the high dais across the grand hall, too far away to overhear, but their every retainer, courtesan, and servant was an eye or an ear. You were never alone on the Isle.

"I cannot discuss with you the secrets of my Masters."

"Know yourself, know victory," the red-haired man said, leaning close. Even whispering, his voice sounded like stone grinding stone. "That is the first law. You know it, and I know it. Right now, you're wondering how I know it, but that's not important. What's important is that we talk honestly with one another. So when I ask what you know of yourself, I am asking a young man who has spent the last eight years of his life investigating that very question. I would like to hear that man's answer."

"I know that I am well trained in the art of Rune magic. I will serve the man who buys my contract faithfully."

"More empty words." The red-haired man waved his hand dismissively. He leaned back in his seat, his face disappearing into shadow. "I don't want to hear you hawk your wares like some common merchant."

No one had ever asked Spider how he felt about his circumstances. In truth, his feelings mattered little. The Masters had spent years training him to become a formidable Rune mage. They had gifted him with powerful spells at great personal expense. He had eaten their food, had drunk their wine, slept under a roof they provided. With his training finished, the time had come to repay the Masters' generosity with his service, even if he had other plans.

"Why are you here if not to make a purchase?" Spider asked.

The candlelight glinted on gold teeth as the red-haired man smiled. "An honest reply for once. It deserves an honest answer in kind. I am here to make a purchase for my employers. They style themselves the Temple of the Undying Serpent, and that is how they wish me to know them. But in truth their order is older than that name and in antiquity they were known as the Cult of the Unseen Empire. You won't find mention of them in the great histories of the West. In the East, their name is cataloged in The Thousand Blasphemies of the mad caliph Khalil Andoweyy. If you know where to look, you will find their snake-headed towers in every great city of the world. Glittering Moraq and its sister city Dabar, grand Pthylop in the Akhaian Islands. There is a tower standing guard over the Yellow City slums in Shaarmai, and another behind the Celestial Theater of the Unified People in Tai-jin. There is even a tower hidden in Antioch City. Every year, the Empire grows stronger, their reach ever wider."

"So you came here to buy them a spellcaster?" Spider asked.

"I came here to buy them a weapon. They trust that I have a discerning eye, and because of that trust, I must perform my due diligence. If I were purchasing an expensive blade, I would ask questions of its smith. The nature of its materials, the manner in which it was constructed, its weight, its strength. If it were a truly unique blade, I might even inquire where the smith was trained. I might ask to see other such weapons he had forged, even to test the blade myself."

"I see," Spider said. A testing, then. That's what this was although he could only guess at what weakness the red-haired man sought to reveal.

"So now you know something of me. Something you didn't know until it was offered. I would appreciate if you returned the gesture. I have told you why I was sent here. Told it truthfully. I wonder the same of you."

"I came here to train, to learn to be the best spellcaster I could be."

The red-haired man shook his head. "No, that's not quite right. Certainly it's true you came here to train. But that's not the whole of the truth."

Spider turned from the red-haired man. He looked to the high dais, where the Masters sat in conversation. Had one of them been watching?

"Tell me." The words seemed to come from the shadows themselves although the dark spoke with the voice of the red-haired man.

The queer sensation from the beach worked its way over Spider's body again. He grew light-headed. Gripping the edge of the table to steady himself, he leaned forward, his face inches from the red-haired man's.

"I was weak before," he whispered. "I came here to grow strong."

"Why?"

"I have promises to keep."

"You guard your words carefully, boy."

"A skill I learned here."

The red-haired man nodded. "I see. Let us return to safer discussions, then."

"What do you wish to discuss?"

"Dungeons." The red-haired man set down his horn. He fumbled in the dark for his ebon pipe, then brought it to his lips and took a long pull. "You've said you know little of dungeons. I myself know a bit. Many years ago, a time so far gone it might well have been a different life, I was acquainted with a man who knew much of them. A tomb robber, he was familiar with the golden age of dungeoneering, that time in antiquity when the great empires were being birthed, and adventurers were looting crypts dug by the primordial ancestors of man. His obsession in life was a particular kind of dungeon and the particular kind of men who would seek to explore it."

"I do not know the different types of dungeons."

"For the sake of simplicity, let us divide them into two groups. True dungeons and false dungeons. A true dungeon is one that houses traps and monsters. And buried deep in such a dungeon is treasure. Let us say, for the sake of argument, that a man doesn't know the nature of the treasure hidden in a true dungeon, but he does know treasure lies there, and so he braves many perils to reach it. If he survives the dungeon and retrieves the treasure, he has enriched his life, earned himself gold and jewels, exotic artifacts, maybe even renown. If he's lucky, the riches he plunders will keep him for all his days, and he need never work again. If he's less lucky, then maybe he finds another dungeon and attempts to pillage its treasures, continuing on in this manner until he no longer needs treasure or until he succumbs to a dungeon. Are you following me, boy?"

"I am."

"I'm talking of dungeons because there are things we cannot say frankly, you and I."

"Of course."

"The second kind of dungeon is a false dungeon. By false dungeon, I do not mean that it stands aboveground where a true dungeon lies under the earth. I refer to it as a false dungeon because it lacks the qualities of a true dungeon. It has some elements of a true dungeon, for sure. It has traps and monsters. But the thing it lacks, the thing that is missing and will forever prevent it from being a true dungeon is treasure.

"A man enters a false dungeon for many reasons. Maybe he suspects it houses treasure, or maybe he enters by mistake. Every level that he descends, he is diminished by what he experiences, never enriched. The dungeon traps him, wounds him, curses him." Here, the red-haired man clenched and unclenched his fists. He breathed deep. "Yet even though the dungeon takes everything from him and gives nothing in return, still the man presses on. The dungeon requires that he compromise his morality at every turn. He wakes the dead, destroys ancient guardians, undoes arcane magic meant to keep evil from entering the world. Nothing will deter him. Can you picture such a place, boy?"

"I can."

"The question I have for you then, indeed the reason I came all this way, is to ask why? Why would a man do such a thing?"

"Madness."

"Yes," the red-haired man said. "Madness would be one reason. But there are others. Obsession. Curiosity. The idea that if you leave before your task is finished, you will be haunted forever by what you failed to see. That false dungeon, still unconquered, will haunt your dreams. Do you understand this, boy?"

"I do."

"Could you picture yourself in such a place?"

"I don't know."

"There are some who would say you've endured such a place these last eight years. That since stepping foot on the Isle of Twelve, you have walked a haunted path. A path that, judging by those who have walked it before you, is destined to end in death and ruin. Do you see it that way?"

"I don't."

The red-haired man shrugged. "I'm an old man. I've had too much to drink and too much to smoke. Perhaps I no longer see things truly."

"Why did you come here?" Spider asked.

"I told you, I was paid to come here."

"I thought we were being truthful with one another."

The red-haired man grinned again, a terrible sight. "My employers sent me to find them a weapon. But I myself am searching for something else."

"What then?"

"A man unafraid to walk the road to hell."

"You think I'm such a man."

"I know it. I can see it in you, could see it from the moment we met. And I believe you've seen it in yourself."

"So you intend to buy my contract?"

"That's exactly right. I have in my possession fifty bars of platinum, given to me by my employers, enough to purchase your contract for a year. In the morning, I'm going to speak with your Masters to arrange the deal. By tomorrow night, you'll be on a ship with me for passage back to the Antiochi mainland. In five days' time, that ship will dock at Astrium, but you won't be on it."

"Where am I going?"

"That's your business. For my part, I will tell my employers that you killed half the crew, subdued me, and commandeered the vessel. You had us put you ashore on the mainland halfway to Borachud."

"And then what will happen?"

"My employers will hunt you. They'll notify your Masters of what you did, and your Masters will hunt you. The price on your head will attract bounty hunters from the far corners of the world. But you will be free."

"Why would you do this?"

"I told you already. I have need of a man willing to walk the road to hell. I believe you are that man, but you don't know it. This will prove it to you."

"What if you're wrong? What if I return to the Isle and tell my Masters of your ploy? You'll be a dead man then."

"I've been one before. That fate doesn't scare me." The red-haired man laughed deep in his throat. "If you return to the Isle, then you're not the man I thought you were. I will have wasted some time and some effort and made a powerful enemy or two, but I will have sussed out your true nature, and so will have accomplished some small part of my goal." The red-haired man paused. "But we both know you won't be returning."

"And what if I don't return? I'll still be gone. You say you have need of a cursed man, but we'll never see each other again."

"I'll find you, boy. That thing gnawing inside you, I know it well. It has a tremendous appetite, and it can only be sated with blood and fire. A man of your skills is liable to leave a great trail of ruin trying to feed it."

2

The storm began at sunup, a heavy rain accompanied by a few rumbling reports of thunder. Cassius sat at the window in his room and breathed the warm, wet air. Through the haze, he watched the city. The sun rose red-orange, the color of heated metal, and the rainwater warmed to mist, and for a moment, the city appeared to be built on clouds, like some mythic land lost since antiquity.

He pictured himself moving through that mist, a hero come to his place of reckoning. He was clad in gleaming bronze, like an ancient Akhaian warrior, Kaliomedes, perhaps, or maybe Great Hippomedon, with a horsehair helm and a heavy ash spear. He dreamed himself tall and strong, with powerful limbs and a full beard, flowing hair, skin tanned by a golden sun.

Something waited for him in the mist. A terrible beast. When he squinted, he could just discern its shape moving through the haze. Massive, writhing, many-headed. A hydra.

He hunted the beast, stalked it through the fog, up wide avenues paved with smooth marble, across the steps of an opulent temple whose columns hid the ivory-fleshed statues of forgotten gods. As he closed in for the kill, the mist parted, and the beast caught sight of him.

The beast reared, three heads hissing, and Cassius raised his spear and loosed a champion's roar and the beast charged forward.

"Cassius," the barkeep shouted.

Cassius blinked. The sound of his own name ended his daydream and made him aware of a dull ache throbbing behind his eyes. He rubbed his temples and rose from the stool. He headed downstairs to answer the call.

The pain behind Cassius's eyes had subsided by the time the barkeep called him for breakfast, but at the table, he was light-headed. The barkeep had fixed a meal of fried eggs and toasted bread, a slice each of pork.

"What did you think of Lowtown?"

"Not as friendly as I'd hoped." Cassius's ears were ringing. He rubbed his temples. His nose began to bleed.

"Trouble sleeping?" Lucian asked.

Cassius shut his eyes against the pain. When he opened them again, he saw the ceiling and a dark shape visible in his periphery. Squinting, he recognized this as the barkeep's face. His mouth was moving, but Cassius could not hear him for the ringing in his ears.

He felt the barkeep's rough hand under his head, then he was being lifted into a sitting position from the floor and propped against a stool.

"—hear me, boy. Just nod." The barkeep inspected Cassius's pupils. "Never seen a thing like that before. You were sitting there, then you fell over."

"It's okay," Cassius said, his voice ragged. He wiped his face, found it damp with sweat. "I'm okay."

"You call that okay?" Lucian slapped Cassius on one cheek, then the other.

Cassius recoiled, shoved the barkeep.

"I get fits." Cassius's hands were numb. He clenched and unclenched them, trying to work sensation back into his fingers. "I've got the falling-down sickness."

"Does that happen often?"

"Only when I cast spells," Cassius said.

"I've never known a spellcaster to do that." Lucian eased back onto his haunches. He reached up to the bar and brought down his cup of wine and took a deep swallow and offered the cup to Cassius, who declined.

"I'm touched." Cassius struggled to his feet. His every movement seemed a half second slow, as though his limbs were delayed in answering his will.

"What does that mean?"

"It's a rare condition. If one in every ten thousand is born with the ability to work the runes, then one spellcaster in every ten thousand is born touched."

"So you're the weirdest of the weird. Congratulations. What does that have to do with your collapsing in the middle of my damn bar?"

"Spellcasters have limits to the amount of energy they can draw on to fuel their spells." Cassius slumped onto his stool. "Different spells require different levels of power. Think of it like lamp oil. A thimbleful of oil will fuel a small flame. A bucketful could start a fire that would burn this bar to the ground."

Lucian snorted. "You'd be doing me a favor."

"But there's nothing you can do to change your limit. Train for hours studying runes and casting, and still you won't be able to draw beyond your capacity. It's fixed at birth, like your eye color."

"So some are more powerful than others. That's the way of the world. You haven't told me anything I don't know, boy. What does this have to do with you?"

"I have no limit to what I can draw."

"That must come in handy."

"At times," Cassius said. "Except that my body, any body, can handle only so much of the rune energies. And drawing on more than I can handle will kill me."

"So the fits come when you draw more than your body can handle but less than enough to kill you?" The barkeep whistled. "Sounds like you're screwed, boy. I suggest you find another line of work."

"It's the only work for me." Cassius forked his food around his plate, then pushed the plate away. He drained a cup of light, dry wine in a single gulp.

"I've got three words for you. Learn a goddamn trade. I've got a first cousin who was dropped on his head as a baby. About as smart as a poorly trained dog. The bastard's a cobbler now. And making good money doing it."

"I'm no cobbler."

. . .

A long awning shaded the steps of the ivory merchant's shop, and under this awning, a shirtless man rested on a stool. He wore loose green pants rolled to his knees, and a cudgel lay in his lap.

"I'm looking for someone," Cassius said.

"Well, I'm not him. So piss off." The man yawned and resettled himself on his stool. He had a harsh red tan, and his chest and arms were flabby, his belly marred with stretch marks.

Cassius stood staring at him.

"Is there going to be a problem, kid?" the shirtless man asked.

Cassius opened his cloak and the shirtless man caught sight of the gauntlets at Cassius's waist. He sat forward, his gut sinking to rest between his upper thighs.

"I'm just looking for a friend, not trouble," Cassius said. "Her name is Sulla."

"Wait here." The shirtless man stood and entered the storefront. A few minutes later, Sulla emerged from the shop.

"How'd you find me?" She stood on the top step, her hands behind her back.

"Spread a few coins around, and you can find anyone in this town," Cassius said. "I've got your money from yesterday. Your commission."

"Hand it over." She looked past Cassius, avoiding eye contact.

"Can we go inside?" Cassius spread his arms wide, inviting her to take in the entirety of the Market. "I'd hate to do this in the open, on the street."

"The street is where I handle my business."

"And you don't mind who overhears?"

Sulla surveyed the busy merchant stalls that littered the square, the crowd of passersby.

"Follow me," she said.

They walked behind the store to a cramped alley. A young boy at the far side of the lane was kneeling to lace his sandal.

"Spare some change for a meal?" the boy called.

"Leave us," Sulla shouted, "before I club you to death and sell the corpse to a hungry Jutlander."

The boy ran.

"I'll take my money now." Sulla spun on Cassius, a pig-iron dirk clutched in her fist and the tip of the dirk pointed at his face.

He didn't doubt her resolve. She'd kill him without hesitation if she thought it necessary. But he was still alive, and that meant she hadn't made up her mind quite yet.

"I'd make a move for my coin purse if I didn't think it would cost me an eye."

Sulla snatched the front of his tunic, pressed the dirk into the soft flesh under his chin.

"Don't mock me," she said.

Cassius lowered his hands. "I'm sorry."

"You could have gotten me killed yesterday. I was doing you a favor. I was trying to protect you. And you used me. Is that the kind of person you are?"

Her anger was plain, but when he looked close, he saw fear in her as well. It was measured, controlled, only hinted at by a faint quiver in her voice, like a bowstring drawn overtight. A subtle sign that someone unacquainted with fear might never notice. But Cassius was not such a person.

"I'm sorry," he repeated, his voice soft, injured. "Things got out of hand yesterday. That wasn't how I planned it."

"Liar. I saw the look on your face. You were there to cause trouble."

"I was."

"You were there to kill Junius."

"No."

"I saw—"

"I didn't want that," he shouted. His voice echoed in the alley, then the alley fell silent. "And to answer your question, I'm not the kind of person to use someone and throw them away. I looked for you in the crowd. You must have slipped away after the finish. I wouldn't have left you. I don't leave friends behind."

"We're not friends, Cassius."

"What are we then?"

"Business associates."

"Well, I have a business proposition," he said. "But I don't negotiate at knifepoint."

Sulla lowered the dirk.

"For yesterday." Cassius removed two silver pieces from his coin purse and held them up between his face and Sulla's face. She released his tunic and snatched the coins with her free hand.

"I don't want to work with you," she said. "You're bad for business. You walked into one of Boss Piso's gambling halls and killed his man in cold blood. And I was your damned escort."

Cassius shrugged. "You can smooth that over. Spellcasters fight. It's in their nature. Piso's lost men before. Loses men every day, I'd imagine."

"Not in one of his own houses. Not at the hands of some stranger who wanders in off the street."

"Explain what happened," Cassius said. "Tell the truth. You only set up the fight to help a friend. Things got out of hand. If you're as resourceful as you say, Piso will know you're more valuable than a second-rate killer."

"What the hell was that about anyway?" she snapped. "Did you think you'd impress Piso by killing one of his men?"

"No, I did it to impress Boss Cinna."

"You're working with Cinna?"

"Not yet." Cassius smiled. "That's why I need your help."

Sulla's face slackened. She stared at Cassius as though trying to spot a scratch on a pane of glass.

"What are you talking about?" she asked.

"I'm talking about making a lot of money." Cassius lowered his voice, fixed Sulla with a pointed stare. "I'm unknown on this island. No one will hire me because no one knows what I'm capable of. Now that's changed."

"No, you're still an unknown. Cinna wasn't there. He didn't see your fight."

"But you were there. And you've got Cinna's ear."

"Do I?" Sulla laughed. "You think every goddamn fence on this island has access to the bosses? I've dealt with Cinna's people before, and even with the man himself a time or two. But I'm not his advisor."

"You don't need to be especially close for this. I just need you to spread word about what happened at Piso's yesterday and make sure Cinna hears of it. Don't make it seem as though we're working together. Make it seem like gossip."

"To what end?"

"A deal with Cinna." Cassius paused, let his words sink in. He watched for Sulla's reaction.

She lowered her eyes, but otherwise, her face remained calm. She was considering the offer and how it might play out, but she did not seem to oppose it on principle.

"I'll present myself to him later," Cassius continued. "Ask for terms of employment. If he takes you at your word, I'll sign on with him immediately. And if he needs a demonstration, I won't have a problem with that either."

"You think he'll go for it?"

"Why not?" Cassius asked. "I know how to fight."

"Good enough to beat one of Piso's lieutenants and brazen enough to do it in one of Piso's houses."

"You're selling already."

"I'll see what I can do." She nodded good-bye and headed for the mouth of the alley.

"Sulla," he called after her.

She stopped and turned.

"I meant what I said about leaving friends behind."

"Why should I believe you?" she asked.

"I'm one of the good guys."

She laughed. "You're in Scipio, boy. There are no good guys."

Sunlight poured through the window in Cassius's room, spilled across the scroll in his hands. It was an old parchment scroll, cheaply made and purchased on the mainland for a few coppers. He had heard that Fathalans produced the best papermakers in the known world, had heard of whole markets in the Empire dedicated to books and scrolls and codices, but their work was hard to find in the Republic.

This particular scroll concerned the Attus epic. He had no need of a richly crafted volume on that subject. These words he knew by rote, carried them with him daily. The page was simply a reminder.

He read for hours. Read till the sun sank below the window in his room, then sank below the earth itself. Read while smoke rose from the city's chimneys to cloud the night sky with oily fog. Read while the sounds of the jungle carried to him from the dark.

When his eyes failed, he lit a few tallow candles and continued the story.

Attus as a hillman on the fringes of the Fathalan Empire. His communing with the first of the four great bird spirits who would guide him on his journey. His revocation of the Fathalan yoke. An uprising. Blood and bronze.

The text did not recount Attus's first kill, but it must have taken place here, Cassius decided. Before this, the great hero was a humble farm boy who had never seen war; after this, the champion of a hundred battles. Nor did the story concern itself with Attus's feelings about the killing. Whether he despaired for his loss of innocence; whether he recognized the bloodshed as transformative. Whether he welcomed it.

The words were plain to see, but their meaning, their truth, still had to be teased out, like a loose thread on the fringe of a garment. He read till he fell asleep, and even sleeping, his mind searched for answers.

A knock at the door woke him. He found Lucian standing in the hallway, a bowl of stew and a pitcher of water in his hands.

"You didn't come down for dinner." Lucian's face was flushed, his ears red, and his eyes bloodshot. Cassius could smell sour wine on his breath.

"I was busy with a few things."

"Am I disturbing you?"

"Not at all."

Cassius motioned Lucian into the room, and the barkeep entered, staggering, spilling wine and stew as he moved. He set down the bowl, then the pitcher on Cassius's nightstand. He paced the room, circled around to the desk by the window, fingered the scroll where it lay between the candles.

"Doing some reading?" he asked.

"A bit," Cassius said.

"More stories about heroes and their destinies? Battles and magic and the like?"

"It's what I enjoy."

"Not much of a reader myself," Lucian said. "I can read, mind you. I'm just not one to spend my days surrounded by scrolls. I'd get bored."

"Not me," Cassius said.

"No, not you. Seems excitement has a way of finding you."

"You heard about the fight yesterday." Cassius took a seat at the desk. He gathered the scroll, rolled it, and set it aside.

"Word is all over the streets of Lowtown."

"I thought you weren't welcome in Lowtown."

"I still hear things," Lucian said. "What were you thinking, boy? I didn't help you find work so you could go off killing people. Prize-fighting isn't glamorous work, but it's honest."

"I'm no prizefighter."

"Damn it, I don't want to aid a murderer."

Cassius started at the word. Lucian sighed, raised a hand as though to offer an apology, but Cassius cut him off.

"I didn't mean for that to happen," he said. "That man attacked me."

"After you provoked him."

"I wanted a fair fight. A demonstration of my abilities. But Junius wanted something else. He killed the man he fought before me, would have killed me, too, if given the chance. I had no choice."

"Do you know why this bar is always empty?" Lucian crossed the room, his steps shuffling and unsteady. He eased himself onto the bed. "Because I don't accept blood money."

One of the tallow candles sputtered and died. Shadows crept forward from the far corners of the room, covered Cassius in near-total darkness.

"Are you telling me to leave?" he asked.

"I'm telling you your next payment is due at the end of this week. That gives you five days to scrounge up enough coin to extend your stay." Lucian stared into the darkness that had swallowed Cassius. "And I don't accept blood money."

Cassius sat silent.

"Scipio wasn't always like this, you know?" Lucian resettled himself on the bed. "Restless? Yes. Violent? Of course. But it didn't use to be so . . . so completely . . ."

"Rotten," Cassius said.

Lucian nodded.

"If I was short with you when first we met, if you thought I was trying to scare you off, it was only because I see too many of your kind here. Naive boys who think themselves strong." Lucian motioned toward the scroll on the desk. "Boys in search of adventure. They don't survive this place."

"I think I've proven myself strong."

"And a survivor?"

"Only time will tell," Cassius said softly.

Lucian heaved himself up from the bed. He stood wobbling, then steadied himself. He patted his belly and loosed a soft belch.

"I think I may have overstayed my welcome," he said. "Enjoy your dinner. I'm not much of a cook, but you can be certain I didn't spit in the stew, which is more than you can say for most places around here. Sorry for disturbing you."

"Why do you let me stay here?" Cassius asked.

Lucian shrugged. "I rent rooms for money."

"You warn off every mainlander you talk to. And you refuse to accept blood money. If you expect me to believe your only motivation is the pursuit of gold, you don't think me naive, you think me stupid."

"You've a sharp mind, boy."

"But?"

"But a bit of a blind spot for the human heart."

Lucian crossed the room to the door. Cassius stood to see him out. They shook hands. Cassius offered Lucian the scroll.

"I don't always read for adventure," Cassius said. "Sometimes a good story introduces you to a new friend."

Lucian set a hand on Cassius's shoulder, ignoring the scroll. "I suppose we can all use one of those."

The Madam's Purse was a three-story building on a dead-end road. No sign hung above its entrance, but two men stood guard at the door. One was bald with a deep underbite, the other squat and bearded. They were dressed in black tunics, and each man wore as a necklace an octan, an ancient Antiochi coin made of copper shavings and iron and having eight sides and a hole through its center.

"I just want a drink," Cassius said.

"This is a private club," the bearded guard said.

"And I'm a man looking for privacy."

Cassius did not realize he was falling because he did not see the punch thrown. When it landed, it broke his nose, numbness spreading over his face. As the earth rose to meet him, he thought he was sinking. He had time enough for only this one thought. And then he hit the ground.

A boot struck his side, and his ribs flared with pain. He gasped for air, and the pain doubled.

Scrambling to his feet, he staggered up the lane, bent and coughing. At the end of the street, he collapsed and forced himself to breathe, his breath coming in shallow gasps, as though he were sipping air.

He stood and fumbled under his cloak for his gauntlets. Tears clouded his eyes. After two deep breaths, he turned and walked back to the bar, blood from his nose dripping down his chin.

The guards advanced on him. He pointed a finger, and the mud in front of him swirled, as though stirred with a stick.

The two men halted.

The air hummed with a loud buzzing, then mud exploded upward, and the sky filled with a swarm of flies.

Cassius felt a droning in his head. He caught glimpses of the world as seen through multifaceted eyes. He wanted to dart away and burrow into a wet, dark place now, the world alive with a thousand new scents.

He cleared his mind. He waved his hand, as though shooing the flies, and they rushed forward as one.

The bald man choked as the black cloud enveloped him. His partner ran for the bar, and as he reached for the handle, the door opened inward, and a half dozen people shouldered outside.

The flies floated back to hover over the sinkhole between Cassius and the bar. They drifted like smoke, black against a black sky.

The crowd at the door parted, and a crossbow appeared in the entranceway, its wielder hidden in shadow. The tip of a bolt glinted in torchlight.

"Move, and you're dead where you stand."

In the back room of the Madam's Purse, Cassius sat with his hands on a large table inlaid with silver and ringed by high-backed chairs. There were two earthenware mugs before him, one filled with a recent vintage Berundian wine and one filled with his own blood. His gauntlets lay in his lap.

Two men entered and took seats at the table.

"Welcome." The man sitting to Cassius's right extended his hand. "My name is Cinna."

Cassius accepted the hand and shook, and his ribs burned with the effort.

Cinna was fat, with a smooth, bland face. His neck was short, and when he lowered his chin, he looked as though he had no neck at all, as though his head were set directly into his torso, like a frog's head. He wore a wig, short and gray-blond, and heavy makeup. His face was powdered, and each eye ringed by black. His fat lips were painted red, as were his cheeks.

"It seems you've injured yourself," Cinna said. He arched his thick gray brows, appraised Cassius with bulging eyes the color of apple rot.

"That's one way to put it." Cassius snorted, spat blood into one of his mugs.

"I know we've just met," Cinna said, "but there are things you should know about me. For one, I don't like when people pick fights at my bar."

Cassius shrugged. "I didn't pick that fight."

The man next to Cinna laughed. He was dark and rat-faced and sat with his hands tucked into his armpits.

"This is my associate," Cinna said. "Master Nicola."

"Tell him he doesn't want to be laughing at me," Cassius said.

Nicola rose from his seat, his hand drifting toward the knife at his hip. Cassius reached under the table.

"Enough!" Cinna slapped the tabletop. One of the cups fell, and Cassius's blood spilled into the silver inlay. The room echoed with the sound of the slap, then fell silent.

"Boy, I let you keep that iron as a courtesy," Cinna shouted. "Because I thought you came here to talk business. If I'm wrong, if you're a blood-mad killer, then I'll thank you to leave."

Cassius placed his hands on the tabletop. Nicola sat.

"Good," Cinna said. "Now I'll be as direct as possible. I know your short history on this island. I know yesterday you killed one of Piso's men in a prizefight. And now you've come here seeking sanctuary. You angered Piso, and I'm the only man who can protect you."

"I don't need your protection," Cassius said.

"You're no fool." Cinna wagged his plump finger. "Maybe in over your head, but not a fool. Remain calm, and we can talk business like civilized men. We're sons of Antioch, after all. We have to be examples for these yellow savages."

"I killed Piso's man yesterday," Cassius said. "I'll kill more for you."

"This isn't a war, boy," Cinna said. "My interests conflict with Piso's, but that doesn't mean I can have you killing people in the street. Order must be maintained. Understand?"

Cassius nodded.

"So tell me, are you any good at what you do?" Cinna filled a mug from a pitcher of wine set in the middle of the table. He sipped the wine, tilted back his head to savor the taste.

"Better than Piso's man. And I'm told he was good."

"Where did you train?"

"I'm from Florea." Cassius watched the flow of his blood along the inlay. "The grasslands between the Delium plains and the mountains. I trained myself. Street fights mostly."

"You're a farm boy?" Cinna didn't bother to hide the contempt in his voice. "How'd you get here?"

"I killed a man in a duel some time ago. He was an officer in the legion."

"And now you've come to Scipio to start over." Cinna shrugged, unimpressed. "I've heard that story a hundred times. I was hoping for something a bit more interesting."

There was a knock at the door, and Nicola answered it. A short man with blond hair entered the room. He approached Cinna with his head bowed.

"I'm sorry to interrupt, Master Cinna. My name is Brieus. I work for you."

"I know who you are," Cinna said. "You stopped a knife fight at the door last year."

"That's right, sir." Brieus flashed a quick smile.

"I never forget the faces of my men. Do you have news for me?"

"We found Cornelia, Master," Brieus said. "The girl from the brothel on the street of jewelers. Blond girl. Young thing. The one who run away last week."

"Yes, I seem to remember."

"We caught her by the city wall a few hours ago," Brieus said. "That's where I patrol. Near the gates. Out by the old west tower."

"Well done, boy. Nicola, make sure our friend here receives compensation."

"Thank you, sir." Brieus nodded, bowed awkwardly. "Back to work now."

"Brieus," Cinna said, "I'd like you to take care of the girl first."

"Take care of her, sir?"

"Discipline her." Cinna ran the tip of his finger along his bottom lip.

"I don't—" Brieus's face paled. He looked to his feet.

"You know how it works, right?"

"Yes, sir."

"We do it to dissuade the girls from leaving. Afterward, she'll tell the others and they'll know the punishment if they run away and they'll know it gets worse each time one of them does it."

"I don't know if I can do that," Brieus said.

"Nonsense." Cinna dismissed Brieus's protests with a wave of his mug. "Take her upstairs. How many men did we use the last time a girl ran away? I think it was four. So take five men this time—"

"It was five last time," Nicola said.

"Five? Well, then take her upstairs with six men."

"Ye-yes, sir," Brieus said.

"Brieus."

"Yes, sir?"

"You as well," Cinna said. "It's five men and you. Do you understand? I want you there to make sure it's done properly."

"I ain't never done a thing like that."

"You will have after today."

Brieus nodded to Cinna and exited the room, his shoulders stooped.

"Good man," Cinna said. "But a bit timid. This will put some steel in his spine. Now would you care to discuss salary, Master Cassius?"

Cassius stood with his hand on his chest and his heart racing beneath his hand. He tried to breathe deep to calm himself, but the smell in the privy behind the Purse was foul enough to make him gag. He was in the dark, though, and that helped. A blackness so complete it mattered not if his eyes were open or closed. A place where no one could see his fear.

He felt his stomach spasm. Leaning forward, he spat, then vomited, not bothering to aim for the pit. His ribs burned with the effort.

He thought about sitting across from Cinna, about the way the man had meted punishment and reward as assuredly as a magistrate well-read in statute and sworn to uphold the rule of law. The thought made his pulse pound in his ears. He felt his cheeks burn, felt beads of sweat collect on his brow.

Here was the root of the fear churning in his guts. Not a fear of the man himself but a fear of his own reaction. Fear that had he sat in that room two minutes longer, he would have leapt across the table and throttled that fat throat. Fear that he had almost lost control.

It would have all been for naught, then. The training, the struggle, the time spent building the willpower and the courage to step off the safe path and find the destiny he knew was waiting for him.

He heard a pounding at the door.

"Hurry up in there," Nicola shouted. "We've work to do before this night is over."

Cassius wiped his mouth with the back of his hand.

"Just be a minute," he said.

He waited until he heard Nicola walk away, his footsteps growing faint, then fading completely.

"Brieus," he whispered to himself in the dark. "Brieus."

He said the name ten more times, said it until he was certain he would not forget, until the very sound became a promise to himself.

"People stay out of your way if they know you're working for Master Cinna." Nicola lifted the octan from beneath his tunic and let it hang on his chest.

It was late, but still the roads were choked with people. Drunks wandered cursing, and on corners, whores plied their trade with impunity.

"You'll be a courier at first." Nicola moved with a hurried slouching gait. "Collection jobs mostly. Master Cinna needs to know you can be trusted with his money."

"That's not a problem," Cassius said. He watched Nicola walk, his steps furtive, his head snapping to one side, then the other at every sound that traveled through the dark.

"Do well with that, and we'll put you on patrol, guarding warehouses and brothels and the like." Nicola elbowed through a clutch of beggars, lashing out at a legless wretch with a poorly aimed kick. "After that we'll give you leave to start your own rackets. And then you'll give a percentage to the boss and keep the rest."

"I see." Cassius discreetly tossed a handful of coppers behind him in the lane, pretended not to notice when the beggars called their thanks.

"Now the key to collecting is that you don't need to scare anybody who wants to pay," Nicola said. "Only get mean when you have to. And even then, you get mean in moderation. Cinna doesn't want his men acting like animals. Always remember that order must be maintained."

The narrow lane terminated at a low, stucco wall, crumbling and marked with charcoal graffiti. Misspelled curses, phalluses, an image of Cinna and a horse engaged in crimes against nature. Nicola leapt, scrabbled to the top.

"Goddamn it," he yelled, swatting his chest. "Spiders. I hate spiders."

Cassius climbed up, and together they descended to a street bordered on either side by well-tended lawns, walled gardens filled with colorful mango trees and bright jungle flowers, man-made grottos.

Gone were the tenements they had come from, replaced by serene domi, or city villas, that would have looked impressive in Antioch City itself. Guardsmen stood outside the doorways of every home, and here and there, slaves toiled in the light of streetlamps, sweeping walkways, pruning shrubs.

"Where are we?" Cassius asked.

"The Street of Blossoms," Nicola said.

"I feel like I've left Scipio."

"I'm the one convinced Cinna to build this place." Nicola flashed a smug smile. "Got the idea from my time in gaol."

"What is this?"

"The most beautiful cage in all the world."

A rider on horseback trotted in the road ahead, the first horse Cassius had seen since his arrival on Scipio.

"These are Cinna's prisoners?"

"No, they're exiles. Forced to flee the Republic by injunction or because they made powerful enemies. They come here for refuge, same as everyone comes here. But these are noblemen, well-heeled merchants, people from influential families. They don't want to live among the rabble, so Cinna built them this enclave, this small slice of home amidst the blood and mud and shit of Scipio."

"And this was your idea?"

"Gaol is like anywhere else in the Republic. The law talks of equality amongst men, but I saw rich prisoners living in luxury while the rest of us fought and killed for bread crusts and gruel."

"They paid for preferential treatment?"

"Not them, they were prisoners. They had no coin to influence anyone. But their families paid. Paid at first for small comforts and amenities. Paid later to ensure a shiv didn't find its way into their loved one's ribs."

"You're extorting these people then?"

"*Extortion* is such an ugly word." Nicola shrugged. "We provide a service. Comfort, Luxury. Safety."

"And if they refuse to pay?"

"Then they can try their luck amongst the animals."

"Does Piso have a similar arrangement?"

"Nothing like the Street of Blossoms. Piso is all force, no finesse. He doesn't have the taste to cater to the elite or the connections to noble families that Cinna does."

They reached the rider on his horse and moved to pass him in the road. The beast shied at Cassius's approach, as some horses did when near spellcasters.

The rider reined in the horse and clicked with his tongue. He stroked the beast's mane.

"Evening, travelers."

They had crossed into the light of a streetlamp, and Cassius saw now that the rider was a tremendous man. On foot, he must have stood near to seven feet tall. He wore a cloak of vibrant red, similar to the flowers of a poppy, and wore also calfskin boots that came to his knees, flowing black pantaloons like those favored by Fathalans, a sable tunic.

"Evening," Nicola said. He stared up at the rider, squinting in the dark. He did not seem to recognize the man.

"Out for an evening stroll?" The rider's voice was deep, edged with a harsh quality that Cassius could not place. He spoke with an accent but not one Cassius recognized although he had heard the tongues of men from most every corner of the earth. "Or are you looking for more sophisticated entertainments?"

Nicola lifted his octan.

"Ah, I see. A man on business, then. Or is it two men on business?" The rider looked to Cassius. "What say you, boy? What brings you here? Business?"

"What else?"

A beam of moonlight pierced the dark of the rider's raised hood. Cassius glimpsed his face. His eyes were big and searching and seemed to reflect the light, like the eyes of some predatory creature that makes its home in caves. He did not blink.

The sight of the red-haired men set Cassius's heart racing. He had not seen the man since they parted company on the sea route to Borachud. He had heard whispers of him for some time. A bar fight in Gaspia, a legendary night of revelry at Queen's Lace in Trajean. But they had never crossed paths.

Cassius had gone long stretches of time without thinking of the man. After a year, he was certain they would never see one another again. Sometimes at night, when his mind wandered, he imagined the red-haired man was not a man at all but a creature from beyond the veil that had come to set Cassius on the path of his destiny or a demon sent to curse him.

Now they were face-to-face again. Strangely, if the red-haired man recognized Cassius, he gave no sign.

"I see no ornament of office around your neck," the red-haired man said to Cassius.

"Very perceptive of you."

"So then you are a man who does not advertise his business."

"I suppose."

Cassius met the rider's stare, searching for any sign of recognition, but he could not hold it long. A queer sensation overcame him, a weakness that spread through his body, so that he felt on the verge of collapse although he remained clearheaded.

He took a step back.

"What about you?" Nicola said. "I don't think I've seen you around here before."

The rider continued to stare at Cassius. Then he turned to Nicola. He smiled. His mouth was wide, and he had a wider smile, one that seemed to split his face in half like a rictus. His teeth flashed in the streetlight. They were gold. Every tooth.

"No, I don't believe we've met. As for my presence in Scipio, why, there are plenty of reasons one might find himself on the edge of civilization. A place where the laws of man no longer hold dominion. I like the excitement of it. I find it invigorating."

A breeze picked up and rustled the rider's cloak, revealing a massive, jeweled kopis, or forward-curving sword, sheathed and hanging from his saddle. It was an ancient weapon, one Cassius had only ever seen once before and that in a house of curios.

"Well, we've got to be going," Nicola said. "See you around."

"No, I don't believe you will."

"What was that?"

"I don't believe I'll be seeing you again," the rider said. "But maybe you, boy. Maybe." The horse snorted and stamped. The rider wheeled his mount. "Be safe, travelers. And I wish you luck in your business endeavors. Both of you."

The rider put heels to his horse and trotted off. When he was out of sight, the queer sensation lifted off Cassius. Nicola continued up the road.

"Now what was I saying before that bastard interrupted us?" Nicola asked. "That's right, order. Order must be maintained."

"What about Piso's men?" Cassius surveyed the road. Overhead, the moon sailed behind a cover of clouds.

"We don't fight Piso's men. Not in the open anyway. Not the way you did yesterday. Piso puts pressure on the people under our protection. We put pressure on the people under his protection. No need to fight anyone."

"Seems a strange war."

"It's not a war. And if we have our way, it never will be." Nicola stopped, turned to face Cassius. "I mean this. You don't lay a hand on a man of Piso's without the boss's permission. Peace is good for business. Beyond that, we don't want to look weak in front of the legion. Quintus lives in the jungle, but word of the city can still reach him."

"And what would happen if he heard of fighting in the streets?"

"He might see an opportunity to replace the bosses."

"Could he beat them in a war?" Cassius asked.

"Not both at once. Boss has fifteen hundred men. Piso the same. Legion has about three thousand men."

"So any fighting between the bosses only strengthens Quintus," Cassius said. "And if the bosses can maintain the peace long enough to build their forces, they'll eventually be able to overthrow Quintus."

"If I were you, I wouldn't say that a second time. You never know who's listening in Scipio."

"But it's the truth, isn't it? It must be obvious to anyone with half a brain. So why doesn't Quintus take notice?"

Nicola chuckled. "Maybe he's down to less than half by now."

They passed into a courtyard overgrown with trees, then reached a squat, stone building with a domed roof. Nicola whistled. Cassius heard the sound of a heavy door open, and a short man in white robes emerged from a darkened alcove. He descended the steps delicately, as if discovering each of them for the first time. He carried a large sack at his side.

"Is this a temple?" Cassius asked. "You collect from temples?"

"Everyone pays in Scipio, boy. Even the gods."

At the door of the Madam's Purse, Nicola offered Cassius a half-silver piece and asked him where he was staying.

Cassius gave him the name of a pension near the city walls, and Nicola dismissed him, instructing him to wait home until someone called.

The night air was cool and as dry as it had been since Cassius arrived. The sky had cleared, and the stars shone ice white and distant, muddied by the smoke and the glare of streetlamps. Cassius's side ached with each step.

Soon he reached the Street of Horrors, a wide avenue in Hightown along which the worst of the city's beggars plied their trade. Cripples and lepers and madmen. They lined the street at sunup to exhibit stumps, boils, sores, empty eye sockets. They called for mercy and for charity.

At night, though, as now, it was mostly quiet. Cassius heard groans and whispers as he walked, an occasional cry for him to look on a tumor. But the lane was dark, and the beggars remained in shadow.

He came to a flat-roofed building made of stone, a private bathhouse. A small woman with a hooked nose escorted him inside.

"What can I help you with?" the woman asked.

"I'd like a hot bath. And two attendants."

"Boys or girls?"

"One girl please," Cassius said. "And a larger woman, about my size. Do you have that?"

"I'm sure we can find someone."

They passed through the front room, which was tiled with a colorful mosaic of a phoenix with spread wings, to a high-ceilinged hallway lined with wooden doors, each door bearing a small plaque with a number. At number eight, the woman stopped and fished inside her dress for a key and unlocked the door.

A low wooden bench ran the length of one wall, and in the center of the room stood a large brass tub. There was a drain nearby, and from under it came the sound of flowing water, as in a sewer.

Cassius took a seat on the floor. His face was numb, and he could not breathe through his nose. His ribs burned.

A short while later, the door opened, and two women entered. The first was a young woman with wide hips and smooth, plump arms. Her hair was dark and straight, her skin the subtle tan of sandalwood.

The second woman was middle-aged, with long gray hair that had been dyed black and was still gray at its roots. She had a fat face and dim eyes. She was an inch taller than Cassius and nearly fifty pounds heavier. Both women wore shapeless gray dresses that reached to midthigh.

They set their jugs next to the tub and stood staring at Cassius.

"Is he all right?" the old one asked. They spoke the Khimir language.

"I think he is hurt," the girl said.

"What does he want from us? Does he think us healers?"

"Speak Antiochi," Cassius said.

"I am sorry," the young one said. "She knows only our tongue. You would like bath?"

"I would."

The women emptied their jugs into the tub, and steam filled the room. The young one produced a handful of soap powder from a satchel and sprinkled this into the tub.

The old woman motioned for Cassius. He rose and walked to her, and she caught sight of the gauntlets as he stood.

"I do not like this one," the old woman said. "He is a killer. They are cruel."

"How many have you ever known?" the girl asked.

"Enough to know they are cruel."

The old woman flashed a nervous smile. She motioned for Cassius to turn and he turned and she undid his belt from behind and let his belt and his gauntlets fall, then lifted his tunic over his head. He winced as her hands brushed his side.

"Do you see that scar?" the girl asked, slipping into Khimir unconsciously.

"It is big," the old woman said. "But I have seen worse. Near the spine, a bad place. But not so bad as to kill him."

Cassius turned to face the women. He was nude, his side purpled with a deep bruise.

The women took the towels from the bench and dipped them into the soapy water and cleaned him. They wiped the mud from his neck, his arms, and his legs. The old one held her towel open and he offered his hands and she scrubbed them.

"Rich hands," she said in slow, strained Antiochi. "Rich hands."

"What is she saying?" Cassius asked.

"She means that your hands are valuable," the girl said. "Because you are . . ."

"What?" Cassius asked.

"You are killer." The young woman stammered. "I'm sorry. I don't know this word."

"That is the word," he said.

"There is a better word."

"A more polite word maybe," he said. "But not a better one."

Cassius stepped into the tub. The water was hot, and he eased back until it rose to his chin.

"How long have you worked here?" Cassius asked.

"A year," the girl said.

"How old are you?"

"Fifteen years."

"Are you mixed?" he asked.

"No. Khimir only. You people say Scipian."

"You speak Antiochi well."

"Thank you."

"Do you work other places?" he asked. "Different baths? Do you ever work in Lowtown?"

"Sometimes," the girl said.

He cupped his hands and splashed water onto his face and washed away the dried blood, and fresh blood dripped into the bathwater.

"How would you like to earn some money?" he asked.

At dawn, Cassius left the bath wearing the old woman's gray dress and a cheap scarf draped over his head so that only his eyes were visible. He carried a small oilskin bundle over his shoulder, stuffed with his own clothes. He was not accustomed to walking in a dress, but he moved slowly and felt he did a passable job. If he was being followed or watched, he trusted that his tail would not be alert for a woman leaving the bath, even a clumsy one.

The sun had not yet risen, but the eastern sky was pink. Whorls of steam rose from the wet streets and the wet roofs. Jungle birds cawed loudly as they dipped through the haze, a blur of beating feathers, red and gold and green, colors so bright they seemed more a product of a hallucinating mind than the natural world.

At the Market, Cassius bought a bottle of expensive wine, fried cakes with honey, and a small pouch of strong tobacco. Afterward, he walked back to the bar and ducked into the stables. The previous day, during their stroll, the barkeep had shown him a hidden door that led into the pantry, and approaching it now, Cassius thought it might be locked, but it was not.

In the pantry, he changed into his tunic. The main room was dark, the barkeep asleep at a table near the wall. He lay with one arm covering his face, snoring dryly.

"I've brought you breakfast," Cassius announced from across the room.

The barkeep started. He spotted Cassius and eased back onto the table.

"Goddamn you, boy," he whispered. His voice was grating, his throat raw from drink. "Can't a man catch a wink of sleep in his own damn room?"

"You're not in your room," Cassius said. "You're in the bar."

Lucian lifted his head and scanned his surroundings in disbelief. Cassius sat across from him. He removed the fried cakes from his bag. He set down the bottle of wine and the pouch of tobacco.

"Will you eat with me?"

The barkeep squinted one eye. He looked to Cassius, then looked to the fried cakes.

"I'm not hungry," he said.

Cassius uncorked the wine bottle. He reached for an overturned cup on a nearby table and poured it full.

"This is a good bottle." Cassius sipped the wine, found it cool and dry with a clear, strong taste. "A nice red from Albatua. I'd hate to drink this alone."

"I'm being more careful about the company I keep."

"Drink enough, and maybe the company will seem better."

The barkeep smiled despite himself. He handed over his mug, and Cassius filled it.

"I'm sorry about yesterday." Cassius spoke softly. "I should have told you about the fight and how it ended."

"Yes, you should have." Lucian drained his mug. "I don't mean to pry. I'm just looking out for you."

"Why?"

"I don't know." The barkeep shrugged. "It's not like you need my protection. Especially if I'm to believe what I hear in the street."

"And what do you hear? You never leave this bar, and I never see any customers in here."

"I keep to this bar, and still I hear." Lucian tapped his ear. "Nothing happens in those streets that I don't learn about. And right now, they're saying you're the best killer since the champion Gracchus. That you're a monster come to life. With enough spells to fight an army."

"How handsome do they say I am?"

"This is no joke, boy. People are talking."

"I don't care."

"Even when they talk of the bounty on you?" Lucian asked.

"Let them try to collect."

The barkeep sat forward. "What if they come here looking to collect?"

"Is that a threat?"

"Of course not," Lucian shouted. "I've no fondness for Piso, the bastard. But I have few friends on this island. And no spells to defend myself. I'm saying I can't protect you. And I'm telling you to be careful. People are asking questions."

"Maybe I've thought of that already," Cassius replied coolly. "And maybe I'm being so careful they won't find any answers."

"Who are you that you've planned your visit so carefully?"

"Just a man looking for work."

"Is that all?"

"What more could there be?"

3

Cassius lay sweating in bed all morning, unable to sleep. He listened to the rain outside his window, and when the rain calmed, to the sounds of the street. Shouts and laughter and dogs barking and children at play. He rose and moved the bed aside and lifted the notched floorboard and settled into the cool dark under the floor. He slept a fitful sleep. When he woke, his legs were cramped and it was night.

He thought he had dreamed of spiders. Or maybe he had dreamed himself a spider. He could not recall clearly. He was certain he had not dreamed of the jungle chase again. Those dreams stayed with him. Those dreams he could not forget.

He fished two massive spell indices from his rucksack. The tomes had thick covers of stretched leather inlaid with gold, their titles spelled in ink made from rare purple pine resin. These were copies of the official codices of runes produced by the Spellwright Collegium, the school of Antiochi arcanists who, in two centuries past, had discovered the ability to codify magic in writing.

Before then, magic was an esoteric pursuit whose secrets were obscured by ritual, offered only to the initiated few. In the primitive lands, they still knew the language of the Primal Ones, and with these shouts and cries, they could command the elements, could rain fire on their foes, call down storms from the vault of the sky, or call up monsters from the belly of the earth.

In Murondia and in the Fathalan lands, noble and ancient families had made terrifying pacts with beings beyond the veil. These contracts granted their descendants great favor. Some learned to craft weapons of immense power, blades whose names would outlive the men who wielded them and the kingdoms they won. Others could change their skins on a whim or bend time to their will. But the most feared were the suzerains, those who could summon the great beings themselves.

In the East, they had discovered the secrets of the lotus flower millennia ago, whose petals, when consumed, turned the mind of the eater into a weapon. Over centuries, botanists and alchemists had purified and enhanced lotus strains until now the great mentalists of the world could move objects with a thought, could invade the minds of their foes, twisting their wills, stealing their memories, trapping them in elaborate prisons of dream.

And in the Southern Kingdoms, the first civilizations had in man's infancy unlocked the secrets of his blood. Through corrupting rituals and obscene rites, they had welcomed into their veins a blight that could be used to animate the dead, to prolong the span of human life to inhuman proportions, to yoke demons and nameless horrors.

But two centuries past, the Antiochi had discovered the runes, a language that codified all forms of magic. With it, they had dragged the most esoteric of arts into the light, exposing it to all who were born gifted enough to power the strange symbols. Now nobles and slaves alike, men and women, if possessing the proper trick of their blood, could wield the runes. And on the backs of these brave new initiates, Antioch had spread its borders wide and made the civilized world tremble.

Cassius arranged the tomes on his bed. He retrieved from his rucksack a jeweler's loupe and a pair of tweezers. By candlelight, he donned the loupe and inspected the first jewel he had won from Junius. Etched in the facets of the jewel was the runic symbol he would have to craft in his mind's eye to cast the spell. Next to this was a notation for the page of the codex that would describe the rune, the effect the spell would produce, the range of the spell, the average casting time, possible counters. Finally, it would name the origin of the spell.

Cassius removed the loupe. He set aside the jewel and opened the appropriate tome and searched for the correct page.

He read. And for a while, at least, he did not recall the nightmares.

. . .

I t rained into the next morning, and Sulla arrived that afternoon.
"Cinna's been looking for you," she announced. She was sitting at
the bar with Lucian, spooning a bowl of thick stew. An open coin purse
lay between her and Lucian, a half dozen coppers spread across the bar top.
"Sent word, but you didn't answer. I thought you were eager for work."

"I've been here all day," the barkeep said. "I'd have noticed if they
sent word."

"They wouldn't have come here," Cassius said. "I told them I was
staying at a pension near the city walls. Few people know I'm staying
here. I intend to keep it that way."

"How did you expect them to find you?" Sulla asked.

"Small island. I figured word would reach me eventually."

"And you have faith I can keep your secret?"

"So long as I'm paying you."

"Secrets are expensive in Scipio." She pushed aside her bowl of
stew and gathered up the coppers and cinched the coin purse, then
tucked the purse away into a fold of her dress.

"Consider this some small compensation." Cassius drew a pouch
from inside his cloak and tossed it onto the bar. "Those are the spells
I won from Junius, the ones I didn't want anyway. I trust you'll be
able to sell them."

"Damn right I will." Sulla snatched the pouch off the bar and
hefted it to test its weight.

"Be careful with those," Cassius said. "If you have even dim magical abilities, you can hurt yourself by touching rune-scribed jewels
with your bare hands."

"Rest easy, boy," Sulla said. "You're the only damned finger wig-
gler in this room. And anyway, you should worry less about me and
more about Master Cinna. He's not a patient man."

T he main room of the Purse was half-filled with patrons. Idle
whores lazed in the heat, Antiochi women dressed in sheer
gowns, Native girls with large, dull eyes, aggressive ladyboys with
painted faces and dyed hair.

Cassius ordered a glass of water and took a seat at an empty corner table.

A pair of spellcasters drinking at the bar eyed him as he waited, their looks both openly covetous of his gauntlets and appraising. Theirs was the natural pose of a spellcaster amongst spellcasters, a type of predatory disdain.

They were wondering if he was as good as the rumors, wondering how many of the jewels in his gauntlets were fakes, there only to project false power. Cassius knew this feeling, had felt it himself at times, and he knew what was underneath it as well.

Fear. Fear that the rumors were true and more than true, that he was stronger than they suspected. Fear that all the jewels were real and that he wanted the curious to find out for themselves.

The spellcasters turned their gaze to a passing server. Cassius sipped his water.

Cinna emerged from the back room and made his way to the table, a long pipe in his hand. His face was sweaty, pasty with old powder. His wig sat crooked.

The sight of him sickened Cassius. He was Antiochi excess personified. Smug, voracious, never sated. Convinced of the rightness and the supremacy of his own hunger.

"The nose doesn't look so good," Cinna said by way of greeting. "It might be broken." He took a short drag on his pipe and blew a smoke ring past his fat, wet lips. The smoke was sweet and pungent, hashish mixed with opium.

"It wasn't such a nice nose to begin with."

"My man is blind now," Cinna said. "The one you attacked the other night."

"He attacked me," Cassius said. "He was overconfident and aggressive, and that cost him."

"Maybe." Cinna shrugged. "Either way. He's blind now."

"Are you looking for an apology?"

"I was looking for a reaction." Cinna motioned the bartender for a drink. "I saw all I needed."

"What does that mean?"

"You seem a cold man, Cassius. That's a shame. It used to be, days gone by, the sons of this Republic were passionate, full of fire." Cinna grimaced, flexed his flabby arms comically. "Eager to explore and conquer. To change the world."

"And now?" Cassius asked.

"Young men care only for money."

"You're starting to sound nostalgic."

"What brings you here today?" Cinna swatted at the flank of a passing girl. Cassius knew not if the girl were a patron or an employee, but she gave no reaction.

"I'm here to work."

"Provided the wage is sufficient, right? Why else? Not out of a desire to serve. Not out of fealty."

"I have to look out for myself," Cassius said. "Who would if I did not?"

"In days gone by?" Cinna asked.

"If that's what you'd like to talk about."

"In days gone by, it would have been your master's responsibility."

"You, then," Cassius said.

"Am I your master now?"

Cassius finished his water and set aside his cup.

"You're the man giving orders," he said.

Cinna chuckled, the sound devoid of humor. "What do you hope to accomplish here?"

"I hope to serve you." Cassius bowed his head, smiling.

"I don't like being mocked."

"I meant no offense."

"Tell me, boy, if you could snap your fingers and make your dreams come true, where would you be?"

The question surprised Cassius. Not the asking exactly, but the idea that he had never before considered the answer. He recalled a trip along the southern coast of the mainland, a training mission while still an initiate on the Isle. That was the oldest part of Antioch, so old most of its history predated the Republic. You could still glimpse the old world there, could see antiquity hidden in the shape of its buildings, in the odd curves of its roads, in the speech of its people.

He recalled a coastal villa with tranquil gardens filled with orange trees, the calming sounds of the ocean, warm breezes. It seemed a place he might lay his head in peace, without dreams.

In truth, Cassius knew the only place he wanted to be was here. He had dedicated years to his arrival. Cinna would learn that in time.

"I would be living in a palace. With an army of servants. A harem of beautiful women."

"So young," Cinna said. "So unambitious. I thought you were made of better stock."

"I didn't know I was being tested."

"You're always being tested." Cinna adjusted his wig. When he finished, it still sat askew. "But don't fret, I have uses for men such as you. Men with shopkeeper's dreams. There is a storefront on the south side of the Grand Market. It is advertised as a bookstore. The man who owns it pays a tithe to Piso. But after your visit, I will be his master. And he will tithe to me."

"All right."

"I sent a man to him some months ago, but still the shopkeeper has not paid. I want you to collect every copper he owes me from that day until today. If he shorts me a single coin, I will hold you accountable for the entire sum. Understand?"

"I do," Cassius said.

Cinna reached into his coin purse and produced an octan. "This is my symbol. Do you know its history?"

"I'm no history student."

"They paid soldiers with these in the early days of the Republic. They're nearly worthless. You'd need a hundred of them to buy a loaf of bread. But they were a promise from a general to his soldiers. It's a symbol of trust between a leader and his men. I give it to you now, in trust."

Cassius accepted the coin.

"Now go collect my money," Cinna said. "You have a shopkeeper's dreams, boy. So I am sending you to keep shop. Do not disappoint me."

At dawn, the shopkeeper opened his store and found Cassius sitting at his desk, his gauntleted hands splayed on the table before him.

"I don't want to hurt you," Cassius said. "Take a seat, and we'll—"

The shopkeeper shouted, dropped his ring of keys, and sprang at Cassius.

The shopkeeper was a full head taller than Cassius and much heavier. They stood wrestling for some time before he managed to hook a foot behind Cassius's leg and push him over. They fell together and hit the floor hard, Cassius on the bottom.

The shopkeeper mounted his waist and began to land wild punches to the side of Cassius's head.

Reaching up, Cassius grabbed the shopkeeper's wrists. The shopkeeper tried to pull free but could not; and then he leaned forward to choke Cassius, and Cassius bit him. He bit the first two fingers on the shopkeeper's left hand, breaking skin and stringy flesh before reaching a bone through which he could not bite.

The shopkeeper screamed. Cassius lurched into a sitting position and hit him in his throat, and the shopkeeper fell backward.

The shopkeeper rolled onto his stomach, crawling for the door.

A flash of light lit the room, and the air rippled with heat. A coil of flame, wire thin, appeared in midair, then whipped down and struck the shopkeeper across his back, disappearing with a hiss.

The shopkeeper screamed and collapsed. The back of his tunic was split from his left shoulder to his right hip, and the line of skin visible beneath was the purple of undercooked beef.

Cassius climbed to his feet.

"Don't move," he yelled, panting.

He stepped over the shopkeeper, straddling him. The man lay unmoving, his breathing slow. Cassius rolled him, and his head lolled backward, his eyes closed.

"Goddamn it."

. . .

The shop was advertised as a bookstore, but inside, there were no books. The first floor of the shop was a single, spare room, devoid of furniture but for a chair, a desk, and three metal chests chained to metal anchors in the ground.

The shopkeeper sat in front of the desk, his hands tied behind his back with the leather straps of his own sandals. He was crying.

"Stop that," Cassius said.

"Please," the shopkeeper said. "Please. Anything. Just don't kill me."

"I won't hurt you."

"Anything," the shopkeeper said. "I'll give you anything."

"Shut up."

The shopkeeper gasped.

The sight of the man disturbed Cassius. He did not like to see a man suffer, certainly not a man so defenseless. And the man was right to attack. Cassius had broken into his store after all. But Cassius had a mission, and sympathy was a luxury he could not afford.

"I don't want to kill you," Cassius said. "I'm only here to get the money you owe Cinna."

"I pay to Piso already," the shopkeeper screamed, spit flying from his mouth. "I shouldn't have to pay both."

"I was sent here to collect for Cinna." Cassius spoke firmly, in the voice you would use to heel a well-trained dog. "I can't leave until I have that money."

"I don't have any money."

Cassius walked to the door and opened it and peered outside. The Grand Market was humming with commerce. On the far side of the square, a troupe of performers held the attention of a small crowd. There were two jugglers and a sword swallower. A fire breather and a tumbler. There was a man walking on a pair of stilts, and as he moved, children threw stones at him.

Cassius closed the door and walked back to the shopkeeper. He searched the pockets of the man's tunic and found his coin purse. Inside were two silver coins and four coppers. One of the silvers was an obvious fake, and all four coppers were shaved.

"How much do you owe Cinna?" Cassius asked.

"I don't owe Cinna anything."

Cassius slapped the man. He did not feel the blow for the gauntlet he wore.

"How much?" he asked again.

"Damn it," the shopkeeper shouted. "Four silver. Four silver a month."

"And how many months do you owe for?"

"Six."

Cassius exhaled sharply, as though struck a blow. He sat on the floor and stared off into the distance.

"Where am I going to get twenty-four silver pieces?" he asked, speaking to himself more than the shopkeeper.

This was no test, he decided. Cinna had set him an impossible task and would level a heavy fine when he failed to deliver. He'd be Cinna's man for sure after today, not by his own choosing but because he was indebted to him. And if he displeased his new master, it was no great scandal to kill a man who owed you money.

It was a harsh lesson, the only kind Cassius seemed to heed. Cinna might look the part of a clown, but the man was no fool.

"I don't know," the shopkeeper said. "Please."

"What's in the chests?" Cassius asked.

"Nothing."

The man's key ring had only two keys on it. Cassius tried them in each of the locks without success. He thought about asking the shopkeeper for the true key, but the man was not likely to give it willingly, and Cassius did not want to hurt him.

He gripped the first of the locks in his palm and drew in his mind the rune for the Cold Touch spell. Frost spread over the lock, and a wisp of mist rose from the chilled metal. Cassius tugged, and the lock shattered in his hand.

The first two chests were empty. The third chest contained an oilskin pouch filled with a half pound of powdered opium.

"That's not mine," the shopkeeper said. "I'm just holding it."

"That's why the keys didn't work," Cassius said. "So who does this belong to?"

"Piso. If you take it, he's going to kill me."

"Give me twenty-four silver pieces, and I'll leave it. Seems a simple trade to me. Your life for some silver. Either you find a way to get me my money, or I take this pouch, and Piso slits—"

"I don't have any money." The shopkeeper started forward, straining against his ties. His face was red, the veins in his neck fat and blue beneath his mottled skin. "You're killing me." He hung his head. "Do it with a spell at least. Make it quick. Piso's men will do much worse."

"It doesn't have to be this way," Cassius said. "I know you don't have my money. I believe what you say. So tell me who does."

"What?"

"You're a man who knows things, right? The way I figure, a man who runs a shop like this has to have information."

"I know some things," the shopkeeper said.

"I don't want this pouch. It's going to take me weeks to sell what's inside, and I don't have that kind of time. But if you told me where I could find some money, I'd leave this pouch and move along."

The man sighed.

"Maybe you know another place like this," Cassius said. "Or a safe house. A high-stakes dice game. Any place of Piso's that will have money lying around."

"Piso's?" the shopkeeper asked.

"Piso's."

The man leaned his head back. "I know a place," he said, speaking to the ceiling.

The statue was twelve feet tall and carved from marble. It was a statue of a nude Native woman with blank eyes that, to Cassius, seemed to survey all corners of the Market. Behind it loomed the council hall.

Small offering bowls were set before the statue, filled with bread or fruit, fresh-picked flowers, scraps of silk, incense, candles.

An old Native man sat with his back pressed against the granite block that served as the statue's base. He was blind, his dark eyes rheumy and unfocused. As Cassius approached, the old man stirred.

"Come for make offering?" He was wrapped in a gray blanket. His arms thin and wiry, roped with fat veins. His skin was warm and earthy, a shade darker than corn.

"How did you hear me?" Cassius asked.

"She take not offerings," the blind man said, speaking Antiochi. "You people give bread, and she eat not. She want it not. You leave, and the bird, he eat."

"Is that right?"

"You call, and she answer not," the blind man continued.

"What good is she then?" Cassius asked.

"For you? She not good."

"Surely, she watches us, one and all, grandfather." Cassius was whispering now. "And although she remains unmoving, she witnesses every act, even the most futile."

"That is an unkind trick to play. To force me to use the tongue of the Outsiders when it was not necessary."

"Forgive me, it was habit." Cassius sat beside the old man. The Market was overflowing with traffic, but if anyone near the statue took notice of him, they showed no sign of it. He pulled his cloak tight about his shoulders and lifted his hood.

"You speak their tongue well," the blind man said.

"I have studied."

"They taught you when you were a child," the blind man said. "That is the only way. One cannot study a tongue enough to speak and fool a blind man the way you did. I thought you were one of them."

"I learned when I was young."

The blind man nodded. "That is their way. They teach a child their language, and as the child grows, their language is the language of its thoughts. That is how they take a child without taking it."

"And what of me?"

"What of you?"

"One who speaks both languages?" Cassius said.

"In which language do you think?"

"Both."

"No." The blind man shook his finger, the way one might signal displeasure to a small child or to a house pet. "How is it possible to think in two languages?"

"I do not know how it is possible. But I know that I do."

"Which did you learn first?"

Cassius considered this. He reached back into his memory for something he could not quite recall, a half-formed image, the sound of a voice, a feeling of warmth and safety. He tried to revive these things, to breathe them to life as one would breathe a spark into a hearth fire. But they vanished and he was left with only a memory of the memory, a false copy.

"I cannot recall," he said.

"Strange." The blind man scratched at his scalp. He was bald on the top of his head, and on the sides, he had long, thin, hair that hung over sagging ears. His hair was white, except at the tips, where it was the yellow of old candle wax. "There must be conflict in your life."

"There is."

"It comes from this," the blind man said. "From thinking in two languages. You war with yourself."

Cassius heard the beat of heavy boots on concrete as two legionnaires passed. They eyed him, then the blind man.

"Your mind never rests." The blind man either did not hear the soldiers or did not fear their presence. He continued speaking as though he and Cassius were alone together for a warm chat. "Am I right? I sense this in you. Sometimes, you cannot sleep for all the thoughts."

"Yes," Cassius said.

"Two languages. That is the trouble. Do you believe me?"

"I suppose you are right," Cassius said. "Although not in the way you think."

"You see? Conflict. Every sentence a contradiction." The blind man adjusted his blanket. "I would not want to live inside your head."

"Maybe not. Although to live under a statue is difficult as well."

"I do not find it difficult," the blind man said. "Mostly I am left alone. Except when the Outsiders come to make offerings."

"Do they come often?"

"More than you would think." The blind man swatted at a mosquito. "Is that why you are here? To make an offering."

"No, I was drawn by her." Cassius looked up at the marble figure. "She reminds me of something. I cannot place it, though."

Since leaving the bookstore, Cassius had wandered the Market for hours. Thinking, anticipating, trying to build a framework for battle in his head as the Masters had taught him hundreds of times. While walking, he had caught sight of this statue again and found himself overcome by a singular urge to sit in the shadow of the goddess. It made him feel safe, like the compartment under the floor in Lucian's bar, although he was not sure why.

"Well, sometimes the Outsiders will leave gifts. They have many gods, as do the Khimir. And yet they take more. They take gods, they take land, they take children, they take magic. But this is futile when the offerings are made to Isvara, the watcher. She will accept offers from no one. She will favor none. She will only stand and watch, as she has done for all time."

"And yet the Outsiders fear her?" Cassius asked.

"Some. And maybe that is how you make good people of them. Let them think they are being judged. Then they are decent. Not because it is good in itself. But because they are afraid of what will come."

"I see," Cassius said.

"Do you agree?"

"I do not know."

"Because you think like them," the blind man said.

"Maybe."

"I say it not to insult you but to make you aware," the blind man said. "You use their language, and you think like them. Even your voice betrays you. You speak with an accent."

"I do not."

"You do. You do not hear it because your ears have grown accustomed to their words. But to one such as me, who remembers a time before their words, the accent is clear. You have been amongst them for too long."

"I was away for some time," Cassius said.

"For how long?"

"Long enough, I hope."

The house was gray and rotted and stood leaning to one side, its foundation sunk into the Lowtown mud. Greasy roaches crawled in the wood of the outside walls. Cassius knocked at the door, the sound muffled by the damp wood. He was alone on the dark street, but he felt as though he was being watched.

"Who is it?" a voice called from behind the door.

"Marcus Tullus sent me," Cassius said.

The door was silent for a second, then, "Who are you?"

"I'm here to drop off a package."

Cassius scratched at his scalp. It was a deliberate gesture, but he did not want it to appear deliberate, only to show that his hand was empty if someone was looking.

"What did he tell you?" the voice behind the door asked.

"He told me to tell you that it is warm under the wing of a dragon."

The door eased open. The man inside was tall and wiry. He had a long, thin face and a scar that twisted from his lip to a half inch below his eye. The knife in his belt was long-handled, with a curved blade nearly a foot long, the kind preferred by knife fighters.

"Who are you?" the scarred man asked.

"A friend of Marcus's," Cassius said. "My name is Jacomo."

"Let me see the package."

Cassius reached for a fold in his cloak but checked himself. He held his hands up, palms outward.

"May I?" he asked.

The scarred man nodded.

Cassius withdrew a pouch.

"Give it here." The man reached for the pouch. Cassius pulled away.

"Marcus told me not to give it to you," Cassius said. "I have a key to a safe inside. He told me to place the package in the safe."

The scarred man nodded. He stepped aside, and Cassius entered the house.

"Safe's upstairs," the scarred man said.

Cassius motioned for the man to precede him.

They climbed the stairs to the second floor, where three men sat rolling dice, with stacks of coins and banknotes at hand.

Two of the men wore daggers tucked into their belts. Cassius could see the long handles of their knives above the lip of the table. The third man sat close to the table, and Cassius could not see his waist nor what he might have tucked there.

"Over there." The scarred man pointed to the corner of the room, where sat a large chest similar to the ones at the safe house. It had an iron lock and was chained to a bolt in the floor.

The scarred man moved to the empty seat at the table. He called for the men to hold the next roll, then pitched a handful of coins into the middle.

"Five or better," one of the gamblers called.

"Hundred I do?" said the man holding the dice.

"Aces," the scarred man shouted. "Aces."

Cassius walked to the safe and kneeled, his back to the table. He set the pouch on the floor and grabbed the lock. He slipped his free hand under the edge of his cloak and into his gauntlet.

Dice clattered on the table.

He began to draw the rune in his mind's eye. A dozen lines, curved like worms and spiraling out from a central circle. The spell was a picture in his mind now, but when he finished, it would be a geyser of unquenchable flame.

He had cast it a hundred times before today. Two hundred times probably. But now he halted.

Four men would be on the other end of the fire. Four defenseless men.

He began to slide his hand from his gauntlet. It trembled.

He balled his hand into a fist.

Four bad men, he told himself. These were no honest citizens. They were thieves, extortionists. Murderers, probably. They would slit his throat for a handful of coppers and not lose a night's sleep over it. He breathed heavily. He closed his eyes.

"Hey, boy," one of the men called. "What are you doing over there?"

"I'm about my business," Cassius replied. "You should be, too."

He heard a chair scrape floorboards. He glanced over his shoulder and saw one of the knife fighters rise from the table. He was a Widsith, a wild man of the Black Forest beyond the borders of the Republic. A large man, with a wide, angry face and shoulders broad as a bull's. He had braided brown hair that hung to his waist, threaded with beads and rings of bronze, and had also a thick beard, a face decorated with tattoos of black ink that stood in striking contrast to his pale skin.

"This house is my business, boy," the Widsith said. "Master Piso pays me to keep nosy urchins like you out."

"I'm here to deliver a package."

"Is that what you're doing? 'Cause it looked to me like you were playing with yourself under your cloak."

The other men at the table laughed.

"Just leave your package," the scarred man said. "And then get out before we lose our patience."

"I have instructions. I'm not to leave this package with anyone."

"We weren't asking." The Widsith drew his massive knife, its long handle carved in the shape of a wolf's head.

"Nice piece of steel," Cassius said. Under his cloak, he lowered his hands to his gauntlets. "Wonder if you've ever used it? Or if it's just a nice conversation piece."

"I've got twenty-three notches on its sheath."

"Didn't think a Widsith could count that high."

The man loosed a roar. Cassius could not tell if he flipped the table and leapt over it or if he had charged forward, knocking it over in his mad rush. Either way, his intentions were clear.

The Widsith's footfalls shook the rickety house. Cassius watched his approach, standing with calm poise. The Widsith dropped the blade low for an underhand stab that would drive steel through Cassius's bowels.

Cassius's cloak fluttered. A sudden blast of heat shook the air.

He heard a scream, and he closed his eyes.

Afterward, Cassius sat with his back to the wall, bleeding. His hands were shaking. He tried to still them by force of will, but he could not. A smell like overcooked bacon filled the room, a smell so strong he could taste it. The air was smoky and burned his lungs.

He removed one of his gauntlets and probed the wound in his belly with the tip of his finger, his flesh like the flesh of an orange, slick and wet. The wound was not deep although it had bled enough to soak his tunic and his cloak. His groin was wet with blood, and blood ran along his inner thighs and pooled on the floor.

It had been quick. He had used fire, which was quiet enough, and there had been only brief screams. The flash did not worry him because the room had no windows.

He rose to his feet and stood holding his belly. He made his way to the overturned table. Some of the coins there were charred and melted into odd shapes, and the banknotes were ruined but for a single bill worth twenty-five silver pieces redeemable at a bank in Meroe, a Shona port town in the Southern Kingdoms.

He checked each of the bodies and found little of value beyond the ornate knives. One man held a corn husk filled with thin cigars, another a snuffbox made of horn. Inside the snuffbox was a fine, gray powder, and Cassius snuffed a pinch and his face grew numb. Garza root, a powerful stimulant.

He snorted, the taste sharp and rank in the back of his throat, then tucked the snuffbox under his belt.

Surveying the room, he found himself discomforted by the sight of the charred eyes and the open mouths, but there was no deeper revulsion and he considered this a victory and the first sign of something he could not yet name. A kind of transformation. He thought on the word he was looking for but could not find it and realized that maybe there was not a word for it yet.

He rose and felt dizzy, his head throbbing. He doubled over and coughed until his eyes watered. He spat something dark.

As he descended the stairs, he broke his necklace and left the octan on the bottom step. Then he exited the house, closed the door behind him, and headed for Hightown.

"Quit whining. I've seen bee stings worse than that."

Cassius lay naked on the bar, a towel draped over his groin. He was breathing in short gasps and focused on the ceiling. The physician stood at his side, needle and thread gripped in one hand and a bowl of soapy water nearby.

Lucian sat at the opposite end of the bar, eating broiled chicken with his hands.

When the wound was stitched, the physician applied a clear salve, then a bandage made of clean, dry linen. He helped Cassius sit up.

"Clean it twice a day and dress it," the physician said. "If it gets red or starts to leak, come see me. And take it easy for a while. Give those ribs time to heal."

Cassius paid the physician three silvers, and Lucian walked him to the front door, then locked the door and returned to his meal.

Cassius climbed off the bar. His legs were bloodstained, his pubic hair matted with dried blood. He dressed in a fresh gray tunic supplied by Lucian, his back to the barkeep.

"Goddamn it, boy," Lucian whispered.

Cassius turned. "What?"

"That scar." Lucian sat staring.

"A souvenir from earlier times," Cassius said, his voice hard-edged. "When I was young and stupid."

"Not like now, when you're old and wise and servant to a big boss like Cinna."

"Is that the word on the street?"

"Yesterday, Sulla came to say that Cinna was looking for you. And tonight you show up with your belly sliced open. I'm no fool, boy." Lucian picked his teeth with a sliver of chicken bone. "And I'll say this about your new employer, he's a thug. Mix with men like that, and you put your goddamn life at risk. Not to mention your honor."

"What do you know of him?" Cassius tore a piece of bread from a loaf set on a nearby plate and chewed it absently, the bread drizzled with oil and garlic.

"As much as anyone would want to know. And I'm telling you to be careful. All business in Scipio is corrupt. But it's also corrupting."

"What does that mean?" Cassius asked.

"It's hard to explain." Lucian licked his fingers, wiped them on the front of his tunic. He filled his cup from a bottle of wine then filled a second cup. He motioned for Cassius to sit by him, and Cassius did. "You'd have to live your whole life here to understand. And that's a fate I wouldn't wish on anyone."

"So why do you stay?" Cassius sniffed the wine in his cup.

"The same reason everyone stays. I can't make it elsewhere. Which is why I have trouble understanding you. And worse, I worry that if you stay, you'll become like the rest of us."

"I'm stronger than most," Cassius said. The words sounded convincing to his own ears. He wanted to believe them.

"So is your new friend Cinna. And look what this island did to him." Lucian gestured for Cassius to finish his wine and Cassius did and Lucian refilled his cup. "Not a topic for polite conversation, though."

"You won't offend my delicate sensibilities."

"This was years ago," Lucian said. "Back before the Uprising. Before the island had two bosses, and Quintus still ruled from the city. The island was a frontier province, long forgotten by the mainland. A cesspool even then."

"And who was Cinna then?"

"Just some merchant from the mainland. Nobody important."

"A shopkeeper?" Cassius asked.

"That surprises you, does it? Well, it's true. That goddamn grotesquerie you see oozing its way through his bar"—Lucian thrust out his already sizeable belly, twisted his face into a leer, grunted lasciviously— "that's what this city made him."

"How?" Cassius scratched at his bandage.

"When he landed, there was some unrest with the Natives, as there often was. These were the Natives who lived in the city, not the tribes from the jungles. Those had been beaten back by Quintus's father a generation before, driven so deep into the jungle, they were almost myth. At the time, Natives in the city outnumbered Antiochi three to one. And they were restless. They rioted, killed soldiers, anything to disrupt the rule of law."

"Quintus's rule," Cassius said.

Lucian nodded, downed another cup of wine. "Our young friend Cinna disliked Quintus's rule as well. And he was rich enough to do something about it. So he aided the Native troublemakers, helped organize them. Regimented their training, planned attacks, offered bounties on legionnaires. All the while acting to the public as an honest merchant."

"Seems a lot of trouble for one man."

"He had help," Lucian said. "From Piso."

Cassius sucked his teeth.

"Like I said, this was a long time ago, boy." Lucian stared off into the middle distance, then nodded, confirming something to himself that Cassius would never know. "Cinna and Piso were friends then. They organized and operated a dozen Native gangs, managed their own Antiochi mercenaries, and ran legal businesses that were making them rich. Illegally, they ran protection rackets."

"And since they planned all Native attacks, they could offer better protection than the legion."

"Exactly. Pay, and you were spared. Refuse to pay, and you were targeted."

"That's genius," Cassius said.

"I admired it at the time, too." Lucian leaned off his stool and spat. He wobbled. Cassius steadied him with a hand. "Cinna and Piso were great at portraying themselves as champions of the Natives' cause. Their moves were covert, but for those of who knew what they were doing, they played the role of revolutionaries, not men grabbing for power."

"Those of us who knew what they were doing?"

"You have to understand, the conditions of the Natives were terrible then, worse even than they are now." Lucian sighed, stared into his empty cup. "They were slaves in everything but name. You couldn't buy and sell them. Officially, they were citizens at this point, living on Antiochi soil, even if they didn't see it that way. And the goddamn Republic would never tolerate open slavery of its own subjects. Foreigners? Certainly. And before conquering a people? Of course. But after the land was part of the Republic, Antiochi law protected the Natives. In theory, at least. In truth, their lives were worthless."

A single peal of thunder sounded in the distance. It began to rain, the downpour loud on the roof of the bar.

"You didn't answer the question," Cassius said.

"Certainly they were right to want change. And maybe they were right even to try forcing it through bloodshed. Hell, I don't know anymore, if I ever did. But that was the state of things then."

"And you?"

"I was a fool." Lucian looked to Cassius and then looked away. He grabbed the bottle of wine. "Eager to change this terrible world. If you want to make money, that's fine. I've no qualms about that. But I wasn't content to work for wealth. Sell myself for gold like some—" The barkeep waved the bottle.

"So you weren't a bartender back then?"

"I was Piso's man." The barkeep made to fill his cup but stopped and raised the bottle to his lips instead. "First time I've said that aloud in years."

Cassius set his hand on Lucian's shoulder. The barkeep lowered his head.

"I thought I was fighting for something worthwhile. Live long enough, and you'll see how rare it is to believe in something enough to risk your life for it. And you'll see how dangerous that belief can make you."

"So how did things get to be like this?" Cassius asked.

"Piso and Cinna grabbed for more power than they could handle.

Quintus ruled from the city then. The legion's fort was still in the jungle, and Quintus split his time between both places. In the fort, he was unreachable, completely protected. But the city was different. One day, there was an attempt on his life at the council hall. He was wounded terribly."

"Piso and Cinna were behind it."

The barkeep shrugged. "Who knows? Neither ever claimed responsibility, but who else could it have been. Afterward, Quintus retreated to the fort. Withdrew his entire army. Left the city undefended against the Native gangs."

"It must have been chaos."

"There were riots for days," Lucian said. "The mob was inexhaustible. The city belonged to Cinna and Piso for a week. A whole damn week. And then Quintus mobilized his legions. Before the coup, he had been fighting a guerrilla war. But after the Natives took the city, he changed his strategy. He marched out of the fort with his entire goddamn army. Twice as many men as Cinna and Piso, and better trained and better equipped. He sacked the city in two days, turned most of Hightown to ash."

Cassius started to speak but then fell silent. When he spoke again, his voice was husky, strained.

"What was the city like?" he asked.

Lucian wiped his face with the back of his arm. He took another swig from the bottle.

"He slaughtered them all," Lucian said. "Civilians, women, children. None were spared. The Native army collapsed and went back into hiding. Quintus had no way to fight an army hidden among his own citizens. So he built gallows in the town square, held public executions for days. Killed thousands. Natives and Antiochi alike. Foreign merchants. Anyone suspected of aiding the Uprising. Anyone he couldn't trust. All to force people to talk.

"They found that Sulla's father was aiding the Uprising and beheaded him in the plaza. We served together us two. He had a family. A terrible thing."

"Is that why you trust her?"

"She's not the type to forget the help I offered her family," Lucian said. "Not much help, but all I could spare."

"And where were Cinna and Piso during this?" Cassius asked.

"Hiding. Planning. They were going to stage a mass exodus of the Native army. They bribed a pirate armada to transport the men to an island near the Turmii Straits. Once there, they would set up camp, train, reequip, hire mercenaries, and plot another attack."

"They were going to start a civil war?"

"Piso was an old army man himself," Lucian said. "His family had connections that ran to the high council in Antioch City. Quintus, on the other hand, had never been to the homeland. Had never set foot in the senate. He simply took his father's place when he died. His men stayed because they were loyal to him, but his country was another matter."

"So Piso and Cinna thought they'd be able to topple Quintus," Cassius said. "Then get the support of the High Senate to install themselves as the new leaders of Scipio. And since no one cared about this province anyway, there wouldn't be much resistance."

"Not so long as the bribes continued to flow."

"So what happened?"

"The day of the exodus came, and the ships arrived as planned," Lucian said. "Two dozen of them. I'll never forget the sight of them speeding toward the docks of Lowtown. Emboldened by the fleet, the Native armies fled their homes en masse. Most had never revealed themselves. Not publicly anyway."

"Weren't you scared of the legion?"

"We knew it would be a fighting retreat. But Quintus had no navy. He couldn't chase us to sea. And once the ships appeared, our ranks swelled. We couldn't have beaten the legion, but we could have fought them off long enough to make it onto the ships."

"But you didn't make it onto the ships," Cassius said.

"Never even docked." Lucian shook his head. "They anchored a half mile out at sea. Watched us fight the legion for a whole day. And after we were beaten, the ships sailed the hell away."

"What happened?"

"It was all a trick. The ships arrived long enough to draw the Native fighters to one place. And then the legion showed and slaughtered us. Cinna and Piso double-crossed the Natives." Lucian drank the last of the wine, then upended the bottle over his open mouth.

"Why?"

"For Scipio." The bottle slipped from Lucian's hand, shattered as it hit the ground. He laughed bitterly. "Piso and Cinna wanted the city. So Quintus gave it to them. In return, he demanded they sacrifice the Native army. Piso and Cinna got to be bosses, and Quintus got to punish the Natives. Everyone won."

"But you said Piso and Cinna don't really run this town," Cassius said.

"They don't. This is Quintus's town. He outmaneuvered them again. He offered to let them rule so long as both those bastards were beholden to him. The council would remain to keep up appearances but wield no real power. Cinna and Piso agreed to his terms."

"Because they never really wanted to help the Natives," Cassius said. "They were just using them to grab for power."

"Exactly."

"So how could Quintus trust them to be peaceful?"

"He didn't," Lucian shouted. "He knew they were lying about serving him. Once they were in control, they would build their goddamn forces again, waiting to stage another coup. So he drove a wedge between them. He split the town in half. Piso got the docks. Cinna got Hightown. Of the two, the docks are worth more. Plus, Hightown was in ruins."

"So Cinna became resentful."

"Both bosses had to pay tribute to Quintus." Lucian snatched Cassius's mug. He patted his stomach, loosed a wet belch. "Piso could afford his, but Cinna couldn't. Not with most of his land destroyed. So Cinna did the only thing he could to survive."

"He attacked Piso," Cassius said.

"And that's what started the first of the wars between Piso and Cinna. It's been like that ever since. Sometimes, there is peace, like now. But then Quintus raises the tribute, and both bosses are forced to take more from each other."

"Which leads to fighting. Which leads to killing. Which weakens the forces of both bosses so that neither can challenge the legion directly."

"All while Quintus grows fat in the jungle."

Cassius shook his head. "This place is a nightmare."

The barkeep raised his mug. "Let's hope we all wake up screaming someday soon."

LEARN TO BE STILL

———

In Celembria, they called him Doe Eyes. He was a boy of six, and he made his home in the narrow alleys near the docks, sleeping amongst stray dogs for warmth. During the day, he subsisted on half-eaten scraps of food scrounged from garbage heaps or else stole apples and pears from fruit vendors. He wore only a threadbare tunic and a pair of sandals, his hair mangy and unkempt. His breath stunk always, and the dogs he slept with gave him fleas. But the women in the red house said he was beautiful, and they named him Doe Eyes.

They might have called him by his given name, but the boy had refused to speak for the last six months, not even to offer his name. His mother had warned him to be wary of strangers and to answer none of their questions. Your speech will give you away, she said. He listened.

His mother had made him promise to keep quiet around others and to run if he felt scared. Most importantly, she made him promise to be strong. His mother was gone now, but every night, he prayed she would return, and every day, he kept his promises to her.

On the outskirts of the docks stood a house with windows lit by red lanterns. A young woman named Flavia lived in that house. She was tall and heavy, with olive-hued skin and dark hair that hung down her back in long, loose ringlets. The first time he met Flavia, the boy saw her knock a man unconscious with a single punch.

The boy was wrestling with a dog over a ham bone that day. A small crowd of old men and beggars had gathered to watch the contest, standing about and cheering, most for the dog. The boy had gotten a two-handed grip on the bone, but the dog was tireless, and the boy was near to losing the contest when he heard a shriek from the crowd. He turned to see Flavia shoving through the press. A raggedy beggar with a wide straw hat tried to stop her from interfering, and Flavia punched him in the face, a clean punch that sent the man reeling. Still charging forward, she kicked the dog in its ribs and the dog slunk away and the boy looked up at her, the bone held before him, and she shouted for him to drop it, her scream scared instead of angry, as his own mother's had been the time he brought her a snake he had found near an old well. The boy dropped the bone, and Flavia grabbed his arm and pulled him out of the crowd and pulled him all the way to the house lit by red lanterns.

Flavia lived with her ten sisters, and when she brought the boy home, some of her sisters cooed and petted him and others shrieked in surprise and shouted for him to leave. Flavia wanted him to stay, though, and she was big enough to get her way.

Flavia fed him milk and bread and an apple, all the while asking the boy his name and where he came from and who his mother was. The boy met her questions with silence. She asked if he were mute and the boy did not respond, so she pinched him. The boy cried out and Flavia said he was no mute and told him to speak or she would send him back out to wrestle with the dog.

The boy did not want to wrestle the dog again. His hands still throbbed from bone splinters. But thoughts of his mother pushed the pain from his mind, and he stood silent. He had promises to keep.

Flavia sighed. She looked down at the boy and frowned and asked what she was going to do with him, asked it as though speaking to someone else although the room was empty but for the two of them.

Later that night, she washed him and shaved his head and dressed him in his tunic, which she had cleaned and mended. She laid him to rest in the basement, piling old cloaks on top of him until he felt warm and safe.

"Do you remember me?" she whispered in his ear.

He stared up at her in silence.

She smiled, her eyes filmed with tears, and wished him good night. For the first time in six months, the boy slept through the night.

Flavia let him sleep in the pantry for most of that winter. Each night, he crawled through a narrow opening in the wooden gate and snuck around the back of the house to the door that led into the kitchen. There he waited for one of the women, usually Flavia, to let him inside.

Sometimes no one opened the door. Usually, these nights saw too many men inside the house, and neither Flavia nor her sisters could spare a moment away from their guests. Other nights, Mother lurked about, and no one opened the door for fear she would catch him.

The sisters fed him often. Cold bean soup, crusts of bread, sour pickles, sometimes a hard-boiled egg. After that, they put him to bed under the pile of old cloaks and with a sack of flour for a pillow. Sometimes he woke to find Flavia sitting nearby, watching him sleep, and other times he heard her singing to him, her songs working their way into his dreams. They were sweet songs, but they were not the songs his mother had sung, songs about rain and a river, and knowing this, they only made the boy miss her more.

Each morning, Flavia's sisters chased him outside, rushing him into the alleyways and warning him not to return while Mother was about. At first the boy misunderstood, thinking his own mother was visiting the house. Once, while the sisters were busy with housework, he snuck through the back gate and caught sight of this new Mother, a thin, old woman with heavy powder layered on her wrinkled face and a small, deformed left hand that she kept wrapped in red silk.

Mother beat the girls with wooden spoons when they were slow at their work, when they sulked or dallied, when they displeased her. When she caught him lapping up a saucer of warm cream left outside for an old tomcat, she tried to beat him as well. She threatened to clap him in chains and sell him like a plucked chicken if he ever returned. The boy kept his distance from Mother after that.

One night, while swaddled under musty cloaks, the boy heard crying from the kitchen upstairs. He often heard noises in the house, strange shouts and grunts, men calling on gods. There were always men in the house at night although none lived there.

He dozed in fits. Sometimes he woke to the sound of crying and sometimes the crying seemed to come from his dreams. The crying scared him, but Flavia had been clear in her instructions. He was allowed to stay in the basement but not to come upstairs. If he came upstairs, they would put him out of the house, and he would spend the night in the cold streets, a threat sister Minna made good on once.

He listened to the crying for some time. Between sobs, he heard voices. It seemed the girl crying was Flavia. He hated to hear her cry. It made him scared. He wondered what was wrong with Flavia, but thoughts of sleeping outside tempered his curiosity. Even in the basement, he could hear the howl of strong winds and knew a night spent in the streets would be terrible. There were not enough dogs in all of Celembria to warm him against that cold.

Sometime later, he heard steps creaking. He looked to see Flavia approaching from the dark, a small candle held before her. She set the candle next to him and kneeled and stroked his head.

She told him that she knew who he was, that she knew from the first moment she saw him.

Her breath smelled of wine. Her hands were rough and clumsy on his head.

She told him that he was her own baby boy, returned to her after all these years. She could see it in his eyes. No one else could look at her as he did.

She was sorry that she had lost him. Mother had demanded it, though. When Mother found out about him, she had taken a switch to Flavia and burned her with an iron and cut off her hair, and still Flavia would not give him up.

Finally, Mother had fed her tea laced with a tincture of Blood Belly, and he had disappeared before she ever laid eyes on him. He was here now, though, and that was all that mattered. She would let no one take him away again.

The boy kept his silence.

4

They talked through the night, and the barkeep was still drunk at breakfast. He smoked while Cassius ate boiled eggs. The tobacco Cassius bought him smelled sharp, and its smoke was heavy and dark. Cassius tried some but found it unpleasant. It made him cough and then he vomited from coughing. The vomiting hurt his ribs, and the barkeep thought this was funny.

Afterward, he shared a mug of warm rum with the barkeep and fell asleep at the table. He dreamed of fire.

He woke to the sound of a knock at the door. The barkeep rose and called out and received no answer. He opened the door partway, and Cassius saw there a small boy limned in the pink light of dawn. The barkeep conferred with the boy, then handed him a copper. He closed the door and turned to Cassius.

"Someone's looking for you," he said.

Cassius was ushered into the bathhouse by a Native woman. She asked what kind of bath he would like, and he asked what kind was best for a hangover.

"You are hungover?" the woman asked.

"No, I'm drunk," Cassius said. "But soon I'll be hungover."

The woman nodded, feigned concern. "Cold bath."

He asked to be attended by a girl named Tadua. The woman led him to a private room, and soon the young girl he had met at the bathhouse the other night arrived, along with the old woman.

"I didn't expect to get your call so quickly," he said.

"It is too soon?" asked the young girl.

"No."

"What did he say?" asked the old one.

"He says that we worked fast," the young girl said.

"Let us hope we are paid as fast."

"Where is—" Cassius left his sentence unfinished.

"Come, we show you." The young girl motioned for Cassius to follow her.

They made their way deeper into the bathhouse, past a swimming pool, then into a room with a fountain and benches, where men sat naked or sat draped with towels. Serving girls and boys offered drinks and tobacco and hashish and opium and coca leaves for chewing, all arranged on trays. They passed through a steam room and down a flight of steps into a dank, stone basement, then through a porthole that led to a sewer.

In the sewer, there was a wide stone ledge that fronted a slow-moving underground stream. The stream was black, and the air stank of excrement and salty urine.

The sewer was unlit except for a few beams of sunlight that leaked through a small grate overhead. It took a minute for Cassius's eyes to adjust to the dark. When they did, he saw a man lying on the stone ledge that fronted the stream. He lay on his back, and his left eye was covered by an eyepatch. He had short dark hair and wore a black tunic and a hooded, short cloak.

"Is this good?" the young girl asked.

"I don't know," Cassius said. "You tell me."

"What is his problem now?" the old woman asked. "Tell him we did as he told us."

"This is what you wanted," the young girl said. "This is Piso's man. We know him. He goes to Lowtown baths. He talks all the time of Boss Piso, and he wears his symbol."

"Show me," Cassius said.

"Tell him we had to pay a boy to bring this man here in a cart," the old woman said. "And then the boy had to drag him into the bath as though he were drunk. Tell him about the boy and the cart."

The young girl walked to the one-eyed man and lifted the sleeve of his tunic over his shoulder. He bore a brand on his bicep. Three diagonal slash marks, the flesh raised and red as wine.

"See," the young girl said. "Piso's man. And he is killer, like you told us to get."

"Is he dead?" Cassius asked.

"No, he is sleeping. We use what you give us. Will this kill him?"

Cassius shook his head. "It only makes him sleep."

"When will he wake?" the young girl asked.

"In a few hours. You need to do again what you did to him earlier. Dip a knitting needle in the potion and then jab him in the thigh. Do this twice a day. At sunup and sundown."

"Where did you find this potion?" the young girl asked.

"That's none of your concern. You only have to know that it is expensive and not to be wasted. Now remember, twice a day. Will that be a problem?"

The young girl shook her head.

"How long can he stay down here?" Cassius asked.

"For a short time," the young girl said. "They clean here once a week. We have four more days."

"That should be enough time," Cassius said. "You need to cover his eyes with a blindfold. And then gag him. You don't have to feed him. But give him water when you poke him. Wet his gag, that should be enough. Do you understand?

"I do."

Cassius walked to the one-eyed man and kneeled by his side. He unhitched the man's gauntlets from his belt, then began to undo the belt.

"Help me with his cloak and eyepatch."

Cassius scanned the front room of the Purse. It was early afternoon, and the crowd was small. The room smelled of cherry-scented incense and smoke, and beneath this, of human bodies, of sweat. Behind the bar stretched a large mural of dancers at practice, adolescent girls painted in pinks and creamy whites. They were dressing, their backs arched, mouths open.

Sulla approached Cassius from a corner table. She leaned against the bar and did not look at him.

"Buy me a drink," she whispered over her shoulder. "Then lean in close. Put your hand on my ass."

"Sulla, I—"

"Don't be weird," Sulla snapped. "Just do it."

Cassius placed his hand on Sulla's ass. She knocked it away.

Cassius ordered a drink, and when it arrived, he handed it to Sulla. She flashed a withering smile and thanked him dryly, then walked off to a corner table. Cassius followed.

"Have a seat," she whispered.

"I thought you didn't want people to know we were working together."

"If you make it seem like you're hitting on me, then people won't think we're conspiring." Sulla looked away, feigned distraction. "They'll just think you're drunk and horny. Touch my knee."

Cassius set his hand on Sulla's knee. She slapped him.

"Damn it." His nose began to bleed.

"Don't act so angry," she said.

"I'm not acting."

"Word is you're Cinna's man now," she said. "So where's my money? Ten percent of any upfront money Cinna paid you. Plus a weekly retainer."

"Take it out of the money you owe me from the sale of those spells," Cassius said.

"I haven't moved them all yet." Sulla gnawed at a fingernail. She caught herself in the act and lowered her hand into her lap. "I have to be discreet. People know you killed Junius. And maybe they know I was there when it happened. If they notice me selling a batch of spells shortly after, then I look complicit."

"Move those spells, and you'll get your money," Cassius said. "In the meantime, I need a favor."

"Ask me for a handjob, and you'll be putting your life at risk."

"Piso's got a man who works for him. A killer. Dark hair. About my height. He's missing an eye. Sound familiar?"

"Servilius." Sulla lifted her mug to hide her lips as she spoke the name. "One of Piso's favorites. Bit of a gambling problem."

"Would people in Hightown recognize him by sight?" Cassius asked.

"They might."

"Would Cinna's men?"

Sulla nodded. "Definitely. But what's Servilius have to do with anything?"

Cassius shrugged. "I heard he might have a problem with one of Cinna's men. He might be coming up to Hightown to settle a score tonight."

"That's a lie," Sulla said. "You're lying to me. No one is coming up to Hightown. Not after the trouble last night."

"What trouble?" Cassius asked.

"Haven't you heard? One of Piso's safe houses was raided. Four of his men were killed. Some of his men suspected it was an attack from Cinna, so they ambushed a patrol of Cinna's guards. Killed two. Wounded two. And the fifth was taken to Lowtown and hung."

"Damn."

"Piso's furious because his men acted without permission," Sulla said.

"Does Cinna know about this?" Cassius asked.

"Of course he does. And he's not pleased. If you speak with him today, it better be to bring good news."

The balcony on the top floor of the Purse overlooked Hightown. It faced west, with a view that was clear to the docks on one side and to the city walls on the other.

A slight breeze cooled the hot night. The sky was overcast, heavy with a coming storm.

"You did a good job getting my money," Cinna said. He leaned out over the balustrade, his girth pressed against the wrought iron, his gaze fixed on the street below. "You're learning, and that's good. After the trouble we had last night, I need men who can follow orders."

"I don't act unless you tell me to," Cassius said.

He scanned Cinna's face, looking for hints of his true feelings about the money. Displeasure, curiosity, maybe even admiration. He was adept at reading subtle clues. It was the same skill he employed in combat, where the only warning he might have of a spell was some small sensory cue, a brief flash of light, the sound of a beast's cry as it breached the veil, the faint smell of flame in the air.

But although he was a formidable spellcaster, he was no expert on Boss Cinna. And that smooth, bland face hid its secrets well.

"I won't tolerate anyone's getting an idea to take revenge," Cinna said. "Is that clear?"

"Of course."

Revenge.

Cassius thought it an ugly word. Base and nasty. Not at all like the high art he had learned on the Isle.

Cinna lifted his nose and sniffed. He closed his eyes. "Rain today."

"Rain every day," Cassius said.

"I suppose." Cinna propped his elbow on the balustrade and rested his round chin in the palm of his hand. "Although if you live here long enough, you don't notice."

"Seems to be that way with a lot of things."

In the distance, a man screamed, a high, wailing shriek that ended abruptly. The streets fell silent again.

"How strong a spellcaster are you?" Cinna asked.

"I've never been formally tested."

"You're my man now. If I'm to pay you, I will see you tested."

"And if I refused?"

Cinna stared at Cassius, his look pointed and searching.

"Respectfully refused," Cassius said. He stepped back, opened wide his cloak, and bowed. The Isle had taught him that discipline and power were necessary for survival. But so were deceit and obsequiousness, in the right circumstance.

"I'd be curious why."

"A point of pride. Professional courtesy. Whatever you like. Spellcasters only benefit from being unknown. My goal during a battle is to get my opponent to overestimate my strength or to underestimate it. But never to know it."

"Kind of like now."

"How do you mean?"

"Maybe I'll think you don't want to be tested because you're weaker than I suspected," Cinna said. "And not worth the money I'm paying. Or else you're much stronger than I suspected."

"And what would be the benefit of hiding that?"

Cinna stroked his slick neck. "I wonder."

The Grand Market was mostly empty and the rain on the concrete loud. Cassius sat at the stone fountain, his cloak heavy on his shoulders. At the council hall, ten legionnaires stood guard. Rain dripped from the wide brims of their helmets and Vorenicus's eagle feathers sagged.

Even at this remove, Cassius noticed those feathers. Shining and pure. They did not belong in Scipio.

The sky flashed bright, then gray. A peal of thunder shook the air, and Cassius closed his eyes reflexively. When he opened them again, the legionnaires were moving across the plaza at a run, Vorenicus in the lead. They navigated the maze of tents and stalls and emerged on the far side of the square as the fire at the shack reached the thatched roof.

Vorenicus dropped his shield in the street and charged into the house. A crowd had formed. Another legionnaire followed him inside just as the fire spread across the roof. Smoke began to roll out the front door, then two people emerged, a man and an old woman. They staggered into the street and collapsed, their faces blackened.

Seconds later, the legionnaire exited the house. He bent double in the lane and coughed and wiped at his face. Behind him came Vorenicus, a small Native child cradled in his arms.

He placed the child on her feet and led her to the old woman, leading her slowly and talking to her as they moved. He handed her off to the old woman, and the woman hugged the child. Seconds later, the roof of the house collapsed in a shower of bright embers.

The old woman was seated on the floor, and she grabbed Voreni-cus's hand as he turned to leave and she kissed the hand and threw back her head and wept in the rain and cradled the child to her heavy body, all while Cassius watched.

With the patch over his left eye and the hood of the cloak raised, Cassius lost most of his sight. The visible world narrowed to the span of four fingers directly in front of him, disappearing completely on his periphery.

The alley was cramped. Large refuse piles, wet from the earlier rains, writhed with vermin. The moon shone above him, a pale sickle in a haze of mist, and by its light, he stared out at the city walls.

A middle-aged fat woman approached him from the street. She had bleached hair and thin lips, and she wanted to know if Cassius was looking for company.

"I am," Cassius said.

"Maybe I could be your company," the woman slurred. She yanked down the top of her dress, flashed her breasts.

"Maybe." Cassius offered the woman a half-silver piece. "What could I get for that?"

"Whatever you want."

"I want to know about a man named Brieus. Blond hair. Works for Cinna. Patrols out here sometimes."

"What you looking for that bastard for?" the woman asked.

"Not a friend of yours?"

The woman spat. "No friend of mine. Always robbing me. I pay enough already. I don't need to give him a cut, too."

"Have you seen him around tonight?"

"Not yet," she said. "But I will. He's always out here."

"If you see him, send him this way."

"What should I tell him?"

"Tell him the truth," Cassius said. "You saw a man with one eye by the wall. He looked like he was up to no good."

She made a sound deep in her throat that was part laugh, part wheezing cough. "Are you playing with me?"

"I wouldn't dream of it."

The woman wandered off, and Cassius stood waiting in the dark mouth of the alley.

Cassius woke in Lucian's stables, his ears ringing and the world distant and unfocused. A smell like a snuffed candle hung in the air and, beneath this, the smell of curdled milk. Next to him pooled pink vomit.

There was a voice in his head. It spoke a tongue he did not understand. He called out to it, and the voice did not answer but instead began to fade, growing faint and distant, like an echo dissipating as it traveled. And then it was gone.

He tried to sit up but could not, his body tense and numb and none of his muscles responding to his will. His face slick with sweat. His hands throbbing.

He tilted his head and scanned the dark stables and spotted his gauntlets, half-covered by the short cloak, which lay crumpled in the dirt. He reached for them and the muscles in his arm strained and he grunted but no sound came, then his hand was folded inside Lucian's hand and Lucian's face was over him and he began to shake and he shut his eyes against the roar in his head.

Cassius squinted against the sunlight through the small window. He was naked, covered in a thin sheet. His hair was wet, and the muscles of his jaw ached. He rolled and spotted Lucian sitting in the center of the room, perched atop a high stool.

"You awake, boy?" Lucian asked.

There was an earthenware pitcher on the floor, a stained towel, and a deep clay bowl, the bowl filled with water and the water scummed with bloody soap and bits of dark matter.

"Where are my gauntlets?" Cassius asked.

"You were carrying two pair. Both are under the bed."

Cassius sat up and retrieved his tunic from the foot of the bed and dressed. His hands were bloodstained. Blood caked in his cuticles, under his nails.

He fetched both pairs of gauntlets from under the bed and hitched his pair to his belt and set the other pair on the mattress and inspected it. It was set with roughly fifteen jewels, the worth of an apprentice spellcaster.

"You want to talk about last night?" Lucian asked. "You were out fighting, weren't you? Had yourself a goddamn fit."

"I don't remember." He did remember, of course. Remembered many things. The hiss of Brieus's short sword drawn from its scabbard. The growling of the wolves, their lips peeled back over slavering fangs. The cries of the watchmen as the beasts set upon them. Brieus calling to the gods for an end to his pain.

And another sound, a voice. One he could not quite place but that seemed familiar nonetheless.

"It was worse than the one you had earlier," Lucian said. "You fell in and out of consciousness. Cried out. I thought you were dying."

"Did I say anything?" Cassius asked.

"You said a lot." The barkeep stood and walked to the window. "You called for your mother."

"What did I say exactly?"

"It doesn't matter," Lucian said.

"It does to me."

"Working for Cinna is your choice, boy." Lucian stood haloed in the light from the window, gray and weary and worn, like the statue of some suffering god who, unique among his kind, was not immortal. "But I don't want any trouble brought to my doorstep."

"I wasn't working for Cinna last night. And I wouldn't have come here if I thought I was followed. I know better than that."

"I hope so."

"Is that my blood?" Cassius asked. He found his boots next to the nightstand, soaked through with blood, as though he had walked a slaughterhouse floor. He reached for them. His hands began to tremble.

"You were drenched in it. But I didn't find any wounds on you."

"It's all hazy," he said. "I forget things when the sickness comes over me."

"Smart man might take that as sign that he's traveling the wrong path."

Cassius did not respond. He sat staring absently until Lucian called his name again. And then he came to attention.

"Did you ever fight during the Uprising?" he asked. He slid his boots on, one and then the other.

"Yes," Lucian said.

"Did you have a hard time with it?"

Lucian shrugged. "I was fat, if that's what you're asking. I tired easily."

"That's not what I'm asking."

Lucian turned from the window. He squinted in the light.

"Doing something unpleasant gets easier with repetition," he said. "Do you understand what I'm saying, boy?"

"I do," Cassius said.

"You have to be careful about doing a thing too much. Otherwise, it can get easy to do. Even if you don't want it to. Even if you regret it afterward."

"Would you call that sacrifice?"

"I'd call it stupid," Lucian said.

"If you put your life at risk for something that is just, or put your soul at risk, or your mind, then that makes you—" Cassius bit back the word.

"Makes you what?"

"If you sacrifice something for the greater good, you are a hero by definition."

"Piss on that," Lucian shouted.

"Just like Attus."

"Are you daft, boy? Attus fought because he was a fugitive slave. He didn't want to lead a rebellion. He needed an army to help him rob desert merchants. And to protect him from his enemies."

"You're being cynical. That's not how history remembers it."

"Don't speak for history," Lucian said. "You should see what Fathalans write about him. They say he was a madman. A savage. A child murderer. And in the Eastern Kingdoms, they don't know his name at all. Don't need to. They have their own warlords to lionize."

"Attus was a spark," Cassius said. "The Antiochi revolution had been fomenting for years. But it took Attus, just one man, standing up and fighting to ignite a fire. A fire that swept the Fathalans all the way back to the desert. A fire that cleared away the brush so something new could take root and grow. It's the same thing you were trying to do in the Uprising. The same thing someone needs to do now."

"Your sense of history is warped, boy," Lucian said. "And as for the Uprising, we were fighting for Cinna's and Piso's profits. We didn't know it at the time. But ignorance doesn't change the truth."

"You thought you were doing something just."

"And I was wrong. Do you know how Piso and Cinna tricked me into believing otherwise?" Lucian stared at the boy in his blood-soaked boots. "Because I thought myself a hero on some damn crusade."

The midday sun broke through a low veil of clouds and shone on the east end of the city, the tradesmen's district. The streets were crowded with foot traffic and mule-drawn carts. Laborers sang filthy rhymes as they toiled. Cassius moved amongst these people, his gray cloak pulled tight and his gauntlets, the instruments of his own work, hidden from view.

There was a hierarchy amongst the craftsmen of the east end, and the layout of the streets matched. At the top were metalworkers. Silversmiths and goldsmiths and weaponeers specialized in rare alloys. They occupied the Street of Silver, the Street of Gold, and the Street of Steel, places near the Market and with easy access to the main avenues into Lowtown, where supplies arrived from the docks. Their shops were large, with dozens of workers and storehouses guarded by famous mercenary companies.

Below this group, and farther from the Market, were masons and sculptors, whose workshops lined the Street of Stone, where statues of gods and heroes and monsters rose half-formed into the open air, straining to break free of their prisons of rock.

After this came papermakers and scribes, textile workers, skilled and unskilled laborers. And occupying a rare niche in this system were men who traded in blood and bone. Vivisectionists, torturers, chirurgeons, physicians. They were outcasts amongst honest workers, their shops small and rude and pushed up against the city wall, with bloodstained stoops and the smell of decay wafting from their doorways. Flesh was cheap in Scipio, and the trade attracted only the desperate or the deranged.

Hidden in the midst of the flesh workers, at the end of Charnel Row, was a curious stucco shop whose sign depicted a pair of crossed gauntlets.

The door to this shop was open, and when Cassius called for the owner, he received no response. He scanned the front room and found it empty and entered the room and was two steps past the door when he felt a thrumming in his chest. He spun and reached for his gauntlets as a Yoruban emerged from a side room.

The Yoruban was in his middle twenties, tall and with a shaved head, a thin, neat beard, ebon skin. He was shirtless, his belly paunchy but his arms long and muscular and slick with blood. He wore a bloodstained wrap tied about his waist, the wrap reaching to his knees, and wore also a pair of jeweled gauntlets.

"Easy," the Yoruban said.

Cassius's hands hovered at his waist. He lowered them slowly, all the while watching the Yoruban.

"I'm unarmed," Cassius said. "I'd feel better if you were as well."

"You're in my shop." The Yoruban had a deep voice. His Antiochi was flawless, and he spoke it with the singsong rhythm of his native tongue.

"As a customer," Cassius said.

The Yoruban nodded, conceding the point. He slid his gauntlets off and tossed them onto a nearby table, the table cluttered with vials of powder and colored liquids, jars of salve and cream.

Cassius had never before seen a spellcaster disarmed this willingly. The Yoruban moved so casually, his expression so self-assured, that he half suspected this to be a trap.

Then the Yoruban smiled, a wide jovial smile so out of place in Scipio that Cassius was certain this was a trap.

"Relax," the Yoruban said. "You have nothing to fear here. What can I help you with?"

"You're a healer."

"I am. Are you in need of my services?"

"I might have broken a few ribs."

"Come."

The Yoruban passed through an alcove hung with a white sheet, and Cassius followed. In the other room, he found the carcasses of two pigs splayed atop thick sailcloth, the sailcloth stained with blood and with flecks of gore and entrails.

"Lunch?" Cassius asked.

"Patients." The Yoruban sat atop a high stool and motioned for Cassius to stand before him. "Or at least practice for the real thing."

"Has business been slow?"

"Business is always slow."

Cassius surveyed the shop. Rich tapestries covered the walls, multicolored weaves that mixed bright greens and yellows with deep reds. Here and there, strong-scented candles burned, casting the room in soft light. Scrolls with intricate, hand-drawn anatomies lay unfurled, some labeled in Antiochi and some in the ideograms of Eastern Kingdoms and some in languages Cassius had never seen before, dead languages written on ancient parchments carried up from the depths of stygian tombs.

"May I?" the Yoruban asked.

Cassius nodded. The Yoruban pressed his large hand against Cassius's side, and Cassius winced. The Yoruban felt along Cassius's ribs with the tips of his fingers, prodding bone and bruised flesh until Cassius yelped with pain.

"Two ribs," he said. "Maybe three."

"Broken?" Cassius asked.

"I believe so. I know a bone-knitting spell. Do you want me to fix them?"

"Maybe."

"Maybe?"

"Why is business slow?"

"Because healing by spell is expensive," the Yoruban said. "And I'm young. And the process is dangerous. The people here don't know me, and I have no one to vouch for my talents."

"So why practice here?"

"It is a hard path to become a healer in the Western Kingdoms. There are guilds and colleges who hold monopolies on healing spells. They stifle outsiders. I didn't want to spend half my life working as an indentured servant. So I came to Scipio, where I could practice my art undisturbed."

"I can appreciate a man who operates on his own," Cassius said. "That's not very common in Scipio."

"This is true."

"There's a lot of pressure in this town to pick a side. For prosperity. For safety."

"I think I take your meaning." The Yoruban nodded gravely. "Rest assured, I serve no master but my art."

"I notice that you haven't asked my name yet."

The Yoruban smiled. "I figured you would offer it when it suited you."

"You're a discreet man, then."

"The privacy of my patients is important to me."

"Privacy is my main concern," Cassius said.

"I see."

"More so even than the ribs."

"Understood."

"I know that healing is expensive, but I'd be willing to pay for it and pay for privacy as well."

"My prices are fair. And you'll get what you pay for." The Yoruban's eyes were amber-colored and heavy-lidded. They were attentive and concerned but not intrusive. "I would, of course, need to be paid up front."

"Do you have many spells?"

"Not many. But I have the right spell for you."

"Do you have a spell to seal a wound?" Cassius asked.

"I do."

"And to staunch bleeding."

"That as well."

"What about a spell to draw out wound rot?"

The Yoruban shook his head. "This is a master-level spell. Maybe a few hundred exist in all the world."

"Would you like to own this spell?"

The Yoruban paused, measuring his words. "I'm afraid I can't answer that before I know your intentions."

Cassius reached into his tunic and drew out a small leather pouch. The pouch was tied with twine, and Cassius handled it by gripping the tip of the twine between thumb and forefinger.

"This is a wound-rot spell. I'm sure you have spell indices here. I'll let you examine the rune, then we'll check the indices and you'll see I'm telling the truth. This spell is worth a fortune and it will be yours if you can keep my secret."

The Yoruban looked to the pouch. He stood and pressed his hands together and bowed and, even bowing, he was nearly as tall as Cassius.

"Respectfully," he said, "I don't believe this arrangement will work."

"Why not?"

"I must be paid up front. And you will want to hold the spell so that I will hold your secret."

"I will hold the spell, but I will also pay you up front. Gold for the healing, every time I need it. And then the spell, no later than three weeks from today, if I find you have kept my secret."

The Yoruban sighed heavily, the distress on his face plain.

"You don't think this is a good deal," Cassius said.

"No, I think it is too good a deal. It makes me nervous."

"You have every right to be cautious but no need to be nervous. I'll prove this to you. For now, we will have a simple transaction. One healing, paid for with coin in advance. What do you say?"

The Yoruban wrung his large hands. "I am trying to say something, but I need to find the right words."

"Say it plainly. That's best."

"I am curious why you want this deal. But I don't want to ask, lest you think I am not being discreet."

"I will tell you this, and hopefully it will put your mind at ease," Cassius said. "You are a man who has an art and has work to do. And you have come to Scipio that you might do that work without interference. I, too, have an art and a job that I am here to do. And I would see it done without others impeding me. Is that fair?"

The Yoruban nodded, his gaze fixed on the leather pouch. "Fair enough."

Cassius lay on the wooden table. There were leather straps set into the table, two at the level of his wrists and two at his ankles. The straps were for restraining patients during healing, but Cassius refused to be restrained.

The Yoruban stood at the side of the table. He held a bowl and brush and with these he slathered Cassius's bare chest with a thin red-brown liquid. Then he set down the bowl and gathered two candles, one in each hand, and brought these to the table and wafted their heavy smoke in Cassius's face.

"Breathe deep," he said.

Cassius breathed deep and coughed.

"You have been healed by spell before," the Yoruban said.

"That didn't sound like a question."

"It wasn't a question. That scar on your back is proof enough."

"I was hurt."

"Badly."

"Very badly," Cassius said. "My back was broken. They thought I would die."

"It's a miracle you did not die."

Cassius recalled a different room. Dark and damp. The ceiling dripping. His hands and feet bound. A strip of leather between his teeth for biting. And a pain so immense, so unending, the thought of it took his breath away even now.

"Sometimes I think it would have been better that way."

"The healing was painful, yes?" The Yoruban set a hand on Cassius's shoulder, as though to apologize for the pain of that healing and for the pain of the healing to come and for his profession in general.

"It went on for days."

"They were trying hard to save you."

"They were testing a spell," Cassius said. "Practicing on me because they thought me a lost cause."

The Yoruban stood stunned. He closed his eyes and whispered something in his native tongue, then kissed his fist and pointed to the heavens. Cassius thought it a prayer, and although the gesture was touching, it was also futile. He had prayed back then, and no gods had answered his calls.

"Who did this to you?" the Yoruban asked.

"My trainers."

"And where did you train?"

"The Isle of Twelve."

"My goodness," the Yoruban said. "You must be quite a spellcaster."

"I suppose."

"They train the touched exclusively."

"They do."

"And the legends of the Isle's cruelty are true, then, judging by your story."

"It was a hard life," Cassius said.

"I am sorry for the hurt they caused."

"There is no need to apologize."

"This, of course, will not hurt as bad," the Yoruban said. "But it will still hurt."

"I understand that."

The Yoruban set aside the candles and brought a cup of milky liquid to Cassius's lips.

"None of that," Cassius said.

"It will help with the pain."

"I need my senses sharp. Just be quick about this."

The Yoruban donned his gauntlets. He stepped to the side of the table and placed his hands on Cassius's side, his touch light and gentle, the iron of the gauntlets cold.

Cassius turned his head and stared across the room. On a far table, the Yoruban's spell indices lay open, and next to the indices lay the jeweler's loupe with which the Yoruban had inspected the jewel. And in the middle of the table, resting atop the leather pouch, sat the jewel itself.

Cassius focused on this small speck of color, a smoky purple that shimmered in the candlelight.

"Take a deep breath," the Yoruban said. "And then exhale."

Cassius filled his lungs. He felt a thrumming in his chest. He exhaled, and as he did, a ripping pain tore through his side. He gripped the table, gritted his teeth. He could feel his broken ribs twisting inside his flesh, realigning themselves. The pain grew, radiated to his flank and his back, deep into his lungs.

The Yoruban stood with his eyes closed, head bowed, constructing the rune in his mind's eye. He held Cassius, pressing down on him with his large, gauntleted hands, and not letting up even when Cassius bucked and screamed.

Another wave of pain hit, cold and shuddering, and Cassius thought this would be the end of him, the final shock that stopped his heart. Then, suddenly, the Yoruban stepped back, and the pain was gone.

Cassius gasped. He was trembling now, his heart racing and his body coated in sweat. He sat up slowly and inspected the site of the broken ribs. The flesh there was still bruised, but when he pressed his fingers against the rib bones, he found them straight and secure, with no pain to palpation.

"Are you all right?" the Yoruban asked.

Cassius nodded to the pigs. "Better than your other patients."

The street leading to the Madam's Purse was blocked by a shoddy barricade of wooden logs. A dozen men stood guard in mail, sweating in the heat.

A guard recognized Cassius as Junius's killer and motioned for him to pass, and Cassius bent under the barricade and moved up the street to find another half dozen guards posted at the door of the Purse.

He entered the back room of the bar and found Cinna seated by himself. The table was set with a large plate of ribs, bowls of fruit salad, cabbage dressed in red sauce, bean curd, a soup of clams and mussels.

"Are you hungry?" Cinna asked. He wiped sauce from his soft chin.

"No." Cassius took a seat at the table.

"Eat something, or I'll be offended." Cinna snapped a rib in half, sucked its marrow. "Have you heard about last night?"

"The accounts vary. I don't know what to believe."

"We were attacked, out by the city gates." Cinna pointed the cracked rib at Cassius. "By Piso's men."

"And what are the casualties?"

"Three dead. Including a spellcaster." Cinna belched, then sneered, as though tasting something unpleasant. "Two more injured. That makes ten casualties in two days."

"Who was it?"

"Witnesses at the scene claim it was a one-eyed man," Cinna said. "Piso has a killer that fits the description. Man by the name of Servilius."

"So what do we do now?"

"We? I didn't realize you were a part of my inner council." Cinna glared at Cassius. His words hung in the air, as foul as his burp. "I have men at work to uncover what happened exactly. In the meantime, I've increased forces in the main avenues leading into Hightown, as well as our presence in the Grand Market."

"What of the back routes and the alleyways?"

"I don't have enough men to cover all the streets. But we need to show force. This is the best way. Piso's doing the same."

"Why attack us now?" Cassius asked.

"I have my suspicions."

No one spoke.

"Do you have something to say?" Cinna asked.

"No."

"You're worried about my suspicions."

"I worry you might think this is retaliation for your hiring me on," Cassius said. "Maybe Piso is seeking revenge for that man of his I killed."

"And if he is?"

"It puts you in a difficult position."

"How so?" Cinna snatched up a cluster of grapes, nibbled them three at a time.

"You don't want to lose more men on account of me. But you can't exactly turn me over to Piso and be rid of me, either."

"Can't I?"

"Would you so publicly betray a man who wore your mark? Roll over for Piso like a beaten dog?"

Cinna sucked his teeth. He tossed aside the half-eaten cluster of grapes.

"No one likes a man who thinks too much, Cassius. It makes people nervous. You don't want me to be nervous, do you?"

"Of course not."

"Where were you last night?"

"At a bathhouse," Cassius said. "And then playing a bit of dice."

"And where did you sleep?"

"In a hostel."

"Why didn't you sleep here?" Cinna asked. "With your new associates?"

"I don't like the company of whores."

"You'll spend tonight here with me," Cinna said. "To be safe. These are dangerous times. Do you have a problem with that?"

"Would it matter if I did?" Cassius asked.

Cinna smiled.

A pair of serving girls entered and began to clear away the plates.

"I saw legionnaires in the streets this morning," Cassius said. "I thought they didn't patrol Scipio."

"They don't. But they want to learn as much about the trouble last night as they can. Do you fear them?"

"I don't fear anyone."

"You have no reason to fear them so long as you're under my protection. Should you leave my employ, though, I don't know how they'd treat you."

"What does that mean?"

"The legion here are notorious for their brutality," Cinna said. "Have you heard about the Uprising yet?"

"Just a little," Cassius said. "Only rumors."

"A difficult time in the history of this island. But there are many lessons to be learned from it. The wrath of the legion, for instance. Do you know what the reward for turning in a runaway savage was during the Uprising?"

"I don't."

"Nothing. Quintus paid not one dirty copper for aiding his cause. But do you know what the punishment was for harboring a savage?"

Cassius shook his head.

"Death," Cinna said. "Death by hanging or by decapitation for the savage. And death by crucifixion for the Antiochi. For sheltering even a woman or a child."

"A stern measure," Cassius said.

"But fair. Quintus was more eager to punish the betrayer, the Antiochi, than the savage. To him, betrayal was the ultimate offense. Such was his sense of honor. Do you know what the punishment was if they discovered you knew someone was harboring a savage but did not inform on him?"

"No." Cassius shifted in his chair.

"They cut out your tongue. If they want to be silent, Quintus said, let them be silent forever."

Cassius nodded.

"This was a great man," Cinna said. "A terrible man. A thousand years ago, they would have written epics about him."

"And now he rots in a jungle," Cassius said.

"And his betrayers rot in graves. There's a lesson in that, boy. You'd do best to learn it quickly."

5

Cassius passed a fitful night in the Purse. He kept himself awake with snuffs of Garza-root powder, which left his nose raw and with a rank dripping in the back of his throat. In the middle of the night, Cinna had sent a young Native girl to his room. Cassius paid her to lie next to him and sing him a Khimir song about rain and a river, a lullaby to put children to sleep. The girl had a sweet voice.

Breakfast was served in the back room of the Purse. Cinna was there and Nicola and a man Cassius had never met, this new man middle-aged and with a pockmarked face. The table was set with platters of eggs and sausage, fresh bread, bowls of sliced melon, pitchers of water and wine.

Cassius sat watching the others eat. A pair of gauntlets rested in the new man's lap, and Cassius eyed these and eyed the new man.

"Why are you not eating, Cassius?" Cinna gnawed a chunk of sausage, his lips coated in grease. "Is my food not good enough?"

"I'm not hungry," Cassius said.

"See, now, this worries me." Cinna talked with his mouth full, spitting flecks of sausage as he grew agitated. "A man not eating my food in my house is a disgrace. It's my duty to provide for you. That's the order of things. I provide for you, and you, in turn, serve me."

Cassius filled a cup with water. He held the cup but didn't drink.

"I don't mean to lecture," Cinna said. "But boys your age have to learn these lessons."

"What lessons are those?" Cassius asked.

"Lessons of loyalty. Of service. Honor. The young don't know these things."

"Or maybe the old don't care to teach."

"Oh, don't you worry about that." Cinna produced his opium pipe and lit it from a nearby candle. He took a long pull and exhaled through his nose. "I intend to teach you, boy."

"You'll find I'm a lethally quick study." Cassius looked to the pockmarked spellcaster.

The spellcaster grinned.

"There's trouble coming," Cinna said. "And if you're to help me in the days ahead, I'll need to know how strong you are. Now I know you're strong enough to beat one of Piso's men in a goddamn street fight. And strong enough to scare a shopkeeper out of his money. But how strong are you really? Today, we'll find out."

There was a knock at the door, and a serving girl entered. She whispered to Cinna and he nodded to Nicola and both men stood and left the room.

"What's your name?" Cassius asked.

"Aulus." The pockmarked man sprinkled tobacco into a wide, dried leaf, then rolled it and licked it sealed, his movements slow and deliberate, as though he knew he was being watched.

"How much is he paying you to do this?"

"What makes you think he's paying me, boy?"

"You make a habit of killing people for free?"

Aulus's mouth twitched. He plucked a candle from the center of the table and lit his cigar and set the candle down.

"If Cinna wanted you dead, he could have killed you last night." The cigar dangled from the corner of his mouth as he spoke. He exhaled a dart of white smoke.

"Maybe. Maybe not. It would have been a lot of trouble if he had tried. The way I see it, though, this match of ours has two outcomes, both of which benefit Cinna. If you kill me today, then Cinna will know I wasn't as powerful as the rumors. And he'll be rid of the headache of my history with Piso in the process. And if I win, well, then he's got one hell of a killer on his hands."

Aulus smiled. "Always so paranoid?"

"It's served me well in the past."

"Spellcasters fight. It's in our nature. Sometimes we die. If you expect me to take it easy on you, then you're in the wrong line of work." Aulus removed the cigar from his mouth and blew on its tip and the ember flared. "Of course, if you're nervous, we don't have to fight. Just set your gauntlets on the floor and walk out of here."

"Are you Cinna's best?" Cassius asked.

"A man like me, who counts modesty as a goddamn virtue, I couldn't answer that question. But if I did say yes, there aren't many around here who would challenge the claim."

The betting odds were against Cassius. He had expected a more favorable spread after his victory over Junius, but Aulus was a skilled spellcaster and a prizefighter of some renown. He had won his last fifteen matches, eight of those fought to the death.

The testing ground was an empty storehouse two blocks from the Purse, a training facility where Cinna's killers could spar with their own without risking their gauntlets and their lives against unknown opponents in the street.

The crowd was small, roughly twenty people, and made up of Cinna's men exclusively.

A short, pale man presided over the fight. He stood by the far wall, near the small cluster of onlookers, and called for silence, and the crowd grew quiet.

A young boy moved across the ring to Cassius. The boy held an earthenware bowl, the bowl filled with sea salt, and Cassius scooped out a handful and tossed the salt onto the floor. The boy then approached the pale man and approached Aulus, each man salting the ground in turn.

"May the gods keep you both," the pale man said.

He threw up his arms. The spellcasters donned their gauntlets. Cassius felt a flutter in his chest as Aulus began to draw on the rune energy.

Without further introduction, the pale man dropped his arms.

Cassius saw his mouth move, but he did not hear the words announcing the start. The sound of fire hit like a rush of wind. A wall of flame had risen in the center of the room, and now it was toppling forward, collapsing onto him.

Cassius crouched reflexively. With his mind's eye, he drew the rune for his fire ward, then felt a great release, a spasm through the muscles of his back, from his shoulders to the base of his spine.

The wall of fire was on top of him now, but he felt no heat from the flames. The fire washed over him and he breathed sharp smoke and shut his eyes against the glare, but he did not burn. When he opened his eyes, the flames had died to low wisps.

Aulus spat, his discharge sizzling as it struck the hot earth. He circled to his right, and Cassius moved counter to him.

Cassius pointed two fingers before him, and the air there grew hazy, like heat waves rising from pavement, then a massive boar stood between the two spellcasters. It seemed a trick of the eye.

The boar was four feet high at its shoulders, with stout legs and bristly hair the color of red mud. It lowered its head, aimed foot-long tusks at Aulus, and charged.

Aulus clapped his hands and spread them wide. Cassius felt a thrumming in his chest. Steam curled up from the floor, and when it cleared, a lizard lay on the ground. It was small, little more than a foot long. It lay motionless, so still that Cassius wondered if it was not an illusion.

The boar started at the smell of this new creature, the dank scent of festering swampland. The lizard hissed, and there was a flash of limbs. Cassius caught sight of the lizard's underbelly, heard the boar grunt in pain. When the struggle subsided, the boar lay on its side, the lizard's jaws sank into its meaty haunch and poison bubbling from the puncture wounds. The boar twitched and kicked futilely; and then it stilled.

Someone in the crowd whistled. There was a smattering of applause.

Cassius held his hands before him, palms up, and a drop of rain appeared in midair and fell. Where the raindrop landed, a crack opened in the earth and from out of the crack burst a vine as thick as a man's arm.

The vine rose ten feet into the air and toppled under its own weight. It hit the ground with an audible snap, like the crack of a whip, then slithered off toward Aulus.

The air rippled. Aulus gestured as though drawing a sword from a scabbard, and before him materialized a flaming scimitar. It floated in midair, spinning, shedding sparks. He motioned at the vine, and the blade sped off whistling. It struck the vine, sliced it in half.

The newly cut vine never slowed but sped onward and wrapped around Aulus's ankle and tugged and he collapsed, landing on his back with a groan.

The vine looped Aulus twice, one of its coils taut around his neck. He gasped, his face red. His eyes were closed, and he was trying to work his fingers into the space between his neck and the vine.

A cloud of black smoke formed over the ring. There was a sound like a candle being snuffed, then the smell of brimstone wafted through the storehouse. Cassius covered his mouth and nose. Behind him, he heard someone in the crowd vomit. A tense, airless quiet reigned for a brief second, then a column of flame fell from the cloud.

The fire struck the ground and exploded outward. The shock wave hit Cassius like a hammer to the chest and knocked the wind from him. The air grew hot. He shut his eyes, blocking out Aulus and the ring and the fire and the crowd, so that his world was reduced to a colorless canvas, with a shining rune drawn upon that canvas.

He opened his eyes to find himself on the floor. His ward had held, deflecting the fire, and all throughout the warehouse small patches of flame danced and shimmered. He rose to his feet and wiped the soot from his face.

The boar and the lizard were little more than charred bones. Most of the vine had been rendered ash and what remained was limp and smoking. Near the wall, several men were afire, and they rolled and screamed, while others beat the flames engulfing them.

Aulus crouched on his knees, dusting himself. He spotted Cassius and raised his hand. The sound of stone grinding stone filled the storehouse. A mound of earth jutted up from the ground, churning and twisting on itself. When it settled, it lay in the shape of a creature whose form seemed impossible, made of flesh and hide and having the legs and arms of a man and having also hooves and a snout, a wide spread of white horns that bent forward and tapered into points sharp as any spear.

Cassius stared in wonder at the creature, the first of its kind he had ever seen. He tried to decipher its parts, to break it into precedents, but he could not tell what was beast and what was man. It rose onto two legs, a man's legs but ending in hooves, and it spread its arms wide, a man's arms but too large for a man, and it shook its head, a bovine's head with ink-black eyes.

Cassius's heart quickened.

The beast stamped and lowed, looking to Cassius, then to the men in the crowd. Across the ring, Aulus pressed his fingers to his temples, sweating and gasping from the effort of will needed to command such a creature. If he could not establish dominance, the creature would heed no will but its own animal instincts or its own human intelligence, whichever reigned in that fearsome skull.

Cassius saw his opening. He waved a hand, and a burst of light flared near Aulus, a bright display but no real threat, a simple cantrip that ended in a loud but harmless explosion.

The beast started at the sound. Sighting Aulus, it fixed its gaze on the spellcaster and tensed and charged. It moved faster than anything Cassius had seen on two legs, and Aulus had time to raise his gauntleted hands but no time to cast.

The beast lowered its head, the huge hump of muscle on its upper back quivering. Aulus managed to twist between the points of its horns, and then the beast lifted its head with violent speed and struck Aulus and knocked him into the air. Aulus sailed over the creature's back, landed in a motionless heap in the center of the ring.

The beast turned. It fixed again on Aulus and tilted its head to aim its horns, and as it dove for the prostrate form, a beam of purple light shot from the sky like a falling arrow. The shaft of light punched through the beast's chest, and although the blow would have floored a full-grown man, it merely stopped the beast midcharge.

The beast stood stunned for a long second, then reached for the purple shaft jutting from its chest and the shaft vanished and the beast sat down in the pool of blood collected at its hooves and, still sitting, died.

The storehouse fell silent.

Cassius crossed to Aulus. He rolled the spellcaster onto his back and removed his gauntlets.

"Finish him," called someone from the crowd.

Cassius did not respond. He slapped Aulus stiffly on each cheek. He ground his gauntleted knuckles into Aulus's sternum, and Aulus groaned and opened his eyes.

At the sight of Cassius, he started and raised his hands and, seeing his hands were bare, he exhaled sharply, resigned to his fate.

"It's over," Cassius said. He pulled Aulus to a sitting position.

"Why?" Aulus rubbed his ribs, winced.

"You fought me fair."

A murmur went up from the crowd, then the crowd parted to reveal Cinna, red-faced, gape-mouthed. He scanned the chaos surrounding the spellcasters as though trying to piece together the chain of events by the sights that lay nearby, a collection of grotesqueries more at home in the realm of nightmares than in the physical world. He looked to Cassius, then to Aulus.

"Aulus, grab your gear and meet me outside with the best killer in this lot." He gestured to the crowd of his men. "I have an important job. And gods help the bastard who screws it up."

"The best killer here?" Aulus asked.

"Did I speak too softly?" Cinna roared.

Aulus nodded toward Cassius. "That's him."

They passed into Lowtown at noon. They had kept to the alleyways and narrow lanes that skirted the Grand Market to avoid the roadblocks and guards Piso had stationed in the main southern avenues, and now Nicola led them through deserted side streets.

"Won't people recognize us?" Aulus asked.

"We won't be here long," Nicola said.

It had not rained that day, and the ground was hard-packed and dry. Cassius could not see the ocean, but he could smell sea salt in the air. Gulls circled overhead. The sky was overcast, but there was no breeze, only a stillness that made the air heavy.

"What are we doing here?" Cassius asked.

"Master Cinna has misplaced something," Nicola said. "We're here to look for it."

"What exactly?" Cassius scanned the lane as he walked, peering up and down each cramped alley. He could not shake the feeling of being watched.

"Money," Nicola said.

"Cinna's money?"

Aulus laughed. "Ain't that what we're always looking for?"

They made their way through a small market in Lowtown's garment district. They passed squat huts and storefronts. Overhead clotheslines hung weighted with brightly colored tunics and dresses, blazing yellows and vibrant greens favored by the Natives, deep reds and rich purples popular amongst the Antiochi. Other more exotic wares were on display as well, ornate Fathalan headscarves and rugs, heavy surcoats and cloaks more suited to a Murondian court than a jungle, robes of patterned silk modeled after those of the eastern Xin. The air smelled sharply of soap and leather, and the dye runoff that trickled through the streets rainbowed in oily patterns.

Past the market, they reached a single-story mudbrick house with a roof of thatch.

"Mind the door," Nicola said. He drew the long-handled knife from his belt and produced a smaller knife from a sheath strapped to his thigh, this knife short and serrated. He motioned for Aulus to follow.

Cassius turned his back to the door. He stared out into the street, which was empty now except across the lane, where small children took turns poking an unconscious beggar with a stick.

He heard the sound of wood splintering as Nicola kicked in the door. He heard Nicola shout, then two screams, a low, guttural one and a high-pitched yell that ended abruptly. He felt a stirring in his chest as someone cast a spell.

An explosion shook the air.

The children started at the sound. They looked to Cassius, and the beggar stirred and swatted at the boy holding the stick, and the children fled screaming down the alley.

"How are things out here?"

Cassius turned to see Nicola in the doorway. A splatter of black blood stained the front of his tunic. His neck and cheek were red with flecks of gore. He held the long knife backhanded and wiped it on his tunic.

"Quiet," Cassius said.

"Give a shout if you see something."

Nicola swung the door shut.

Cassius heard another scream.

Little foot traffic passed in the street. People seemed not to notice Cassius or else took notice discreetly and continued on their way. After a time, the beggar across the lane rose and urinated in the doorway. He wiped his hands on his tattered tunic and staggered off into an alley.

The door opened again, and Cassius turned and saw Aulus in the entranceway. He motioned for Cassius to step inside.

Nicola sat on the floor in the main room. He held a wad of banknotes in one hand and in front of him stood three stacks of similar notes smeared with mud.

A man lay in the corner of the room. He lay on his belly, his hands and feet bound and tied together with leather straps. He was blindfolded and gagged, missing both of his thumbs. Blood from these wounds leaked down his hands and pooled in the small of his back.

"What is this?" Cassius asked.

"Four hundred, four fifty, four sixty-five—"

"What's going on here?"

"Goddamn it," Nicola shouted. "Shut up before I lose count."

Cassius glanced down the hallway that led to the back room of the house.

"Seven hundred." Nicola set the stack of banknotes on the floor. "Plus thirteen makes an even two thousand."

"Is that it?" Aulus asked.

"No, it should be three."

"Tell me what's going on here," Cassius said.

"Easy," Aulus said. "No need to get excited."

Nicola stood. He picked his long-handled knife off the floor.

"Yesterday, this man robbed a delivery to one of Cinna's gambling halls." Nicola pointed the blade at the bound man. "Cinna's informant said he was an independent, but I had a feeling he was Piso's man. We cut him up pretty good though, and still he claimed no allegiance. He gave us everything else. Who told him about the delivery. How he pulled it off. A description of the man he killed during the robbery. I believe him."

"And there's no brand on him," Aulus said.

"Right. No brand, either. I'll tell you, though, whoever he is, he's coldhearted. We cut that kid to pieces, and still he wouldn't say a word. Not until those thumbs came off."

"What kid?" Cassius asked.

Nicola shrugged. "The hell should I know? Just some kid that was in here with him."

Cassius looked to Aulus, and Aulus lowered his eyes and turned and spat.

Cassius walked to the back room. It was poorly lit, and most of her lay in shadow. He saw her feet, dirty and pale. He saw her hair.

He returned to the front room.

"Why—" He took a deep breath. "Why did you—"

"He wasn't talking," Nicola said. "I needed an answer."

"What did she have to do with anything?"

"I just told you, I don't know who she was."

"Everyone relax," Aulus said. "Let's just finish the job."

"Why'd you do that to her?"

"I needed an answer," Nicola shouted. "And, anyway, go screw yourself. I don't report to you. The man said the rest of it was buried in the back. So you two get to digging."

The floorboards in the back room were rotted. Aulus noticed that two of the boards had loose nails, and he pried these up and he and Cassius sat hunched over the opening, digging at the dirt below with their bare hands. The dirt was warm and thick with worms. It smelled of mold and came up in loose clumps.

Aulus sat facing Cassius, and over Aulus's shoulder, Cassius could see the shape of the girl in shadow. From under the exposed floorboards, roaches crawled across the room. Some wandered into the pool spreading from beneath the girl and drowned there.

Cassius was sweating now, and his chest felt tight. He told himself this was from the Garza root and from the lack of sleep. It was not because of the sight of the body. He had hardened himself against that. He had taken the first step toward becoming the thing of which he had dreamed for so long and in the process had scoured himself of his weaknesses, his softness.

But now he was sick.

He rose from the hole, shook the loose mud from his hands, and left the room.

"Where are you going?" Aulus called.

He walked to the front of the house. Nicola was tying the last of the banknotes with strips of twine. The bound man lay in the corner, awake now, struggling against his binds and grunting into his gag.

"You find that money yet?" Nicola called.

"No."

"Then get your ass back in there and dig." Nicola noticed the bound man moving and he cursed and drew his knife and crossed the room.

"I need some fresh air."

Cassius opened the door and stepped outside. He trotted across the lane and into the alleyway. He doubled over. His mouth watered, and he spat to clear away the taste. His stomach contracted, and he vomited up a thin, milky liquid. Warm and rank, it leaked from his nose and left his throat raw. His eyes watered and blurred. He emptied his stomach, then stood gagging until, finally, his body was sore with the effort and he stopped.

Overhead, he heard thunder. In the distance the sound of rain beginning to fall. A wind swept in from the north, and the air smelled of jungle. Cassius donned his gauntlets.

. . .

Nicola sat hunched over the man in the corner of the room. He looked up as Cassius entered and Cassius walked through the front room and into the back room and found Aulus squatting over the hole.

Cassius cast his fire-ward spell.

Aulus started with a curse and raised his hands, but it was too late.

Cassius held his hand out, palm open, and a circle of fire appeared on the floor. A coil of flame rose from the circle to the ceiling and spread outward like spilled water. The flames swept from wall to wall with a sound like a gust of wind, and Cassius stood in the inferno. He heard a scream and smelled the sharp scent of burned hair, the greasy smell of burned flesh. The scream died almost instantly, and Cassius stepped out of the back room. He passed through the flames, and when he was clear, he saw Nicola racing for the door.

The entranceway grew hazy, and a smell like stale water, like the inside of an old well, wafted through the room. A spider the size of a large dog stood just inside the doorway. It was black with flecks of green on its mottled shell. It had stiff red hair, and its torso hung low in the cradle of its legs. It eyes were red and asymmetrical, a burning star cluster set above its crab maw.

Cassius urged it forward. The spider tapped the ground with its front two forelegs delicately, like a blind man sensing with a cane. Nicola reached for the dagger at his waist, and as he drew it, the spider was on him.

He stabbed for its head, and his blow glanced off a spindly leg. His dagger struck the creature's shell with a sound like metal striking hardened clay, and the spider punched its fangs into his thigh and he screamed and fell and then lay silent and twitching and then he stopped twitching.

Cassius waved his hand, and the spider disappeared in a shower of sparks.

He shut the door and sat down and slid off his gauntlets. His hands shook, but otherwise, the room was quiet and still.

. . .

He sat for hours, thinking of the child in the back room. He decided that he did not like the sight of her body, and he was displeased with this realization, with the weakness it implied. How could he move forward from here, do what was necessary, when such things troubled him? The task at hand required fortitude. There would be more bodies to come.

He had acted rashly, and now there was the chance he had undone all his work of the past few days. And for what? A child whose name he did not know. This was the work of a rank initiate, not a true strategist. The Masters would be displeased.

Still, when he thought of what he had seen in the back room, he felt his pulse pound and his skin grow hot and he knew if the two killers were with him now, he would do it all again. He had been a nameless child himself once, one who would have gone unmourned and unavenged in death. He had avoided that fate, though. Now he was here, seeing to his work.

He had come this far. With a clear head, he would go further. He was changing, growing, becoming something stronger, something more suited to the island. Nothing was going to stop that.

He remained in the small house until the sun set. Then he rose and walked to the back room and dug in the hole beneath the floorboards. The fire had dried the mud, and under all that brittle earth, he found an oilskin parcel, the banknotes inside worth a thousand gold pieces.

He gathered Aulus's gauntlets from the floor, then returned to the front room and collected the other banknotes and stuffed them all into the oilskin parcel. He took Nicola's long-handled knife and removed the octan from Nicola's neck. He wiped his hand in the congealed blood pooling on the floor and walked outside. He stabbed the knife into the door and hung the octan from the knife. With his bloodied fingers, he wrote "War" on the outside wall.

STRIKE FIRST AND STRIKE
WITH OVERWHELMING FORCE

—◦◦◦◦—

I n Scylacium, they called him Two Cups. A boy of eleven, he prowled the Viper's Belly slums with a gang of boys known as the Pinchpennies. His brothers were orphans, pillow slaves, runaways escaped from labor camps and legion servitude. They spent their days scamming dice games and fencing stolen goods nicked from the storehouses of the largest trading companies in the Republic. They lightened the purses of travelers and missionaries foolish enough to venture into the Belly, always alert for Vigil patrols. At night, they snuck away to the city proper and burgled the estates of wealthy patricians, eating for weeks on stolen jewels and silk gowns.

These were wild days. He lived like a feral dog more than a true boy, perpetually unwashed, nearly naked, always half-starved. But in all his short life, he had never felt so alive.

He made his home in the burned husk of an old tenement on Hangman's Road. A revolving band of boys squatted with him. Calub, Limper, Sheepsfeet, Bonesaw, Manius Dento, Manius Naso. The house had room enough to sleep eight, but they were never less than ten, sometimes as many as twenty. They shared everything. Food and drink and bedrolls. In the winter, they shivered together, and in the summer, they sweated together. And they fought every day, sometimes against Vigils or marks, sometimes against other slum boys.

Two Cups was not much of a fighter. Short and skinny, he lacked the raw strength needed for street fighting. Moreover, he had no taste for violence. The boys teased that he was softhearted and tender. They called him Mother Hen. It shamed him greatly, but he knew it to be true. He did not appreciate cruelty as the other boys did, never enjoyed tying rats together by their tails or splashing mud on the white gowns of young nuns on their way to temple.

He liked stories of heroes and great battles, though, could sit for hours listening at the knees of the graybeards in Philosopher's Square as they recited the legends of old. Tales of Ulpius the Bear, the finest soldier ever to don a centurion's helm, rugged Barbatus, who forfeited his senatorship and his life of leisure to become a pirate hunter, Diokles of the Black Cloud, slayer of gorgons and harpies, who carried lightning in his ash spear.

These tales filled him with wonder and he dreamed that someday he would win glory on the field of battle. Not in fistfights with other slum boys but in a proper battle, where men fought for honor, men whose acts of valor echoed through the ages.

The graybeards taught him the hero's code. A hero was strong. A hero fought for what he believed. A hero was loyal. He did not strike first. He did not kill the defenseless. He needed no reward but honor. He was not afraid of death.

He was kin to these men. He could feel it in his blood. They shared the code.

Every man needed a code, Two Cups knew that. Calub told him as much. Calub who had fifteen years to Two Cups's eleven and so was wiser than most. Calub who was tall and strong, with heavy shoulders and hard fists, who had never lost a fight.

"Stick with your brothers," Calub said. It was a chill autumn night, and the boys huddled indoors around a small fire, roasting potatoes on sticks. Two Cups sat massaging a bruise on the side of his head.

That morning, two rival slum boys had caught him and Sheepsfeet walking home after stealing tomatoes from a grocer. The slum boys were older than Two Cups, probably thirteen or so. He recognized one of the boys as Fullo, a tall, fat bully with big arms and crooked teeth. Fullo was famous in the Belly for his teeth. He liked to bite during fistfights, had once bitten Avino's cousin's ear off in a fight outside the Staghorn Pub.

Fullo lived well by slum-boy standards. He never had to steal or beg. Instead, he trawled the alleys for the prettiest boys he could find and sold them in the city. No two slum boys agreed on where Fulla made his sales. Some said slavers or whorehouses, others believed he had ties to a dark temple where initiates fed boys to a giant rat god. Two Cups never believed the story about the temple, but he believed Fullo was trouble.

At the first sight of Fullo in the alley, Two Cups had dropped his bag and run. He shouted over his shoulder for Sheepsfeet to follow, but Sheepsfeet was only eight and slower than the older boys. As Two Cups fled into the market crowd, he heard a scream, then felt a burst of pain on the side of his head. He found himself on his hands and knees, a bloodied rock lying next to him. His mind had only a few seconds to piece events together, then he was up on his feet again, staggering away.

"You have to look after one another." The fire cast shadows on Calub's high cheekbones, his strong jaw. "You have to protect one another. You want to be men, don't you? Not little, crying slum boys but real men, right?"

Low mumbles answered from the dark.

"Speak up," Calub shouted. He hopped to his feet and leaned out over the fire. The smoke and the flames drew up higher, as though answering his challenge. "You want to be men, don't you?"

The boys hollered their assent. Two Cups shouted with them. Whenever Calub spoke, he felt something stir in his chest.

"Well, then you need to stand for something. You have to be strong and proud. You have to look after boys littler than you. Weaker than you. You can't take shit off of anybody."

Two Cups sat outside the light of the fire, listening, learning. That morning, he had fled at the first sign of trouble, and he was sorry for that. But he knew now that running had not been a choice. He acted without thought, on instinct alone. He would be better next time, would choose to be better. He was certain of that. Calub's words convinced him.

Sometimes Two Cups pictured Calub as one of the old heroes in the graybeards' stories. He imagined Calub in the early days of the Republic, fighting the Widsith barbarians in some black forest, or as a gladiator facing down wyverns and manticores in an ancient coliseum. He wanted to picture himself there alongside Calub, armored and brave, but each time he tried, it ruined the illusion. He had not earned his place next to Calub. Not yet.

That night, he slept bundled up with Sheepsfeet for warmth. Sheepsfeet winced when he wrapped his arms around him. The boy had bruises along his back and chest and arms, a bite to his shoulder. Calub had given him a pinch of whiskey to help with the pain, and Sheepsfeet had not cried since. He was a tough boy, Sheepsfeet, and one quick to forgive. He had said nothing of Two Cups abandoning him in the alley, although everyone knew the truth of it, Two Cups especially.

Sheepsfeet was an ugly boy as well, with a lazy eye and a face pitted with scars from the same pox that had killed his family. A lucky thing those scars, or else he might never have made it back home from that alley. He shook as he dreamed.

"I'm sorry," Two Cups whispered to the sleeping boy. "I'll make this right. I promise I'll make this right."

Two Cups woke early the next morning. He went outside and circled around to the back of the hovel, where the boys kept a small stash of weapons hidden under a large plank of wood. Sharpened sticks, a few rusted shivs, a fire-hardened club, a heavy chain. He picked through these until he came upon the cestus, or battle glove, made of leather straps threaded over strips of iron. Calub had pinched it from a gymnasium months ago, but Two Cups had never before worn it.

He slid the glove over his right hand. It was large for him, but he liked the weight of it on his arm. When he made a fist, his hand felt heavy and strong.

"Do you think you'll hit him with that?"

Two Cups turned to find Calub standing behind him. Suddenly he felt small and silly.

"Answer me, boy," Calub said. "Do you think you'll be able to hit him with that?"

"Who do you think I want to hit?" Two Cups asked.

"I know exactly who you want to hit. And I know his arms are longer than yours. And that thing on your hand is heavy as a brick. You won't be halfway through your punch, and he'll have you knocked out."

Two Cups lowered his hand. The cestus seemed heavier after Calub's words.

"Go back inside," Calub said. "Get some sleep. It's too cold to be out this early."

"I won't," Two Cups said. "I have to look after the little ones. You said it yourself."

"That's right. You have to look after the little ones. And when there's a fight, you have to be there. But what do you think you're going to do now? Walk down to the Staghorn and call for Fullo to come out and fight you?"

"That's exactly what I'm going to do."

For a second, he expected Calub to laugh. It was the worst thing he could imagine. If Calub had yelled at him or called him a fool or even knocked him down and ripped the cestus off his arm, Two Cups could have endured it. But laughter would have broken his spirit.

Instead Calub smiled and, bending down, lifted up a fire-hardened club and swung it over his shoulder.

"Well, if one of us is fighting, then all of us are fighting."

There were nine Pinchpennies sleeping in the house, and within minutes, Calub had roused every one of them. They made their way to the far edge of the Belly, where the twisting corridors that gave the slum its name began to crest the first of the twin Lupine Hills, and where the Staghorn Pub sat on the edge of Dustmaker's Lane. Sometimes the boys marched, mimicking legionnaires at drill, and sometimes they ran flat out, like a pack of dogs after a hare. Each boy wielded a weapon, and as they moved, the boys stabbed and swung and cleaved at their imaginary enemies.

Two Cups walked with Calub at his side, the older boy whispering strategy in his ear.

"As soon as he steps outside, you rush him," Calub said. "You're quick. If you can knock him down, you might get a few punches in before he can make a move."

"I can't hit him first," Two Cups said. "What about the code?"

"What code?" Calub asked.

"The hero's code. Like the graybeards teach. A hero doesn't hit first."

"Listen to me." Calub grabbed Two Cups by his shoulders, stopped the boy in the lane. "Graybeards never been in a fight. They don't know what they're talking about. Now you hit him first, and you hit him with everything you have, understand?"

Two Cups nodded.

It was midmorning by the time the boys arrived outside the Staghorn. The slums had woken and the lane bustled with foot traffic. On the walk over, Two Cups had rehearsed in his head the words he would say to call Fullo out of the pub. But Fullo stood outside when they arrived, laughing and chewing Kaota leaves with a few other boys his age. The laughter stopped when Two Cups approached, Calub at his side.

"What's this about?" Fullo asked. He turned and spat a chewed brown mess onto the ground.

Fullo had addressed Calub. The two boys knew each other by reputation but had never had much interaction. Fullo seemed not to notice Two Cups at all and certainly did not recognize him from the events of yesterday.

"Seems you had a little trouble with my friend here," Calub said.

"Is that right?" Fullo looked to Two Cups.

Two Cups started to speak, but his voice caught. He took a breath. He pictured himself and Calub as horse-haired Akhaian warriors on a blood-soaked plain, ash spears and heavy shields in hand, back-to-back, as a horde of howling, painted barbarians bore down on them.

He clenched his fist and tested the weight of the cestus. His hand felt strong.

"My name is Two Cups, and I'm a Pinchpenny." He stepped forward, within arm's reach of Fullo now. "Same as Calub, same as all these boys. Yesterday you hurt one of my brothers. Little Sheepsfeet there. You caught us in an alley and put the boots to him. Instead of helping, I ran away. But I'm here now to make that right. And so me and you are going to step out into this square and—"

Fullo's fist caught Two Cups on the chin, and Two Cups collapsed, tumbling off the porch of the Staghorn and into the dirt of the lane. He was unconscious when he hit the floor, but if his eyes had been open, he would have witnessed Calub and the Pinchpennies charge, a glorious charge worthy of a true epic.

6

—◦◦◦—

Cassius held his belly as he walked. Ahead of him in the road, a couple stood kissing beneath a sputtering streetlamp. The glow of the fire cast the lane in a pale haze, and the couple glanced at Cassius and retreated into shadow.

At the Purse, he walked to the back room and asked to speak with Cinna. The guard at the door said Cinna would not be taking visitors until morning.

Cassius lifted his hand from his belly, and the wound there was black and ran with black blood that dripped to the floor, with a heavy, wet sound, like the rain of a storm.

"I can't wait that long."

Cassius lay in a dark room on the second floor of the Purse. His bed was small, and the gray sheets smelled of come and sour wine.

A guard stood at the door, a tall man with jowls and short, stiff hair. A sword hung sheathed at his hip.

When the door opened, the light from the hallway was blinding.

"Don't move," Cinna said. He slammed the door shut, and the room was dark again. "I'll kill you where you lie if I lose sight of your hands for a second."

Cassius held his hands in the air.

"Now you just keep them there," Cinna said.

"I need to see a healer."

"And I need answers," Cinna roared. He kicked a nearby chair.

"You give me what I need, and I'll think about giving you what you need. Understand?"

"Yes."

"Good. Now, where's Nicola?"

"Dead."

Cinna clenched his hand into a plump fist. "And Aulus?"

"Dead."

"And yet you're just fine."

"I wouldn't say fine," Cassius said. "I'm hurt, and I need to see someone about my injuries."

"Where'd the gut wound come from?"

"One of Piso's men."

"Piso's men?" Cinna shook his head. "What were they doing there?"

"Coming to pick up the money."

"That's a lie. The man who took my money wasn't with Piso."

"It was Piso's men at the house," Cassius said. "A man and a woman. Nicola got to work on the kid, and the man started to talk. He was with Piso. Nicola didn't believe him at first, so he got to work on the man, but the story was the same. He was Piso's man, and he was just holding the money until the pickup."

"That doesn't make sense. The robbery was too sloppy. He took the money and left a trail for us back to him."

"That's what Nicola tried to figure out. But we couldn't get a straight answer. And then the rest of them showed. Six of them. And then it all made sense. The whole thing was a setup. The thief was a lure, and he didn't even know it. Led us right to an ambush."

"But you managed to get out?" Cinna's voice was low and searching.

"Wounded."

"So let me go over this again. Just to be sure I've got it right. I sent three men to retrieve my money. You three arrived at the house and found the thief and found the money. My money. And then suddenly Piso's men arrived.

"They killed Aulus, one of the best spellcasters on this godforsaken rock. They killed Nicola. A man who was like a brother to me.

Yet you, who I've known a week, somehow you escape. Go missing for hours. Show up on my doorstep with a scratch on your belly. And now my money is gone. Is that about right?"

"Not exactly," Cassius said.

"Well then, explain. And you had better do a good goddamn job of it."

Cassius reached into his cloak. Cinna shouted, and the man at the door reached for his sword.

"Easy." Cassius drew an oilskin pouch from a fold in his cloak. He tossed it to the floor and raised his hands again.

"You didn't search him?" Cinna asked the guard.

The guard lowered his head. "He said if I touched him, he'd burn this place to the ground."

"I could kill you right now. Go get that for me."

The guard retrieved the pouch and handed it to Cinna. Cinna untied the pouch and looked inside, then withdrew a stack of bound banknotes. He thumbed the notes and looked to Cassius.

"Is this all of it?"

"I don't know," Cassius said. "It's banknotes, and I can't read. But it's all that was in the house."

Cinna tossed the bundle to the guard. "Count this. And be diligent. A man's life depends on it."

The new stitches itched. They were thicker than the old ones and tied with an overlong knot. The area around the wound was caked with dried blood, and the wound itself was raw. Cassius knew enough about wounds to know that it would leave a scar when it healed.

The physician had arrived in the night. He had been curt when addressing Cassius and unconcerned when Cassius flinched from the pain of the needle. He did not ask Cassius his name and did not supply his own. He thought the wound looked strange, as though it had been stitched recently.

Afterward, Cassius lay in bed, his tunic wet. There was no longer a guard at the door, or if there was a guard, he stood outside the door now. The light through the window was gray, early-morning sunlight filtered through a cloud cover.

He was tired now, so weary his joints ached. Beneath his exhaustion, he felt warm with anger.

He rose and walked to the window. In the streets below, a pair of old women argued. They began to yell, then one old woman spat on the other and they grabbed and slapped and fell in the mud.

A long-haired man entered and stood staring at Cassius, as though he had not expected him to be there.

"We're going to meet someone," the long-haired guard said.

"Who?" Cassius asked.

"Don't worry about that."

Cassius adjusted his cloak. He made his way to the door, walking with a hitch in his step.

"Leave your gauntlets here," the guard said. "You're in Master Cinna's house. There's no need to be armed."

"I won't leave my gauntlets."

"I could take them if I wanted to." The guard eyed Cassius. He had a knife tucked into his belt, and a truncheon hung at his hip.

"You don't want to."

The guard stood silent.

"Keep your hands where I can see them," he said finally.

With a flourish, Cassius slid his arms out of his cloak, like a stage magician preparing for a trick.

The main room of the Purse was cleared of all tables save for one. The table could seat ten but now seated only Cinna and Vorenicus.

Vorenicus was dressed in a red tunic trimmed with yellow. His skin was tanned, and he had close-cropped hair, as befitted a soldier. His eyes were dark and deep-set. He looked to be about Cassius's age, and behind him stood another soldier, much older.

"Cassius, this is Master Vorenicus." Cinna motioned toward his guest.

"Nice to meet you, Cassius." Vorenicus offered his hand, and Cassius shook it, the hand small but the grip wiry and strong.

"This is about the incident in Lowtown yesterday. Vorenicus is here to gather information."

"What does he care?" Cassius asked.

"I'm the head of the city guard." Vorenicus's wide-brimmed helmet, with its two long eagle feathers strapped one to each side, lay on the tabletop.

"I thought the legion didn't interfere in Scipio business," Cassius said.

"I don't know who told you that. But I assure you, I'm very interested in what you have to say."

"Tell him everything he needs to know," Cinna said. "Start from the beginning."

"I was in Lowtown around noon yesterday."

"What were you doing there?" Vorenicus filled a cup with wine.

Cassius looked to Cinna. Cinna nodded.

"I was going to collect money," Cassius said. "Money that was stolen from a gaming hall."

Vorenicus lifted his cup. He stared into it and sniffed, then set it down.

"Who was with you?" he asked.

"Me and Nicola and Aulus."

"Just the three of you?"

"Yes. We tracked the man to his house and entered and found him and a child inside." Cassius paused. An image of the back room flashed through his mind. He breathed deep, tried to calm his racing heart. There was strength in stillness. He knew that well. "We questioned them, and they confessed to stealing the money and told us where it was hidden."

"Questioned?" Vorenicus looked deep into Cassius's eyes. "Their bodies were mutilated."

"It's my understanding," Cinna interjected, "that the thieves weren't cooperating at first. My men were in enemy territory. They needed to find our property and leave as quickly as possible."

"Who ordered that?"

"The questioning?" Cassius's hands, lying on the table, began to shake. He buried them in his lap.

"The mutilating."

"Nicola did it. I'm a spellcaster. I don't know how to work a knife that way."

"What happened after that?" Vorenicus's eyes seemed always to be searching. His gaze moved from Cassius to Cinna and back again, looking to see every change in expression, whether prompted by questions or even certain words.

"We found the money buried under the back room. Nicola counted it and said it was good. We left and stepped outside into an ambush. Piso's men were everywhere."

"How do you know it was Piso's men?" Vorenicus reached for his helmet, ran his fingers along its brim.

"Who else would be down there?"

"So you don't know for sure."

"I didn't ask to see their papers," Cassius said.

"It's important." Vorenicus leaned forward. "Piso claims that he didn't send anyone to that house. Claims the men inside weren't even his."

"Of course he does." Cinna had forgotten his makeup, and his naked face was mottled and red. "What good would it serve him to take responsibility for this?"

"Please finish your story, Cassius."

"We were outnumbered, and it was over fast. Nicola fell first. Someone stabbed me. I managed a fighting retreat. Aulus was still standing last I saw him. But he was hurt pretty bad. All burned up."

"And what happened to the money?"

"The money was—"

"Taken." Cinna slammed a fat fist onto the table. "From the corpses of my men. Whatever restitution Piso is forced to pay should also include the stolen money."

"And how much was it?"

"Five thousand gold," Cinna said.

"We'll have to look into that."

"Well, you had better make it quick," Cinna shouted. "I've got a thousand men under my command. And every last motherless one of them is calling for blood."

"Keep your men in line." Vorenicus stood. He gathered his helmet and placed it on his head and, for a second, it caught the candlelight, and he seemed wreathed in golden flame.

"I'm doing the best I can." Cinna leapt to his feet. "But they don't like when their associates are murdered in broad daylight. They want some goddamned justice, and if you don't give it to them, they're liable to take it for themselves."

"I'll do what needs to be done," Vorenicus said. "But I won't abide open violence in the streets. If you can't control your men, you'll be forcing me to take action."

"I assure you," Cassius said, "that's something no one wants."

That night Cinna came to Cassius's room and Cassius pretended to wake from a deep sleep. He ordered Cassius out of bed and together they walked to the third floor, Cinna's private apartments. At the top of the steps was a small anteroom, the far wall draped in a rich purple tapestry embroidered with an ancient battle scene, Aemillius Attus and his troops fending off Fathalan horsemen.

Cinna's bed had a large brass frame and was draped in a mosquito net. A young girl lay amidst the blankets, curled and naked. She looked fourteen at the oldest.

There was a bottle on Cinna's nightstand and two mugs and Cinna collected these. He crossed the room to a set of double doors and opened the doors and stepped out onto the balcony. He poured the mugs full of wine and leaned against the balustrade, gazing over the city. In the middle distance, to the east of the Grand Market, a fire raged. It was three blocks long, and smoke from the flames hung thick.

"What's this about?" Cassius asked.

"Can't a man have a drink with a friend?"

"Is that what we are now?"

Cinna smiled. "Of course not. You work for me. We can't be friends."

"So I still work for you?"

"Unless you've resigned your post."

"I've been locked in that room," Cassius said. "I thought I was your prisoner."

"Boy, I don't make a habit of leaving prisoners armed. I kept you locked up at first because I needed to learn the particulars of the situation. There was a lot of money at stake. Not to mention the loss of lives. I don't know you well, and it was too much of a coincidence that men loyal to me were dead while you yet lived."

"But all the money was there?" Cassius walked to the balustrade. In the street below, a drunk Native man wandered singing.

"Every note."

"I told you as much. I don't steal."

"I know that now." Cinna raised his mug to Cassius and sipped it. "And I want you to know that's a quality I appreciate in my men."

"So why keep me locked up after the money was accounted for?"

"It's my job to control the flow of information to my men. They don't like to hear of their own dying. That's news I have to break to them."

Cassius leaned back against the balustrade. "So what happens to me now?"

"You can resume work if you'd like."

"Two days ago, I thought you had a mind to kill me."

Cinna smiled. He stared off. "Why would I kill you?"

"Because I was more trouble than I was worth."

"And now?"

"I have a feeling you may need my services in the coming days."

"So then rest easy."

Cassius sniffed at his mug. He sipped the wine and found it sweet and heady, unwatered.

"An acquired taste," Cinna said.

"They say unwatered wine makes you dim and crazed."

"I find that it can be invigorating. In moderation."

"*Moderation.*" Cassius smiled. "I didn't think you were familiar with the word."

"And why should I be when I can have as much of everything as I want?" Cinna spread his arms, gesturing to the city and beyond the city, to the horizon.

"But not of unwatered wine?"

Cinna stared in silence. "The first wine I ever drank was unwatered," he said after some time. "I was a boy then, maybe ten. I grew up in a small border town, near the Crean Desert."

"That's Fathalan land."

"This was fifty years ago. Now it's Fathalan land, but back then, it was part of the Republic, and there wasn't a summer went by the legion didn't fight those animals for it. One night, a raiding party came across the desert and raced through the town, slaughtering, raping."

"Fathalans?"

"Of course." Cinna spat. "The pigs. They burned everything. The legion arrived, and there was a huge spellfight, one of the greatest I've seen to this day. The ground was shaking, and I was certain I was going to die that night. The next morning, I wandered out onto the plains. Me and Nicola."

"You knew him then?"

"Even before then. Our families have been friends for generations. We were raised together."

"I didn't know that."

"Why would you?"

Cassius shook his head.

"Nicola and I wandered out of the town to the countryside. There was a winery there. Nicola wanted to see his first dead body, and I wanted to find something of value. Of course there was nothing at the winery worth taking. We searched the whole ruins. Stole grapes and ate them in the fields of ash. Later, we came upon a sinkhole."

"From the battle?" Cassius set his mug of wine down when Cinna wasn't looking.

"Some spell had punched a hole in the ground. There were tunnels below for storing the wine. We found the barrels destroyed, goddamn tunnels flooded. Some of the wine had gelled inside the barrels from the early-morning cold. Nicola and I ate it."

"Did you get drunk?"

"Of course. Nicola's father was furious. He beat Nicola when he saw him drunk. Right in front of me. Nicola was crying, and I was crying. His father asked where we had gotten the wine, but Nicola never told him. Certainly never told him I was the first one down the hole. That it was my idea to eat the stuff. My idea from the start."

Cinna turned to face Lowtown. Streetlamps sputtered under an overcast sky and the city was mostly quiet and the sounds of the jungle loud. Crickets, birdcalls, the howls of monkeys.

"He didn't want a funeral. He wanted only to be burned. He wanted his dog killed and burned with him, but beyond that he asked for nothing."

"I respect that," Cassius said.

"So do I." Cinna looked to Cassius. "But if he hadn't sworn me to his last wishes, I'd build a funeral mound. A mausoleum. A goddamned pyramid to rival the ones those apes in the Southern Kingdoms build. High enough to blot out the sun."

Cassius thought about Nicola standing over the butchered man, his bloody knife gripped in his fist, his rat-face locked in a twisted grin.

"That's a good sentiment," he said, speaking of the funeral wishes of a man he himself had killed. He looked Cinna in the eye while he said these words, and never once did his voice waver.

He had come very far to be here, he thought in that moment. And he knew now there was no place else that he belonged.

"What worth is good sentiment?" Cinna asked. "Hell, they're not even going to return his body." Cinna sipped from his cup. He spat, then hurled the cup over the balcony. "That bastard down at the docks is laughing his sick ass off. Bad enough he outmaneuvered me with that ambush. But he killed my friend as well."

"And what will you do?"

"I don't know yet. The men want blood. That fire is their handiwork."

"One of ours started it?" Cassius asked.

"Who can tell? Piso will claim that we started it. And the men will swear they were attacked and only defending themselves. The outcome is the same either way."

"And what's the outcome?"

"Fifteen dead for us. Twenty for Piso. Twice as many injured. Plus the property damage. And it'll mean another visit from Vorenicus tomorrow."

"Why is that?"

"He doesn't like when we burn the city," Cinna said. "He's a bit strange that way."

"I thought Quintus benefited when you and Piso fought. Nicola said it meant you weakened your own forces, and Quintus grew stronger in the process."

"That's true. But Vorenicus is different from his father. Fancies himself a lawgiver. Thinks it's his job to keep us bosses honest. He doesn't have the foresight of the general. And he's idealistic besides. I suspect if there's more bloodshed, he'll want it contained to our personal armies. Any more business like this"—Cinna motioned toward the fire—"and he'll want to get involved."

"Will his father let him?"

"Who knows?" Cinna was sweating. He wiped his brow. "That crazy bastard is liable to do anything."

"And will there be more fighting?"

"I don't know. The men are right to want revenge. Hell, I want it. But it's not that simple. What would you do?"

Cassius's wound began to ache. He rubbed it while he thought, his mind working intuitively to decide a true answer to the question, then counterintuitively to find the answer Cinna would expect of him. He recalled what the blind man in the Market had said the other day about warring with himself, about his every thought being a contradiction.

"I'd sue for peace," he said.

"Only days ago, you said you wanted to join me to kill Piso's men."

"There's more money in peace, though."

"Money isn't my only concern," Cinna said. "What about the way people look at me? Is it okay for them to think they can kill my men with impunity?"

"No."

"And what of the guards they killed the other night?"

"You're sure that was Piso's man Servilius who did that?"

Cinna threw up his hands. "Oh, who can ever be sure? The only witnesses were whores. But they said the man told them the streets were no longer safe. It was war now. War. The same message left at the house in Lowtown, spelled in the blood of my men."

Cassius stood silent.

"My men cry out for revenge," Cinna yelled. "Should I deny them? If I do, they'll think me weak. And what about honor? About loyalty and justice? My friend is dead. Don't I owe him vengeance?"

"What worth is vengeance? It's not something you can hold."

In the distance, one of the burning buildings collapsed, and a cloud of embers rose into the sky.

"In the early days of the Republic, before the courts were created," Cinna said, "vengeance was the only justice. Families and clans used blood feuds to settle their grievances."

"These are not the old days."

"A shame, if you ask me."

"It must have been chaos then," Cassius said. "People killing each other over the smallest insult."

"That's not how the feuds worked. There was a price that needed to be paid for minor infractions. Assault. Theft. Rape. These things were negotiable, could be mended with the exchange of gold. But other crimes—murder, slavery—these had to be paid in blood."

"A dark time, to be sure."

"Dark time? That was the age of heroes, boy. Don't you know your history?"

"I haven't studied it much."

"You know what they say of the young and history." Cinna sighed. "It was a different time then. Men cared still for personal honor. For a moral code. Back then, a man's honor could not be satisfied with gold. It could only be repaid in blood. So murder demanded murder for retribution. And sometimes more than one."

"How do you mean?" Cassius asked.

"The death of a servant or a friend demanded one death. The death of a brother or a son, two. The death of a father, five."

"And what of a mother?"

"The law only applied to men. Although there is the legend of Aemillius Attus and his mother."

"I'm not familiar with it."

Cinna clutched his heart dramatically. "You should be ashamed, boy. He's the father of the Republic."

Cassius did not respond.

"After Attus escaped from slavery and began to war against the desert rats, they killed his mother to break his spirit. In response, he destroyed the city of Al-Bujah."

"Al-Bujah is the name of a desert."

"It was a city once. He destroyed it totally. Turned it to ash and salted the earth so nothing would grow again."

"And that was justice?" Cassius asked.

"In the old days. When heroes walked the earth."

7

In the morning, Cassius called on Cinna and learned he would not be seeing visitors until after noon. He thanked the guard and exited the Purse through the front door and never set foot inside again.

He wandered out to the Grand Market and purchased a loaf of bread sprinkled with olive oil. He made his way through the crowd to sit by the statue of Isvara, cool in the shade of the goddess. The blind man was there. They split the loaf of bread.

"Why have you come here today?" the blind man asked.

"I like to sit under the statue," Cassius said. "It helps me to think."

"You may be the most pious young man I know."

Cassius laughed. "If you knew me well, you would not feel that way. In truth, I like your company."

"It is nice to be noticed. Sometimes I sit here for days, in this busy market, and no one says a word to me. They treat me as part of the statue."

"They are moving too fast to notice the important things in front of them."

"You are flattering me, boy."

"I am paying my respects to an elder."

"Nothing is free in Scipio. Not bread and not kind words. What do you wish of me?"

"I like to hear stories," Cassius said. "Stories of heroes. I know many Antiochi heroes. No one ever told me stories of Khimir heroes. You must know some."

The blind man smiled wistfully. "I do, boy. I do."

"In Antioch, they have a hero named Attus. The man who freed them from oppression."

"I see."

"Do the Khimir have a hero such as him?"

"We have many heroes."

"And what of one such as him? One who set the people free."

"We have never needed to be set free. We were unconquered until Antioch arrived."

"And now?" Cassius asked. "Is it time for such a hero?"

"I have waited a long time. He has not shown himself."

"Let us talk of the older heroes then."

Cassius's mind wandered as the blind man told him of Keeyalhe and the great basilisk he slew with his stone ax. He looked south and in the widest avenues entering the Market from Lowtown, barricades were raised to block traffic. A hundred men stood guard at these posts, some geared in scoured mail and brandishing Fathalan scimitars or short, stabbing, Antiochi blades, some wielding greatswords from the famed weaponeers of Murondia, and even a few armed with spellcasters' gauntlets.

The guards questioned every man passing into and out of the Market. It was a futile gesture. Any who wanted to avoid the checkpoints could easily utilize the warren of lanes and alleyways that snaked through the city. But as a show of force, it was effective, a message to all that Boss Piso would not suffer violence quietly.

To the north, an equal force was assembled in the avenues to Hightown. And at the base of the council hall stood scores of legionnaires.

Cassius sat observing this arrangement for a time, until the blind man had finished his tale and finished his bread. Then he stood and looked up.

"Watch me be strong," he whispered to the statue.

He bit his palm hard enough to draw blood, then reached out and rubbed his hand on the feet of the goddess.

The Street of Horrors was crowded with people, and the beggars along the lane called to Cassius as he passed.

"Please, Master."

"Anything at all."

"Spare a copper."

"A veteran, sir. A veteran."

He saw the stumps of two amputated arms, a tumor the size of a peach pit, a child born with its feet fused, a leper, a burn victim.

At the baths, he asked for a private room and asked to be attended by Tadua. His room smelled of mildew. He stripped naked and lay on the cool, tiled floor, his head ringing with a sharp pain. He closed his eyes against the dark and tried to will himself to sleep. He dozed in fits and dreamed that something clawed its way up his chest and strained to break out of his throat as a newborn snake will break through an egg.

He thought about a burned beggar who had cried to him, the sight of the scarred flesh.

He considered the man that he was now and the thing he needed to become to do his work, and he wondered at his chances of reconciling the two.

There was a knock at the door, and he dressed himself and answered it. Tadua entered and took a seat on one of the low, stone benches.

"Where is the old woman?" he asked.

"Still at work. We work another bath together, and she stays late."

"And our other friend?"

"He is good," the girl said. "Still secret."

"Does he know where he is?"

"No, we keep blindfolded. And with the medicine. He thinks he is dreaming all day. Will you take him soon?"

"Tonight," Cassius said. "Can you call the boy with the cart who helped you?"

"It will take time. Maybe one or two hours."

Cassius told the girl where he wanted the man moved, and she left and returned an hour later. She carried with her a small satchel and an oversized jug of steaming water.

"The boy is on his way," she said.

She emptied the jug into the tub and dusted it with the soap powder, then called to Cassius and undressed him and wiped the loose grime from him.

The water was hot. She stared as he washed, her hands clasped together as before an animal that is wary of sudden movements.

"You look like you have something to say."

"Will you kill him?" she asked.

He wet his face, the bathwater brown now and the scum that floated the bathwater the color of old blood.

"Why do you want to know?" he asked.

"I just wonder."

"If things were reversed, would he care what I would do to you?"

"I don't know," she said.

"I know. And so do you if you're honest. He would sell you to me without caring what I would do. This is a bad man."

He ran his fingers through his wet hair. With his hair slicked back and his face cleaned and exposed, he looked very young. The girl feared him, feared his scheming and his magic and his strange potions. But looking at him like this, that fear seemed foolish.

"You know this man?" she asked.

"I know all I need to know. I know who he serves. I know the work he does. That is how you judge a man."

"Only I wanted to know if you would kill him. Sometimes they steal people and hold them for money. The old woman, this is what she think you do."

"Do you regret what you've done?" Cassius asked.

"I don't know," she said. And then, "I don't want you to kill this man."

"Those aren't my plans."

"There is too much killing already. I worry there is more coming. That it never ends."

"It will never end," he said.

"Maybe someday. When everyone gets tired."

"No." He sat forward, and she recoiled, startled by him and by her reaction to him.

"In the old days it was not this," she said. "It was nice."

"How old are you?"

"I told you already. Fifteen."

"And do you know what happened on this island fifteen years ago?"

She nodded. "I hear about it."

"You were a baby when it happened, so you don't remember."

"When I was young, it was not like this."

"You misremember."

She closed her mouth tight. Her lips disappeared in a thin white line.

"I'm eight years older than you," he said. "Do you want to know what I remember?"

"Tell me," she said.

Cassius started to speak but then stopped. The words would not come. When was the last time he spoke of such things? He could not recall. He had locked those words away, and now they were beyond his reach.

"Do you have a family?" he asked instead.

The girl nodded.

"The old woman. Is she your mother?"

"No, but I look after her. She has no one. No child to care for her. She says my brother and I are the children she never carried."

"You look after your brother as well?"

The girl sat quietly. She looked concerned, as though she had revealed something she should not have.

"I meant nothing by the question," Cassius said. "It's nice that you take care of him. He's a lucky boy."

The girl smiled, despite herself. "He is strong boy. The strongest of all his friends."

"Is that right?"

"He likes to wrestle. No one can pin him. Not once."

"A real fighter."

"When he is older, and I have money saved, I take him to Akhaia. We have an Akhaian man on our street. He teach us words every day. My brother will go to a wrestler's gym. He will be my champion. My little champion."

"I think that's a great plan."

"The old woman says I am fool. She tells me it will take two lifetimes to save that money."

"I don't know if that's true."

"You have traveled," she said. "What do you think?"

"I think you're determined. I think nothing will stop you."

The girl smiled inwardly, looked away. "My little champion," she said softly.

"You worry for him," Cassius said.

"Every day I worry. This is dangerous place for a child."

"Only because of the bosses. If there were no bosses, this would be a place safe for children. Safe for everyone."

"No bosses? There have always been bosses."

"No." Cassius shook his head. "Not always. That's what they want you to think. But in truth, they've been here only a short time."

"Get rid of bosses, and new bosses will take their place."

"It doesn't have to be that way."

"Who would rule here instead?"

"The Khimir."

The girl seemed surprised. "My people? They can't drive out the bosses. They're not strong enough."

"They are," Cassius said. "And they can. They just need someone to show them how."

A crowd had gathered to watch the fight. Inside the hog pen, two mastiffs circled each other warily, one favoring a front paw and the other with a gash along its muzzle. They moved under the glow of a streetlamp so dim Cassius could not see the blood on the floor of the ring.

Sulla was shouting above the noise of the crowd, cursing her fighter as a worthless bitch. She caught sight of him from the corner of her eye and moved deeper into the press.

A great cheer erupted. Cassius glanced in time to see the dog with the injured paw now fallen and its opponent moving to kill. When he looked back, he had lost sight of Sulla.

He broke free of the throng just as the cheering reached its loudest. A sustained whine rent the air, followed by more cheers.

"Enjoy the show?" she asked.

He could barely make out her form in the shadow of a nearby alley.

"I find this unsettling, actually," he said.

"Strange criticism from the likes of you." She stepped into the light of a streetlamp. The chemical fire pooled in her pupils. "Didn't seem so averse to bloodshed when we first met."

"I was fighting for my life then. Not for the amusement of gamblers."

"Does a distinction like that help you sleep at night?"

"I don't need to sleep," he said.

"I envy you that. Now why are you following me? If this is about your money, I don't have it yet."

"Does it normally take this long to sell some spells?"

"I've had trouble," she said.

"Something I could help with?"

"Maybe you should lie low. Leave the troublemaking to others for a while."

In the near distance, the crowd began to disperse. Two men staggered up the lane, arguing over their wager.

"You seem eager to get rid of me." He moved closer to her.

"People have a habit of getting hurt when you're around."

"I don't see it that way."

She backed out of the light of the lamp. He halted. He would not follow her blindly into a dark alley. He did not fear her exactly, she had never threatened him nor shown that her aims conflicted with his. But nor did he trust her. She was too resourceful, too ambitious. He respected her too much.

"Come now, Cassius. I'm a gambler, but even I couldn't calculate the odds on the coincidences that follow you." Her voice was low and teasing. "You know that man of Piso's you asked about? That one-eyed bastard? Well, a few days ago, he went missing. And then the night you asked about him, someone fitting his description attacked

Cinna's men. Afterward, he disappeared again. Coincidence. Big co-incidence."

Cassius wormed his shoulders under his cloak. "I'm just here to earn money."

"You had banknotes worth three thousand gold in your hands the other day."

"How did you hear about that?"

"Small island." Her voice came from off to his side. She had flanked him from the shadows. "Word travels fast. Now tell me to my face why a man with three thousand gold wouldn't run from this garbage heap."

"Believe what you want."

"I believe what I see." She stepped into the light again, her eyes wolf gray and tight. "And when I work both sides, I see more than anyone."

"Is that meant to impress me?"

"What happened in Lowtown?"

"We went to pick up money." Cassius turned to face her. "Things got out of hand."

"And the message at the house?"

Cassius shrugged. "I don't know anything about that. My guess is someone just declared his intention to escalate this conflict."

"Who? Piso or Cinna?"

"I couldn't say."

"Well, someone has to answer for all those bodies," she said.

"There's violence every day on this island."

"That doesn't make it right."

"What are you saying?"

"You cut that girl to pieces."

"I didn't have anything to do with that."

"You were there."

"No," he said. "I was outside."

"Then you let it happen." Her eyes were frantic. She tried to make her face a mask of calm strength, but her fear was plain to see. It shamed him so that he had to look away.

"You think I'd do that?"

"Would you stand by while someone else did?"

"I wouldn't." His voice was thin, near to cracking. His chest sank, and it was easy to see now that he was still a boy. When he spoke, there was always the feeling of a cold intellect working beneath the words, ever guiding, and it made him seem older if only because the thing that fueled it was old. But clearly he was not its equal. "I didn't lay a hand on that girl. I only learned of it after the fact."

She looked off into the middle distance. He turned to follow her stare, but the street was empty.

"And then you killed them," she whispered, more to herself than to him. "You discovered what they did and killed them. I couldn't figure out who did it. But it was you. It makes sense now."

"I don't know what you're talking about."

"We both know there wasn't a firefight in Lowtown. Just because Cinna can't trust word that comes out of Lowtown doesn't mean that I can't. That money was the only reason Cinna didn't kill you. You gave the money back, and after that, your killing those men didn't make sense. Your even going back to Cinna's didn't make sense. Not if you robbed him. So Cinna figured if you weren't out to rob him, then you had to be telling the truth. And so he thinks Piso did the killing."

Heat lightning lit the sky.

"I'm smarter than you," she said. "Most people stop liking me when they realize that. I wonder if you will, too."

"If you're so smart, tell me why I'd risk my life doing this."

"I don't know yet. But it's clear you're up to no good. If I can see it, others will eventually."

"Not before I'm finished," he said.

"Finished tearing this city apart?"

"And what do you care for this nest of rats and snakes."

"This is my home."

"And what does that say about you?"

"You self-righteous pig. At least there's no blood on my hands." She stepped close to him, their faces inches apart. Her hand dipped into a pocket in her dress. Cassius did not need to see the hand to know that it now gripped her dirk.

"No one in this city can say that."

"What do you mean by that?"

"Nothing," he said.

"Liar. You were talking about the Uprising. No one in this city has clean hands because of the Uprising. That's what you meant."

A bent old man emerged from an alleyway. He was naked, and he declared himself a great prophet, alive some hundred thousand years, and declared also that he carried the word of god for all to hear and that any man who laid a hand on him in anger would turn to stone.

"If I were you, Cassius, I would be very careful with that sort of talk in the future. Cinna may need your help now, but if he hears that kind of thing, he will end you."

"I don't work for Cinna anymore."

"What?"

"That's why I came to talk," he said. "I'm going to Lowtown tomorrow. If you told Cinna that I was defecting, how would he react to that information?"

"You're a madman. You know what his response will be."

"I meant what would be his response to you. Seems he might reward someone who came to him with advance knowledge like that."

"Might reward me if I gave him your whereabouts as well," she said.

"You'd be giving up Lucian, too." He paused, let his words sink in. "They'd want to know who was helping me. They'd torture me. I would talk. I wouldn't want to, but I would."

"I could tell them to wait in ambush for your carefree ass. No interrogation, just a simple hit, and everyone could go on with their lives as though you'd never set foot on this island."

"Would you help Cinna kill me?"

"I might," she snapped.

"I wonder what he'd do to me if he caught me. Maybe behead me in the Grand Market for all to see."

"What does that mean?"

"Give me over to Cinna, and sure as I'm standing here, there'll be gold in it for you. But I wonder if you wouldn't be cheating yourself in the long run."

"Cheating myself how?" she asked.

"There are debts; and then there are debts."

The barkeep was singing. He sang a sailor's chantey that listed a number of ports, then listed a number of women. Cassius entered the bar from the pantry just as the song was turning to tales of a jail cell.

"Cassius, old boy." The barkeep filled his mug from a wine bottle. "I was just thinking about you."

"That was quite a song. Were you once a sailor?"

"No. I've never been anywhere."

"What about the mainland? You lived there."

"A long time ago," Lucian said. "And I didn't travel much then."

"Only to Scipio."

"Yes. When I was a little younger than you. I still regret that. I should have seen the world. Or at least the Republic."

"You're not too old to travel," Cassius said.

"I'm old enough to have lived here too long. Old enough to be stuck here." The barkeep slid his mug across the bar. "Here. Have some of this."

Cassius drank. The wine was warm and sweet.

"Are you all right? When's the last time you slept?"

"I slept a bit today."

"And before that?"

"Not since I slept here."

The barkeep shook his head. "Are you hungry?"

"Very."

The barkeep fetched a half loaf of stale bread and a bowl of cold chicken thighs from the kitchen. He set the bowl down before Cassius, and they sat in silence as Cassius ate.

"I've got a bit of business in the morning," Cassius said after he had finished half the chicken. "I wanted to see you before I left."

"What kind of business?"

"Lowtown business."

"Like your business in Lowtown the other day?"

"You heard about that?"

"I told you, boy. I hear everything."

"I didn't do that to that girl," Cassius said solemnly. "I didn't lay a hand on her."

The barkeep nodded.

"And if I did—" Cassius checked himself. He took a deep breath. "If I did a thing like that, you wouldn't talk to me anymore, right?"

"Why are you asking that?"

"It's important to me. I need to know you're not like the others, Lucian."

"What others?"

"Like everyone else on this island. You're not numb to it. You wouldn't eat with a man who did a thing like that, would you?"

"Of course not."

Cassius peeled the flesh from a thigh and popped the tough meat into his mouth. He washed it down with a sip of wine from the barkeep's cup. His hand began to tremble, spilling wine into his lap. He set the cup down and lowered both hands beneath the table.

"That was a bad piece of business," the barkeep said. "I warned you not to get involved in this sort of stuff. This isn't your fight."

"I know how to pick my battles."

"And this bit tomorrow?"

"I think this will be the worst yet," Cassius said.

"How so?"

"I'd rather not say."

"Because you don't trust me?"

"Only because it's a thing you shouldn't say aloud." Cassius reached into his cloak and withdrew a small pouch, cinched tight with a knotted drawstring. He tossed the pouch onto the table, and it landed with the sound of coins clinking. He nodded to the old man.

"What is that?" Lucian asked.

"A bit of money. Not much, but all I could spare. It's in case you need to leave here suddenly."

"Why would I need to leave?"

"There are people who want me dead."

Lucian snorted. "Not such an exclusive club, I'd imagine."

"There will be a lot more after tomorrow. And maybe they'll want to hurt people who were close to me."

"I've had my life threatened before, boy. And anyway, why would they come looking for me?"

"They might learn you were giving me shelter."

"Where would they hear that? Only you and Sulla know."

"And what of Sulla?"

"Never." Lucian shook his head. "She wouldn't say a thing."

"For the right price, she'd tell. The woman's a wolf. You're a fool to think otherwise."

"She's had some trouble recently." The barkeep lowered his gaze. He looked as though he was nerving himself up to say something.

"What kind of trouble?"

"She won't tell me. But I think she's into someone for a lot of money. That doesn't make her dishonest, though. She's loyal. To me at least."

Cassius nodded. "So what if I'm the one who gives you up?"

"Would you do that?"

"If they were torturing me, I might."

"Who's they? And why would they torture you?"

Cassius did not respond.

"It's no crime to house a man," the barkeep said. "Even if he does get into a bit of trouble. And if I did need to leave, I have my own money."

"There's a note in there also."

"What's it say?"

"It has instructions on where to go once you're gone. Places on the mainland I know to be safe. A few names."

"Will it be that bad tomorrow?"

"Maybe," Cassius said.

"When will I see you again?"

"I don't know. So I need you to take that to put my mind at ease."

The barkeep took the pouch and made a show of clenching it.

"Thank you for this," he said. "But I still trust everything will go well."

"And if it doesn't, you'll get your chance to travel."

ADAPTATION IS YOUR
ONLY ORTHODOXY

—◦◦◦—

I n Quirthoge, they called him Olivetto. A boy of sixteen, he was
two years into his training on the Isle of Twelve when he made his
first trip outside the Republic. He played the part of a novice priest
of the Curio order, a fanatic who had traveled across the Ebon Sea to
bring the yellow light of his god to the heathens of the Southern
Kingdoms. In truth, he came only to bring fire and death.

Olivetto was excited to see a foreign land, especially one as re-
nowned as Quirthoge, with its mosaic walkways and gilt fountains.
Quirthoge was famous for its fountains. Thousands of them adorned
the city, each bubbling with water dyed a unique color. No two fountains shared a color, and legend held that if a man drank from every
fountain in Quirthoge, he would live forever. Olivetto had not come to
chase immortality, though; he had come to learn about destruction.

As a second-year initiate, he was seasoned enough to accompany
older initiates on their annual appraisals. The Masters had taught him
advanced spellcasting, had gifted him with a basic ideology of victory
and conquest. Now it was time he learned these lessons firsthand.

He traveled with Master Keno and initiate Alaric, who in only a
few short months would graduate to peerhood. They had reached
Quirthoge by boat, after a stormy two months at sea, and landed
during the height of a plague. On every street corner and in every
dusty lane, Quirthogi children sang the rhyme of the Weeping Sickness. *Red as a beet, Dry as a bone, Blind as a bat, Dead as a stone.*

The Weeping Sickness had swept into the city on the hot winds
blown up from the witchlands, or so said the old men who sat playing

senet on the harbor front. To the Quirthogi, the witchlands birthed every illness and malady in the Southern Kingdoms. There, hidden in sunless valleys, Blood mages hatched endless curses in their bid to reclaim the land they had ruled for thousands of years. The old men were certain of this, they told Olivetto. They were less certain of how to stop the sickness.

Some told the boy to smear boiled onion paste on his chest, others to stuff bits of dried clove in his nostrils. Most everyone in the city had taken to sleeping with veils over their faces, silk if they could afford, cotton or linen for the poor. The old men agreed the veils helped keep away unclean spirits, but it was the only thing they agreed on. That and the fact Antiochi gods were powerless here, and the help of these outsiders was unnecessary and unwelcome.

Master Keno agreed. He had no intention of helping the sick. The Masters cared only for wealth and power, and the opportunity for both had brought them to Quirthoge. As Olivetto understood it, the head of a local merchant concern had purchased the services of two experienced spellcasters, Master Keno and Alaric, to help cripple a rival. The merchant had no idea he had enlisted the aid of the famed Masters of the Isle of Twelve.

Appraisal missions were clandestine affairs, often arranged under aliases so as not to attract attention and because botched assignments could tarnish the reputation of the Masters. These missions served to teach initiates how to behave while on contract. Master Keno was here to observe the ways Alaric interacted with his employer, how he dealt with the locals, how he overcame his enemies. More importantly, Master Keno ensured that Alaric did not betray the Isle's secrets.

Olivetto aided his companions with both their real mission and their cover mission. He spent the first three nights in the city wandering its streets and its public gardens, practicing the language, eating savory pastries of goat meat spiced with cumin, and eyeing dusky, dark-eyed girls in sheer gowns. He preached on street corners to orphan boys who made his heart ache for his friends of old. And all the while, he bore witness to an expert lesson in crushing your foes.

His fourth night there, Master Keno asked him to burn a granary.

No easy task; Olivetto had to enter the compound where the grain was stored, destroy it, and escape with his life. Olivetto had done all three without being noticed, but that night, lying awake in bed, he wondered what good came of burning a granary during a plague. It was not his place to worry over such things aloud, so he kept the question to himself.

"How long did it take you?" Alaric asked the next morning. As a senior initiate, he was expected to assist in the training of junior classes and to discipline them for any transgressions.

"Less than an hour," Olivetto said.

They bunked in a small room on the upper floor of a tavern. The tavern owner had worried that these outland priests would shame his customers away from drink and whoring and gambling, but Master Keno assured him that Curio priests cared only about aiding the sick and the poor. They liked to travel amongst outcasts and lived in squalor to better serve their god. The tavern owner thought them mad for pledging themselves to a god who kept them destitute, but he accepted their coin without complaint.

"How did you get in?" Alaric was in his early twenties, tall and thin-boned, with a long face and an aquiline nose that hinted at a strong Antiochi heritage. Nearly bald, he clung to the few tufts of light brown hair still atop his head, brushing them forward to cover his scalp in a way that seemed pleasing to him alone.

"I dressed as a laborer, snuck in under cover of night."

"Where did you buy the clothes?"

"A market on the far side of the docks." Olivetto kept his answers short and vague. He knew Alaric's debriefing had little to do with assessing his performance and more to do with doling out punishment, warranted or not. Alaric would use the boy's words against him, to prove him inept and unworthy, regardless of his actions. The Masters taught that cruelty was the secret to power and obedience. Alaric was a believer.

"So someone in the market saw you."

"I hired an urchin boy to buy the clothes. The merchant dealt only with him."

"So the boy saw you?"

"The boy saw someone in a cloak. He could not identify me."

"I see." Alaric ran his fingertips through the front of his hair. He sat at the room's one small table, a pitcher of water and an earthenware mug set before him. A small rucksack lay at his feet, open enough to expose the butt of Master Keno's lash. "How did you get past the guards and to the granary?"

"My disguise got me into the compound. To reach the granary, I used a spell of illusion."

"And the spell worked?"

"No one saw me."

"No one stopped you," Alaric said. He spoke softly, never made eye contact. "That doesn't mean no one saw you. You might have been followed all the way back here."

"I didn't notice anyone following."

"That doesn't surprise me." Alaric reached down and retrieved the lash from the rucksack. It was a fearsome thing. Half as long as a man's arm, made of Murondian thornwood, ringed by bands of iron for added weight, with a corded grip and, at its head, twelve strips of scored leather. The sight of it turned Olivetto's stomach, but he refused to give Alaric the satisfaction of seeing his fear. "How did you burn the granary?"

"A spell of hot embers carried on a slow breeze."

"Did it burn quickly?"

"It did."

Alaric rolled the lash in both hands, as though savoring the feel of it. "Much faster than a simple arson, would you say? So fast that reasonable men might suspect the work of a spellcaster?"

"I performed my task successfully."

Alaric brought the lash down onto the table. The pitcher spilled, the mug clattered to the floor. The noise rang, then the room fell silent.

"That was not the question I asked you," Alaric said.

That night, Olivetto snuck down to the harbor. He sat watching great ships from the far corners of the world as they sailed under the glow of a bone-white moon. Akhaian triremes and Murondian trader-cogs and even a few large junks from the far east. His back ached from the lash, throbbing with raw pain. He thought about leaving.

It would be simple enough to find work on a ship and sail out of the harbor in the next few days. He was able-bodied, could learn to tie knots or mend sails or cook or clean as well as anyone. Or maybe there was a ship in need of a spellcaster. The boy was without his gauntlets—Master Keno kept them on him at all times—but he could still prove his abilities if put to a test. He could sail away from it all, the Isle and the Masters, the fear and the lash. High adventure was waiting for him out on the seas.

All he had to do was run.

He had run once before. He still relived that night in his dreams. Not every night, but often enough that he never forgot. There was no shame in running then, he was just a boy. Weak. Helpless. But he had determined to grow strong. He had made promises.

The lash didn't make him strong. Even in his short life, he knew enough of pain to know it only diminished, never strengthened. But if he could bear the lash, the secrets of the Masters were open to him.

It was a warm night. The sweat from his back made his wounds sting. He shut his eyes against the pain.

Pain. He had been dealt a strong measure of it during his time on the Isle. Pain was not the goal of the Masters though, he knew that much. Pain was their tool, the instrument by which they molded, same as a sculptor's hammer and chisel. It was this pushing and shaping that wore on him the most, the sensation that he was losing something of himself, some small part he tried to keep locked safely inside but which the Masters seemed always to be reaching for, flaying him open so that they might touch it. The question then was not whether he could endure but whether he could adapt.

He did not know the answer to that question. He did know he had suffered the lash tonight, and still the part of him locked inside had remained locked. The Masters had not gotten to it this time. That was a kind of victory. And maybe that was all he could hope for. One small victory a day, every day, until this was finished.

On his way back to the tavern, he passed a fountain bubbling with coral-colored water. A withered beggar wrapped in loose robes sat beside the fountain and cried out to the boy as he passed.

"Mercy," the beggar shouted in Antiochi. "Mercy."

The boy had forgotten he was wearing the robes of the Curio. He fixed his cowl and approached the beggar, kneeling down to say a brief invocation over the suffering man. He placed a hand on the man's head and began to speak a blessing when a beam of moonlight caught the beggar's face. Olivetto saw the man's flushed cheeks, his cracked lips, his rheumy eyes and tear-stained cheeks.

Red as a beet, Dry as a bone, Blind as a bat, Dead as a stone.

"Help me," the beggar muttered. "My eyes. I'm nearly blind."

"There now, friend," Olivetto said. He drew the small square of silk he carried with him from his pocket and wiped the man's eyes. "Have a drink of water. Try to get some rest."

Olivetto helped settle the beggar comfortably, then took the man's hand and ran it through the water of the fountain so he knew where to drink. He offered one last prayer and then he left the man.

When he returned to the room, Master Keno was out on business, and Alaric was sleeping. Olivetto closed the door gently behind him, taking care to make as little noise as possible, but still Alaric woke. The Isle cultivated light sleepers.

"Who is it?" Alaric shouted. He sprang up in bed and snatched the silk veil from off his face, squinting at Olivetto until he recognized the boy in the dark. "Just you, boy? Keep it down."

"Of course," the boy said. He undressed and set aside his robes. He retrieved the silk square from his pocket and settled onto the floor, lying on his side as the pain in his back was still too great to lie flat.

"Where have you been all night anyway?"

"There's an emerald fountain near the city gate. They say it helps keep away the Weeping Sickness."

"How does it do that?"

"You dip a cloth in the fountain and sleep with it over your face. It keeps you from breathing foul dust and air."

"You went there to wet your own cloth and didn't think to take mine as well? You selfish cur. You deserve to catch sick and die." Alaric held out his hand. "Give it here."

Olivetto hesitated.

"Give it now, or I'll fetch the lash again."

Olivetto handed over the cloth. Alaric took the square with a sneer. He unfurled it and lay back in bed and placed the cloth over his face.

"Cool and damp," he said smugly. "I'll sleep well with this tonight."

8

~~~

Cassius passed the night in the hole and left the bar at dawn. Outside, he watched the sun rise, the horizon melting from pink to warm gold. He thought about leaving now, and he wondered what he hoped to save by leaving and he wondered what he would lose. It seemed immeasurable in any real way.

His work had driven him for so long, he was unsure life could exist apart from it. For all his days, he had strived to grow stronger, to protect himself where others had failed, to find solid footing in an unstable world. But that had changed when he discovered Attus.

The graybeards in Philosopher's Square had taught him of Attus, the great warrior who had thrown off the yoke of Fathalan slavehood and carved a nation out of the lost and wandering tribes of the Antiochi plain. Attus who had sparked the fires of revolution, fed those fires until they grew to uncontrollable flames, and in the process earned immortality.

After learning of Attus, Cassius had found a new mission in life. He would grow strong that he might spark a fire of his own. He would see tyrants brought low, would see a great and proud people restored to their glory, would follow Attus's footsteps into immortality.

Or so he had dreamed. The reality of Scipio did not match his dreams, though. The mud and the grime. The savagery and greed. The complacency. How could he hope to overcome it all? At best, he did not know. At worst, he thought the task impossible.

The question that remained was whether his life was worth living without this work, without this dream, or if losing it would burden him for all his days, and at death, he would know his accounts stood imbalanced and, knowing this, would die a man cheated by his own hand.

His palm began to ache. He picked at the loose scab absently. Blood ran down his hand, and he lifted his hand to his lips and swore an oath on his own blood.

At sunup, the Grand Market was mostly empty but for Piso's men guarding the main avenues south, Cinna's men guarding the main avenues north, and the legionnaires stationed at the council hall. Here and there, a merchant was erecting his cover or laying out his carpet.

Cassius cut across the square. He passed into an alleyway and walked south through the network of narrow lanes, moving in the company of stray dogs.

He emerged on a Lowtown road that was unpaved and strewn with trash. Melon rinds, offal, scraps of cloth, rotted lettuce, chicken bones. Crowds of Native children huddled seminaked in the doorframes of steaming shacks. If they were young, they stared out at him openly, and if they were older, they stared and tried to appear as though they were not staring, employing a sidelong glance with lowered head that was commonplace in Scipio.

He made his way through an avenue of glassblowers and witnessed their craftsmanship and compared it to his own work, which he knew was never beautiful, and he wondered which would last the longer, their glass or his orchestration, to which he had not yet put a name.

He caught sight of his reflection in a polished mirror and saw himself as others saw him, short and thin, unshaved, covered in a filthy cloak and an oversized tunic, with blackened eyes that were turning a green-yellow at the edges of the bruise. For all the damage, his face still looked soft.

He was harder on the inside than he looked. He was certain of that, had proven it time and again on the Isle. He hoped he was hard enough.

He made his way deeper into Lowtown, and now he could hear the docks in the near distance, the dockworkers shouting orders. He heard birdcalls and the snap of sails in sea wind.

He reached a dirt plaza built on the intersection of three unpaved lanes and here was a tall, mudbrick-and-wood building. On the opposite side of the plaza were colorful huts, their garish paint peeling to reveal wood the color of sun-bleached bone. The boy and the cart were nearby, in the shade of an alley. The boy sat with his feet dangling off the cart and pretending to sleep.

Cassius approached the cart and made a clicking noise with his tongue. The boy snapped awake. Cassius palmed a coin into his hand. Across the lane, a half dozen men were engaged in a dice game. Nearby, a pair of watchmen dressed in leather armor were sharing snuff and eyeing Cassius.

Cassius moved aside the bundles of firewood in the cart and threw off the blanket to reveal the one-eyed man, Servilius, lying naked and unconscious, his mouth open. Cassius pulled him off the cart and lifted him from under the armpits. The man was a head taller than Cassius and when Cassius walked, the man's feet dragged the ground.

The building was five stories tall, with a plastered facade painted salmon. Cassius knocked at the door, and there was no response. He banged again, louder this time, and shouted for the master of the house. He heard the sound of wagon wheels behind him, and he glanced in time to see the muscular boy pushing his cart out of the plaza at a run. The door opened, and a squat man with a drooping mustache stood in the entranceway.

"Out of the way," Cassius shouted.

He shouldered inside, and the man with the mustache backed away and stared dumbly. Cassius eased the one-eyed man to the floor.

"Get a healer," Cassius called.

The man with the mustache ran off, and Cassius could hear his cries for help in the still house.

The front room was large, furnished with a half dozen long tables and benches. There was a tall counter, the kind used in chow lines, and on the front wall a mural of an ivory-colored man, the traditional Antiochi figure of Death, leading a line of people to the gates beyond the veil.

Cassius took a seat at one of the benches. The man with the

mustache returned, and behind him scurried a fat, old man. They approached Servilius cautiously, as though he were a rat they had happened upon in the pantry. The fat man kneeled and pressed his ear to the one-eyed man's chest. He felt for his pulse.

The room filled quickly. A dozen men whispering as the fat one set about his work.

"Where'd you find Servilius, stranger?"

"I seen that little bastard before. I know I have."

"Which whorehouse you visit?"

"You play cards down at the Chum Bucket?"

"He's one of Cinna's."

The room fell silent.

"He's the one killed Junius," the same man called.

Cassius rose and reached to his waist, taking care to keep his cloak still, hands hovering near his gauntlets.

"I know it. Little guy. I remember. He's all bruised up now, but I remember."

"Is that true, boy?" another man called. "Speak, damn you."

"Enough."

The crowd parted as a massive figure emerged from the hall. He stood six and a half feet tall, with powerful legs and a broad chest. His head was shaved, and he had wide cheeks, hazel eyes, skin the color of pistachio shells. His shoulders were knotted with muscles, and he had three diagonal slashes branded into his left bicep. The short sword tucked into his hide belt seemed a knife for the size of him.

He approached the one-eyed man, and the crowd parted. His steps were loud on the wood floor.

"How is he?" the tall man asked.

"Alive," the fat one said. "Breathing. But barely."

"What's wrong with him?" The tall man turned to Cassius.

"He's drugged," Cassius said. "And he'll be dead within the day if you don't get him the proper medicine."

The tall man spat at Cassius. He made to step forward, and Cassius lifted his cloak with a flourish, and at sight of the gauntlets, the tall man checked his advance.

"Look around you, boy," the tall man said through gritted teeth. "You're outnumbered."

"I am," Cassius said. "But I'll be sure to start my killing with you."

"If he dies, you won't make it out of here."

"I can save him," Cassius said.

"Then you better get to work."

"I want to see Piso first."

"You look like hell, boy."

Gnaeus Piso was square-jawed, with thick gray hair that he wore cropped short and slicked with lard. He was doughy, with big hands and a high, firm gut. He smelled strongly of musk. A massive burn covered the right half of his face, from his forehead to his neck, the scar tissue an angry pink.

"It's been a rough week," Cassius said.

Piso sat behind a large, oak desk. The room smelled of the same musk as the man himself. Maps hung tacked to the walls, and there were shelves set with odd trophies, nicked half helms, a tiger pelt, ornate Fathalan fighter's robes now torn and bloodied. On a high shelf sat a clear jar filled with dark water within which floated a human head, the head with two holes where its eyes should be.

"What are you?" Piso asked.

"How do you mean?"

"You don't look Antiochi. Not full Antiochi anyway." Piso was missing his right ear. His right eye was barely visible under its drooping lid, and the corner of his mouth curled permanently in a demented smirk.

"I am."

"You sure you're not some mongrel? Maybe your mother got drunk, rutted with some Fathalan, huh? Or a big, black Shonite maybe? I was in the legion, son. Fought those black bastards for ten years. Seen with my own eyes, daughters of the Republic swoon at the sight of those animals. Nipples hard as diamonds with thoughts of . . ."

Cassius looked away.

Piso laughed. "Oh does that offend you, son?"

"I'm not your son."

"What?"

"You called me son," Cassius said. "I'm not your son. And that's the last I'll hear from you on the subject of my mother."

"See, I like that." Piso shook a finger at Cassius. "Shows you have honor. Back in my day, if a man challenged your blood, then you fought that man. Showed him your worth."

"And today?"

"Today, few boys are built that way. But I half suspect that if I'd continued down that path for two sentences longer, you'd have jumped over this desk at me." Piso smiled. "Or maybe summoned a wolf to do the jumping for you."

Cassius stared at Piso's face, appraising the burn openly. The skin was like dripping candle wax, and a small pool of spittle collected in the corner of his lip. Piso noticed Cassius staring but did not seem to mind. He had been a handsome man before the injury but not a vain one.

The sight of the burned skin unsettled Cassius, a reminder of the fate that might await him should his fire ward ever slip.

"It was one of your kind give me this." Piso motioned toward the side of his face.

"A killer."

"That's right. Back in the army. You ever served in the legion?"

"No."

"Soldiers hate killers. You know that? It's one thing to try sticking a sword in a man's belly, that's just honest work. But it's another thing to burn someone alive. Besides which, every killer in the world is protected from fire, so he doesn't share the risk a common soldier does."

"Fire wards don't offer total protection," Cassius said. "Most killers die by fire themselves."

"Good is what I say to that. Me, I'm a soldier at heart. Can't stand you goddamned finger wavers."

"That doesn't mean you don't need us."

"We'll see about that." Piso smoothed his black tunic, his motions direct, purposeful. "What happened that day with Junius?"

"He attacked me."

"Maybe. Maybe not. Who can tell? Half the witnesses were probably drunk. So what the hell is the difference, right? Except here you are in my house. In front of my face." Piso slapped his large hand onto the desk. "Now I've got to consider you. And what to do with you."

"You should hire me on immediately," Cassius said. "I think that's clear."

"Why would I do something like that?"

"Because you know how good I am."

"And what of my men? If I hired on the man who killed their brother, I'd have a goddamn riot on my hands."

"Was Junius that beloved?" Cassius asked.

"I liked him well enough."

"He was a fool. He attacked someone he didn't know, walked straight into a spell trap. He was overconfident, and it cost him his life. On the mainland, a half dozen killers die that way in every city every day. His death isn't a tragedy. It's a cliché."

"What of your debt to me?"

"Those gauntlets were mine by right of combat."

"I don't give a damn about the gauntlets." Piso smiled, the look full of menace. He wiped a string of drool from his burned lips with the back of his hand. "What of the blood debt? You took my man from me."

"And I gave another back. Now that doesn't exactly make us even, but the way I figure, this is about as square as you and I are ever going to get."

"And what happened to Servilius?"

"Cinna had him kidnapped."

"By you?"

"No, but I knew of it. And I brought him back to you at great risk to myself."

"Why?"

"To prove my intentions." Cassius paused, watched as the muscles of Piso's face twitched unconsciously. "I want to serve you now."

Piso breathed loudly through his nose, like some snouted beast. "How could I trust you? You worked for Cinna."

"You trust a yellow to fight alongside your men, but you wouldn't trust me?"

"You mean Hoka?"

"The tall one."

"He's only half savage." Piso stood from his desk. He walked to the far wall, where a weapon rack hung. He lifted a scimitar from the rack, its steel polished to a shine, its pommel set with a massive pearl. "And I only halfway trust him. But at least he never worked for Cinna."

"Cinna's a fat, effete fool. I don't work for him anymore."

"Why?" Piso twirled the blade. It whistled as it sliced through air.

"Because there's a war coming. And I want to be on the winning side. Cinna's a great whoremaster. But he's no general."

"What makes you think there's a war coming?"

"Look around you," Cassius said. "What's the death toll for the last few days? Fifty? More than that? I was at the firefight in Lowtown the other day. I know what's coming."

Piso shrugged. "The people killed in Lowtown the other day weren't mine. Why should I give a damn what happened to them?"

"Cinna thought they were your people. That's why he killed them. Doesn't that speak to his intentions? And the message he had us leave? Could it be any clearer? The kidnapping. The deaths in Lowtown. The ambush at the safe house. The fires two nights ago."

"Why now?" Piso stared off. He ran his thumb along the edge of the blade, testing it absently. "Things have been quiet for years. Not peaceful, of course. But there hasn't been open war either."

"Have you ever considered that he might not be in his right mind?"

"How do you mean?"

"Nothing. Just rumors. I shouldn't have even brought it up."

"Tell me."

"There's talk of Cinna being sick," Cassius said. "Whore's disease. They say he's had it for years."

"Dick rot?" Piso laughed. "That dirty bastard."

"Over time, it drives you mad, you know? You start acting on impulse. Grow paranoid."

"And you'd have me believe all this without proof?"

"You can believe what you like. But the fact remains, I've ruined my relationship with Cinna to come here. There's nowhere else for me to go on this island. Even if you don't trust me entirely, trust my desperation."

Piso nicked his thumb on the blade. A drop of dark blood dripped to the floor. He brought his thumb to his lips and sucked the wound.

"How do I know this isn't some ploy by Cinna to plant a spy in my ranks?"

"You'll have to test my loyalty."

Cassius's room was cramped and smelled of sweat. He sat cross-legged on a fusty cot, one of ten in the room, his cot covered with an old blanket, gray and rotting. On the opposite wall, an open window revealed a cloudless, midday sky and a blazing, unrelenting sun. A church bell sounded noon. Cassius heard men move about downstairs, heard them talk of him in whispers.

In the front room, ten men sat at the long table near the door, the table set with earthenware plates and mugs, dishes of salad and bread, fresh fish, dates, sliced oranges, cheese. There were pitchers of wine and water.

Hoka, the large man who had spat on Cassius earlier, sat at the head of the table. There was an empty chair opposite him, and Cassius sat in this chair, the men at the table watching him warily as though he were some creature loosed from a cage.

Hoka forked two fish fillets onto his plate and began to eat, and he was the only man eating, and no one spoke.

"I can leave if you want," Cassius said after a while.

"No one asked you to do a goddamn thing," Hoka said.

"I make people here uncomfortable."

"You're a murderer," some man announced.

"I killed Junius in a fair fight. That doesn't make me a murderer."

"Doesn't make you our friend neither," Hoka said. "If boss says you bunk with us, that's fine. If boss says no one touches you, that's fine, too. I'll make sure you're safe. But boss never said we had to listen to you. So shut your mouth and let us eat."

When the meal was finished, the men rose and cleared the plates and left the house, and Cassius was alone.

That night, Cassius listened to the men sleeping around him. His heart was racing from Garza root, his nose running. He heard a series of faint cracks, then an explosion. He walked to the window and looked east, where, halfway across Lowtown, a stream of salmon-colored flares rose and arced and burst in a bright display, then fell sputtering.

He made his way downstairs. Few people loitered in the dark square. He stood gazing over the low rooftops to the east, and when next he saw a column of fire spiral upward, he recognized the spell by sight alone.

He heard the approach of footsteps as a young boy, about ten, sidled up beside him. The boy was shaved bald, probably to save him from lice.

"What's that?" The boy pointed to the sky.

"Cone of fire."

There was the sharp cry of a beast. He listened but could not place the sound.

Wisps of green phosphorescent smoke drifted over the distant rooftops, then slowed and began to settle like dust. Moonlight glinted in the haze.

The boy cursed softly.

A gust of wind swept back the smoke, curling it.

Darts of purple light arced skyward through the retreating smoke. They halted in midair and hung motionless, each the size of a broomstick. One at a time, they flared bright and shot downward with the speed of falling arrows.

The boy gasped.

Cassius recalled the way spells had excited him as a child, their bright displays and loud reports, the explosions that shook his bones. It was great fun to watch from a distance, and that far from the action, he never heard the cries of the wounded and dying. He had thought spellcasters dashing and brave then, but he knew the truth of them now. Butchers with better tools than most.

More people had gathered in the plaza now. Men stood staring out doorways, some gape-mouthed and pointing to the eastern sky, others already geared for battle. A few raced off toward the sight of the skirmish.

Cassius was sitting on the stoop of his bunkhouse when Hoka returned the next morning. His face and neck were bloodstained, his tunic streaked with grime. In his hand he held what looked a slice of burned ham but was instead a human scalp. Thin and ragged, coated on one side with sparse, greasy hair.

"Recognize that?" Hoka shook the scalp at Cassius. "Maybe was a friend of yours."

9

The dining hall was filled with thirty men, most gathered at the long table in the middle of the room. It was early morning, but many were already drinking, some even drunk.

Cassius was not hungry, an aftereffect of the Garza root he had snorted to keep himself awake last night. He could not allow himself to sleep beside these men. Better to rest in a viper's pit. Snakes, at least, did not pretend to be an ally before they bit.

He sat at an empty corner table, smoking a thin cigar. All around him, men whispered his name. He heard spellcasters debating the worth of his victory over Junius, heard them swear they would never have stumbled into a trap as he had. Cassius ignored them. Talk was worthless. Truth lies in the ring, as the old gladiator maxim held.

"Can I sit?"

Cassius turned to find Servilius at his side. He nodded to the empty section of table across from him, and Servilius dragged a chair to the table and sat. He set down his mug and placed his hands on the tabletop, palms flat. Almost unconsciously, Cassius did the same.

"I came to thank you for what you done for me," Servilius said.

Cassius shook his head. "No need for that."

"You saved my life. You have my gratitude. If you'd like me to repay you by leaving you in peace, I wouldn't be offended."

"I don't mind company."

"Can I ask you a question?"

"That depends on the question."

"Where did you find me?"

"One of Cinna's warehouses," Cassius said. "Do you remember any of that?"

"No. Last thing I remember was heading to the baths. I go to a place in Ashkani Row. It's cheap. I was looking to get a blowjob from this tart I see sometimes, and the next thing I remember was waking up at Piso's, all the boys standing over me."

Tart. The word turned Cassius's stomach. It took an act of will not to sneer. He wondered if Servilius was talking of Tadua, but then quickly put the thought from his mind. On all sides, men plotted his death. He had to remain focused.

"Cinna probably had you waylaid. After that, you were drugged."

"No recollection of that either," Servilius said. "Just strange dreams."

"It wasn't me that did it."

Servilius considered this.

"How'd you know where I was?" He adjusted his patch and set his hands back on the table.

"I was one of the guards at the warehouse."

"Guarding me?"

"Guarding everything in there."

"Did they do anything to me?"

"What do you mean anything?" Cassius asked.

"I don't know. Anything."

"I don't think so."

"Well, that's a small blessing. An untouched asshole, and I'm still breathing." Servilius patted his chest. "What more could you ask for? And the spells, too. Most people would've kept those. Especially another killer."

"They weren't mine to keep," Cassius said.

Servilius surveyed the room. He looked back to Cassius. "You know what everyone's thinking, don't you?"

"I'm not sure I do," Cassius said.

"Maybe Cinna's men work differently, but around here, we're brothers. That's how you know you can trust the man next to you, the man fighting at your back and sleeping in the bunk across from yours.

Because he's your brother. And you know what makes a man your brother, don't you?"

"Blood."

"That's right. Blood. The only way to make a man your kin."

"I see," Cassius said.

"Do you? Because when I say it's the only way, I mean it. A man can claim to be your brother, but that doesn't mean people see him that way. Not even when someone important tells them they should. Understand?"

Cassius nodded.

"And if people don't love a man like kin," Servilius said, "they're liable to do terrible things to him. You understand me, stranger? You seem a smart man, but I want to make sure you're hearing what I'm saying."

Cassius rolled his cigar between his thumb and forefinger. "I do."

"Good. Now take a sip of my mug. Do it and make sure everyone can see you do it."

Cassius took a long sip, then set the mug back on the table, and Servilius drank from it immediately.

"That's so everyone knows we're having a cordial discussion over here."

"I appreciate that," Cassius said.

"I'm a person who believes one act of kindness deserves another, stranger. But there aren't many like me around here."

The streets of Lowtown smelled of smoke. Ash floated through the air, remnants of the previous night's fires. The sky was clear and the sun overhead small and very bright. Cassius squinted against the glare.

He moved through a lane of hovels. Women stood cooking just outside their doors, Khimir women and Antiochi. They called to each other from all directions, their grilles hissing and sputtering. Someone spotted a rat. Another yelled for some flour.

He purchased two salted sausages and received them wrapped in flat bread. The cook was large and old. She smiled as she took his money and told him there were ways for a man to earn a discount when haggling with her. She grinned lewdly. Cassius blushed, and the other women laughed.

At the end of the lane, he turned north, and now he was moving through the site of last night's spellfight. The ground was powdered with soot so thick, he left footprints as he walked. Two dozen houses were charred and nearly as many had collapsed into rubble. Here and there, the street was stained with dried blood, and he saw limbs protruding from under ruins and even whole bodies stripped naked, lying faceup in the sun.

He came to a section of paved road spiderwebbed with thin cracks. He leapt across the chopped earth and continued up the street, walking through shallow craters.

At the end of the street, he came upon a hound rooting in the wreck of a tenement. The hound was gaunt and had a patch of raw mange on its left hind leg. It stiffened at the sound of his approach, then circled to face him and hung its head as though embarrassed. Its muzzle was filthy with gore and Cassius did not look to see what it had been eating but instead moved more quickly through that place, and although he was sweating, he pulled his cloak tight around him.

I n the Grand Market, he found the blind man asleep at the statue of Isvara. He was sleeping with his eyes open or else was feigning sleep. Cassius took a seat next to him and called to the blind man, and the blind man stirred.

"Did I startle you, grandfather? Were you sleeping?"

The blind man flashed a faraway smile. "You have heard the old saying, have you not? Never tire in your duties. For Sleep is the sister of Death."

"I have heard this."

"Then know that I never tire in my duties. Now why have you come, boy?"

"I have food, grandfather," Cassius said. "Will you eat with me?"

"I do not have money for food."

"I did not ask you for money."

"And I did not ask you for food. I am not a beggar." The blind man sat up straight, fixed his blanket.

"You will share your company, and I will share my food."

"What is your name?"

"What do you care?"

"When I eat with a man so often, I would like to know his name." Cassius leaned close to the blind man and whispered.

"That is a good name," the blind man said. "A very traditional surname as well. Your father must have come from one of the oldest tribes."

"It is my mother's name."

"That is not how the people name their children. Boys carry their father's name. That is the way."

"I do not have my father's name. I was named for my mother's father."

"Are you sure of this?"

"As sure as one can be."

The blind man was sitting cross-legged, with his blanket on his thighs and his chest exposed. Cassius passed a sausage into his hand. The blind man broke a piece and deposited it in his mouth. He worked the meat with his gums and swallowed.

"What do you wish to discuss?" he asked.

"The Uprising."

"I was old even during the Uprising. I have no great war stories for you."

"Tell me what you remember."

"Fighting in the streets. Every day, you would hear the fights. No one could sleep."

"Did you have a family then?" Cassius asked.

"They were slaughtered when Quintus sacked the town."

"I am sorry."

"It was not your fault."

"What do you know of him?"

"Of Quintus? I know what everyone knows. He was an accomplished spellcaster in his youth. As was his father before him and his father before him. Rune magic is strong in their people. So is madness."

"I see," Cassius said.

"You were hoping I would say something else."

"I am just glad to hear you talk."

"Do not lie," the blind man said. "If you want something from me, only tell me what it is."

"I was hoping for stories about him. Something to illuminate his character."

"You want to hear horror stories? There are plenty of those. Ask in any bar, and they will tell you of Quintus's brutality during the Uprising. You do not need me to recount it."

"You must know something," Cassius said.

"I will tell you the only thing you need to know about our general. When his father died, Quintus took control of the legion. His father was a tremendous man, yet Quintus did what his father could not. He broke the Khimir."

"Are the people broken now?"

"Either they live in the jungle and pay him tribute, worship him as a vengeful god come to walk the earth. Or else they live in his city and pay tribute to those who pay tribute to him. I call that broken. You can call it what you like."

"He will pay for what he has done."

"The gods do not punish every man according to his crimes," the blind man said.

"Maybe it will be a man who holds him accountable."

"It would take a terrible man to overcome Quintus."

"Why would he have to be terrible?"

"Because Quintus is terrible. And how could one less than him overcome him?"

"But this man would not need to be terrible to do so."

"What would he need to be?"

"A hero."

The blind man wiped his greasy hand on the blanket. "Ah I see," he said. "I see now."

"You do not agree?"

"I did not say that."

"Then tell me how you feel about it," Cassius said.

"You will be offended."

"I will not."

"This is an Antiochi thought," the blind man said.

"How can you say that?"

"Because it is the truth. The Antiochi respect those who can do what normal men cannot. To hear the stories of their heroes, you would think they talked of gods, so great are their exploits. Tales of men who sack entire cities, men whose wealth is equal to that of small kingdoms. But do you know what a man must sacrifice to become so great? His humanity. The very thing that makes him a mortal man."

"That is foolish."

"Do not call me a fool, boy," the blind man shouted, a fleck of spit arcing from his lips. "I do not insult you, and I expect the same treatment."

"Forgive me."

"You think because I am a pauper you can talk to me like I am a beggar. This is the Antiochi in you."

"Let us not say things we will regret."

"I know these people. I have known them longer than you have been alive. And this is the truth of them. They think themselves gods. Who but a god, or an Antiochi nobleman, can turn every whim into reality? Who but a god, or an Antiochi general, can kill whole races with no feeling of remorse?"

"You oversimplify things," Cassius said.

"I do not. I have seen them at their worst. Have seen the unimaginable."

"I believe you."

"Do you, boy? You would think me a madman if I told you the truth of what I have seen."

"I would not."

"I have seen their Death," the blind man said. "You know him, this Death? His skin is pale, white as bone, his mouth black as a pit."

"He is an ancient figure. The Antiochi paint him on murals and vases. They raise temples to him. They make offerings so he will spare their loved ones."

"I am not talking of paintings and temples. I have seen him in the flesh. As a younger man, when I still had my sight. I was out hunting boar, and he passed through the jungle of a night. You will think me a liar, but it is the truth."

"I do not think you a liar."

"His eyes were black as a starless sky. His gaze was fixed ahead as he walked, and I was grateful for that. If he had turned to stare at me, I would not be sitting here with you. Of that I am certain. He takes all that he sees."

"That is what they say."

"He is like all Antiochi in that way," the blind man said.

"I suppose."

"You think me a foolish old man."

"Of course not."

"You do. Why else come today to talk of the Uprising. About Quintus and the horrors he has wrought. To justify the terrible things you dream of doing to him? To kill your guilt for having those feelings? I would not do it even if I could. I would rather you stay a man forever. I would see you saved even from yourself."

He watched the Market for most of the afternoon. He sat by the dried fountain and drank lemon water from an oversized pitcher, the water floating with thin slices of strawberry. He dozed in fits and dreamed himself in faraway places. Sometimes when he woke, his eyes stayed unfocused for whole minutes, and he thought he heard whispers spoken in a familiar voice.

He watched the crowds conducting business. It seemed a kind of dance. Chaotic at a glance but upon inspection something much more formal and structured. He put the number of people in the square at a thousand although he figured that a conservative estimate. The noise of the square was loud enough to interrupt his thoughts. Sounds of haggling, laughing, shopkeepers shouting at thieves, crowds of young boys calling obscenely after women, quiet whispers of secret meetings, investment tips, gambling, talk of Piso and Cinna and Quintus, children fighting. After some time, the voices mixed into a low, featureless roar, and in this quiet, he told himself his work was inevitable.

When he finished the lemon water, he rose and headed north. He came upon a fruit vendor and paid the man a half-silver for an apple and for the location of a bar favored by Cinna's men. The vendor was reluctant at first, or else he was feigning fear, Cassius could not tell which.

"The Drunken Monkey," the vendor whispered. He spoke into his shoulder so that Cassius had to lean close to hear him. "By the north side of the Market. They eat and drink for free in there."

"Thank you."

"Will there be trouble?" The vendor grinned knowingly.

"I certainly hope not," Cassius said.

The vendor nodded knowingly. "I take your meaning."

The bar fronted the north edge of the Market. A Native man lay sprawled in its doorway, naked but for a pair of bleached pantaloons. His beggar's bowl rested on his belly.

"Charity for the poor," the beggar said.

Cassius stepped over the man and into the bar, and the man cursed him as heartless and rolled onto his side and farted.

The room was hot and dim. A stone grille smoked behind the bar, the smoke thin and smelling of roasted goat. Cassius ordered a mug of wine and made his way to the back corner.

A short time later, three men entered the bar, one man with a pair of gauntlets dangling from his belt. The men settled at the bar and ordered a pitcher of spiced rum and three plates of goat meat. They ate quickly and ordered more food and more rum. They finished their meals and made to leave.

"What kind of place is this?" Cassius called. "A bar where men eat and drink for free?"

"You don't know what you're saying," the bartender said.

"Is my next meal free as well?" Cassius asked. "Or have these men made other arrangements?"

The three men stopped.

"Shut up, boy," the bartender said.

"You dogs come here and take everything," Cassius said. "You may scare this cur, but you don't scare me."

The bartender turned to the men at the door. "Don't mind him. He's drunk."

"I'm not drunk," Cassius said. "And in case you three didn't hear, I just said I'd whip the three of you in a fight."

"I'll break your face." The last of the three men lunged for Cassius. He was large and pale, a Jutlander maybe or even a Kell, who made their homes in the dark forests at the end of the world. He had a mess of red-brown hair and thick muttonchops. The bartender leapt over the bar to hold him.

"Outside," the bartender said. "Wait for him in the streets."

The red-haired man hooked his thumbs into the neck hole of his tunic and lifted out an octan suspended from a leather cord.

"You see that, boy. That's what's waiting for you outside."

The three men exited the bar.

Cassius finished his wine. He stood and donned his gauntlets and crossed the room and stepped over the beggar into the light of the Market.

"If they kill you," the beggar called, "can I have your boots?"

As Cassius emerged from the bar, he squinted against the glare of the midday sun and felt a stirring in his chest. He spotted the red-haired man and the killer standing ten yards ahead of him, the killer with his gauntleted hands raised. Cassius began to draw the rune for his fire ward, but before he finished, he noticed a blur on his periphery, then felt cold pain on the side of his head.

His vision dimmed as he pitched forward. He raised his hands to break his fall but his movements were sluggish, clumsy. He landed facedown and rolled. That's when he saw the third man from the bar standing over him, his heavy truncheon held high, stained with Cassius's blood.

Cassius lashed out with a kick to his groin, and the man with the truncheon collapsed. The smell of manure filled the air as the killer in the Market finished his casting.

Cassius lurched forward, spurred by blind panic. He grabbed the man with the truncheon and rolled, pulling the man atop him. As the flames descended, Cassius felt the heat of the fire, intense heat, a sensation he had not felt for some time. The man screamed and thrashed as the flames licked his back, but Cassius gripped his tunic tight and held the man in place, using him as shield against the blast.

When the fire cleared, he tossed aside the man and stood. Wisps of smoke rose from his tunic and from his singed hair. He beat a lick of fire that had caught the edge of his sleeve.

He felt another strumming in his chest.

Without thought, he cast his fire ward and raced to flank the two remaining attackers.

Cassius's vision clouded. He blinked, then dragged his forearm across his head, wiping away blood. When his eyes cleared, he judged the red-haired man to be about twenty paces from him and closing fast.

The red-haired man held a knife in each hand, and behind him, the spellcaster had called forth from the void a pair of shambling corpses, their rotted flesh hanging in strips that left their gray bones exposed. They wore molded half cloaks over ancient bronze cuirasses, their helmets plumed with horsehair and shrouded in cobwebs, their spears and round shields rusted.

Here, in these two forms, was the essence of Antiochi magic made clear. The original spell had most likely originated in Awanu, one of the Southern Kingdoms. There ibis-headed priests practiced Blood magic, manipulating the passageways into the afterlife so that they might hold dominion over their dead long after death. The imitation spell though, the rune, was wielded by no priest.

Instead a mercenary Antiochi had summoned to modern-day Kambuja a pair of deceased Akhaian spearmen, warriors so ancient they might well have died at the dawn of western civilization, guarding the cyclopean Lion Gate against barbarian hordes.

All thoughts of ritual and custom were disregarded. Time and magical tradition itself were cast aside for raw immediacy, the mysteries of the arcane arts commodified in service to speed and violence. Antiochi magic.

The Market crowd fled, some calling for the legionnaires to aid them, others imploring the gods for protection.

Cassius swept his hand forward and out of the ground curled violet smoke. When the smoke cleared, a sleek panther crouched in its midst. The panther stiffened and hissed at the red-haired man, its fangs stone gray and dripping.

The spear struck the panther in its flank. The panther lifted off the ground, then landed hard and lay bleeding.

"Stand down. Or the next spear goes through one of you." Vorenicus was approaching from the south side of the Market. He moved with a legionnaire on each side of him, the man on his right a spellcaster with his gauntlets raised.

The red-haired man checked his advance.

Vorenicus motioned to his spellcaster, and the spellcaster moved to aid the man afire, who was still now and no longer screaming.

"What the hell is going on here?" Vorenicus shouted. "Your name is Grinmall, isn't it?"

"That's right," the red-haired man said.

"Doesn't Cinna have enough to worry about without two of his own fighting in the streets?"

"Cinna's man?" Grinmall looked to Cassius. "You're Cinna's man?"

"He's the one who killed Junius," Vorenicus said.

"That doesn't make me Cinna's man," Cassius said. "Not any longer."

The legionnaire had extinguished the fire and was trying to calm the burned man, who rolled and groaned and called for his mother.

"Grinmall, take your men home," Vorenicus said. "Make sure that one sees a healer."

"I don't take orders from you."

Vorenicus tilted back his helmet, his eyes wild and manic.

"If I see you lingering in this Market for longer than it takes to collect your friend," he said, "you won't be taking orders from anyone any longer. Now move your ass."

Grinmall stood glaring for a minute, then sheathed his knives. He looked to Cassius and spat, then made his way to his comrades.

"You." Vorenicus pointed to Cassius. "Come with me."

Vorenicus's chambers were in the basement of the council hall. The rooms were neat and sparsely furnished, cool enough to offer respite from the island's oppressive heat.

"Am I under arrest?" Cassius asked. He sat at the only table in the room. His head still throbbed, the pain sharp and cold, radiating down into his back. He felt like a mule had kicked him, pained and embarrassed in equal measure.

"I don't usually house prisoners in my room." Vorenicus unstrapped his cuirass and laid it on his bed. It was a muscle cuirass, of the kind favored by high-ranking officers in the legion, sculpted to represent an idealized physique and with a frontispiece bearing an elaborate relief. This particular relief depicted a human representation of one of the cardinal Antiochi virtues, blindfolded Justice holding a sword in one hand and scales in the other, a twisting serpent at her feet. An elaborate piece of armor, but not one relegated to an art object. It bore the nicks and dings of practical use, scorch marks that could only have been earned in spell battles.

Vorenicus fetched a pitcher of water and two earthenware mugs. He removed his helmet and placed it on the table, then sat across from Cassius.

"If I'm not your prisoner, what do you want from me?"

"Answers," Vorenicus said.

"I gave you enough of those at Cinna's bar." Cassius rubbed the side of his head. A knot had formed just above his ear, tender to the touch and matted with dried blood. A throbbing ache settled behind his eyes.

"What happened out there? Was that to do with your switching sides to work for Piso?"

"No."

"What was it about then?"

"The price of wine at a bar."

Vorenicus's helmet shone, its twin eagle feathers stiff and tall. Cassius could see his face reflected in its polished surface, eyes blackened, nose swollen and bent.

"I'm curious why you decided to change your allegiance," Vorenicus said.

"Better pay. Better food." Cassius shrugged. "What does it matter?"

No one spoke, and the two men sat, appraising one another.

"Where do you come from, Cassius?"

"Ivalia. Near the Murondian border."

"Who was your trainer? Did you serve with one of the spellcaster guilds? A mercenary house maybe?"

"Are you trying to recruit me into the legion?"

"I've made inquiries about you. Do you know what I found?"

"How would I know that?"

"Nothing." Vorenicus spoke softly. He was young, probably no older than Cassius, and although not an imposing figure, he had mastered a kind of calm menace more intimidating than Cinna's flagrant displays of power or Piso's fits of rage. "Does that seem strange to you?"

"No, I'm just a mercenary. Hundreds of us pass through this city every year. We're common as copper. What is there to find?"

"There's always something to find. Not always something interesting, of course. But always something. About when you arrived in Scipio, how you got here, your habits on the mainland. Something. But when I asked about you, I found nothing. How is that possible?"

"I guess I'm not a memorable person," Cassius said.

"Maybe. Or maybe you've made arrangements so that no one would remember."

"Why would I do that?"

"That's what I intend to find out."

"Surely you've got bigger problems to worry about." Cassius leaned back in his chair. He retrieved the box of horn from his pocket and pinched a measure of Garza-root powder and snuffed it. His heart-beat quickened. A tight pain settled in his chest, then passed. He snorted, swallowed the rank taste at the back of his throat.

"The other day, when we discussed the incident in Lowtown, you were clear that Piso's men had ambushed you. Would you care to amend your statement?"

"Why would I amend it?"

"Considering your new employer, I thought maybe you'd want to revisit your story."

"Doing a thing like that would make me a liar, wouldn't it?" Cassius asked.

"I only meant that maybe now you'd be free to say things you weren't before."

"I was as free then as I am now."

"So your story stands," Vorenicus said. "Piso's men ambushed you and killed Cinna's men and robbed Cinna's money. Do you realize how that story casts your new boss? It might seem that Piso's responsible for the violence of the past few days."

"My story stands. I told it to you the way I understood it."

Vorenicus nodded. "And if Master Piso has a different account?"

"Well, then, I guess that makes us two men with two separate accounts of the same incident. Not such an uncommon circumstance, I'd imagine."

"Seems you're in a position to tell more clearly than most who's responsible for the violence of the past few days."

"Maybe, but I'm not sure I'm fit to judge." Cassius wiped his nose. "The deaths in Lowtown last week contributed. But so did the safe-house deaths and the kidnapping of Servilius and any number of of-fenses against Master Piso. If I had to lay blame, I'd say both parties deserved a share."

"It's my job to maintain the peace. If you would only help me understand—"

"What's that?" Cassius stood and walked to the mantel above the hearth, where a small plate was set. The plate held a sliver of ivory and a sliver of bone, a small metal scale.

"That's an altar to Tithemia."

"The goddess of justice. You have a shrine to justice in your home and yet you share a drink with a man who just had a spellfight in the Market?"

"I'm giving you the benefit of the doubt. There were three of them, one of you. And, being a loud-mouthed son of a bitch and all, it's not hard to picture him starting a fight. Am I wrong in that assumption?"

"You talk like them," Cassius said.

"Like who?"

"Everyone else on this island."

"I meant no offense," Vorenicus said.

"I'm not offended. It's just a bit strange."

"Strange how?"

"Those words don't fit you. You sound like a man acting a part."

"It's important to be able to communicate with those out there." Vorenicus pointed a finger straight up, indicating the street. "Sometimes harsh words are necessary to make yourself heard. Especially here. But I won't use them again if they make you uncomfortable."

"All right."

"And what happened this morning, that doesn't happen again either. Not in my Market. And I'm not asking. If Piso and Cinna want to hack each other to pieces, they can do it in their parts of the city. But the Market is under protection of the legion."

"Because the Market is where all the money changes hands." Cassius fingered the sliver of ivory on the altar.

"Because this is where the council hall stands. Now I intend to tell Piso and Cinna as well. But you're new here, so I thought you should hear it from me. No more violence in the Market. Or else the legion gets involved. Understand?"

Cassius turned to face Vorenicus. "I saw you save that kid the other day, in the fire. I've never seen anything like that before."

"You're a spellcaster, you see men move through fire all the time."

"That's not what I meant."

"What did you mean?"

"Why do you care about this place? Why risk your life trying to maintain order in a place without any laws?"

"Scipio is unusual," Vorenicus said. "On the mainland people are accustomed to order. But people come here to escape the rule of law."

"So what hope is there for justice?"

"All things change with time."

"Do you really think Piso or Cinna would upset the order of things here? Or even the good general, for that matter?"

"They won't be around forever."

Cassius did not speak.

"Don't misunderstand me." Vorenicus lifted his helmet. He buffed a small bit of grime on the brim with his tunic sleeve. "I'm not angling for control. I would never raise a hand against my father. He's a great man. I love him dearly."

Cassius looked away.

"But the men in power now won't be in power forever," Vorenicus said. "Just as my grandfather ceded control to my father, my father's time will come eventually. And Cinna's and Piso's as well."

"And then what?"

"Then maybe the island will be ready for the rule of law. Maybe we'll finally be able to join the rest of the Republic."

"And how do you think the savages would respond to that?"

"That's a distasteful term, Cassius."

"I learned it here."

Vorenicus sighed. He considered his words.

"Officially, the Natives are already citizens of the Republic," he said. "They live on Antiochi soil. I'd like to show them the honor in that. There's no denying they've had a difficult history with the Republic, but that can change. Nothing in the past can be altered, of course. But we can show them that the rule of law will ensure they receive the same treatment as any other citizen."

Cassius had not expected such a sentiment from Vorenicus. He had assumed the son would share his father's hatred of the Natives by reflex. Lucian and others had spoken of the commander's fairness, but an even hand did not preclude a desire to subjugate. Benevolent masters were masters nonetheless.

"You think I'm mad," Vorenicus said.

"No," Cassius said. "I just don't agree with you. From what I've seen of the Natives, they need an iron fist to rule them. They'll respect nothing less."

"You don't know them as I do. They're a proud people, noble in their own way. Inquisitive. Hardworking. With a great love for family and friendship."

"They click and squawk like beasts in the field."

"Come now, Cassius. You don't know the first thing of their history. Before the legion arrived, they were divided into small tribes, each ruled by a chieftain selected from amongst the best warriors. No divine right of kings, no crown passed from father to son. They chose their leaders. Just like in Antioch."

"You'd have us let them vote?"

"Every citizen has the right to vote. The Natives should elect their local council, same as any other province."

Cassius thought again of Attus, of a single spark igniting a great fire. He was closer to his dream than ever before, the island like dry brush beneath his feet, waiting only for a flash of lightning to set it off. Yet now it seemed the legion commander himself had been stacking kindling.

"You're laughing at me," Vorenicus said.

"I'm not."

"I've been laughed at before, it doesn't offend me. Many people on this island think me a fool."

"I don't think you're a fool. Just idealistic."

"Men of vision shape the world. Tellium said that after the truce at Parnay."

"What he actually said was, 'It is the burden of men of vision to shape the world.' And it wasn't at Parnay. It was before the war, in his plea to the senate to raise an army."

"A student of history, I see."

"I've studied all the classical heroes," Cassius said. "Tellium, Equitius, Plinius."

"Attus?"

"I know every word of the Attus epics by heart."

"Where did you study?"

"Nowhere."

"Just something you picked up on the streets of Ivalia then?"

Cassius shook his head.

"I'm not mocking you," Vorenicus said. "That's quite an accomplishment. My father paid for a team of mainland tutors to instruct me since I was a boy. And still I don't think I ever made it through all of the Attus epics."

"Surprising what you can do with a little conviction."

He was three blocks out of the Market and heading south into Lowtown when Sulla caught up with him. He did not see her approach. One minute he was walking by himself and the next Sulla was walking beside him. She did not call him by name, nor did she acknowledge him by gesture.

She moved ahead of him and crossed directly in front of him. He kept pace behind her, and when suddenly she darted over a refuse heap and into a stinking alley, he followed after her.

They moved to the end of the alley, the ground wet with excrement from emptied chamber pots. A rat brushed Cassius's leg and he shouted from surprise and kicked at it and Sulla wheeled on him and told him to keep his voice down. She crouched, motioned for him to do the same.

"What the hell was that in the Market?" She was whispering. Her right eye was bruised.

"I had to prove to Piso and his men that I wasn't a spy. The only way to do that was to attack Cinna's men."

"You interested in doing that again?"

"What does that mean?" Cassius asked.

"Don't act so indignant. It's what you do, isn't it? Killing people? I'm asking if you're looking for work?"

"Does this have something to do with the eye?"

"It does." Sulla's lips peeled back into a sneer.

"Who did it?"

"A man named Iustus. One of Cinna's."

"And this is the man you'd have me kill?"

Sulla bowed her head, looked as though she were calculating odds. "If you're interested," she said finally.

"Why did he hit you?"

"I owe him money."

"Gambling debts?"

"What business is that of yours? I owe him, that's all you need to know. And I'm good for it, but he's been beat by some other debtors recently, and he's looking to make an example of me."

"Will he kill you if you don't pay?" Cassius asked.

"I believe he might try."

"Can you pay him with the money you owe me?"

"That money"—Sulla shook her head—"that money is gone, Cassius. And even if it weren't, it wouldn't put a goddamn dent in what I owe."

"I don't just kill people, Sulla. I'm not a monster."

"What about today? You were prepared to kill that man, weren't you?"

Footsteps sounded from the mouth of the alley. Cassius and Sulla fell silent. They waited. Two men appeared on the street but continued moving, lost in their own whispered conversation.

"That man had it coming," Cassius said.

"Why? Did you pick a fight with him like you did with Junius? Or is it just because he was one of Cinna's, and it served your purpose?"

"To hell with you. I'm not on trial here. You came to me."

"For help."

"It's not that simple."

"It would benefit you," she said. "I know a way you could do it and take down others if you wanted. Cause some trouble and score a nice bit of money as well."

"What does that mean?"

"What?"

"Cause some trouble?"

"The conflict with Piso and Cinna. The one you're trying to orchestrate. Or did you think I hadn't noticed."

"If I do this for you, I'm going to need you to do something for me. Something big."

She hesitated before speaking, then reached out her hand. Cassius stared at it without moving. It hung soft and insistent.

"Go on," she said. "I don't have plague."

He gripped her hand. She pulled him close.

"When I make a deal with a demon," she said, "I shake his hand."

Piso's quarters smelled heavily of musk and beneath this of rancid meat. Scented candles burned weakly. The door to the side room was closed, and a black cloth was draped over the entranceway.

"Have a seat," Piso said.

A scream rent the air, high and sustained, followed by hushed voices. The noise had come from the next room, but Piso seemed not to hear it.

"I'd rather stand," Cassius said.

"Suit yourself." Piso produced a wad of shredded tobacco from a pouch at his hip and tucked the plug into his lower lip. He worked his tongue over his teeth, smoothing the wet mass until it lay evenly against his gums. "Tell me, Cassius, have you been to war before?"

"Is this a war now?"

"It's a war, boy. I didn't exactly want one, but one's what I got. Only thing for me to do now is try to win it."

"Is it too late to sue for peace?"

"Much too late." Piso eased back onto the edge of his desk. "You saw what Cinna did last night. Sent spellcasters down here to cause trouble. He's getting more brazen with each attack. Now answer my question."

"No, I've never been to war."

"And yet you'd come fight for me."

"How many spellcasters do you have?" Cassius asked. "Eighty? Maybe ninety? Cinna has a hundred and twenty."

"Do you expect me to believe that?"

"I'd know better than you."

Piso stared up into Cassius's face, sitting motionless, waiting for the lie to reveal itself.

Cassius stood tensed, his cloak pulled tight, his arms tucked inside to hide their trembling. His heart pounded in his chest, and beads of sweat rolled down his neck. On the Isle of Twelve, he had learned to stand calm in fire. Panic meant death. But if you could move past panic, then no fire in the world could harm you.

He had no spell to protect him from Piso's gaze or his sudden rages. But the lesson still held. He was safe if he was calm.

And if he chose his attacks wisely, waiting for his opening and striking with overwhelming force. It was a lesson that took years to learn, a lifetime to master. Cassius was no expert, but he knew an opening when he saw one.

"I'm an adept spellcaster," he said. "And I've shown I'm willing to fight Cinna's men. You don't have the luxury of turning me away. Not now."

Piso sniffed. "The men are still upset about Junius. I can't offer you my brand."

"If your word is any good, I don't need the brand."

"It's two silvers for every man of Cinna's you kill," he said. "Four if the man's a spellcaster. I don't pay for women or children. But I don't frown on it either."

"All right."

"But no more of what happened this morning. You can't be that careless. Not in the Market at least. That's legion territory."

"What do you care?" Cassius asked.

"I care because the legion has twice the men I do. Trained cut-throats every one. I don't need Quintus sticking his nose in this. So you stay clear of the Market."

Another scream rent the air.

"Goddamn it." Piso spat. He sprang from his chair and moved to the door opposite the entrance. Cassius followed him inside.

A man lay on a table, naked to the waist, and two men stood over him. The man on the table had deep burns to his arms and chest, his flesh the caramelized brown of cooked pork skin. He was trembling, and one of the men was trying to hold him. The other man, a spellcaster, cradled the burned man's left arm, clutching it at the wrist and at the elbow. The flesh of the forearm was unlike the other flesh, smooth and pink as though freshly sunburned but with no severe trauma.

"Are you healing him or twisting his dick off in here?" Piso shouted.

The spellcaster stood at the sound of Piso's voice. He was old, with a wide brow and a wrinkled, thin-lipped mouth.

"Can't you give him something to ease the pain?" Piso asked. "There are monkeys in the jungle who can hear him carrying on."

"I gave him all I can," the healer said. "Any more, and we risk his going unconscious. Can't have that. Need to be able to hear him to know how much of this he can take. When to keep going and when to back off some, give his heart a chance to rest."

"How much more is left?"

The healer shrugged. "He's hurt bad. It's going to be a slow healing."

"Are you certain he'll recover?" Piso asked.

"Recovery isn't the problem. Spells I got can heal any wound a man can sustain. I can regrow you two lungs if needed. But they won't be any use to you if your heart seizes up while I'm doing it. So we go slow, and we hope he doesn't die before I get all the way through him."

"How slow?"

"I wouldn't want to put a time to it if I didn't have to."

"You have to," Piso said.

"Thirty or forty hours."

"At a half-gold per hour, he had better make it out of this alive."

"I'll do the best I can."

The healer returned to the table. He took a fresh grip on the arm and closed his eyes. Cassius felt a stirring in his chest and the flesh of the burned man's bicep began to bubble. A smell like rotted ham rose from the arm, and the burned man kicked his legs and screamed. The flesh dried as it bubbled, then sloughed off in great calcified flakes, and the skin left beneath was bright pink and smooth.

Piso exited the room and Cassius followed and closed the door behind him.

"Goddamned washed-up old killer." Piso kicked his desk. "He's robbing me."

"That's generous of you to pay for that man's healing," Cassius said. "I'm sure your soldiers respect you for it."

"Don't be an idiot. I don't pay to have every man in Lowtown treated by healers. That's my sister's son in there. She'd have my balls if I sent him back to the mainland in that condition."

"Is that why Cinna attacked last night? To hurt your nephew?"

"I don't know. He thinks I killed his friend. And that fat old pervert wants revenge. Probably he just wanted to kill someone, anyone, and got lucky with the boy."

There was another shout. A long wail that tapered off into a breathless gasp.

"Aren't you worried that screaming will spook the other men?" Cassius asked.

"All healing is painful. If the men don't know that now, it's time they learned." Piso crossed the room to his desk. He searched through his drawers until he found a bottle of spiced rum. He poured a measure of this into a mug and drank it in a single gulp.

"About the fight last night," Cassius said. "Do you know how many people were killed?"

"Five of Cinna's. Three of mine. Three if him in there lives. Four if not."

"And civilians?"

"What?"

"How many civilians died?" Cassius asked. "I saw the ruined houses while walking this morning. The destruction was terrible."

"What do you care? They don't pay taxes to you, do they?"

"I was just wondering."

"I don't know. Go ask around if you're that interested."

"All right."

"I don't have enough trouble as it is?" Piso shouted. "Worrying about this fat bastard trying to kill me? Worrying about that maniac in the jungle and exactly how much damage I can cause before he decides enough is enough and marches his army over the whole damn town? Now I've got to worry about how many of these yellow animals died under a collapsed tenement, too? Is that what you're telling me?"

"I was just wondering."

"Are you a physician, Cassius?"

"No."

"A priest maybe?"

"I'm not."

"No, you're a killer. And we do ourselves a disservice to deny our nature." Piso jabbed a finger at Cassius. "So put the suffering of the masses from your mind and do the job you came here to do."

"Why do you practice Rune magic?"

Cassius sat on a high stool in the healer's shop. The Yoruban stood next to him, probing the painful lump on the side of his head with his large, gentle hands.

"The same reason you do," the Yoruban said. "Because it is my gift and a means for me to make my way in this world."

The Yoruban pressed the base of Cassius's skull, felt along his occipital bone, felt along his temples. He looked into Cassius's ear and dipped the tip of his index finger into the ear canal and withdrew it, inspecting for blood but finding none.

"Yorubans must have their own magic."

"A kind of nature magic," the Yoruban said. "Handed down from elders to initiates that my people may use these secrets to tame the wilderness and protect our kingdom."

"But you weren't interested in Yoruban magic?"

"I was not able to study it. Initiates are chosen from only a handful of families, their secrets well guarded. Rune magic is different, though. You have the ability to work the runes or you don't. If you do, you need only acquire spells and learn the runes. You need permission from no one."

The Yoruban moved in front of Cassius. He pulled down Cassius's lower eyelids to inspect the red flesh there. He examined Cassius's pupils. He held his finger in front of Cassius's face and asked him to follow it with his eyes while tracing an H in the air.

"Did you ever train as a killer?" Cassius asked.

"For a time. When I first began to practice."

"But no more."

"No more."

"Why?"

The Yoruban tilted back Cassius's head and looked up his nose. He tapped a fingertip on each of Cassius's cheeks, and Cassius winced with both touches.

"Rune magic is an open system," the Yoruban said. "More so than the magic of my people. But it is also a predatory one."

"How do you mean?"

"The only way to grow powerful is to gain spells. You can't study your way to being a better Rune mage. The spell is not in your mind, you have to own it physically."

"That's not true," Cassius said. "You grow better through training and practice, the same as any other discipline."

The Yoruban moved to the table by the far wall. He shuffled through a pile of gruesome instruments, an amputation saw, vein hooks, suture needles, a bone mallet and chisel.

"But still there is the matter of acquiring spells," he said. "If you're rich, you can buy them. But if not, you have to take spells from others, from those who can't resist. The strong devour the weak. And the weak, hoping to become the strong, devour the helpless. I was neither rich nor strong. I didn't like my position, so I had to change it."

The Yoruban came to a vial of green liquid. He held it up in the light of the room and sighted through it, measuring its color and its cloudiness. He uncorked the vial and sniffed it and then moved back to Cassius's side.

"Owning many spells doesn't make you strong," Cassius said.

"Of course it does."

"Is the man with the most swords the best fighter?"

"Not necessarily. Although he may have the advantage of always having the best blade."

"You still have to learn the runes."

"They teach runes to children."

"Easy to learn. Difficult to master. Again, a sword has few movements: Stab. Slice. Parry. I could teach them to you in a day. It doesn't mean you would be a great swordsman. It is the same with spellcasting. You must learn to use your spells in conjunction with one another, learn progression and diversion, trapping maneuvers, when to counter and to feint, how to predict spells by sensory clues."

"I suppose," the Yoruban said.

"You can have two gauntlets full of jewels, but if you don't know how to fight, you're just an easy target for a trained killer."

"This is true. But at its heart, Antiochi magic is about taking. You take arcane secrets from other cultures and make them into runes. You transfer these runes to jewels, then you try to take the jewels from one another. I don't mean to offend you, or disparage your art. It is my art, too. But this is the nature of our magic."

The Yoruban sprinkled a few drops of the green liquid on his fingers. He rubbed the liquid over the lump on Cassius's head, and the skin there tingled and grew cold.

"So why become a healer?" Cassius asked.

"A killer's life is endless strife. He fights to acquire his spells, and in acquiring them, he becomes stronger. But being stronger makes him a bigger target. So he has to grow even stronger to keep his enemies at bay and maintain his power. It continues like this until one wrong move in a fight gets him killed. Then his gauntlets are stripped by another spellcaster, who will one day meet the same fate. It's not for me."

"Do you like helping people?"

"I do."

"Did you ever kill anyone?" Cassius asked. "Before you became a healer, I mean."

"I did."

"Do you think the good you do now makes up for that?"

"This is not for me to judge," the Yoruban said.

"Then who will judge?"

"The gods."

"And if a person doesn't believe in them?" Cassius asked.

"Then you must make your own code, and you must live by it," the Yoruban said. "A wolf kills, but you wouldn't jail him for it. It's his nature."

"And it's mine as well? Is that what you're saying?"

"Wolf or killer, what's the difference?"

The Yoruban wiped his fingers on his wrap. He patted Cassius on the shoulder.

"I'm afraid that is all I can do for you," he said. "I don't have a spell to reduce swelling."

"That's okay," Cassius said.

"I wish I could offer more help."

"You helped enough."

After dinner, a troop of men gathered in the plaza before Piso's hall and made a show of dressing for their patrol. Fifteen men in total. There were two spellcasters with them and also two mastiffs. A crowd gathered. Cassius watched them from the window in his room.

The men left the plaza in loose formation, and a few hours later, five of them returned. No spellcasters. No dogs.

The men were bloodied and stripped of their weapons, and one man had a terrible stomach wound.

That night, Cassius lay awake on his cot, his chest tight from the effects of the Garza root, and thoughts of sleep so distant, he began to think the condition unreachable. He listened to the men at play with dice in the downstairs room for hours; and then he rose and dressed himself. He scratched at his belly absently and winced as he pulled a stitch. He lifted his tunic and looked down to see that the area around his stab wound was inflamed. Red and swollen, and the lips of the wound a deep wine color.

The men cleared a place for him at their table. They stood over him and told him filthy jokes and poured him wine. The first drink of wine he had accepted from his enemies. He choked as it slid down his throat, settled in his stomach like a fist. They laughed when he rolled poorly, their hands rough on his shoulders.

Some man had produced a lyre and begun to play and there was dancing and the floor groaned under Hoka's leaps. Cassius lost fifteen silver pieces and stood to leave and accepted the last glass of proffered wine and smiled and drank it in a gulp and smiled and shook hands and laughed and smiled.

Later, in bed, he lay awake and whispered to himself a passage of the middle verse of the epic of Aemillius Attus. The hero at rest in the Proncius Pass, asleep amidst wolves.

The horizon through the window was orange, a false dawn of a tenement fire.

EVERY ENEMY IS A RESOURCE

On the road to Rocino Novi, they called him Drussus. A boy of thirteen, he had paid for the trip with everything of value he could muster. One Fathalan silver embossed with a wolf's head, six bare coppers, a chipped amethyst, a leather belt with a brass buckle, two pouches of Gaspian tobacco. No large sum, but it had taken the better part of a year to save it. He was happy to pay, though; happier still to leave everything behind.

He rode in a flatbed wagon, his rucksack tucked under him for cushion. Three other passengers journeyed with him, an old man with a crooked back and two women veiled and dressed in black as befit mourners. The women rode up front with the driver, but the old man settled in the flatbed with Drussus, and side by side, they sat facing backward and watched the road as it stretched behind them.

Drussus pictured the road as a river carrying him downstream. He liked the feel of moving, especially the feel of moving toward something. Before this, he had traveled frequently but never with a destination. He had moved only for the sake of moving, his journeys trips of opportunity. He was getting older now, though. He needed a plan.

He knew no one in Rocino Novi. Only the legion waited for him there. At thirteen, he was old enough to sign on as an auxiliary troop and learn to be a scout or runner or slingman. He had no love for the life of a soldier, no love for the legion in particular, but serving the Republic meant three rations of food a day, a roof over his head, clothes enough to keep him warm.

It meant also a sword and the training to use it.

The dreams drove him to Rocino Novi, more than anything. They had troubled him as a boy, gave him fitful rests and kept him awake with fear of what waited in the dark. All boys had nightmares, but Drussus had only one nightmare, had it most every night.

He was alone in the dream, running through a damp, dark jungle while legionnaires in full battle gear gave chase. The soldiers had hounds with them, and the sound of dogs barking made his heart race. Behind his pursuers, a wall of fire devoured the jungle. The heat from its flames burned him like fever.

He ran with heavy legs, his feet sinking into warm mud. The legionnaires gained ground with every step until, finally, he felt a hand on his shoulder and turned to find a terrible beast reaching for him. Red-limbed and fanged and covered with steel.

In all the years he had had the dream, Drussus never once made it out of the jungle. The beast caught him every time.

As he grew older, the dream lessened in frequency until even his memories of the dream faded. Then last summer, a heat wave swept the city, and most nights saw Drussus sleeping on rooftops for cool comfort, sweating in the dark. The dream returned then, the chase and the legionnaires and the hounds and the beast in all its horrific splendor.

He was too old for such dreams, he thought. Too tired to run anymore. It was time to face his fears. But first he needed to grow strong.

Rocino Novi stood two days' ride from the Ox, the great river that marked the edge of the Republic and the beginning of Fathalan land. It was a fort city, little more than a legion garrison with a surrounding civilian camp. Old Rocino had been different. A proper city, modest for a provincial settlement but large for a frontier post, until the Bloody Dervish Nasr ibn Ya'qub put it to the torch last winter. Now its walls were charred husks, and not even carrion birds called it home.

"Shame of the Republic," the old man said. Here the road drew within a dozen leagues of the old city's outer gates.

They had ridden for five days without much talk, but something about the walls had stirred the old man.

"Wouldn't have stood for it in my day." The old man sat with his head cocked, his eyes squinting against the setting sun, which painted Old Rocino in blood-red light. "We had Mad Malleolus in the senate then. The Hammer of the West, the desert folk called him. He would have ridden across that river and brought those jackals to heel after something like this."

"Is that right?" Drussus asked.

"You better believe it." The old man turned to Drussus. "These senators treat the legion like it's a plaything. They need to let the generals do what's right."

"And what's the right thing to do?"

"We should be watering those deserts with Fathalan blood." The old man gripped his cane tightly. "Kill them all. Women, children. Line every avenue in the Republic with their crucified dead."

"You'd have the legion kill innocent women and children?"

"I'd do it myself if I were thirty years younger." The old man sneered at Drussus. "And there's no such thing as an innocent Fathalan. They have blood on their hands going back hundreds of years. It's time we put an end to them."

"To all of them?"

"Is there another way?" The old man pointed toward the walls of Old Rocino. "You see that city? They burned it to ash no more than a year ago. We already have a new one built. And if they burn the new one, we'll rebuild that one in a year. There's no end to it. Not until we die or they die. Remember that when you swear your oath to the legion."

At Rocino Novi, the legion recruiter made his office in a dusty guardhouse, stockpiled with broken armor and rusted weapons, crates of old linens, carpenter's tools, great scroll racks covered in dust. The recruiter was middle-aged and trim, beardless, with a shaved head and a neat uniform. He greeted Drussus with a wide smile and an easy handshake, but his charm could not hide the hunger in his eyes. He was a butcher, after all, a man who traded in flesh. He needed meat to fuel the Republic's great war machine, blood to grease its gears, and Drussus had just offered himself for slaughter.

The recruiter made Drussus walk twenty paces, checking for a limp, then made him run a half mile. He had the boy strip naked, bend at the waist, bend at the knees, flex and extend his arms. He noted the scars on his body, the condition of his teeth, tested his vision for nearsightedness and farsightedness. Finally, he asked if the boy could spell his name.

"I can read and spell most anything," Drussus said.

The recruiter eyed him curiously. "Who taught you to read?"

"Old men who gathered at the orator's square. I would listen to them for hours. They took a liking to me."

The recruiter fetched a scroll from one of his many racks, unfurled it, and placed it on his desk. He called Drussus to come closer and pointed to a line of text on the scroll.

"Read this," he said.

Drussus scanned the words. "Four dozen chickens, two hundred eggs, nineteen lambs, forty sacks of barley, eleven casks of beer."

The recruiter nodded, rolled up the scroll. "You should have said something at the start. You'll be a good fit for the supply corps. We don't put those boys through the normal paces. No one cares if you can march so long as you can read."

"Supply corps?"

"That's right."

"I don't want to be in the supply corps," Drussus said. "I want to be a soldier. I want to learn to fight."

"We have boys who can fight and boys who can read. We don't mix the two. The supply corps is a good appointment. Plenty of those out drilling under a hot sun right now wish they were supply corps."

"I'm not one of them," Drusus said. He had paid every coin he owned, left behind every friend he knew, and ridden for a week in the back of a rickety wagon to reach this place. He wanted to become a great warrior, not a bookkeeper.

"Be honest with yourself." The recruiter's warm smile had faded. "You're no fighter, and you're certainly no soldier. You wouldn't survive half a day of legionnaire training. But you can still serve the Republic."

Drussus made to respond, but the recruiter silenced him with a raised hand.

"Take a minute to think it over, boy." The recruiter moved toward the door. "I need to find a fresh copy of the supply-corps contract. I'll take your answer when I return."

The recruiter left, and Drussus was alone in the guardhouse. He felt gut punched, weak in his legs. He had come so far only to find himself stranded on the edge of the Republic, in some godforsaken fort city where no one knew his name. He would be back to stealing his meals and sleeping in alleyways by nightfall.

It wasn't supposed to end this way, he was certain of that. But what choice did he have?

On the far side of the recruiter's desk, he spotted a rusted gladius placed longwise across a scroll. The sight of it filled him with a sudden urge to hold a blade, if only to see if the recruiter's words were true. He thought himself a fighter at heart, but maybe he was delusional.

He circled the desk. Next to the gladius rested an old, iron gauntlet. He donned the gauntlet and took hold of the sword's hilt, then hefted the blade, slicing it through air a few times. The movements felt natural enough to him. Was there something else he should be feeling?

He set the blade back on the desk, unfurling the scroll so that the blade rested in its original position. The scroll bore a single symbol, unlike any he had seen before. It was five lines, arranged in a pattern that nearly recalled a star. It wasn't a word, at least not one he recognized. Drussus had seen many languages, even the picture-words of the men from the East, but this was not the same.

He set his hands on the desk and leaned down, trying to decipher the image before him, when suddenly he felt a rush of warmth up his spine. The sensation of pins and needles crept over his hands. He noticed that a single jewel was set in the dorsum of the gauntlet, and the jewel now flared red.

"What are you doing over there?"

The sound of the recruiter's voice startled Drussus. He stumbled back from the table, reaching out with his gauntleted hand to steady himself on a nearby shelf, and caught sight of the glowing jewel as it streaked through the air, like a falling star, like some terrible portent.

10

The morning sky was cloudless, and the sun rose white and small. The city steamed. Great swirls of mist curled up from the streets, from the roofs of decaying huts and tenements. The air still smelled of last night's rain, and to the north, the smoke from the fires had faded. Cassius sat on the stoop of his barracks house and waited for the city to stir to life.

His eyes itched. His body ached from lack of sleep.

The plaza was mostly empty. In an alleyway nearby, a gaunt beggar sat warming scraps of rat meat over a fire of twigs and weeds.

Hoka emerged from the doorway behind Cassius. He was three paces into the plaza when he vomited, the sound of his heaving loud in the quiet morning. Green stew pooled on the hard-packed earth, washed over his bare feet. He spat and blew his nose. He wiped his face, looked over his shoulder at Cassius.

"Come, boy," he said. "Time to eat."

"I'm not hungry," Cassius said.

Hoka cupped a hand over his ear, feigning as though he had not heard. He walked back to the steps of the barracks house, stood looming over Cassius. He stank of liquor, his eyes bloodshot.

"That's your problem, boy. You never eat, and so you look like this." Hoka jabbed a finger into Cassius's side. "Eat, and you'll grow strong like me."

"I'm stronger than you."

Hoka laughed. "Tiny, soft mainlander. I've been killing your kind since I was a child."

"Is that right?"

"I was fifteen the first time. That was a knife fight. And him a grown man." Hoka dragged his thumb across his midsection and made a wet noise through pursed lips. "Spilled his fat guts in the street. Before I hadn't even made it with a girl yet."

"Why?"

"He called me a monkey."

"And that was during the Uprising?" Cassius asked.

"What do you know about the Uprising, mainlander?"

"Only what I hear in the street."

"No one recalls the Uprising. People in Scipio are famous for their short memories."

"What about your memory?"

Hoka spat.

"Did you fight for Piso then?" Cassius asked.

"Piso and Cinna. There was no difference then."

"And what of your people?"

"I'm a half-breed. I don't have people. And you should know, boy, talk of the Uprising can get you hanged to this day. I'd mind my tongue if I were you."

Hoka made to leave, then stopped.

"You see that man there?" Hoka pointed to the beggar roasting the rat. "In the afterlife, the soul of every king who once walked the earth would trade places with that miserable bastard in an instant."

"Does that mean you fear death?"

"I'm alive." Hoka slapped his chest. "And I wouldn't trade places with those who died. None of them. But I don't fear anything."

"Why won't you talk to me about the Uprising."

"I don't trust you."

"Because I worked for Cinna?"

Hoka threw wide his arms. "Because I don't trust any man who won't eat with me."

"Why the sudden urge to fight?"

Hoka scooped the last clumps of oatmeal from the bowl

with his fingers. He licked each finger clean, then wiped his wet hands on his tunic. He set down his bowl and reclined on the steps of the barracks house, resting on his elbows, and loosed a massive belch.

"Just thinking about something Piso told me," Cassius said. He tossed a small green pear hand to hand, his breakfast this morning although it remained unbitten. "About doing the job I'm here to do."

"Boss wants you to start earning your keep, then?"

"I'm not officially part of his organization."

"I know it, boy. Why do you think he keeps me near you?"

"I thought you just liked my company."

"In this plaza, you sleep in the midst of a hundred and a half of the Republic's most vile cutthroats. And yet you don't share our brand. Lucky for you, I'm here. If not, you wouldn't last a single night."

"Maybe. Although the business with Servilius might have changed a few minds."

"Servilius vouches for you, and that carries weight with some. But we're talking about men who think with their dicks or their blades. Hard to change their minds because their minds don't make their decisions."

"Those are exactly the kind of men we need right now. We have license to march into Hightown. We should take advantage of that. There's a fortune to be made up there in loot and scalps. In a matter of days, we could earn enough to live on for a year."

"Like those last night?" Hoka asked.

"They were ill prepared. Most likely they walked right into one of Cinna's patrols. Or else hit a target that wasn't vulnerable."

"But you'd be able to plan better?"

"I know the lay of the land," Cassius said. "Places where Cinna is unguarded."

"Well, you've caught me at a bad time, boy. Today's my day off. And, anyway, if Servilius is such a good friend, why don't you bother him with your schemes of theft and murder."

"I'll need help. And so I need someone the men will follow. Servilius doesn't command the respect you do."

"How many do you need?"

"Six."

"Us and four more?" Hoka asked.

"Us and six more."

"I call that eight, boy."

"Eight, then. Eight total."

"And what would be our haul?"

"We could take ten scalps," Cassius said. "With little resistance. It's a gambling hall, so there'd be opportunity for looting as well."

Hoka considered this. He mumbled to himself as he calculated the potential haul spread out over eight participants.

"I get two shares to everyone else's one and first pick of all loot. And a share of any spells recovered."

"Fine."

"And half of your share." Hoka sat forward, pulled himself up to his full height. "That's nonnegotiable. I don't like to haggle, and I'm hungover besides. If you don't like my terms, you can find someone else to help."

"I don't have a problem with any of that."

"Good."

Across the plaza, two children mimed a spellcaster's duel. They waved their hands at one another and made noises with their mouths, then one clutched his chest and collapsed and lay twitching in the dirt.

He met Sulla by the docks. She stood in the center of a near-deserted lane, brandishing her knife and yelling at a stray pig that was trying to bite her dress. She caught Cassius's eye and motioned toward a pub across the street with a tilt of her head.

He walked past her to the pub, which was damp and nearly empty. He took a seat in the corner and ordered wine and a dish of potatoes fried in chicken fat and spiced with black pepper. His food arrived and he began to eat and he finished the entire meal and a second glass of wine before Sulla arrived.

She ordered a drink and paid for it, pressing the coin into the bartender's hand and holding it there while speaking to him, an obvious bribe. She made her way to his table.

"You didn't order the potatoes, did you?" she asked.

"I did."

She shook her head. "You're a brave man, Cassius."

"I have to be, in my line of work."

"Always talking business. That's what I like about you."

"I spoke with Hoka earlier."

"He's quite the conversationalist, I'm sure."

"He's going to help me handle your problem."

"You didn't tell him it was a job for me, did you?" Her voice hovered just above a whisper, despite the empty bar.

"I'm not an idiot. I told him what he needed to know and nothing else."

"I'm sure he'll be a help in the fight. Did you give any thought to what it is you need me to do in return?"

"A little."

"You going to tell me? Or make me drag it the hell out of you one question at a time?"

Cassius drained his mug and set down his cup. "I want you to burn one of the storefronts that line the Market."

"You should know that me and Piso have exactly one thing in common," she said. "A deathly fear of fire."

"Find someone to do it. I wasn't asking for you personally."

"Which storefront?"

"I don't care."

"You do want it to be one of Cinna's, though."

"Damn it, I don't care about that, either," he yelled. The sound of his own voice seemed to startle him. He took a deep breath, raised his hand as a gesture of reconciliation. When he spoke again, his voice was low and weary. "Just make sure it's near the Market."

"Why?"

"What does that matter?"

"It matters. I'm not Hoka, to do a thing without question." Her voice was firm without being confrontational. She had seen men near to breaking before, men who had wagered their last copper on a roll of dice and lost it and lost their future as well. They were dangerous. And although she had never seen Cassius place a bet, she knew he was risking everything here nonetheless.

"I have my reasons. Besides, we had a deal."

"I came to you because I needed help. Because there was no one else to ask."

"I don't believe that," he said. "You know plenty of people on this island. Why come to me?"

"You tell me why." Sulla leaned in close. "Since you have all the damn answers anyway."

"Because you know I'm up to something, and you want to help."

"At the risk of sounding cruel, you should know I don't care for you very much, Cassius. Don't take it personally, though. There aren't many I do care about. My purse, on the other hand, that's something I do—"

"This is bigger than money. If it wasn't, if it was just a job, you wouldn't concern yourself with my reasons. And anyway, can't you figure it out for yourself? You're smart. What would happen if a storefront in the Market burned down?"

"Stores in the Market are practically built on top of each other. The collateral damage would be huge. The legion would have to fight the fires. If he thought it was arson, Vorenicus would be furious. He's already on edge about this war."

"And maybe a legionnaire or two would get killed in the process." Cassius looked to her again. "I bet that wouldn't make him too happy, either."

"And what does that net you? Vorenicus and the legion being angry with the bosses?"

"Maybe nothing. Maybe something. It doesn't concern your purse, so what do you care?"

They dressed in the barracks house after dinner. The men who owned armor helped one another with shirts of iron mail and shirts of scale, with the buckles and straps of cuirasses and greaves. One man had kept his centurion armor after deserting the legion, and his top of segmented steel plate was an object of considerable envy. Each man produced his blades and compared them with the blades on display, short, stabbing swords, long-handled knives, throwing axes, a pair of spiked cesti. They talked of the kills attributed to each weapon, lying to one another as though all were strangers.

There was a spellcaster with them as well, a man only a few years older than Cassius. His gauntlets were set with nearly fifty jewels, and Cassius could tell by sight alone that most of these were fakes. He was a squint-eyed man, a pale mouth-breather who stared openly at Cassius's gauntlets, a covetous look that lacked any real nerve.

Once dressed and armed, they waited until the midnight bell, then they left the plaza in a pack, Hoka in the lead, Cassius at his side, the six men fanned behind. They headed north.

They walked to the southern edge of the Grand Market, then doubled back and cut along the periphery of the square. The streets were sparsely peopled, and they walked in silence and were well into Hightown before any man realized Cassius was now leading.

The gaming hall stood near a strip of houses gone to rot and squatted by beggars and the abject poor. Along the way, it began to rain and the rain was heavy and warm and the streets flooded. They waded through running water that reached to midcalf. Their boots sank in loose mud, and the water was dark and smelled foul as people emptied chamber pots from overhead windows.

"Scipio," Hoka cried. "A city that simmers in its own gravy."

The front room of the hall was long and had a low ceiling. It smelled of stifled air, hot from a lit fireplace. Torches sputtered along the walls, and Cassius had to squint to discern shapes in the near dark. In the center of the room, he saw a man lying with his hands clasped to his belly and Hoka stood over this man, his sword slick with blood.

The rest of Piso's men entered the room in a rush. They kicked over chairs, toppled tables. An old man behind the bar lifted a crossbow to his hip and fired. The bolt loosed with a loud snap, glanced off a table, and skidded clattering to the floor.

Hoka slapped the bow from the man's hand with the flat of his sword and the man raised his arms over his head and shouted please. Hoka made a furtive stab with the knife he held in his off hand, and the man folded to the floor.

The room was still now. Hoka moved off to the hallway and shouted for Cassius to keep up. They came to stairs that led to the second floor and climbed the steps at a run. Halfway to the top, Cassius felt a faint tug in his chest.

Hoka shouldered into the door at the top of the steps, and it exploded off its hinges. In the center of the room, two tables were set on their sides to serve as fortification. Dice and coins lay strewn about the floor, and two men stood behind the tables, each armed with a dagger. Hoka advanced with a shout. He kicked at the tables and swung his sword and caught one of the men on his forearm.

The man screamed and dropped his dagger. Hoka stabbed at the other man's belly.

Cassius stopped at the door. The rest of the men charged past him, screaming.

The smell of brimstone carried through the air.

Cassius covered his ears and crouched low, and still the explosion stunned him. The cloud of fire mushroomed out from the far corner of the room, the rush of air a physical blow. Shrapnel stung his arms and face, wooden splinters, chips of earthenware cups, glass.

The flame spilled over him, curling like surf, and he did not feel it though the air grew hot, and he smelled burned hair and burned flesh, and around him, men screamed and died. The flame dissipated in a flash, and the air rang with the force of the explosion and then settled. Cassius stood and brushed himself. A cold pain worked its way up his arms. His forearms were shredded and bloodied, pitted with bits of rock and splinters. His eyes watered. The sight of his ravaged flesh made him nauseous.

Before him, the men were laid low, slumped motionless, like sated bodies at an orgy. Soot powdered the floor.

The young spellcaster who had followed him up the steps sat with his back pressed against the wall, face upturned and eyes open, a broken chair leg buried in his chest.

Cassius caught sight of movement on his periphery. Across the room were two shuttered windows, and in the space between these windows rose a short, balding man. His face was gaunt, and he had a long, aquiline nose perched above plump lips. He wore a tan tunic and leather sandals and wore also a pair of gauntlets.

He was covered in dust from the explosion but he bore no mark of the flame, and Cassius stared at him as a man in a foreign land will stare at a countryman he has chanced upon, feeling somehow connected and yet still strangers for all that link. There was a brief acknowledgment between them, a silent thing that arrived and passed and was never visible. They were spellcasters, and they shared in their blood secrets that most men would never know, and this bound them to one another and to what would inevitably follow.

In the vision, Cassius saw himself sitting in the dark room, hunched forward. He saw this from behind, as though viewing himself over the shoulder of another. When the voice spoke, it was a stranger's voice, although it was familiar.

"Rise, boy." The voice seemed to come from nearby and below him, as though he were a small bird perched on the speaker's shoulder. *"This is no safe place for you."*

He watched himself stir.

"Rise, boy. And continue about your work."

And suddenly the vision was gone, and he saw nothing and heard only a low whine that was very distant. After some time, he realized this was the sound of his own scream, and he woke then.

He opened his eyes and blinked away tears. He dragged himself into a sitting position. Across from him lay the body of the bald-headed spellcaster, twisted over the corpse of a jackal called from the nameless void, their limbs entwined so that they might have been sleeping companions from some illustrated storybook rather than instrument and object of murder each.

His head was heavy with numb pressure, and his jaw ached from grinding his teeth. He was aware now of sharp pain in both arms.

It took a minute to recognize his surroundings and his purpose there and to understand the danger he was in now. It took another minute for words to return to him. When they did, he told himself to get up, calling himself by his true name, which was the one he had used most infrequently in his short life although he had spoken it to the blind man in the Market the day before so that it was fresh in his mind and the first name that came to him.

He stood slowly, clomping heavy-footed. When he had steadied himself, he scanned the room for any bit of clothing that could serve as a shroud. He found a hooded, short cloak and donned this and made his way to the exit. He checked himself at the door and looked out over the room again. The gaming tables were overturned, some burned nearly to ash. Coins and a few singed banknotes lay scattered everywhere.

Fire covered the far wall, and its smoke rose through the massive hole torn in the ceiling. The flickering light seemed to animate the faces of the dead.

Lightning flashed in the sky outside.

He searched the room until he found Hoka's knife, then he was in that place for another half hour, and by the time he finished, he had vomited again, and his hands had begun to shake. Through this, he told himself to be strong.

The sun had risen by the time he reached Piso's hall, but the sky was still overcast, the small plaza filled with men. People stood gawking. Cassius had shed the hooded, short cloak, and as he moved through the press, men drew out of his path, staring as though he were a plague victim. He asked no man for help.

"By the gods, are you all right, stranger?" The crowd parted as Servilius, the one-eyed spellcaster, stepped forward. He hooked his arm under Cassius's arm and walked with him to the hall.

It took two hours to remove the shrapnel from his wounds. Cassius lay on the table in Piso's quarters, arms spread cruciform, while a physician and his two assistants worked with tweezers to pluck the shards of wood from his flesh, root out the bits of rock and broken pottery. He bled so much, he stained the tabletop.

Afterward, they soaked his arms in hot, soapy water, coated them with pig fat and honey, and then wrapped them, from elbow to wrist, in strips of clean linen. All the while, Piso ate his breakfast of fried eggs and sausage.

"Wound rot will be a problem," the physician said. He spoke to Piso, as though consulting a parent on the treatment of a child. "No matter how clean he keeps them, there will be complications. I recommend healing by spell."

"No," Cassius said. "I don't like healers."

"You won't like losing both your arms, either."

"Leave us," Piso said.

The physician gathered his instruments and his wraps, jars of salve and soap powder, and departed with his assistants.

Alone, Cassius and Piso sat in silence. Cassius listened for cries from the adjacent room, but heard none.

"What happened?" Piso asked.

"We attacked a gaming hall."

"I know that part. The part I don't know, and the part I need you to tell me about, is the part where eight of my men leave for Hightown and only one of them comes back."

"We made it to the hall without any problems."

"Who was leading?" Piso stood and began to pace. He carried his plate in one hand, scooped eggs into his mouth with the other.

"Hoka. Before we broke into the hall, I cautioned him to watch for killers lying in ambush. But he said he didn't give a damn about spellcasters. That there wasn't a spell in all the world that could protect a man from a sword in his belly."

"Now that has the ring of truth to it. Go on."

"We cleared the bottom floor and made our way upstairs," Cassius said. "There was a killer up there. First spell he cast cooked everyone in the room, even his own men."

"Everyone but you."

"And him."

"Then you two fought. And you managed to beat him?" Piso dropped his plate onto the desk. It clattered and settled. He crossed the room to stand over Cassius, trailing musk.

"That's right."

"That must have been one hell of an ambush." Piso looked over Cassius's arms. "You didn't feel anything before it happened? Don't all you freaks have some sort of extra sense, that you can feel when another of your godforsaken kind is doing whatever the hell it is that you all do?"

"I didn't feel anything until a second before the spell triggered. This man was skilled. He cast quickly, before any of us had time to think." Cassius flexed his arms, tested their range of motion. The physician had given him a tincture to help with pain. But the tincture, coupled with his blood loss, made him faint, and the pain still lingered, dulled and ever-present just below this haze.

"Except you," Piso said. "Who had time to shield himself from the fire, right?"

"That was pure instinct. Had I even thought about what was happening, I would have been too slow to cast. It's Hoka's fault, if you ask me. He should have been more careful. He was careless, and he got those men killed. I barely made it out of there myself."

"Still, you made it out. Better shape than the others, all things considered." Piso made to swat at Cassius's arm but thought better of it and slapped the table instead.

Cassius did not flinch. He stared into Piso's eyes.

"You think this is a double cross? I left five of Cinna's men dead in that hall."

"Which is, of course, hard for me to verify. The bodies being in Hightown."

Cassius made to reach into his cloak, and Piso stiffened. Cassius checked himself and Piso nodded and Cassius slipped his hand into his wrap and withdrew a pouch knotted with a drawstring. He dropped it onto the table, where it landed with a wet thud.

"What's this?" Piso asked.

"Your proof."

Piso lifted the pouch by its strings. He untied it and peered inside, his face impassive.

"Scalps," he said. "This is your proof?"

"That's right."

"This doesn't mean anything to me. I have no proof these came from Cinna's men. At the risk of sounding devious beyond redemption, what's to convince me you didn't turn my men over to Cinna and bring back their scalps as proof for your lies?"

"Count them," Cassius said flatly.

"Didn't you hear what I just said? It doesn't matter how many there are if I don't know who—"

"There were eight of us. Me and Hoka and six others."

"And how many scalps are here?"

"Twelve. Hoka, plus your six, plus the five we killed at the gaming hall."

"You scalped my men as proof of your loyalty?"

"I figured you'd question me. It's ugly, but it had to be done."

"I believe I just felt something I haven't felt in ages," Piso said.

"What's that?"

"A chill up my spine."

There was a knock at the door.

"What now?" Piso roared.

The door flew open, and the man standing in the entranceway was red-faced and out of breath. His tunic was torn, and he had blood on his head although he did not appear to be wounded.

"Sorry, sir," the bloodied man said. "But there's a riot in the Market. Legion's been fighting a fire there for an hour. There was some looting, then a mob formed."

"How many is it?" Piso asked.

"Two hundred maybe, sir. Legion's only got fifty men there now."

"Is the mob getting the better of them?"

"Hard to tell."

"Go find Dexius," Piso said. "He should be in the barracks. If he's sleeping, rouse the bastard. Then tell him to take a hundred men down to the Market, armed. Ten killers as well."

"Yes, sir."

"Tell him he's to wait in the avenues just south of the Market. If any of the mob crosses over, he's free to defend himself. But he shouldn't make a move otherwise."

"What if Cinna goes into the Market?" Cassius asked.

"What?"

"If Cinna goes to help the legion, and you don't, how will that look?" Cassius asked. "It might seem to Vorenicus that you were leaving his men to get cut to pieces in the Market."

Piso shook his head. "If my men and Cinna's men are in the Market together, there's going to be trouble."

"Did one of yours start this fire?"

"Not on my orders."

"Well, then, probably one of Cinna's did. And to cover that up, Cinna might offer the legion aid. Then he can pin this on you and win Vorenicus's favor."

"Sir," the bloody messenger said, "do we know this was arson?"

"I can feel it in my goddamn bones," Piso said. "Tell Dexius to take his men into the Market to aid the legion. If Cinna's men are there, he's not to confront them unless attacked first."

"Sir, as sure as I'm standing here," the messenger said, "that's going to end in bloodshed."

"Don't question my orders. Just act on the task you've been given."

The messenger nodded and left the room.

"Gods almighty." Piso rubbed his temples. "It never ends."

11

⚋⚋∿∿⚋⚋

"Want some wine, sir?"

The boy with the shaved head, the one Cassius had met his first night in Lowtown, held a bottle of wine tucked against his chest. He glanced about the dining hall nervously.

"No, thank you," Cassius said.

"It's good wine, sir. You should try some."

Cassius fixed the boy with his stare. "No. Now run along."

The boy placed the bottle on the table.

"Someone wants you to have this bottle," the boy whispered. "It's yours. No charge."

"Who wants me to have this?"

"I couldn't say."

Cassius retrieved a half-silver piece from his coin purse and passed it to the boy.

"I don't have a name," the boy said. "But she wants to meet in Butcher's Lane in the east end."

"All right."

The boy looked over the table, which was set with a plate of fish and bread, a bowl of warm stew, all untouched.

"Are you hungry?" Cassius asked.

"They won't let me eat in here. They beat me once for lifting scraps of bread."

"Answer my question."

"I'm not going to let you bugger me just because you gave me stew."

"Watch your mouth." Cassius pulled up a stool. "If you do, you can stay and eat. No one will beat you while I'm here."

The boy settled himself at the table. He spooned the thick stew. He looked around the room.

"Is something wrong?" Cassius asked.

"They're staring at me."

"You get used to it."

From the plaza, he could see smoke rising in the north. It curled slowly, spreading like a drop of ink in water. The men gathered in front of the barracks were talking of the fight this morning. Some were geared in chain mail and some wore iron helms and, to a man, they spoke of the help they could have done.

"Makes no sense. Sending in a hundred men to get chopped to pieces."

"Could have sent in five times as many."

"Everyone wanted to go."

"The old man better not send me into no fight without backup. 'Cause if I live through it, he'll wish I didn't. I'll slit his throat for him."

Cassius passed through their ranks in silence.

The streets of Lowtown were nearly deserted. Shops stood shuttered, small markets abandoned, and no children played in the lanes. The silence made him uneasy, and the feeling of being watched returned. He wondered if this was a product of being in Scipio or of the work he was doing or if the thoughts he tried to deny at night were true and he was losing his mind.

In Butcher's Lane, he came upon two mastiffs fighting over a bone. They shied at his approach, teeth bared, then growled as he passed.

The lane had been abandoned quickly. Carcasses of pigs and cattle still lay quartered on chopping blocks. Gutted chickens hung from poles. The metallic smell of blood was sharp in the air.

A soft voice called to him. At first he thought it was the voice that accompanied his seizures, but then it came again, louder this time and more clearly female. He crossed the street and the front shutter of a shop opened and Sulla was in the window, motioning him inside.

She wore a man's tunic, drab gray and oversized, with her hair braided and tucked under a small cap. Her face and arms were filthy.

He climbed into the window, and she closed the shutter behind him.

The shop was a single open room with a low ceiling. There was a cellar door in the floor and a large counter in back with a top scored by slice marks. An array of knives, cleavers, and meat hooks hung tacked to the wall.

"Is this your place?" Cassius asked.

"Yes," Sulla said. "Yes, it is. You've guessed my master plan. Bide my time until I could open my very own butcher shop. And now I've asked you here to be my partner. What do you say, Cassius? We've had a rough go of late, but I just know we can make an honest living, you stupid bastard."

"Iustus is dead," he said offhandedly, as though this followed from Sulla's remark.

"And what of Hoka and the others?"

"What do you care?"

"I'd like to know the particulars," she said.

"Everyone is dead."

On the floor by the counter lay a large rucksack. Sulla kneeled and opened it, rooting inside.

"You're hurt," she said.

"I'll live."

"You sure of that? After that fire this morning, I have a feeling there's going to be more bloodshed."

"You did a good job with that."

"Go to hell." Sulla lifted a small wineskin from the sack. She uncorked the skin and drank.

"Why would you say such a thing?"

"Don't patronize me. I'm not some stupid kid to be congratulated by you. I know what I did this morning. I saw the fires. I saw what followed. Good job doesn't describe it."

"Are you having regrets?" Cassius asked.

"Have you been to the Market?"

"I haven't."

"There were bodies everywhere." She pressed her thumbs to her temple, as though trying to massage away a headache. Her palms covered her eyes. When she dropped her hands, she looked tired. "Did you know that would happen?"

"How could I have known?"

"Don't match a question with a question. Say something. Declare yourself. Did you know that would happen?"

"I suspected."

"How?"

"Vorenicus made it clear there was to be no more fighting in the Market. I knew that, and knew he'd be the first to respond to a fire. I saw him pull people from a burning building once." Cassius fished inside his cloak for the box of horn. He snuffed a pinch of the gray powder. "When word of the fires reached Piso, knowing that the legion would be on the scene, I mentioned that the fire might be a ploy by Cinna. He responded by sending men into the Market. He knew that Cinna would take that poorly, especially after last night's killing, but he was left with no choice. He had to act or risk getting outmaneuvered by Cinna. So he acted, and everything else followed in course. The fighting between both sides. The legion trapped in the middle. All of it."

"Piso could have said no."

"The decision was already made for him." Tightness seized Cassius's chest. He took a few deep breaths, and it subsided. "He needed only to respond in the manner that hurt him the least. It was out of his hands."

"Any number of things could have gone differently."

"And if they had, I would have corrected my play accordingly. But there wasn't any need to. The only thing I wasn't certain about was you."

"Well, then, to hell with me for playing along," Sulla said.

"If it helps, know that it wouldn't have stayed quiet long. Tomorrow I'd have found another reason for Piso's and Cinna's men to be in that Market with the legion between them."

She turned her back to Cassius and ran her hands along the

countertop. She pulled a knife the size of her forearm down from the wall and tested its blade with her thumb.

"Why are you doing this?" she asked.

"Why did you help me?"

"Answer a question with a question one more time, and I'll cut your precious hands off."

"I'm trying to illustrate a point. Why did you want to help me?"

"I didn't want to help you," she said. "I needed someone to take care of Iustus."

"You could have found a dozen other people to do that. But you came to me. And you came asking a favor so that I would ask you one in turn."

"You're crazy."

"Self-deception is dangerous, Sulla. I won't tolerate it in a friend."

"Are we friends now?"

"We've killed for each other. That makes us more than friends. But since there isn't a word for what we are, let's stick to familiar terms."

"Remember the other day, when you told me you were switching sides and heading to Lowtown?"

"Yes," Cassius said.

"You said something to me then."

"There are debts; and then there are debts."

"That's what you said." Sulla lowered her gaze. "And you said it knowing about my father, from Lucian or from somewhere else, didn't you?"

Cassius did not respond.

"I had a dream about him that night," she said. "Long time since I dreamed of my father. I was so happy to see him. Sad, too. But when I woke, I was embarrassed by the whole thing."

"There's nothing wrong with missing the dead."

"I'm not the little girl he knew. I don't know that he'd be pleased to see me."

"You're a survivor," Cassius said. "He'd respect that."

"Maybe. Surviving is important. But again, there are debts; and then there are debts."

Cassius nodded.

"I thought that maybe helping you a bit would be the right thing to do," Sulla said. She looked up again and met Cassius's stare. "And then I thought that was stupid. And then I figured if you could help me with something first, then it wouldn't be stupid helping you. It would just be good business. Now are you going to tell me you planned it all that way? Saying one sentence to me like that, at some damn dogfight, knowing it would lead to all of this?"

"Guilt is very powerful," Cassius said, his voice bitter and knowing.

"I don't like to be used."

"I wasn't using you. I was giving you the chance to help that you wanted but didn't know how to ask for."

"After seeing those bodies today, I know helping you isn't the right thing to do."

"Better to let Piso and Cinna run this city? To let them kill at will?"

"Don't do that," she shouted. "Don't misdirect me. I'm talking about the deaths in the Market today. That's blood on your hands, and on mine, as much as the bosses'."

"It's different."

"Killing is killing. You had a hand in the proceedings."

"But they kill to maintain power."

"And why do you do it?"

"For justice," Cassius said.

"Are you the arbiter of right and wrong now?"

"No, but the people I work for are."

"Who do you work for?"

"The senate in Antioch City." Cassius clenched his jaw as though steeling himself, as though he had uttered the lost name of a wrathful god, and the very act of saying this aloud would cause some terrible doom to befall him, a bolt of lightning maybe or maybe a meteor.

They stood in silence.

"No," Sulla said finally. She still held the massive knife. "That doesn't make any sense."

"I'm an agent of the Falcon Guard."

"The consuls' secret police."

"I'm the first wave of an offensive planned by the mainland legion. My job is to act as an instigator. Get the bosses fighting amongst themselves, then drag Quintus's forces into the fray."

"Why?"

"To weaken all parties against an eventual coup."

Sulla set down the knife. She stared at Cassius, then looked away.

"The senate is going to send forces down here?" She squatted, wrapped her arms around her stomach. She looked like she had just been gut punched.

"Commanded by General Tremellius from the northern front. Three legions' worth."

"Why now? They've got plenty of reason to want Quintus gone. But the bastard's been here for years, and they never raised a hand against him."

"I don't know," Cassius said. "Maybe one of the consuls has plans for this place or thinks it will give people something to talk about in the next elections. Or maybe Quintus was just late with a bribe. The reasons don't matter to me. I'm here to do a job."

"Kill as many potential resisters as you can, in the shortest time possible, is that it?"

"I'm here to see a legitimate governor installed on this island. To see these criminals brought to justice."

"You should see your face when you say things like that." She stared up at him. "This look comes over you. Like a boy glimpsing his first pair of tits."

"Don't mock me."

"Don't get self-righteous."

"Someone has to be held accountable for this place," Cassius said.

"Even if it means killing innocents?"

"Can you think of another way? Because I'd hear it."

"Piss on you," she said.

"I'm almost finished here. When Quintus learns of the fight this morning, he might mobilize his forces immediately."

"You don't sound sure of that."

"Vorenicus is for peace. This morning may have changed his

mind, but I don't know just yet. Even if it didn't, though, one more incident like that, and the general will call for blood. He can't tolerate this kind of violence. It makes him look weak."

"And once the general declares war, how long until the mainland legions arrive?"

"Less than a month," Cassius said. "The forces are assembled and ready to sail. They're waiting on my order."

"And you need my help in causing this next incident? Like I helped this morning?" She stood. She took a fresh grip on the knife. "I don't know, Cassius."

"There's been a lot of bloodshed. But we're almost finished. If we stop now, all those deaths will be for nothing. If we continue, any innocents killed will be martyrs for our cause."

"More like sacrifices." Sulla chopped the knife into the counter edge, where it stuck.

"When the mainland legions arrive, everything will change. The new government will need people with knowledge of the island then. People with connections. You can start over."

"Meaning I could serve the new masters?"

"Meaning they could find you a place in the new government. Using your talents to their fullest. You've got an opportunity here to remake yourself."

"Avenge my father's death and become an honest citizen. It seems too good to be true."

"Then how could you pass it up?"

"I couldn't," she said. "It's almost like the decision is out of my hands."

He left Sulla in the shop on Butcher's Lane and made his way deeper into Lowtown. It was late afternoon, and through the cloud of smoke spreading from the direction of the Market, the sky was a melt of blood-red sunlight. The streets were still empty. Shops were shuttered, homes barricaded. Occasionally, he passed people who were moving hurriedly through the lanes, and these always made for uncomfortable exchanges, the passerby fingering the hilt of a blade or wielding some blunt weapon, Cassius with his hands hovering over his gauntlets.

He was not used to seeing the city this way. Before, it had seemed a teeming, writhing thing, like a wound infested with maggots. Now it was calm, almost idyllic. Even the tenements seemed quaint in the absence of the squalid life they supported.

He thought about Sulla as he walked. She needed time to think, she said. She would consider his offer and send word if she was interested. She did not say what she would do if she was not interested.

As he neared the Grand Market, he raised his cloak so that it covered his mouth and nose against the smoke. He figured the main avenues to the Market were barricaded, so he crept into an alley off a less-traveled lane.

He moved through garbage heaps and streams of foul runoff. His eyes watered from the smoke and from the smell. He heard movement ahead of him, but here the alley rounded a gentle curve, and he could not see far. He reached for his gauntlets.

He waited but heard no sound of approaching footsteps. He started forward again. It took a second to spot the blind man. He lay in a pile of refuse and seemed part of the heap himself, torn and filthy as the discarded offal about him. He was wounded, his stomach split by a gash that ran crosswise to his right hip. His eyes were closed, his face shiny with sweat.

Cassius felt his stomach turn.

The blind man did not hear him. His hands were folded over his belly wound, and from between his fingers, black blood leaked and ran down his wrists.

"Blessed and merciful. The one true mother. Queen over us all. Keep me safe in your grace."

Cassius could not see the full extent of the wound, but what he could see looked severe. The blind man would be a long time dying and spared no measure of pain before it was through.

"Let me never grow hungry. Let me never grow parched. Let no hand strike me in anger. And if I die today, walk with me to your sacred forest, where I will abide for all time."

Cassius retreated until his back was pressed against a damp wall. His legs were weak. He kneeled in the lane.

"Who is it?" the blind man called. He looked up, his milk-white eyes rolling wildly. "Whose man are you?"

"It is me," Cassius said, slipping into the Khimir tongue.

"Oh." The blind man seemed to deflate. "Oh my."

"I can get you to a healer."

"No."

"Stay calm. I will lift you onto my shoulder."

"I am a dead man," the blind man said, as though just realizing this. He licked his dry lips with a dry tongue.

"Not for a while yet."

The blind man coughed and spat blood. He swallowed hard. "Will you make me ask for it?"

"For what?"

"The mercy I need."

"Do not ask," Cassius said. "Because I will not grant it."

"What is it to you? You have killed before. What will the life of one old man mean to you?"

The garbage heaped under the old man wriggled. A rat nosed out from under a head of molded cabbage. It made to move toward the blind man and Cassius leapt forward and swatted it, and the rat dove deeper into the heap. He was standing over the blind man now.

"Can you not see why you are here, boy?" The blind man tilted his head. His eyes continued to dart while he spoke. "To release me. The gods have answered my prayers."

"Do not say that."

"I asked for mercy, and they sent me a killer. Their will is undeniable."

"No, I can help you," Cassius pleaded.

"Do not fight this."

"Why will you not let me save you?"

The blind man chuckled, then winced from the effort. "We are past that now. You know it."

Cassius did not respond.

"And knowing that," the blind man continued, "and knowing that the gods do not act against their own plans, that your being here is part of their design, what must they want from you?"

"I do not believe in the gods."

"That does not amount to much. Not when they believe in you."

Cassius kneeled next to the blind man. He touched the blind man's folded hands.

"You even came wearing the instruments of your destiny." The blind man smiled at the feel of Cassius's gauntlets on his skin. "Now do what you are here to do."

The blind man closed his eyes. Cassius placed two fingers on the blind man's forehead, and the blind man began to pray again.

The spark that jumped from Cassius's fingers made the blind man's body jerk. He exhaled slowly. He seemed about to sit up, lifting from his chest, then he settled back down and his hands shook and his legs kicked and a tremor passed through his body and he was dead.

Cassius folded the corpse's arms across its chest. He composed the legs and the head so that if the man were alive, he would be lying comfortably. He removed his cloak and draped it over the corpse and pressed a coin into the corpse's palm, for any payments that might be required of the soul when passing into the land of the dead. He felt a hypocrite for doing so, but doing so made him feel better.

When he reached the Market, he found the dead piled along the main avenue. Workers were hauling the unclaimed corpses, which had been picked clean by the men of both bosses, into mule-drawn wagons. The wagons, supplied by churches, would transport the bodies for burial in unmarked graves. The rest would become pig feed for ranchers in the jungle.

The fires had mostly died although a few of the stalls near the Lowtown border still smoldered. Many of the storefronts were now charred husks, and wide sections of the Market proper were ash. In that moment, he wanted nothing so much as to make of it all a funeral pyre large enough to blot out the sun.

ENTER BOLDLY

In Diadora, they called him Marcellus, or the Little Warrior. A boy of fourteen, he spent his days begging and stealing, his nights angling for pickup matches at the pit-fighting dens and back-alley rings of the Marble Hill slums. He possessed only a few spells and so fought only other novices like himself, boys who owned at most a fire ward and one or two offensive spells, enough to give a crowd a show and earn a few coppers from a fight promoter.

Over the last six months, he had made something of a name for himself. He was known as a tenacious fighter, fearless of fire, and unwilling to throw a match. The last helped grow his following amongst the degenerate gamblers who stalked the Hill for action. If Marcellus was fighting, it might not be a spectacle of spellfire and monstrous horrors summoned from across the veil, but it would be a fair fight at least.

Spellcasters flocked to Diadora. It had a large coliseum, a rich black market for rare spells and spell indices, and most of the great mercenary houses maintained guild halls in the city. It was also the closest port in the Republic to the Isle of Twelve.

Marcellus had heard about the Isle while still training with the legion. On the drill field one day, while sparring with other spellcasters in his unit, a fit had overtaken him. One minute, he had been standing upright, preparing to snuff a wall of fire with a gust of wind, and the next he was on the ground, his trainers standing over him. He was unsure what had happened, and the trainers did not offer much information. They talked amongst themselves for a while, then canceled the drill and ordered everyone back to barracks.

When another of the boys told Marcellus he had taken a fit, he thought this the end of his career in the legion. How could he fight if his body betrayed him on the field of battle?

"Don't you know anything?" his bunkmate Claudius said that night. "You're touched."

"What does touched mean?"

"It means you're going to be a great spellcaster. It means you don't belong here."

He had fled the legion within the month, making his way down to Diadora by wagon train and by foot, Along the way, he heard many stories of the Isle of Twelve. Most everyone warned him away. Demons ruled the Isle, they said, or creatures that fell from the stars or vile cults intent on birthing their dark gods into this world. No two people agreed on who controlled the Isle, but they all agreed the Masters were powerful beyond measure. That was enough for Marcellus.

On the Hill, they said the Masters themselves stalked the streets of Diadora. They dressed as beggars and missionaries and prowled darkened alleys, searching for others of their kind, eager to seduce the young and touched, that they might pass on their dark arts. Marcellus knew better than to announce that he was touched. More than just the Masters of the Isle hunted such spellcasters.

In Murondia, inquisitors from the Order of the Stag viewed the touched as abominations against the gods, killed every one of them they found. And agents from the Spellwrights College in Antioch City performed unspeakable experiments on the touched, in search of the secrets locked in their blood.

Marcellus wanted no such trouble. Better to remain discreet, save his coin, amass spells. He would find his own way to the Isle then. The trick was not to lose his gauntlets, or his life, in the ring before that moment.

He fought four or five matches a day. Quick bouts that usually ended with one man or the other pushed from the fighting ring. At his level of skill, neither spellcaster had the power to force a man to yield. The matches did not tax him much, but with the frequency of the fights and the training he did each day to test the limits of his powers, he feared overextending himself. He had not suffered a fit since that first one in the legion, but he knew there would be more. The fear of it weighed on him daily.

The inevitable happened on an overcast night in early summer, while standing in the ring behind the Club and Fang. He had just chased his opponent out of the ring at the point of an ice lance and was basking in the scattered applause and drunken catcalls of the crowd, when he felt his scalp grow hot and his eyes lose focus. He kneeled down in the ring, not wanting to fall from standing, and found himself floating in a void.

A dark so total it seeped into his body through his mouth and nose and ears, filled him inside with shadow. He seemed to float in the void forever, adrift between this world and the next. He was afraid. And then the voice called to him.

"I worried I would never see you again." The voice came from behind. Deep and strong, it filled the void around him and within him.

"Where am I?" the boy asked.

"The place between. And I have been waiting for you."

"Who are you?"

"You should know," the voice said. *"You brought me here."*

"You speak in riddles."

"You know everything you need to know. You just don't remember."

"Then help me," the boy said.

"You have fire in your blood," the voice said. *"It will burn your mind. Others will tell you to be afraid of it."*

"But what is the truth?"

"The fire is cleansing. It burns only weakness, like steel in a forge."

Marcellus opened his eyes. The sky above him was dark and overcast. The air felt still. He sat up and saw that the ring was empty, the alleyway deserted but for stray dogs. He wondered how long he had been out.

His feet felt cold and, looking down, he saw they were bare, his sandals missing. His belt and his dagger were missing as well. He reached for his coin purse but found the inside pocket of his tunic empty. He thought about his gauntlets, then cursed loudly.

He staggered to his feet, wondered where he would spend the night. He had no money and nowhere to go. No gauntlets. No spells.

He was just a boy again. Alone. Helpless. The thought nearly crushed him.

But there was another thought in his head, one spoken in a dark and quiet voice, a thought that felt alien to him, like a hand that has fallen asleep.

Steel in a forge.

He could not recall where he had heard that.

Two days later, he was sweeping horse stables to earn a dinner when a small girl approached him. She was olive-skinned, with long dark hair. She wore a sackcloth dress and wore also a knotted black kerchief that marked her as a mute orphan, the kind sent to the richer parts of the city to beg coins off patrician women. She brought him a small oilskin bundle and left without incident.

He found his dagger tied to the outside of the oilskin bundle, its blade polished to a sheen, its old sheath replaced by one decorated with three onyx stones bound by black silk. A folded piece of vellum was tucked into the sheath, and this he removed and unfolded and brought beneath a nearby candle to read. The note was written in red ink that shimmered like dancing flames.

We heard about your recent misfortune. It troubles us to learn when one of our brotherhood suffers such a setback. You'll find your dagger returned in good condition. We were unable to retrieve your gauntlets. The thief had sold them before our arrival, but we managed to secure the contents of this bundle from him as payment instead. Please accept them in good faith. And if you ever wish to further your arts, you need only visit us. Your sheath will serve as ticket of passage for any ship in this port.

Marcellus refolded the note and tucked it into his inside pocket, along with the dagger. He untied the oilskin bundle and, reaching inside, felt something cold and wet. He held the bundle up to the candle, and by its light, he glimpsed two severed hands.

12

Piso's nephew died in the night, and the next morning a priest arrived to supervise the preparation of the corpse. Afterward, he remained in the plaza and offered blessings to any who cared to receive them. He was a young man, this priest, and timid. He had dark hair that was shaved on the crown of his head, and he wore the rose-colored robes of the order of the goddess Vinalia, the goddess of beauty, of art and poetry. She had few worshippers in Scipio. But the boy had been born under her sign, had been anointed by her priests at birth, had passed into manhood in her temple.

From the front door of the dining hall, the priest stood with a bucket of water mixed with rose petals at his feet and he dipped his scepter in this water and shook the scepter at the crowd and the people knew themselves blessed.

At midday, a crier emerged from the hall and announced that the nephew's corpse would be sailed back to the mainland for burial. There was to be a pig roast at dusk to commemorate the boy's passing.

In the plaza, the same tasteless joke repeated for hours. "If I knew we'd get a pig roast out of it, I'd have killed the kid myself."

Twoscore spits were assembled. Tents to house the butchers and cooks. Casks of wine and mead arrived by the cartload. The pigs were slaughtered in public, each killing overseen by the priest and the last performed by his own hand with his own dagger. Blood was streaked on the door of Piso's hall, and bowls of salt and blood were set in the lanes as offerings. Vermin gathered to feed, rats and stray dogs and scavenger birds.

When the legionnaires arrived, they were thirty strong, geared in full armor, segmented steel plate that lent the men the look of strange, carapaced insects, wide-brimmed helmets that blazed in the light of the sun, bowed shields, glittering spears. A contingent of Piso's men escorted them through the crowd that had formed in the plaza although it was not clear if these men were protecting the crowd from the legionnaires or the legionnaires from the crowd.

At the front ranks, Cassius could see Vorenicus's helmet and the white eagle feathers standing tall. Vorenicus entered the hall along with a dozen of his men, and the others assumed a post outside the door, some of the men visibly wounded from yesterday's skirmish.

From the window of his barracks, which was empty now, its occupants all dead but him, Cassius watched the crowd swell and the first of the spit fires lit. He watched as the legion entered the hall, and he knew then that his work of the last few weeks was nearly ruined, if not completely destroyed. He decided it was time to leave this place.

He had seen enough of Scipio. Enough of death and killing. The Masters had dedicated themselves to the idea that few could stand against many, could overcome great odds with power and strategy. But Scipio resisted him at every turn.

Maybe he had not learned his lessons well enough. Maybe he had abandoned his training too early. A few more years of peer training might have left him better prepared, but opportunity arrived with the red-haired man. Not knowing when it might arrive again, Cassius had taken it.

Too soon. There was no other explanation. Unless Scipio itself had bested him, a force unlike any the Masters had trained him to face. Savage, primal, cunning, unyielding. He had no way to predict its responses, the way it wore on him. Every day, he seemed diminished, his careful facade melting in the damp heat. It even filled his dreams. He had no respite from it.

None but escape.

What of those he was leaving behind though? Lucian and Sulla. Tadua and the old woman. The Yoruban. He had used them as pawns in his schemes, and now he would abandon them to this chaos. Defenseless in the company of cruel and powerful men.

It had already cost the blind man his life. He would not let that happen again. There was still time.

The plaza was lit by streetlamps, and a great bonfire burned in the center of the square. The fires from the spits still smoldered, and although it was a clear night, the glare from the flames blotted out the stars. Hundreds of people had gathered, and Cassius could only guess at the number lurking outside the light, in alleys and dim lanes.

The sound of the combined voices was loud, and drummers were at work in the center clearing, hammering out rhythms in the dark. Whores moved through the crowd, calling prices for their services. A pack of dogs stole a pig carcass and, in a corner, they fought over the charred bones, barking, snapping.

Cassius stood at the edge of the crowd, near the barracks house. He ate none of the meat offered and accepted no drink from any man. Nearby, he heard the Vinalia priest calling upon men to prepare themselves for their coming deaths, to ready themselves like brides to the altar.

"Death," the priest said, "is the culmination of life. If a man does not recognize his own death as such, he will find himself unprepared for what follows, and the dead are dead longer than the living alive."

Behind him, a boy of four or five stood naked but for grime, limned in the white light of the bonfire. Drunk, he ambled about in imitation of the priest, mimicking his hand gestures. From the surrounding dark came laughter and catcalls and even a few copper coins, which twirled ringing through the air to land at the boy's feet.

From across the plaza, Cassius spotted a figure all in white moving through the crowd. He lost sight of it briefly but spotted it again as passersby fled its path.

The figure was slim and shaved bald. Its head was painted white, as were its face, arms, and legs. It was dressed in a bleach-white tunic and a white, short cloak. Its teeth and tongue were stained blacker than the surrounding night and, from his remove, Cassius could not tell if it was man or woman.

The figure in white did not speak. It moved through the crowd with an operatic grace. It fussed over each small encounter, grinning menacingly at children, staring with ominous intent at drunks and whores. As it passed, some stopped to follow its movement while others laughed nervously or made symbols with their hands that would grant them the protection of gods. None dared meet its gaze for long.

One fat old woman clutched her chest as the figure drew near. She fell to her knees and threw herself prostrate before the figure and cried out the names of her dead, husbands and parents and grandparents buried for ages, imploring them to call her home.

Cassius tracked the figure until it was lost in the press, and never once did it turn to match his stare and he knew this to be a false Death by its indifference to him.

There was a table arranged under a large tent outside Piso's hall. Piso sat at the head of this table, Vorenicus on his right. Throughout the night, people entered the tent, offered their condolences, and departed. And all the while, Piso and Vorenicus talked. A great feast was laid before them, but they ate little.

Near the edge of the plaza, a troupe of tumblers was performing for the crowd. While the men flipped and somersaulted, a dwarf stood off to their side and worked a lyre. When the tumblers finished their routine, the dwarf moved through the crowd with his small hat held before him and people tossed coins into the hat and the dwarf thanked them each to a man.

Someone tossed a piece of half-chewed pork into the hat, and the dwarf fished out the meat and threw it to the ground. He began to scold the man who threw it, and the man kicked him in the stomach.

The dwarf fell, and the coins spilled from his hat. Onlookers rushed to gather the coins, and the tumblers dove into the fray to recover their money. A melee ensued, and the crowd near the fight swelled.

"Hell of a show, isn't it?" Sulla stood with a mug clutched in both hands. She glistened with a thin sheen of sweat, a pair of daggers tucked into the belt cinched around her small waist.

"What's with the steel?"

"Dangerous times. A girl has to be prepared for the worst."

"Did you see Death was here?" Cassius asked.

"See him? He hit on me. Said he had a room on the fourth floor of Piso's hall if I was interested."

Someone hurled a bottle from the crowd. It struck one of the tumblers in the face, and the man fell, bleeding.

"Aren't these people meant to be mourning?" Cassius asked.

"Everyone grieves in their own way."

One of the men in the fight slipped. He landed on his back, and before he could rise, a tumbler stomped his head.

"Have you heard anything about Vorenicus's visit?" Cassius asked.

"No."

"Would you have?"

"Maybe. Watch out!"

A man reached for the dwarf where he lay facedown in the muck. He gripped the dwarf by the hair, and the dwarf twisted and bit the man's fingers.

"What do you think?" Sulla asked.

Cassius looked to Piso, who was leaning close to Vorenicus's ear. Both men touched their mugs together and drank.

"I predict peace by morning," he said.

"That's awfully optimistic of you."

"Why do you think Vorenicus is here?"

Sulla shrugged. "To pay his respects. Kiss a little ass. Why does anyone come to these things?"

"No better time to talk peace than a funeral."

"Vorenicus has been trying to talk peace since day one. Why would Piso listen now?"

The man howled and swatted at the dwarf, and the dwarf drew a knife from his waist and lunged for the man. In the dark, Cassius could not see the blows landed, but the man collapsed, and the dwarf wheeled on the crowd, knife held before him.

"Piso never wanted this war," Cassius said. "And with Piso's nephew dead, maybe Cinna feels his honor has been repaid."

"That doesn't make any sense."

"You wouldn't understand. I'm closer to this than you are. I can see more angles. And that smile on Vorenicus's face means this thing is over."

"You sound disappointed," Sulla said.

"I want to leave. I'm sick of this place."

"Now you're starting to sound like a real Scipian."

"I'm serious. I need you to book me passage on a ship to the mainland."

"Just yesterday, you were telling me to prepare for revolution," Sulla said. "And now it's all over? Because Vorenicus and Piso are having a toast?"

"Book the passage and meet me at Lucian's in the morning. Be discreet, Piso can't find out. Or Cinna, for that matter. I have a few loose ends to wrap up before the night is over."

"You're not kidding. You want to go home."

"I don't have a home," Cassius said. "But I don't want to be here anymore."

"Because of the peace?"

"Because I'm tired. And I want to lay my head someplace where I won't have nightmares."

By midnight, the cooking fires had died to embers. The last of the pig meat was gone, and the crowd had thinned to a few revelers come to warm themselves by the bonfire. Vorenicus and the legion had left, and Piso had retired to his room. Alone, Cassius ambled through the plaza with his arms folded inside his cloak.

He settled into the mouth of an alley. A church bell sounded in the distance. He figured the time until sunrise to be about five hours, too late for Vorenicus to call upon Cinna.

He thought about sleep. His head hurt. He closed his eyes and pressed his palms against his face and sat holding his head and trying to think as Piso thought, as Cinna and as Vorenicus thought.

He opened his eyes and spotted Junius's brother in the plaza. He was filthy and disheveled. He had an arm draped over a whore, and he leaned into the girl heavily as she tried to steer him toward the dining hall. They disappeared together into the dark.

Cassius felt sick now. His stomach was empty, and the smell of pig meat was everywhere. He felt the urge to vomit but did not. He heard footsteps behind him. He shifted to listen more closely, and the footsteps stopped. He reached for his gauntlets inside his cloak.

"Announce yourself," he said.

"I meant no harm."

"Come closer."

The bald boy advanced.

"You nerve-wracking idiot. Are you trying to get yourself killed?"

"No," the boy said.

"Then why are you skulking around in an alley?"

"This is where I sleep."

Cassius lifted his hands away from his gauntlets. "Forgive the intrusion. Are you hungry?"

"I had some of the pig."

"Did you save some for tomorrow?"

"No."

Cassius handed the boy a coin.

"What are you doing here?" the boy asked.

"Thinking."

"You can sleep here if you're tired."

"Do you know of a bath around here?"

"There are plenty."

"Do you know of one near Ashkani Row?"

The nationless Ashkani who lived in Scipio made their homes in the northeastern edge of Lowtown. Theirs was a modest, clean neighborhood, known for its metalworkers, its parchment makers, and its scribes. The neighborhood had a single stone bath. It stood at the edge of a courtyard, and on either side of its entrance loomed two statues of sea nymphs.

The bath manager was a thin Antiochi. He wore loose blue pantaloons and a billowy, bleached shirt, and had longish hair. The man escorted Cassius to a private room and said he would send an attendant.

"I was hoping for someone specific," Cassius said. "A young girl. Native."

"We have those," the manager said.

"Her name is Tadua."

"That doesn't sound familiar."

"She works here. I know she does. I only want to be seen by her."

"I'll see what can be done."

The manager left, and when he returned a short time later, he was alone. Cassius asked him about the girl, and the manager shook his head. He wrung his hands.

"I'm . . . I'm sorry."

"Does she not work here?" Cassius asked.

"No."

"Do you know where she does work?"

The manager mumbled something incomprehensible.

"The girl," Cassius shouted. "Tadua. Does she work here or not?"

"She's dead."

Cassius's knees grew weak. He exhaled slowly, as though a heavy weight had been lowered onto his chest. He steadied himself against the damp stone wall, then crossed to the far side of the room and took a seat on the low wooden bench.

"When?"

"I'm told last night. This is the first I'm hearing of it. I didn't work with her often. I had no idea this—"

"How?"

"I'm afraid I don't know the exact—"

"How, damn it?"

"I just don't know," the manager said.

"You've heard things."

"I couldn't say."

"You had better find a way to say." Cassius rose and crossed the room. When he lifted his cloak, the manager groaned at the sight of the gauntlets and backed to the door.

"Please." In the near dark, the manager's eyes shone with a film of tears.

Cassius checked his advance.

"Here," he said. He offered his open hand, and the coin in his palm glinted silver in the light of the room. "Take this."

The manager accepted the coin.

"She worked with an old woman sometimes," Cassius said.

"Yes."

"You know her?"

"I don't."

"But you'll be able to find out who she is, won't you?"

"I will."

"If she's working now, you'll send her to me directly. And if she's not, you'll find someone who knows where she lives. You'll send someone to find her and bring her here. I have questions for her. Nothing more."

"I'll do my best," the manager said.

"You'll do it."

The manager looked to the coin again and slipped it inside his pants pocket. He turned to leave, then stopped at the door.

"Did you know her well?" he asked.

"What is that to you?" Cassius asked.

"Just a question."

"People on this island get their throats slit asking too many questions. I'm not paying you to ask anything other than the whereabouts of that old woman. So be about your business."

The room was windowless, and Cassius had no means to measure the passage of time. He sat for hours and dozed in fits, never for more than a few minutes at a stretch. The dreams that came to him were brief and violent.

He saw rows of spits set over fires and the meat hanging in the smoke was Junius's flesh and he was eating this flesh and made full by it. He saw the blind man lying faceup in a muddy lane, the wound on his belly a mottled red-black, and from out of the gash poked a massive crow. He saw the figure in white as it stalked through the plaza, and in its hands it held the head of a dark-haired woman who sang a lullaby about a river and rain.

A knock at the door woke him. He rose and cracked the door and stared out into the hall, where the manager stood.

"She doesn't want to be alone with you," the manager said.

"What?"

"She was very specific about that." The manager looked over his shoulder.

"Is she here?" Cassius opened the door and found the old woman in the shadows of the far wall. She looked to the manager.

"I need to speak with her alone."

"She said that she'd only—"

"I'll pay her. Tell her that. I just need to talk with her."

The manager crossed the hall and conferred with the old woman. The manager spoke to her in slow, loud Antiochi, and she said nothing but instead shook her head at each of the manager's requests. The manager returned to Cassius.

"There's no use talking with her. She simply won't budge."

"Grandmother," Cassius called softly in Khimir. "I mean you no harm. Come closer please."

The old woman stepped forward. In the light of hallway candles, Cassius could see that her left eye was swollen shut, half her face bruised.

"You speak the tongue of my people," she said.

"I do. I will speak it with you if that will put you at ease."

"Why did you not speak it before now?"

"It is my secret," Cassius said. "A secret I am sharing with you. But I am not a man who likes to share secrets with many, so I ask that we speak in my room."

The old woman lowered her head.

"I will pay you for your time," Cassius said. "You have nothing to fear from me."

The old woman stepped into Cassius's room and crossed the room to the bench on the far wall, but she did not sit.

"Are you well, grandmother?"

"I am not your grandmother. Do not use this term with me." The old woman looked as though she might strike Cassius.

"Has someone seen to your eye?"

"Did you bring me here to talk of the eye? The eye is fine. Do not worry over it. Ask your questions and give me my money."

"I would have news of the girl Tadua," Cassius said.

"She is dead. That is the only news I have."

"How?"

"She was killed. In this house."

"By who?"

"The one-eyed man. He appeared drunk last night. He asked to see her. He began to question her about the day he was drugged. He did not remember much, but he remembered her."

"And what did she tell him?" Cassius hung his head.

"Do not fear, boy. She admitted nothing. Not even your involvement. When she would not cooperate, he beat her. A terrible beating. Such a little girl." The old woman shook her head. "Still she held her tongue. In the end, he strangled her."

Cassius stood silently. He paced, then took a seat on the floor. He sat with his back pressed against the door and stared up at the ceiling.

"You were here when it happened?" he asked.

"I was."

"And do you fear for your life now?"

"If this man wanted to kill me, he would have done so. But he had no memory of me, and with her silence, the girl protected me. A shame no one protected her."

"Did no one raise a hand to stop him?" Cassius asked.

"I did. I fought him as best I could."

"Of course."

"I am an old woman, and still I fought him. I." The old woman punched her chest

"I did not mean to imply that you sat idle. I only wonder why no one else came to her aid."

"He is one of Piso's men." The old woman was shouting. "Who can stand against Piso? Of what value is the life of a single girl against this man's life? And him a killer. Who would fight such a man?"

"It should not be that way."

"Do not waste my time with talk of what should and should not be, boy."

"I hold her life precious," Cassius said. "I value it if no one else does."

"What did you say?" The old woman stood. She crossed the room to Cassius and stared down at him. "Say it again."

"I will not forget this."

"Why not?" she asked.

"It matters to me."

"What does?"

"Her life."

The old woman slapped him. Her blow landed clumsily on the side of his head. His ear burned. She slapped him again.

"Then you should have taken better care of it," she said. "You used her, and this is what came of it."

"How can you say that?"

"There is blood on your hands, boy. No bath can wash that off."

"I did not—"

She cocked her arm for another blow, then heaved with a sob. She fell forward onto him and gripped his tunic, her hands balled.

"She was just a child," she said. "You used her."

"I am sorry."

"What good are your apologies? They will not raise the dead." Her hair was unbound, and it hung in his face now, thin and dry. She smelled of wine. "I wish they were all . . ." The old woman's words tapered off into a groan.

"Say it."

The old woman trembled.

"Say what you wish," Cassius commanded.

"I wish they were dead."

"Wish it of me."

"What can you do?"

"I need to hear the words. I need you to say what you wish, or else I cannot do it. Ask me."

"What would you have me ask?"

"Ask me to do what you want to do yourself, grandmother. Ask me now, or I will leave this place forever and you will live the rest of your life knowing that you did not ask."

The old woman loosed a sob. She kneeled between his legs and pressed into him, less like a hug than like a wrestler trying to gain leverage against an opponent.

"Kill this man," she breathed into his chest.

"Say it again."

"Kill him."

"And what else?"

Her body shook. A light trembling that carried through her frame and into his.

"Kill them all," she said.

Cassius closed his eyes.

"Did you hear me?" she asked. "Kill them all."

Cassius clenched his hands into fists. "I will, mother. I promise."

13

~~~

The sky was overcast. The sun was risen but not visible, and a light rain misted the courtyard, the rain warm and with an undertaste of sea salt. The lane was deserted but for a pair of Ashkani women. They wore shawls to protect against the rain, and their hair was thick and dark, nearly blue-black, their skin pale. They averted their eyes at the sight of Cassius and whispered amongst themselves in their own language. When they passed into an adjacent lane, the street was empty and Cassius stood for a time and the rain washed over him.

He felt thin, dissipated. The aches that had plagued him these past days were fresh, the throbbing in his face, the sting in his stomach, the burning in his forearms. These feelings tethered him to his body and to the physical world, but otherwise he felt himself a ghost come amongst men, a thing hollow and insubstantial.

When he walked, his footsteps on the concrete sounded distant.

He approached the Grand Market through the main south avenue. Small crowds had gathered on street corners, smoking, drinking, rolling dice. Only yesterday, these people had hidden in their homes for fear of violence. Watching them, Cassius recalled Hoka's words about the short memories of Scipians.

Hoka, whose skin he saw melted over his face.

The path to the Market was guarded by forty of Piso's men. The barricade was set to the side of the road so that a team of mules pulling a flat wagon could pass into the square. Cassius moved around the wagon, but before he reached the Market, he heard someone call him to stop.

"What business do you have here?" The guard was tall and large, heavy around his chest and shoulders. He was dressed in a shirt of leather and scale mail and had a spiked mace at his hip.

"I have something to attend to," Cassius said.

"We've got orders today. No fighting. We're to man our post until relieved. But nothing else. Not so much as a dirty look north."

"When did those orders come in?"

"First thing this morning."

"What do you make of that?"

"Hell if I know." The guard turned his head and spat. "But Piso was very clear. Not a drop of blood to be spilled today. If I were you, I'd stay out of that square. Those boys up north won't like the sight of you. And if a fight breaks out, the boss is liable to twist your balls off."

"If our orders are to stand down, doesn't it seem likely Cinna's men were told to do the same? Piso wouldn't lay down his arms when someone means him harm."

The guard squinted to the opposite side of the Market.

"Have you seen anyone over there causing trouble today?" Cassius asked. "Any firefights?"

"No."

"Well, when's the last time you went half a day without at least hearing of something? This is a lull that is leading to truce talks. And it's the perfect time for me to slip into the Market and attend to my business. I'll be out in no time. And if something goes wrong, I'll be responsible."

"What's this about?" the guard asked.

"A girl."

The guard smiled. "A girl?"

"That's right."

"Well, make it quick."

"Won't take but a minute."

The storefronts were open and most of the makeshift stalls assembled. The main avenue was cleared of the dead. Blood stained the concrete, and the smell of smoke was still strong, but seeing the staggering volume of commerce, Cassius wondered if he was the only person to notice these things.

A group of legionnaires spotted him from the steps of the council hall. They pointed, conferred amongst themselves, then two men raced down the steps and out into the Market in pursuit. Cassius continued north, keeping to the avenue that bisected the city. Ahead of him, two-score men were posted by the roadblock into Hightown.

He opened his cloak so that his gauntlets were visible. He walked straight and purposeful. As he drew closer, the men at the roadblock stirred.

Still moving, he unhitched his gauntlets and donned them. His arms burned with hot pinpricks as he cast his fire ward. The spellcasters on guard at the roadblock shouted and reached for their gauntlets, the men around them drawing their weapons.

He pointed and the air grew heavy. There was a rushing sound, like a great intake of air. Overhead a white flame sparked to life and streaked across the sky, a tremendous jet of liquid fire that engulfed the roadblock.

Before the flame had cleared, Cassius felt a series of tugs in his chest. The air rippled in front of him, then fell still, remnants of a counterspell cast too late.

The roadblock was in flames. Several men writhed on the ground, beating at the fires consuming them. Three spellcasters held their ground near the barricades, but otherwise, the men unharmed fled their post, some retreating to Hightown, others to the alleys.

A shock wave rent the air. A cone of fire flowered near Cassius's face, but the flames died as they reached his ward. Before his vision cleared, he heard whistling overhead. An explosion to his left staggered him. He stumbled and fell to one knee. His arm grew numb. A low ringing settled in his left ear.

He spared a quick glance over his shoulder, in time to see the two legionnaires racing back to the council hall. The Market crowd was a stampede. When he faced forward again, he found a gorilla in the lane. It stood on all fours, knuckles down and with its haunches raised so that its back curved, sleek and gray. Its eyes were deep-set, and it had a severe brow with a plume of red-brown hair on its forehead. It appeared startled at first, frightened of the flames and the smoke. It made to charge forward, then checked itself and tensed, flashing teeth.

Cassius cupped his hand, and a shelf of earth jutted up from the street and struck the gorilla and the gorilla bent double and fell, its back twisted at an odd angle.

The air hummed with crossbow bolts. He ducked and saw now a dozen fighters gathered before the flaming roadblock. He tapped the concrete, and a wall of fire rose from the ground. It was seven feet high and a dozen feet wide, stretching between him and the archers. He sighted carefully, and a plume of black smoke appeared behind the wall. And then a fireball shot from the smoke and sailed through the wall, catching the men by surprise.

The air stank of sulfur. His chest ached, and beneath this pain, he felt the familiar thrum. He glanced to his side and saw a lanky killer, garbed in a bright green tunic, approaching with arms raised, a line of bulls racing before him. The lead bull stood five feet tall at the shoulder, and it was roan-colored, with patches of white on its chest. It ran with its head low, the ridge of muscle on its back quivering and the tips of its massive horns a stark white. Behind it, the other bulls bucked and thrashed wildly. They seemed an avalanche of flesh.

Cassius backed deeper into the Market. Behind him, he heard shouts and the sound of running.

He shook his hand as though rolling a die. There was a high, delicate sound, like glass breaking, and a sheet of ice spread across the pavement. He continued backward, walking with measured steps and steady, never giving sign of panic.

The bulls, willed forward by the lanky spellcaster, gained speed. As they reached the ice, the lead bull slipped and fell. It snapped a foreleg as it collapsed and slid out into the Market. The other bulls toppled in short order, crushing stalls as they dropped.

The lanky spellcaster circled wide. Cassius pointed with two fingers, and behind the lanky spellcaster, the corpse of the gorilla twitched. Its fur undulated. Its sides split, and out of the ruptured flesh emerged a host of spiders, slick with blood.

Cassius felt the pull of another's casting. He could no longer tell if this marked the work of the lanky spellcaster or the killers from the roadblock or some other killer approaching from elsewhere in the Market, maybe even a legionnaire. There were too many players with whom to contend. He checked his flanks but could not see past the cluttered stalls. People scrambled aimlessly.

The lanky spellcaster had reached the sheet of ice. He stepped onto it carefully, and the first of the blood-soaked spiders leapt onto his leg, sinking its fangs into bare flesh. He swatted at the spider, and two more leapt onto his hands. He wheeled, screaming, and now the entire wave was upon him. He slipped on the ice, disappearing under the horde.

Looking past this scene, Cassius could see a fresh company of men from Hightown headed to the square, the spellcasters amongst them walking with their gauntlets raised and with summoned beasts at their sides like escorts. He clapped his hands, and a coil of green light rose into the air, and when it disappeared, a giant snake lay at his feet. He felt the concrete vibrating beneath the snake's scales, tasted the warmth of the nearby fires on its tongue.

He willed the snake to follow him and moved south, the creature curling over itself to keep up.

He felt a rush of air and turned in time to see a fireball smash through a wooden stall. The fireball struck the ground and bounced past him. As it tumbled back up into the air, he dropped to his knees and covered his head with his arms, and the fireball exploded. Bits of rock showered down on him. Several stalls caught fire, and people within the blast radius collapsed, their screams louder than the flames.

Two spellcasters emerged from the clearing opened by the fireball, one wearing an iron cuirass and one with his hair shaved into a rooster's plume. The armored man cut his hand in a diagonal arc, and there was a hiss, a smell like vinegar, and a jet of mist washed over the snake. The snake stiffened, its flesh bubbling and bleeding.

Cassius turned from the spray and raised a hand. A stiff wind picked up and blew clear the spume but still some landed on his neck and shoulder. His skin burned as though splashed with hot grease. He beat at his tunic where it smoked and ducked around a clothing merchant's stall.

The two killers wheeled on Cassius, their hands raised. In quick succession, a pack of gray wolves appeared before them, a pair of warthogs, an oversized wolverine. A falcon descended to alight on the armored man's gauntlet, and with a yell, the men advanced on Cassius and their beasts moved before them and all were of a single mind to do him harm.

He was in the middle of the Market now. A cloud of low black smoke roofed the north end of the square, and fires burned in all directions. He retreated toward Lowtown, moving backward without breaking into a run. Explosions sounded in the distance, and he could only guess at how near the rest of Cinna's men were.

He bent low as he moved and touched the ground. A wall of fire began to rise. Suddenly, he felt a sharp pain in his forehead as a counterspell wiped clear the rune from his mind. He blinked to clear the discomfort, and the wall of fire was gone before it had fully risen.

The wolves were nearly upon him. He cupped his hands, and a ten-foot crack spread along the ground. He glimpsed the world as near blackness, and when his vision cleared, the cracked ground sank, then burst skyward. Three large gray tentacles emerged from the hole.

The tentacles were as wide as tree trunks, fish-belly white and mottled with suckers. One tentacle swatted aside the two wolves, breaking their bodies on the pavement. Another snatched up a warthog, squeezing until blood ran from its eyes, then hurled the beast at the spellcaster with plumed hair.

The falcon loosed a shrill call and took flight over the reach of the tentacles. Once clear, it dove for Cassius. Cassius clapped his hands and opened them, and a glowing ember drifted into the air and exploded into a flurry of white-hot ash. The falcon fell smoking.

One of the tentacles had latched onto the spellcaster with plumed hair. It gripped his knee and tugged him toward the open hole, and the man flailed, and sparks fell from his fingertips. Another tentacle swatted at the remaining summoned beasts so that they cowered out of reach, the fear in these beasts greater than the will that sought to move them.

The armored spellcaster approached the pit with an orb of purple light suspended between his outstretched hands. A tentacle struck his hip, and the man fell. As the orb hit the ground, it shattered like glass. A dark purple mist rose from the shards. The armored spellcaster blanched and covered his face with his hands as violent spasms overcame him.

A spear struck the ground next to Cassius. It skidded along the concrete to land at his feet, then two more passed overhead. He turned from the killers and saw a troop of legionnaires assembled in one of the narrow walkways leading west. Thirty men in total, they stood three abreast and carried heavy, bowed shields, spears on their shoulders. Vorenicus's eagle feathers were visible in the middle ranks, and the air around the men seemed hazy, the result of some misdirection spell.

The soldiers loosed another volley of spears, and with a curl of Cassius's hand, a swift wind knocked the spears off course. The centurion who commanded the front ranks pointed one of his swords down the lane and, at his word, the front line advanced, the rest of the troop in lockstep behind them.

Back on the main avenue, Cinna's forces had regrouped, and crossbow men fired at the tentacles. A wave of liquid fire washed over the lane, and an explosion shook the pit. When the air settled, two tentacles lay severed, and the third was limp and still.

Cassius retreated east, ducking out of the main avenue into a smaller lane but keeping in sight of the legionnaires. The soldiers followed. He pointed his fist to the intersection he had just vacated and the ground blackened in the shape of a circle and from this circle rose a column of gray smoke.

Cassius waited until the smoke was thick enough that he could not see through it, then he turned and ran. He took shelter alongside a merchant's abandoned stall. He crouched and drew with his mind's eye the rune for a camouflage spell. Strange colors flowed across his skin like painted shadows, blending neatly with the wood of the stall. When he finished, he sat very still and watched the intersection.

The legionnaires marched through the smoke and into the main avenue. A crossbow bolt struck the centurion commanding the front ranks. The bolt hit in an unarmored spot at the base of the centurion's neck, and he stiffened and looked up. The helmet tipped backward off his head and he opened his mouth and exhaled a spray of blood then collapsed.

More bolts rained down on the legionnaires, and they raised their shields against the sky. Vorenicus took up position on the left flank, from which the fallen centurion had commanded. He shouted, and the lines circled to face north. The men in the front line lowered their shields, and the men in the second and third lines lifted their spears and laid them forward so that the spearpoints bristled past the shield wall.

Seconds later, the men from Hightown were at the intersection. A few seemed to slow as they sighted the legionnaires, having expected to find Cassius in the smoke, but the rest were in full charge. After the legionnaires had loosed a volley of spears, no man gave any thought to who was the enemy but instead raced into the ranks of the soldiers, who held fast and broke the charge with shouts for Quintus and for Manius, who Cassius assumed was the fallen centurion.

The fray that ensued played out against a backdrop of smoke, so that the fighting was difficult to see from Cassius's vantage. But the sounds of the skirmish, of metal striking metal, of shouts and screams, rang clear.

Cassius stood and closed his eyes. He lowered his head, and a weightless feeling settled over him. His stomach turned. To anyone watching, it would have seemed his shadow was reaching up from the floor. And when the shadow had enveloped him fully, it sank back to the ground, and Cassius was gone from the lane.

Cassius opened his eyes. His vision blurred, then cleared.

He was nauseous now and his legs weak. He kneeled in the lane and bent double. He folded into himself and pulled his knees to his chest and all the while a thin finger of pain worked through his guts and down into his groin.

"You all right, stranger?" A passerby set a hand on Cassius's shoulder, and Cassius sprang at the touch.

He steeled himself against the pain in his guts and took his bearings from the sights nearby, the makeshift shops and tents. Judging by the council hall, he stood now in the southwest corner of the Market.

"It's a massacre out there," the man said. He was heading for one of the thoroughfares leading to Lowtown, and he shouted over his shoulder as he ran. "Find cover, boy."

Cassius lifted a thick blanket from the ground and shook off the hand-carved trinkets on display. He wrapped himself in the blanket and ducked behind an abandoned booth, and from this position he had a clear line of sight to the roads into Lowtown.

Piso's men stood guard in five of the main thoroughfares. Two-hundred-odd men. A handful of spellcasters. Their barricades had toppled as hundreds fled the Market, the sheer number of bodies more than the makeshift fortifications could withstand. In the streets, guards set about slaughtering the riotous mob, fighters wielding swords and spears, spellcasters fire. Near the southern storefronts, corpses were piled two and three high.

The mob was mostly unarmed but outnumbered the guards ten to one. Each time a guard fell, the mob set upon him. Men on both sides took to cutting off ears and noses, cutting out tongues, and from all directions came the cries of the trampled.

Cassius headed south.

As he moved, a toothless man in the rear of the press spotted him. The man called to his brothers in arms, and a handful turned.

"It's one of them," the toothless man shouted. He wielded a large, fire-hardened slab of wood, most likely an old table leg. He pointed to Cassius. "At him, boys. 'Fore the bastards flank us."

A dozen men charged Cassius, some with knives and staves and some, like their edentulous leader, with makeshift weapons. Still others attacked bare-handed, armed only with rage and panic.

Cassius raised one gauntleted hand, a warning to the crowd that went unheeded. He shouted for them to stand down, but his words were lost in the chaos of the battle. As the men drew closer, he let his eyes unfocus and by rote the colorless canvas appeared to him and he began to sketch the shining rune. Overhead, black smoke swirled. The fireball that rocketed out of the cloud moved as swift as a shot arrow. It struck the ground with a sound like a roof collapsing, then bounced back into the air and exploded over the attackers, the men falling, some to fire, some to shrapnel. Still others in the mob, who had not been hit, fled at the sound of the blast. A narrow wedge opened in the throng.

With some of the mob scattered, Piso's men fought their way forward. Their ranks were sloppy, a massive, unwieldy formation over which several men argued for position. They did not try to block the roads to Lowtown, a futile task given the number of alleys available to the fleeing crowds. Nor did they try to fight the fires or impose order amidst the riot. They huddled together for protection and killed any who came near, man or woman or child.

Cassius circled east. He checked behind him as he moved, and in the middle of the main avenue he saw the battle between the Hightown forces and the legionnaires still engaged. The legionnaires had held formation and prevented a flanking maneuver. He could not see past their ranks to count the Hightown dead, but he knew there were many.

He turned to face Piso's forces again. He moved toward the knot of men, and when he was within a hundred yards of them, he pulled the blanket tight around himself and he shouted for Hightown and he shouted for Cinna.

His calls were answered by arrows.

He balled his hand into a fist and the warmth that spread down his spine made him shiver. The shape in his head was a net of lines and sharp angles that had taken him years to commit to memory. It folded into itself and was without edge.

His hands trembled. His palms burned. Dust drifted and curled in the street. A white-orange flash lit the sky and a column of fire rose from the ground.

It stood five stories tall. A pillar of flame that roiled and bubbled, with great jets of white-hot gas arcing from the main body. The column began to spin, and renewed screams went up from the mob at the sight of this, a blight worthy of some vengeful god. It swept toward Piso's men.

The thrumming in Cassius's chest was too strong to gauge counterspells as Piso's killers frantically tried to snuff the fire. Instead, he watched for signs of spells and responded with counters of his own. Few in the crowd, or even amongst Piso's men, noticed this meta-battle, though. When the column of fire did not slow or dissipate, many of the guard figured themselves unprotected by their own spell-casters and they dropped their weapons and fled. Less than twenty men stood their ground against this rolling inferno, and most of these were men frozen by fear. As the column enveloped them, their screams were lost to rushing air.

Cassius clapped his hands, and instantly the column lifted into itself and vanished. In its place stood a heap of charred bodies and charred metal and two spellcasters where ten had stood before, both men trembling but unsinged.

When Piso's troop re-formed, they scanned the street and noticed first the bodies of their comrades, then Cassius, wrapped in his blanket with his arms held before him. The men seemed to measure these sights against each other and a low cry picked up amongst their ranks. A stream of arrows rained down around Cassius. He retreated, moving quickly but still facing the Lowtown forces, who were charging now.

A crossbow bolt glanced off his hip. His side stung with cold pain and he nearly dropped the blanket but managed to hold it and with one hand pressed against his bleeding wound, he hobbled north up the main avenue. Piso's forces grew as they gave chase.

Explosions shook the air above him. He moved with his head down and backed through tapestries of flame and sheets of hot ash, Piso's men within fifty yards now. He pointed his fist to a spot in the street, and again there was a silent flash, a blackened circle on pavement. From the circle rose gray smoke that enveloped Piso's men.

Cassius turned north and faced the rear of the legionnaires' lines. He held his palms to the sky.

The bolt of lightning fell silently, followed by a report of thunder.

The rear line of legionnaires turned to face Cassius. He shouted for Piso and for Lowtown.

Behind him, Piso's men emerged from the smoke, and they were scattered and coughing, some with their eyes closed.

The two forces were fifty yards apart and between them stood only Cassius. Then Cassius kneeled in the lane and lowered his head. His shadow reached up from the floor and enveloped him, then sank back to the ground, and Cassius was gone.

Piso's men were at a full run now, and Vorenicus shouted for his lines to hold fast. On the other side of the lane, the men from Hightown fought forward. And at the intersection, under a roof of smoke, all three forces collided.

Most of the Market was in flames. A cloud of smoke had settled over the plaza, and as the winds blew south, embers drifted into Lowtown and already a few tenements had begun to smolder.

The teleportation spell dropped Cassius on the western side of the square. He shed his blanket and made to rise, but the pangs in his gut stopped him. He kneeled and dry heaved, the pain like worms burrowing in his intestines. The cut along his hip ached, as did the acid burns to his shoulder and neck. But the pain behind his eyes was greater than all that combined. He crawled under the remnants of a merchant's stall and lay waiting for the fit to overtake him. An hour passed. He dozed briefly. When he came to, he thought he had woken from a seizure, but his jaw did not ache, and he had no memory of the other world. Realizing that he had napped during a battle, he almost laughed.

He stood and began to walk. The thrumming in his chest had quieted but was still noticeable. Thick smoke curled overhead, and he scanned the sky for signs of the spellfight but could not see well. He turned into a narrow walkway and found there, at the end of the lane, the remnants of the legionnaires marching in lockstep. They were less than fifteen total and all but a few were walking wounded and they carried no injured man who could not move under his own power.

The men shouted at the sight of his gauntlets, their discipline shattered by their injuries. Cassius lowered his hands. He said that he meant no harm, said this calmly and repeated it. He kept very still.

"Who are you?" a legionnaire cried. He held a spear in both hands.

"My name is Cassius."

"Whose man are you?"

"Piso's man." Vorenicus stepped from behind the soldier. "Or is it Cinna's man now? I have a hard time keeping track."

Vorenicus's helmet was streaked with soot, the eagle feathers on either side of the wide brim bent and dirty. He had a cut above his left eye, and his steel cuirass, the one depicting the figure of Justice trampling the serpent of Corruption, was dented, and Justice's face smeared with a bloody handprint.

"Are you all right?" Cassius asked.

"I'd be a lot better if you dropped that iron."

Cassius placed his gauntlets on the ground and lifted his hands.

"I didn't have to do that," he said. "I did it of my own free will. And to answer that soldier's question, I stand before you as no one's man but my own."

"Kick those gauntlets over here."

"Listen to me, Vorenicus. I meant what I said. I serve no one. You're light on manpower just now. And it looks like you have no spellcasters to defend you. You could use my help."

"Just kick those gauntlets over," Vorenicus shouted. "I'm taking you prisoner for the part you played back there. You instigated that entire fight."

"That's not how it—"

"The rest of the legion will be to town shortly. We can decide what to do with you then."

"The rest of the legion isn't coming," Cassius said. "You know that as well as I do. You didn't have a man to spare out there. But if you did, and if you sent him for help, there's no guarantee he made it to the fort. Cinna would have killed him at the city walls to prevent reinforcements. And if he did make it out, it'll be half a day before the soldiers are geared and mobilized. That's a long time to be alone in enemy territory."

"We'll manage."

"Listen to me, Vorenicus. This is—"

"Shut up. If you're going to make me take that iron, I will. But I will not—"

The last of Vorenicus's words were lost to the sound of a piercing whistle. Cassius did not hear the explosion. He felt his legs give out, then he was on the floor, and the air was heavy and quiet. His arm burned. The familiar fatty scent of cooked flesh came to him, and he realized then his cloak was on fire. He rolled and stripped off the cloak and beat it against the ground until the flames died.

Stalls on both sides of the walkway were afire, and all the legionnaires lay crumpled. Most were still, and the ones who were not still were trembling. As the ringing in his ears faded, Cassius heard a man call out to the gods.

He retrieved his gauntlets and slipped them on. His left hand ached. He felt a stirring in his chest. He cast his fire ward and scanned the lane for movement.

Two men were approaching from the south, spellcasters both. One held his hands forward and, at the sight of these men, Cassius prostrated himself in the lane, hands folded under his belly. He stilled his breathing.

He heard footsteps. He heard the sound of a blade being unsheathed, then a muffled scream. The man who had been calling for the gods fell silent. Cassius turned his head and opened an eye and saw the two men kneeling over the corpse of a legionnaire, one man searching a coin purse, the other inspecting a gold-hilted dagger.

Cassius waved his hand, as if shooing a fly. A cloud of silver dust rose into the air. Both men wheeled suddenly, and as they turned, Cassius closed his eyes, and a series of staccato explosions sounded above him. He opened his eyes again, and the spellcasters lay unmoving. He hobbled toward them and stripped the gauntlets from both corpses.

In the distance, he heard explosions and the cries of men and beasts. He headed north, stopping to look over Vorenicus's body. He kneeled over the body for a time and whispered in his ear. He kissed the side of Vorenicus's warm head, then tucked a coin into his hand and the hand closed around his own, squeezing lightly.

He waited a minute and it came again, a faint squeeze.

He stripped off one of his gauntlets and touched two fingers to Vorenicus's neck, and the pulse beneath his touch was strong and steady.

He unbuckled Vorenicus's chest plate and peeled it from his body. He did the same for Vorenicus's steel greaves and gauntlets; and then he unhitched the sword belt and removed the helmet.

He lifted Vorenicus, wrapped an arm around his waist, and headed for the edge of the Market, Vorenicus limp at his side.

WHEN YOU DESTROY, DESTROY COMPLETELY

—◦◦◦—

In Lorium they called him Numerius. A young man of twenty, he was six years into study on the Isle of Twelve when he received his first assignment, a two-month ride with the Scarlet Stallions. The Stallions were mercenaries, a company of ex-legionnaire cavalry hired by Governor Tulloch to put down a rebellion of veterans from the Widsith Wars.

Tulloch was known as the Mad Bull of Burnum, a stern patrician with a desire for consulship and no tolerance for sedition. He gave his mercenary companies great liberties in breaking the rebel army. The Stallions had left scorched villages and fields of dead rebels the length of the southern coast, but their ride ended at Lorium. There, beneath the crumbling walls of that ancient city, the last of the rebellion collapsed, crushed in a trap orchestrated by the Bull himself.

Numerius spent most of that last night on guard duty, sitting his horse, a trim Anatolian, outside the city gates. He watched the stars wheel in the heavens above while out on the dark plain, men lay dying, their blood watering fields that had been tilled since antiquity. Lorium was an old city, older even than the Republic, its walls raised when Antiochi kings still sat the Ivory Throne. It had been deserted for centuries now, a hollow ruins home only to scavengers and night hunters. History wrote of a great earthquake destroying the city, but the people of the southern coast told a different tale. The gods hurled a fiery star down onto the Loriumites, they claimed, to punish them for their wickedness.

Looking skyward, Numerius wondered if the gods were watching that night. Certainly, he had heard men calling for them during the fighting, still heard some calling now. No star had fallen to punish the wicked, though, and no god had shown. Not even bear-helmed Aureus, god of valor and war. Aureus, who carried a massive stone shield chiseled with the face of a fearsome gorgon, with which he protected men who fought bravely and with pure hearts.

Maybe Aureus had been busy elsewhere, Numerius thought. Maybe only cowards had died this night.

"Something for you to see inside, boy." Master Gallard stood under the shadow of the gate, dressed in a cavalryman's leather armor and tall boots. He looked the part of a Stallion, grimed with dirt and blood, reeking of sweat, with a long cloak of deepest red, a broad-bladed sabre on one hip, his gauntlets on the other. A plug of tobacco swelled his bottom lip, and around his neck hung a thong of coppers claimed from the fallen.

Numerius walked his horse to the nearest hitching post and dismounted and hitched the reins. He followed as Master Gallard led him deeper into the city.

It was strange to witness one of the Masters away from the Isle. At home, Master Gallard was haughty and cold, unpredictable, vicious without warning. Amongst the Stallions, though, he played the part of a typical mercenary, fearless on the battlefield, warm with the other men, eager for a drink, quick with a joke. He only showed his true nature in brief flashes, and then only to Numerius, a quick glance or change of tone, a whispered threat. Numerius had no love for Master Gallard, but he admired the man's fluidity.

Deep in the city, they reached the outer courtyard of a ruined palace. Here, low stone walls had once housed an exotic garden now overgrown with moss and toad ivy. Cracked flagstone walkways led to a central clearing lit by a large bonfire. A man lay next to the fire, bound at hands and feet by heavy iron shackles.

"What do you see, boy?"

Numerius looked. The light of the fire showed the man was middle-aged, strongly built and with a shaved head. He was missing his left eye and two fingers on his left hand, as well as the tip of his nose. Wide scars covered his arms and chest and legs. These were his old injuries. There were fresher wounds as well. Deep gashes to his head and belly that oozed dark blood, bruises to his cheeks and shoulders and back. His right arm appeared broken, both his legs pink with fresh burns.

The man should have been dead but, as Numerius watched, his chest rose and fell with strong breaths. Starlight lit the man's good eye, which burned with naked hatred.

"I see a ruined man," Numerius said.

"This is Centurion Balthus," Master Gallard said. "He's the commander of the rebel army and a warrior of some repute. He fought with the legion for twenty years before retiring to a small horse farm in the southern coast. He breeds workhorses, strong and stubborn, much like the man himself. He rallied these men when Governor Tulloch attempted to take their land and relocate them to the northern provinces."

"His capture means the rebellion is over."

"Not his capture, his death."

"Forgive me, Master. I misspoke."

"You made a good point, boy," Master Gallard said. "Although I'm certain you didn't mean to. This isn't the first time Governor Tulloch has captured Centurion Balthus. Two years ago, he arrested the man for trying to foment rebellion. He made Balthus pay a fine and released him after a few months spent in the copper mines, thinking some hard work had taught the man his lesson.

"When his old soldiers saw the way Balthus had been treated, they rallied to his cause by the hundreds. If the governor could treat a loyal servant of Antioch such as Balthus so cruelly, what would he do to a common man, they wondered. Later, about six months into the fighting, Tulloch routed Balthus at Shatterspear Pass. Most of the rebels managed to retreat, but Tulloch captured Balthus and his honor guard. He crucified the men, leaving them to die in the harsh winter cold, but Balthus didn't die. No one knows how he survived. There are rumors, of course, but only the good commander here knows for certain. So when you say that Balthus's capture signals the end of the rebellion, you again have made the mistake Tulloch made."

"I see," Numerius said.

"Do you?" The light of the flames seemed to twist around Master Gallard, reaching for him but unable to touch him, a familiar sight from the hundreds of duels Numerius had witnessed on the Isle. In this new light, the trappings of the man's outfit disappeared, and he no longer resembled a common mercenary, willing to kill for drink and plunder, but instead became a Master spellcaster again.

"I believe so."

"Do you think this war mattered?" Master Gallard asked.

Numerius was silent.

"To Governor Tulloch and Centurion Balthus, I'm certain it did," Master Gallard continued. "But as a study of war, nothing of consequence transpired here. Two armies fought. Sometimes well, often poorly, and in the end, the force that was better equipped, better positioned, and considerably larger won. In a few years' time, everyone will have forgotten there even was a war. Everyone but you, boy."

Master Gallard sprang forward. He grabbed Numerius by the back of his neck and squatted, pulling the boy with him, until both were inches from the face of the dying centurion.

"This is the face of a man who can't be reasoned with," Master Gallard said. "A man who can't be stopped, short of death. Tulloch twice let him live, and instead of walking away with his life, this man returned stronger and more determined. This is why you must never wound an enemy. You must destroy them completely. Remember this."

Numerius looked over the centurion. He would not live to see the light of morning, Numerius was sure of that. Even a man as dull as the governor was not likely to make the same mistake three times. The lesson Master Gallard wished him to learn was plain to see, writ on the broken body of the man. But Numerius thought he saw something else as well.

The centurion had fought bravely and as best he could, leaving pieces of himself on every battlefield of the war, yet still he soldiered on. Looking down on him, Numerius thought that sometimes, the ruin of a thing was remarkable in itself.

14

It was dark inside the looted storefront. Cassius sat in the front room and peered between the slats of a boarded-up window, surveying the Market by the light of the fires consuming it. Behind him, Vorenicus lay unconscious on the floor, amidst bolts of shredded silk and broken wine bottles, overturned pots of spices whose heady fragrances hung thick in the cramped room. From time to time, Vorenicus stirred. His eyes fluttered. He groaned. When he spoke, he called for his mother or uttered words too soft for Cassius to hear. And once, while Cassius was kneeling over him, Vorenicus opened his eyes and stared up at Cassius and reached.

"Father," he called. "Father." Then he shut his eyes again.

The hearing in Cassius's left ear was still impaired and half his face numb. When he felt the familiar queer sensation work across his scalp, he walked to the back room and lay on the floor and waited for the fit to overtake him.

In the other place, he heard the low voice calling to him again, calling him by his true name. It was a man's voice, speaking in a strange language but one he understood.

"Let me die," he told the voice.

He could feel the presence of the voice near him. It was like the sensation of being watched.

"You don't want to die," the voice said.

In the dark, he could feel his body but not its place in the world or its relation to other objects, yet it seemed the voice was calling from behind him and drawing closer.

"I failed her again. All the years, all that I thought I had become. It wasn't enough."

"You are confused." The voice was strong. It shook his bones.

"No."

"What happened to her happened long ago."

"It happened again today," Cassius said.

"Today was different."

"I wanted to be her hero."

"You will be. You are something great and terrible now."

He felt a tremor pass through him. He heard his own groan, distant and strained.

"You thought you were dead, and you should be dead," the voice said. *"There are hundreds of dead outside. But you live. What does that mean?"*

"It means that it is not my time."

"A lesson you learned years ago."

"Yes."

"But sometimes a reminder is in order."

"Yes."

"You know what must be done when you wake," the voice said. *"You have come too far to abandon this road. The time spent training, the sacrifices, the struggle, what was it for if not to bring you to this very moment?"*

"I don't know."

"You do know. You know what I am going to say before I say it. But still you want me to say it, and so I will. You die when you flee your true path. Until then, there is nothing in this mortal world to stop you."

"How can you know that?"

"Because it was true for me." The voice seemed to waver.

"Who are you?"

"You know the answer." The voice was far away now, fading.

"Attus?"

His chin was wet with spit when he woke. His head ached, as did his jaw. The ringing in his ears was low, and beneath it, he heard whispers. He saw the world through unfocused eyes, a soup of browns and grays. When his vision cleared, the world took on a pointed sharpness, as though his eyes had carried defects before but were now set right.

He found Vorenicus lying in stupor, as he had left him. He stood staring for a time, struggling to envision the way forward from here. That was the lesson he had learned on the Isle of Twelve, the importance of position and of projection. To anticipate the moves of an enemy, you had first to assess his position, assess it honestly, then judge the best action available to him.

Who were his enemies now? Cinna and Piso both, after today.

And how would each man react? There would follow a period of confusion as the bosses gathered information about the fight. Each would blame the other. Both would know Cassius was at fault, but they would not yet understand why. It was this small uncertainty that would allow him to stay a step ahead of both bosses.

But where was he to go? There was no place in the city to hide. Every stranger would want him dead. He could disappear into the jungle, maybe meet with one of the lost Khimir tribes. But they were just as liable to kill him as an interloping Antiochi than welcome him as an ally.

He looked again to Vorenicus. The way through was clear.

He left the looted storefront and found the square limned by starlight and fire. He walked with one arm hooked under Vorenicus's shoulder, the legionnaire sagging heavily against him and his feet dragging in the lane.

The fight in the center of the Market had ended with neither side a clear winner. After the skirmish, fires had burned uncontested for hours, and whole sections of the square were now ash.

Cassius set his burned cloak on Vorenicus, to cover the legion uniform, and moved slowly, dragging Vorenicus with each step.

Near the council hall, he spotted the young priest of the Vinalia order who had presided over the funeral rites of Piso's nephew. His rose-colored robes were bloodstained, as was his face. He moved from corpse to corpse and at each body he bent and said a prayer.

Cassius cut west toward the alleys leading from the Market. Outside a dilapidated storefront, a man stood loading bodies into a mule-drawn wagon. He was an old man and big, with a high forehead and thin gray hair. A dozen bodies lay at his feet, the ground beneath them foul with piss and blood, mounds of feces. As Cassius watched, the man lifted the body of a woman by the armpits and laid it over the lip of the wagon, bent forward, then hoisted the body up into the wagon.

"Evening," Cassius called.

The man turned to face Cassius. His face was pockmarked and one eye milky with a cataract. The front of his tunic was stained, and he kept one hand behind his back.

"Something I can do for you?" the old man asked.

"You moving these bodies?"

"Any of these your kin?"

"No."

"Then what business is it of yours?"

"Can I ride with you a bit?" Cassius asked. "My friend and I are hurt. I don't know how far we'll make it on foot. I'd be willing to pay."

The man looked to his cart. He looked down to the pile of bodies.

"How much?" he asked.

"Half a silver."

"That'll do the job." The man hooked a thumb at Vorenicus. "Is he dead?"

"I don't believe so."

"Good for him. Now help me with these here, and we'll get moving twice as fast."

"I think I may have broken my hand." Cassius lifted his hand, showed it as proof of its own dysfunction. He was aware of the pain, the constant droning ache that wracked his body, but it seemed detached from him. Or maybe the pain was with him, and it was his body that seemed detached.

"How's the other hand doing?" the old man asked.

"Fine, I guess."

"Then give me one hand's worth of help." The old man turned and Cassius saw a cleaver tucked into his belt, at the small of his back. "Your friend there can ride in the back. It smells like hell itself, but I don't imagine he'll care."

"Would you think it strange if I asked to ride with him?"

"I might."

"Would you object?"

"I wouldn't. Where you headed anyway?"

"Hightown."

The mule rode slowly, and twice the wheels of the wagon stuck in loose mud.

In the back of the wagon, surrounded by the dead, Cassius wondered if he was not dead himself, and this entire scene some cruel trick to cross him into the afterlife while he yet thought himself alive. When the wagon stopped a third time, Cassius heard the old man climb down off his perch and the sackcloth covering drew back.

"This is it," the old man said.

The streets were deserted and unlit. Cassius climbed out of the wagon, and the old man helped lower Vorenicus onto his shoulder. Cassius paid the man and thanked him, and the man acknowledged neither. He climbed back onto his cart and cursed his mule and whipped the animal once, and the mule started forward at a lazy trot, the wagon rocking side to side as it rolled, like a dog drying itself.

The door in the stables was unlocked, and Cassius entered the bar silently. He placed Vorenicus on the pantry floor and walked out into the dim front room. He found a lit candle at the bar. He walked upstairs and checked first the guest room and found it empty, then checked Lucian's room, where Lucian was snoring in bed.

He called out, and Lucian sprang up shouting, eyes wide, hands clenched into fists.

"Lucian, it's all right. It's Cassius."

Lucian punched the wall. "Goddamn it, boy. You're going to give me a heart attack. Like a thief in the damn night you come to me."

Lucian wiped his eyes. He took up one of the wine bottles from his nightstand and found it empty. He rose from bed, naked in the soft light of the candle, and walked to the corner and stood urinating into a chamber pot. Cassius turned to leave.

"Where are you going?" Lucian asked. "I need that light to piss by."

"Ever the gracious host."

"Maybe I'd have more time for niceties if you gave fair warning once in a while. Instead of dropping in on me whenever the hell it suits your purpose."

Lucian gathered a large tunic from a stool near the window. He shook the tunic and donned it, then wiped his hands on its sides. He crossed the room and stopped before Cassius.

"You don't look much the way I remember," he said.

"You doubt it's the real me?" Cassius asked.

"The real you?" Lucian stared down into Cassius's face. "What could I use for comparison?"

Lucian exited the room, his feet heavy on the wooden floorboards. He descended the steps to the bar, and Cassius followed.

"You looking for a place to stay?"

"That and one other thing," Cassius said. "I've got someone with me."

Lucian stopped. "Someone with you? Why would you bring someone to my bar?"

"I had nowhere else to go."

"Do you realize the position you're putting me in?"

"Relax." Cassius had meant to sound calm, but the fear in him, the pain and rage and maddening uncertainty, twisted the word. He paused, composed himself. "I've got everything under control."

"Just like always, huh? Where is this stowaway?"

"In the pantry."

Lucian walked behind the bar. He entered the pantry and squinted into the gloom. He motioned for Cassius and Cassius came close and, in the dim light of the candle, Lucian saw General Quintus's wounded son lying on his floor.

"Damn, boy," he said. "I knew you'd make a dead man of me yet."

. . .

The bean soup was cold, and the feeling of a full stomach discomforted Cassius. The wine was light, and he finished off a single mug to Lucian's three.

"You want more?" Lucian asked.

"I'm not very hungry," Cassius said.

"How's that hand?"

"I think it's broken."

"Let me see."

Cassius lifted his hand and Lucian accepted it with both of his own, as one might accept a large plate. He stared at it for a time, turned it over, inspected the palm. It was swollen and stiff, marred with nicks and cuts. Black grime was worked deep into the creases, and the fingernails were chipped and broken, with congealed blood in the cuticles.

Lucian nodded, as though confirming a suspicion. He released the hand.

"Is it broken?" Cassius asked.

"How should I know?" Lucian poured the last of the wine into his mug and lifted the mug and tapped it against Cassius's.

"What are we toasting?"

"To not trusting first impressions." Lucian drained the mug.

"When do you think Sulla will show?"

"I don't know. She was here for most of the day, waiting for you. But then she left after sundown."

"Will she be back before dawn?"

"Either before dawn or after dawn, I should think. Or maybe never. She was talking of booking you passage on a ship off the island. Maybe she did the smart thing and kept the ticket for herself."

"I need you to send for a healer," Cassius said. "He's a Yoruban. He has a shop in the east end."

"What's his name?"

"I don't know."

"You don't know his name?"

"He didn't give it to me. I didn't ask." Cassius sighed. "Look, just—he's a Yoruban spellcaster living in the east end. How many people fit that damn description?"

"Okay," Lucian said. "Relax. If he's still alive, I'll find him."

"Thank you." Cassius stared into the hearth. No fire burned there, for fear that smoke might attract attention.

"You still thinking about that?" Lucian asked after a while.

"About what?"

"About leaving."

"No."

"I guess business picked back up this morning."

"It has a way of doing that sometimes."

"Do you need me to tell you that I'm nervous about this arrangement?"

"I've got it under control." Cassius clenched and unclenched his injured hand.

"Housing you is one thing," Lucian said. "That's a risk I took with my eyes open. Or about as open as they could be, dealing with a bastard like you. But this is something else."

"I've never done you any harm."

"Dragging Quintus's near-dead son into my bar is harm on a scale you can't imagine."

"Maybe you should see how this shakes out before you lose all faith in me."

"In you?" Lucian wiped wine from his lips. "Cassius the master plotter?"

"Have I wronged you so far?"

"A month ago, I was a bartender in a provincial town. I made an honest living, and no one bothered me. Now half my city is on fire with war. Look at the trouble you've caused here."

"The trouble I've caused?" Cassius's face was weary, his eyes heavy-lidded.

"Who if not you?"

"A month ago, you were a retired mercenary from a failed rebellion. You lived in a refuge for debtors and criminals and exiles. Ruled by a bastard general with a bastard army. And governed by two crime bosses. All three with the blood of thousands on their hands. And yet you think I caused this trouble?"

"If you're so innocent, then why don't you ever sleep?"

"Sleep is the sister of Death," Cassius said.

"An old Khimir proverb. Pick that up in the last few weeks, did you?"

"When else?"

Lucian stood suddenly, knocking over his chair. He leaned down into Cassius's face.

"When you slept here earlier, every time you slept here, you moved the bed in your room. I could hear you moving it. Why did you do that?"

Cassius did not respond.

"You know what's under that bed?" Lucian asked.

"I moved it, didn't I?"

"So say it. Tell me what you found."

"Loose floorboards."

"Loose floorboards. And underneath a hidden compartment. You know what that's for?"

Cassius's hands began to tremble. He lowered them into his lap. "Hiding things."

"People."

"I don't know what you're talking about."

"When will you learn that playing dumb doesn't suit you?" Lucian's eyes were fierce under his severe brow.

Cassius looked away.

"When the war ended," Lucian said, "Quintus had the remnants of the Native army rounded up. He killed the men. Killed them in public. Slaughtered them in the market square. The women and children he sold into slavery."

Cassius did not speak.

"You hear me, boy? He sold them into slavery. These weren't war captives. These were citizens of Antioch, same as me or you. And he sold them as goddamn slaves. Shipped them off to Fathalan flesh markets in the dead of night, for fear the senate would learn of it and send an army down here to capture him for crimes against the Republic."

"A devious man."

"But some of us still loyal to the Native cause tried to help. We harbored escapees. Chartered ships to ferry them to the mainland. There was a network of safe houses where we hid them while they waited for passage."

"Like this bar?" Cassius said.

"Like this bar."

"In the space under the floor?"

"That's right," Lucian said. "Probably we saved about three hundred people."

"A lot of lives."

"Hell, there were thousands of Natives in the city then. We saved only a handful."

"You did the best you could," Cassius said.

"You know what I sometimes think about, when I think about that time?"

"What's that?"

"The orphans we saved. Children whose parents were sold off as slaves. Or who died. Sometimes I wonder what kind of life we condemned them to on the mainland, all alone."

Cassius's jaw clenched. He swallowed. "Better a hard life than no life at all."

"I used to think that," Lucian said. "But maybe I'm wrong. Can you imagine how hard it would be for a child like that? What he would have to become to survive?"

"It was a long time ago, old man."

"A long time ago." Lucian lifted his overturned stool and slouched back down onto it. "And my memory is bad already. Maybe in a few years, I won't remember it at all."

"What a dream that would be."

Lucian stared at Cassius for a time, and Cassius did not raise his head.

"Where will this end?" Lucian asked.

"I don't know."

"But you're not satisfied with where it's at now?"

"My work isn't finished. If that's what you're asking."

"You could have killed them both," Lucian said. "Piso. Cinna. You were close enough to do that."

"And what would that have accomplished? Kill them, and new bosses would take their places. And I'd be dead. And even if I'd managed to kill them both—" Cassius shook his head.

"Quintus would still be alive."

Cassius did not respond.

"You've hurt them both these past few weeks," Lucian said. "And you could hurt Quintus now."

"You're talking about killing Vorenicus?"

"I didn't say that."

"You implied it," Cassius said. "Do you think I hadn't thought of that? Consider where it would leave me. And besides, what crime has that man ever committed?"

"Are we playing gods now? Judging the worthy and the unjust? What about those people in the Market today?"

"How many of them served during the Uprising?"

"Not everyone who died served Piso or Cinna," Lucian said.

"How many cheered the executions in the Market? How many turned in fugitive Natives?"

"I don't know that number. Neither do you."

Cassius looked up, his eyes filmed with tears. His face was covered in sweat, hair unkempt, like some mad hermit come from a deep cave to impart secrets he had brooded over a lifetime.

"There was no other way." His voice caught. "If there were, I would have found it. I would have found it. But there was no other way. And someone had to—"

Cassius left his sentence unfinished. They sat in silence for a while, then Lucian took the bowls to the kitchen.

Cassius lay sweating in the dark for hours. The air stank of spoiled meat and dried blood and urine, stains worked deep into the fabric of his tunic. He whispered to himself a late verse of the Attus epic. The hero communing with the third of the four great birds, the hawk spirit that would lead him to the Battle of Maghrib. The hawk warning him that he would suffer a terrible injury in that battle and advising him to think of the wound as a sacrifice one would make to the gods, but instead a sacrifice of himself and to himself.

When he slept, he dreamed of worms in his belly. His gut distended with a foul egg.

He woke nauseous from the smell in the hole. He climbed out of the floor, but still the terrible odor clung to him. He tried to form his left hand into a fist but could not.

He undressed and paced the room, naked, grimed with mud down his legs and arms. Streaks of blood covered his chest and belly, and the filth on his neck was so thick the dirt came off in beads. The bruises along his ribs were green now, the stitched flesh of his belly a bright red and slick with pus.

I am rotting inside, he thought.

There was a knock at the door. He dressed himself and answered the knock and Sulla entered.

"Cassius," she whispered, startled by his appearance. She was dressed as he had seen her in the butcher's shop, in an oversized tunic and cloak, her hair bundled up under a white-felt hat. "I don't know whether you're unkillable or the risen dead."

"Either way, I feel terrible."

"Either way, I'm astonished to find you upright." She held a cup of wine and pressed it on Cassius. "Drink some of this. It might help you feel better."

Cassius drained the cup. The wine was strong, with a pungent aftertaste.

"What time is it?" he asked.

"Not sure. About two hours before sunrise I think."

"I need a favor."

"A favor? After what Lucian just showed me in the pantry, it seems you need a lot more than a favor."

"Can you get me some discreet transport?"

"Discreet transport to the docks, you mean?" She flashed a pained smile. "For passage to the mainland using the ticket you asked me to buy, right? That's what you mean by transport, isn't it?"

"Not exactly."

"Oh no? To where exactly then? Somewhere else in Hightown? That doesn't seem right. Cinna would kill you as soon as look at you. Lowtown perhaps? No, I'm sure Piso is still furious over this afternoon's festivities. So where exactly, Cassius? Where in the world would you like someone to drag the island's most notorious man and the near-dead son of General-fucking-Quintus?"

"The jungle."

Sulla cocked her head. "What?"

"I already explained myself to you."

"You said you were here to start a war. Seems to me you did that already. Can't you just send word to the mainland to begin the invasion? The armies of the bosses are devastated."

"But Quintus's legions are still at full force. We need to weaken them as well, or they could turn the tide against the invasion."

"If you wanted to get Quintus to attack the bosses, you wouldn't need to go to the jungle. You could do that by taking a knife down to the pantry."

"I won't do that," Cassius said.

"I could find you someone who would." Sulla's voice was calm.

"I won't allow it to be done either. Just find me a way to the jungle."

"And what if you don't make it out of there? What becomes of the invasion?"

"I'll leave you instructions. People to contact on the mainland. And a coded message that names you as my ally and a valuable resource for the invasion forces."

"What does that mean for me?" Sulla asked.

"It means you'll be taking my place in all of this."

"I'll be a freedom fighter?"

"And everything will change," Cassius said. "You can't go back to being the best fence on the island once you do this. Probably you won't even be able to stay on the island."

"I have to stay."

"Why?"

"I'm Scipian. There's no hope for me in normal society."

"Now isn't the time for jokes."

"Of course."

"We're writing history with our actions here."

Sulla stared at Cassius's face, searching. "Remarkable."

"What?"

"It's like you truly mean it. I almost believe that you believe it."

"Of course I believe it. It's the truth."

"Agent of the Falcon Guard? Freedom fighter? Do you think me that stupid?"

"I don't think you're stupid at all." Cassius took a step back. In an instant, he seemed to transform from an overwhelmed boy to something formidable. He squared his shoulders. The pain and exhaustion vanished from his face, hidden behind the cold mask he had worn throughout his stay on the island, as he talked with Cinna and Piso, as he stared down experienced spellcasters, monsters from the void, living flame, a bloodthirsty mob. He dropped his hands to hover near his gauntlets.

"Then you thought offering me what I desired most would blind me to reality," she said. "That the idea of a fresh start would be too much to ignore, no matter how unlikely it seemed."

"What are you saying, Sulla?"

"I'm saying I don't want to be part of your games anymore."

She did not appear armed. Probably, she still bore her dirk, hidden somewhere in her clothes, but the steel daggers she had worn on display at the funeral were gone. Cassius was unsure if she meant him harm or if she was simply making her position clear. He had time only for that brief moment of uncertainty, then his head grew heavy and his vision blurred.

He fumbled for his gauntlets, his hands cold and numb. The room keeled. He tripped and landed on his knees.

He recalled what she had told him about not finishing a drink bought for you, about the bad luck it brought. And then the world turned black, as though a curtain had been drawn over his eyes.

He woke in the main room of the bar, seated at a small table. He blinked to clear his vision, then wiped his eyes and, realizing his hands were unbound, he reached for his gauntlets.

His belt was gone, his chain and his gauntlets as well.

"You'll have to forgive me for taking your iron, stranger," a voice called from behind him. "I respect your abilities too much to leave you armed."

Servilius circled around the table and took a seat opposite him. He was dressed in a shirt of mail overlaid with a hard leather cuirass. He had three fresh cuts on his left cheek, one scabbed and deep enough that it would probably scar. Scratch marks, Cassius realized.

"Is that why you drugged me?"

"Wasn't my idea. Sulla thought you might react poorly when you spotted us in the bar. So we disarmed you. But we were gentle. Didn't hurt you while you were out. Nor shackle you. I hope those small kindnesses speak to our intent."

"Our?"

"Me and a few of the brothers."

Cassius turned to see two men stood behind him at the bar. One geared in mail and leather and the other in an old steel chest plate, salvaged at some run-down market, but otherwise unarmored so that he looked like a half-dressed Murondian knight. The man in mail wore a longsword sheathed at his hip. The ill-dressed knight had a spiked cudgel resting to hand on the bar. Cassius saw no sign of Sulla, no sign of Lucian.

"What are your intentions?" Cassius asked.

"We're here to talk," Servilius said. "Boss needs answers about what happened today. I need answers."

The bar was sparsely lit. Small flames flickered in the tall candelabrum near the table, cast grotesque shadows along the walls.

"There was a fight in the Market," Cassius said.

"You're not telling me anything I don't already know. What I want to hear is the role you played in that fight?"

"Survivor."

"Quit toying with us," one of the men at the bar called. Cassius didn't turn to see which.

Servilius raised a hand to call for quiet.

"Why not come back to Lowtown after the fight," he asked. "Join your brothers as they regrouped?"

"I ran into something unexpected."

"Is that the something in the pantry?"

"It is." Cassius struggled to keep his voice calm.

"What were you planning to do with him?"

"I hadn't decided yet."

Servilius considered this. He adjusted his eyepatch, as though it were obscuring his view of the truth.

"Why not bring him to Lowtown?"

"Transportation was an issue. That's why I came here. To get help from Sulla."

"But that didn't go as planned."

Cassius shrugged. "I don't know what she told you, but you can't believe her."

"I know that devious bitch can't be trusted. That's why I came up here personally. I wanted the truth. And I intend to get it."

Servilius nodded to the men at the bar. They entered the back room and emerged a moment later, herding Lucian and Sulla before them, each gagged and bound at their wrists and their ankles so that they moved with short, shuffling steps. As they reached the table, the armed men forced Lucian and Sulla onto their knees. Even in the dim light, with their faces awash in shadow, Cassius could see that both were bruised and bleeding.

"What is this?" Cassius asked.

"This is a negotiation. And these are my terms." Servilius pulled a knife from his belt. Candlelight danced along its edge like white flame. "I'm going to ask you questions. And you're going to give me answers. If you give me the wrong answer, if I even think that you're lying, I start to cut on your buddies here."

"You don't need to do this. We can just talk."

"I hope so, stranger. I very much want to believe you've been straight with me. But the girl here has been telling stories. And I'm starting to have doubts."

"This isn't the way to get your answers." Cassius sat forward. "What do I care about a broken-down old bartender and some second-rate fence? You have my word as a brother in arms that I'll be truthful."

"We're not brothers," Servilius said. "Not yet. You don't bear the brand. And the more I learn about you, the more I start to think you might be just a little too tenderhearted for our club."

Servilius brought his knife up under Lucian's ear. Lucian grunted into his gag and made to stand, but the ill-dressed knight held him down by the shoulders. Servilius secured the ear with his free hand, tugging so that the skin drew taut, then advanced the blade.

"All right," Cassius shouted, leaping from his seat. He slapped the tabletop. "Talk to me. Ask your questions, damn it."

Servilius paused. He smiled and withdrew the blade. He flicked Lucian's earlobe playfully.

"There it is." Servilius sat. He pointed the tip of the blade at Cassius's seat, and Cassius sat as well. "See, I knew you were a do-gooder at heart. A man of honor who can't bear to see an innocent suffer. Isn't that right?"

Cassius did not respond.

"Say it."

"Say what?"

"That you're a do-gooder."

"I'm a do-gooder," Cassius said.

"Excellent. An honest exchange. Maybe the first we've ever had. But certainly not the last." Servilius kicked Lucian in the ribs, and Lucian gasped and toppled.

Cassius gritted his teeth and looked away.

"I wonder who this old man is to you," Servilius said. "Are you two in on this together?"

"In on what?"

"Whatever the hell it is you're doing here."

"I'm a mercenary spellcaster. I came here for work."

"A familiar story. Yet you find yourself in some unfamiliar territory."

"The bartender introduced me to Sulla." Cassius breathed deep, tried to stop the words from spilling out in a rush. It was reasonable for him to be nervous. But a show of fear would be his undoing. And Sulla's and Lucian's. "She was supposed to find me prizefights at a gaming hall. I had an argument with Junius at the fights, and it escalated. Afterward, I fled to Hightown because I thought Boss Piso would want my head. I needed Cinna's protection."

"Cinna, who had me kidnapped?"

"That's right."

"Maybe, stranger." Servilius leaned back so that his chair rested on two legs. The light from the candles flashed over his face and, for an instant, cast the shadow of a grinning demon on the far wall. "It does all seem to fit. A misunderstanding. A fight. Someone gets killed. Could have happened to anyone. Now the girl though, Sulla, she seemed to think you were up to no good. She didn't know what exactly, but she thought you were the one who instigated the trouble at the Market today."

Sulla started to speak, her words muffled by the gag.

"She came to me saying she couldn't bear to see the killing anymore," Servilius continued, ignoring the cries of protest. "Told me she knew where you were hiding, would tell me for free if I came to get you, put an end to all this chaos. Free. Can you imagine? Of course, nothing is free in Scipio, so I wonder if maybe she isn't working an angle of her own."

Servilius stood and approached Sulla from behind. He gripped her hair, pulled back her head to expose her neck. He lowered the blade till it rested over her pulsing jugular.

Sulla glared up at him, her eyes raging and defiant.

"Should I slit her throat for making up these vicious stories?" Servilius caught sight of Sulla's withering look and smiled. He lifted the blade so that its point rested in the corner of her right eye. "Or maybe just take out one of those pretty eyes. That way she'll always have something to remember me by. What do you say, stranger? Tell me she's lying, and I'll teach her a lesson."

"I kidnapped you," Cassius said.

Servilius looked up. "What?"

"I paid the bath attendants to drug you. Had you carted to Hightown. I used a draught of Stone Sleep brought up from the Southern Kingdoms to keep you in a stupor until I made my move to Lowtown."

Servilius took a fresh grip on his dagger. "Why?"

"I needed to imitate one of Piso's men to cause some trouble in Hightown. And I needed someone who was recognizable and easy to impersonate. We're about the same height. We're both spellcasters. In the dark, when I'm wearing an eyepatch, we're practically twins. It was nothing personal."

"I'm going to kill you slow, boy."

Servilius flung Sulla aside. He lunged for Cassius and at that moment Lucian sprang up from the floor, shouldered into him, and sent both men toppling to the ground. Servilius hit first, his head striking loudly on the wooden floorboards.

Cassius raced for the bar. He vaulted over it and landed on his feet and crouched and searched in the dark with his hands. He overturned amphorae, knocked cups and plates to the floor. Then he felt the smooth stock of the crossbow. He hefted it and stood. By the light of the candles, he saw it was already loaded. It was also heavy. He had to balance it on his hip to aim.

Lucian and Servilius were still on the ground, Lucian atop the dazed spellcaster. He lay sideways, pressing his girth across Servilius's arms, pinning him. The ill-dressed knight was rushing to help, while nearby the man in mail unsheathed his sword and approached Sulla. He straddled her prone form, raised high his sword, and the crossbow bolt struck his neck. A spray of arterial blood arced in the light of the candles, and Sulla kicked up, striking the man in the groin. He dropped his blade and staggered off into shadow, and Cassius heard the sound of blood hitting the floor, wet and dull, then the sound of the man collapsing. His chain mail rang, then fell silent.

Not knowing if Lucian had another bolt at hand, or if he'd be able to find it in the dark, or load the bow, Cassius hoisted the heavy bow overhead and hurled it at the ill-dressed knight. It struck the man on his side and he turned, eyes wide with murderous intent, and charged at Cassius behind the bar. The sword from the shadows struck him at the base of his skull, an executioner's swing. The force behind the blow was enough to kill but not enough to separate head from body, and so the head lolled forward at a gruesome angle as the body finished its halting step and collapsed.

The sword hung in midair, as though wielded by some hidden wraith or a shadow come to life. And then it clattered to the floor and Sulla emerged from the dark. Her hands and feet were still bound. She screamed into her gag and muffled as it was, Cassius still recognized Lucian's name.

He vaulted the bar again and, with his good hand, snatched up the discarded sword mid run. As he approached the struggling forms of Servilius and Lucian, he switched to a backhanded grip and aimed and drove the point down into the flesh between Servilius's shoulder and his chest.

Servilius screamed. His hand clenched, and a tremor carried up through his arm. Cassius tried to lift the sword for another strike, but its tip was stuck in a floorboard.

Servilius's gauntlets lay under Lucian's large thigh and Servilius reached for these awkwardly with his good hand and Cassius stomped on the hand and felt a crunch underfoot.

Cassius kicked the gauntlets out from under Lucian, and they skidded across the room. He helped Lucian roll onto his back. He retrieved Servilius's knife from the dark and cut Lucian's binds and ungagged him, then did the same for Sulla.

Still holding the knife, he stood astride the prone Servilius and, with his free hand, shook the sword still buried in flesh and bone and floorboard. Servilius writhed and screamed, his arm spasming.

"Tadua," Cassius said. He stopped shaking the sword long enough to hear a response.

"What?" Servilius gasped.

"The girl you killed. The bath attendant. Her name was Tadua."

"What does that mean?"

"Say it."

"Go to hell."

Cassius rattled the sword again. Servilius groaned.

"Say it."

"Tadua," Servilius shouted. "Tadua. Her name was Tadua."

"The last word you ever speak." And, leaning down, he slit Servilius's throat.

Cassius sat on the floor of the bar, his heart pounding so forcefully he could hear its beat in his ears. Time slowed. He measured its passage by the spread of blood pooling beneath him, the blood of Piso's men. He was aware of voices speaking behind him but not of the words spoken.

He felt a heavy hand on his shoulder and looked up and saw Lucian looming over him. He gripped the barkeep's tunic and pulled himself to his feet. He hugged Lucian.

"I didn't know," he said. He was trembling. "If I had known . . ."

"It's okay, boy."

"I wouldn't have let them hurt you."

"I know."

"I would have died before I let that happen."

"I'm okay. We're all okay."

Cassius stepped back. He wiped his face, his hands coming away wet with sweat or with tears or maybe with both. Sulla stood nearby, leaning her weight against a table.

"Are you hurt?" he asked.

"I'll live." Sulla was panting, her breath coming in shallow gasps. She eyed him warily. "Unless you have other ideas about that."

"I think there's been enough bloodshed in this bar tonight."

She nodded. And by that short exchange, a few words, a simple gesture, they agreed not to kill one another. The most informal of peace treaties.

"My gauntlets?"

"In the back near Vorenicus."

"Are there any others that we should be worried about?"

"Servilius only brought two men," she said.

Cassius scanned the room. Every shadow seemed full of menace.

"You could have gotten us killed." His voice was barely above a whisper.

"I didn't want anyone to get hurt."

"Why?"

"I wanted you to stop. You wouldn't listen to reason."

"You betrayed me to Piso. What did you think he would do?"

"I knew he would kill you if I told him everything I knew," Sulla said. "That's why I never told Piso."

"Only Servilius then?"

"I thought you two had an understanding." Sulla rubbed her sore wrists. "More so than any of the other men. I told him you had something to do with the fight in the Market and that you were working your own agenda. That's it. Nothing more. I thought he would take you back to Lowtown and maybe discipline you. Bring you in line. I never thought this would happen."

"You didn't think at all," Cassius said.

"You forced my hand."

"Don't blame this—"

Sulla flipped a nearby table. It landed with a crash.

"Someone had to stop this madness."

"Did you really believe they wouldn't kill me?" Cassius asked.

"Do you think I wanted you dead? I could have slipped poison in that glass of wine I gave you. You would have drank it and never woken up. But I didn't. Think about that. And believe what you will."

Sulla moved for the door. Shadows swallowed her as she stepped beyond the candlelight.

"Where are you going?" Cassius asked.

"I don't know."

"It's dangerous out there."

"No more dangerous than being near you."

The door opened with a sustained creak. A strong breeze swept the room, snuffing the flames of the last few candles. Her footsteps halted.

"Lucian." Her voice was soft, sorrowful.

"Yes, girl?"

"I'm sorry."

The door swung shut, and the room was dark and quiet.

T he Yoruban arrived while they were eating. They ate by candlelight in the main room of the bar, a meal of fish and boiled potatoes, day-old bread. They drank a sweet port.

They had cleared the bodies from the front room, moving them
out into the lane, then dumping them in an alleyway, where three
discarded dead would not raise much suspicion on a normal day and
certainly not tomorrow, when the dead of the Market would number
in the hundreds. They scrubbed the blood from the floorboards as
best they could. Probably the wood had stained anyway but in the
dark, the Yoruban did not notice.

The Yoruban accepted a glass of wine and thanked Lucian for his
hospitality, his tone formal and polite even as the city burned outside
the front door.

"You are in need of healing," the Yoruban said.

"For myself and for someone else," Cassius said.

"You are in bad shape."

"The other is worse."

"You then?" The Yoruban looked to Lucian. Lucian shook his
head.

"Come."

Cassius stood and walked to the pantry. The Yoruban followed.

At the sight of Vorenicus, the Yoruban made a low grunt and
muttered a prayer in his native tongue.

"That is who I think it is," he said.

"Yes," Cassius said.

The Yoruban kneeled over the prone figure. He felt for the pulses
in Vorenicus's neck, listened to his chest as he breathed. He peeled
open Vorenicus's eyelids, one and then the other, and felt his forehead
for fever.

"This is beyond my abilities," the Yoruban said.

"Is there nothing you can do?"

"The wound is in his mind. I have no spells to help that, have never even heard of such a spell." The Yoruban spread his hands like some pious supplicant, as though appealing to Cassius and to his own gods and to the shades of all healers who had come before. "If I could help, I would. But I don't believe I can. And worse, I may injure him in trying."

"I understand," Cassius said.

"How did he come to be here?"

"Do you want to know?"

"No, my friend, I do not. Nor do I want to know what you will do with him. I suppose I asked by reflex."

"Can you help with these?" Cassius held up his ravaged arms. "I believe the hand may be broken as well."

The Yoruban removed the bloodstained bandages, surveyed the wounds as a general surveys the terrain of a battlefield, considering whether success was even an option.

"It will take time," he said

"Hours?" Cassius asked.

"Days."

"No."

"This cannot be rushed," the Yoruban said.

"I don't have time," Cassius said. "Can you clean the wounds and bandage them? And then treat the hand?"

"The hand can be done in a few hours. I am confident of that."

Cassius fished inside his tunic. He produced the leather pouch that contained the wound-rot spell, holding it by its straps so that his bare hand was far from the jewel inside.

"This is yours." He offered the pouch to the Yoruban by its strap.

"Because I've earned it?" the Yoruban asked. "Or because I will not see you again?"

"Either," Cassius said. "Both."

After dinner, Lucian stepped outside to smoke his pipe, and when he returned to the bar, he asked Cassius to help him scour the plates.

"I think you'll be dead soon," he said, when they were alone in the kitchen.

"Not such a controversial opinion, I'd imagine," Cassius said.

"I'm not joking."

"You've been warning me about my death since the first drink I ordered."

"This isn't a warning," Lucian said. "I know there's no use talking with you. You've set your mind to whatever it is you intend to do, and you'll be goddamned if you're going to listen to sense."

"I can handle myself."

"Spoken like a man who has never faced Quintus."

"Have faith in me."

"It doesn't matter," Lucian said flatly.

"What?"

"This thing you're doing. You think it matters, but it doesn't."

Cassius was silent.

"Not to me anyway," Lucian said. "And I was there. Not to the people of this city either. Most of them think you a murderer. Would kill you if given the chance."

"I don't care what they think. Much less what they would or wouldn't do, in light of opportunity."

"The dead are dead. It's childish to think you can alter their condition."

"Talk of Quintus brings out something strange in you."

"Fear, boy," Lucian said. "But it brings out a rage in you. Might be wise to hide that when you meet the man himself."

15

The streets of Hightown were empty. For the second night in a row, no streetlamps were lit and all houses were shuttered. The two men waited in a dark interrupted only by starlight. Cassius kneeled over the prone Vorenicus, who had begun to mumble.

The coach that stopped in front of them was an old sprung wagon drawn by a pair of sickly-gray horses. Two men sat on the perch, one holding the reins, the other a lantern made of tinted glass so that the light it gave off was pale green. The carriage had a cloth roof and room enough to seat six although it was empty now.

The lantern bearer leaned down off the perch. He was wearing a hooded cloak, and the hood was raised so that Cassius could not see his face.

"Looking for a ride?" the hooded man asked.

"Were you sent by a friend?" Cassius squinted up into the shrouded face.

"I don't have any friends in this world. But an associate said I could find a man here who was in need of a ride. And willing to pay for it."

"I'm your man."

It began to rain as the wagon turned onto the main thoroughfare, and by the time they had ridden past the city gates, a storm broke. At each report of thunder the horses shied, and after a time, the driver steered them to the side of the road. He and the hooded man unharnessed the horses and hobbled them and pressed close to them and talked to them in low voices.

In the carriage, Vorenicus stirred. His head rolled to one side, and he groaned, a long, low wail like a mourner at a funeral. He arched his back, as though trying to pull himself up from his shoulders. After a few minutes, he settled down again, and Cassius sat staring out into the rain.

He was aware of the jungle around him. He could not see it for the rain, nor hear it for the thunder, but he knew it lay just beyond the road, and he felt as though it were waiting for him in all that dark and had been waiting for some time.

He told himself this was his imagination. He told himself it was the same as the feeling of being watched that sometimes followed him in the city. But he could not deny that this felt different.

The other had been a kind of restless anxiety. It had seemed conquerable. If he could stay ahead of the searching eyes long enough, they were nothing to fear. But this new dread carried with it a sense of the inevitable, like following a river to the sea.

The rain cleared after an hour, and they set off again. The sky was the blue of near dawn, and staring out from the carriage, Cassius spotted small camps of huts, cruder even than the tenements of the city. Chalk-white cattle antlers and the tusks of wild boars hung above doorways, and the Khimir moved about nearly naked, some with bones threaded through their hair and weaves of feathers tied to their arms and some with stranger charms on display. He glimpsed figures smeared with red and black paint or with odd camouflages of leaves and vines that hid the forms of the wearers so well, their faces appeared to float disembodied in the overgrowth.

The sun rose red as they passed into the clearing where the fort stood.

A deep embankment surrounded the compound, filled with sharpened stakes and pricker bushes. Above this rose a wooden palisade and a rampart. Upon the rampart stood a wall of stone and mudbrick and wood, layered from repeated rebuildings. Along the wall spired crenellated guard towers manned by legionnaires.

They were twenty yards from the main gate when the wagon stopped.

"What's the problem?" Cassius asked.

"No problem," the driver said. "This is as far as we go."

"I paid to be driven to the fort."

"And there it is, straight ahead. Can't go any farther without those soldiers asking us questions. Don't matter how much you paid, that's not something I'm comfortable with."

"This doesn't involve you," Cassius said. "They won't care."

"You're half-right there."

Cassius pulled Vorenicus down onto his shoulder and stepped clear just as the driver wheeled the wagon in a circle, driving fast.

He continued down the road to the fort, struggling for footholds in the loose mud. The legionnaires stationed at the front gate watched his approach calmly. He wondered if they were used to visitors from the city, maybe even Natives. He was anticipating their line of questioning when his cloak fell from Vorenicus's shoulders to reveal the legion uniform beneath.

And then he had no time to think.

H e woke to a shock of cold. The water splashed his face and ran down his naked body and before he could sit up, the guard was standing over him with another bucket. A boot on his chest pressed him to the floor and frigid water hit him again. He gagged and spat, wiped at his clouded eyes. The boot lifted off his chest, and he gasped for breath.

The guard snatched him up by his hair. He swatted helplessly, bound as he was in heavy iron manacles that bit into each wrist.

The punch glanced off his cheek. If it had been a clean hit, probably his face would have numbed from the blow. Instead, his head rang, and he toppled, landing on the cool stone. A kick to the belly knocked the wind from him. His chest was on fire, and he could breathe only in short gasps.

Hands on his shoulders rolled him onto his back.

He could see the guard now. A fat man, deeply tanned, with a long brown beard that reached nearly to his chest. Three black lines were drawn on each of his cheeks and on his forehead was a red shape like a diamond. He wore the crimson tunic of the legion, but it was threadbare.

The guard leaned over him and seized his throat with rough hands. Cassius grabbed for the man's eyes, but the chain of his shackles hindered his reach. He snatched a handful of the man's beard, and the man grunted and began to laugh. As his vision darkened, Cassius spat at the guard. Then, just as his eyes closed, the hands around his neck opened. He breathed slowly, his chest burning with the effort, and two quick slaps to the face brought him around.

He found the guard standing over him, fingering the edge of his beard where Cassius had ripped out a tuft of hair.

"Lot of fight in you, boy." The guard smiled. "Something to be proud of."

He spat on Cassius and exited the cell.

He probed his manacles in the dark, searching for any small defect. He had tried to sleep for a bit, to conserve his strength, but lying of the cool floor proved impossible. The raised bruise on the back of his head stung no matter how he positioned it.

Probably this was the blow that had laid him unconscious. He could recall his approach to the main gate and the rush of the guards when they saw he carried a legionnaire. A half dozen men surrounded him in the road, many more backing them with ranged weapons from the wall, archers with crossbows, spearmen, spellcasters.

He remembered talking calmly even as the sight of an injured Vorenicus panicked the guards. He explained that he was trying to help. And then he remembered nothing until he woke in the cell.

Had one of them circled behind him? He could not remember, but it seemed possible. That was a careless mistake, one he could not bring himself to forgive. Maybe exhaustion was wearing on him, the litany of injuries that plagued him finally overcoming his will to see this finished.

He was at their mercy now. All the plotting of the last few weeks, the manic improvisation in the face of impossible odds, had brought him only to a prison cell. Stripped even of his gauntlets. His face burned at the thought of it.

Sometimes he heard voices at the door. He thought this a

precursor to more beatings at first, but no one entered the cell, and so he listened closely to the muffled words and waited.

When next the door opened, the torchlight from the hallway hurt his eyes. The man who entered was not the bearded guard. He was tall and thickset, with long hair tied behind his head and threaded with a red feather. His hair was dark but graying, and the stubble on his jaw was all gray. Dabs of bright blue paint arced above each of his eyebrows.

"Cassius?" the long-haired man asked.

Cassius nodded.

The long-haired man removed his crimson cloak and folded it twice over his arm, so that it would not drag on the floor. He squatted onto his haunches.

"Look at me, boy."

Cassius squinted against the light.

"I'm here to ask you questions," the long-haired man said.

"All right."

"I trust you met legionnaire Flavius."

"The bearded fellow?" Cassius asked.

"That's him."

"We did meet briefly."

"What I'm telling you is the truth," the long-haired man said. "You might not believe me now, but you will. If you don't answer me, or if you lie to me, I'm going to leave Flavius alone with you again. And if you still won't talk after that, I'm going to let him kill you. Do you understand? Because you're alive only so long as you're useful. And you're useful only so long as you have answers. So be smart."

The long-haired man left the room, and when he returned, he carried a wooden stool. A lit cigar dangled from his lips. He placed the stool before Cassius and sat and took a long drag on his cigar.

"What happened to Vorenicus?" He tilted back his head, exhaled smoke.

"Is he still alive?" Cassius asked.

"Will it affect your answers?"

"No."

"Then what does it matter?"

"I dragged him out here to save his life. I'd like to know his condition."

"I'll keep that in mind." The long-haired man bit the end of the cigar and held it in his teeth. He spoke from the corner of his mouth.

"What's your name?"

"I'm sorry?"

"I'd like to know your name." Cassius wormed his shoulders and then settled.

"My name is Galerius."

"And who are you to Vorenicus?"

"That's none of your concern." Galerius removed the cigar from his mouth. He picked pieces of loose tobacco from the tip of his tongue. "And more to the point, this isn't the time for you to make inquiries. I'll let you know when that time comes. Until then, answer my damn question."

"Vorenicus was injured by a spell. I don't know what kind of spell. There was an explosion, and he collapsed. I thought he was dead at first. The rest of his men were. But then I noticed he was breathing."

"Who attacked him?"

"I don't know. It happened in the Market. The place was a battlefield by then. It could've been anyone."

"A battlefield?"

"Piso's and Cinna's men were fighting," Cassius said. "It was total war."

"And why was Vorenicus there?"

"He was trying to stop the fighting."

"I see." Galerius tapped his ashes onto the floor. He blew on the lit end of the cigar.

"You don't believe me."

"I didn't say that. I'm just wondering why Vorenicus didn't send a runner for reinforcements. He had roughly fifty men stationed with him. Seems odd that he would march out into—what did you call it, a battlefield? Seems odd he would march out into a battlefield undermanned."

"The fight escalated quickly." Cassius felt his calm returning now that his world had shrunk to a cell, his options limited, and his fate all but sealed. There was strength in knowing you were already dead. "I can't speak to his intentions. But maybe he thought he could contain it when it first started, when the fighting was on a small scale. And then once Piso and Cinna's forces grew, the best he could do was a fighting retreat."

"Well, that would make sense. But why haven't we heard word from the legionnaires in the city about this skirmish yet?"

"Because they're dead. Weren't you listening to me? They're all dead. And Vorenicus would've been too if I hadn't pulled him out of there."

"How noble of you." Galerius rolled the cigar between his thumb and forefinger.

"What do you think? That I kidnapped him? Kidnapped him and brought him to the legion's fort? Does that make any sense?"

"Very little of this makes sense."

"Send scouts to the city. Have them check the Market. They'll see it's ash now. Tell them to look for legionnaires. I'll bet they won't find one still breathing."

"Bet your life on it?"

He sprang awake when the door opened. He had been sleeping sitting up although he did not know for how long. Snippets of a dream returned to him, a dream about the bathhouse attendant Tadua. He could not recall it in detail, but a sense of sadness lingered.

The bearded guard stood in the doorway, grinning smugly, his hands behind his back. Cassius decided this would be the end. The guard would beat him again, and during the beating, Cassius would provoke the guard until he killed him.

He had not considered this for very long. The guilt that accompanied the realization made him feel reduced, as though his bones had been hollowed. But he could not endure another beating like the first. Not without the ability to fight back. It was too much to ask of him. Naked and unarmed, shackled in a lightless cell. There were no angles for him to play.

If he could even talk to someone again, there at least he could make a play, turn a man's heart, exploit his weaknesses, his greed or vanity, break his will or embolden him to an action that suited Cassius. But with hands at his throat, there was no chance for words.

He tried to comfort himself with the thought that he had come this far when others would have failed to accomplish even that.

And then he recalled a voice that was not his own. He did not remember where he had heard it, but he was certain of the words.

You die when you flee your true path. Until then, there is nothing in this mortal world to stop you.

The guard stepped into the room, his hands still hidden. Cassius rose to his feet.

"Safer for a prisoner to kneel when a guard's present. Otherwise, it might seem he's of a mind to do something stupid."

Cassius remained standing.

"Insolent little bastard, aren't you? Well, I've got something for you."

"I've been hurt worse," Cassius said. "And by better men than you."

"What makes you think I've done my worst?"

The guard glared at Cassius, and Cassius met his stare silently. The guard laughed.

"Hell, boy. You are something else." He pulled his hands from behind his back and he held a bowl of porridge in one and a half loaf of bread in the other. "But no dancing for you tonight. Just a bit of grub."

The guard offered the food to Cassius and Cassius made no move to accept it.

"Not hungry? I'll just leave it for you to pick at." The guard dropped the bowl and the bread. The bowl landed right side up and he kicked it over, spilling the porridge into the stagnant water. He turned to leave.

"Tonight?" Cassius said. "That means I've been here a full day?"

The guard checked himself, just a brief pause but one Cassius noticed. Then he stepped through the doorway and closed the door behind him.

. . .

There was a rat in the cell. Cassius heard it creeping through the water. It was trying for the food but not making a direct move. Cassius wondered if it could see him in the dark or if there was another sense at work. Smell maybe or sound? Or maybe something else entirely, some vague conception of a malignant force hovering in the near dark.

After a time, he could hear the rat scraping at the bread and he stomped his foot down into the water and the rat raced away and he listened to hear which wall it had wormed into.

The door opened suddenly. He shielded his eyes from the light. Galerius's voice greeted him.

"Get up," he said.

Cassius rose, and Galerius tossed him a tunic.

"Dress yourself and follow me." Galerius stepped outside.

It was not Cassius's tunic, but a fresh one, slate gray and stiff from a recent washing. He tried to don it, but his shackles made that an impossible task. He entered the hallway naked.

Galerius was standing with the bearded guard, who held a pair of sandals.

"Hard of hearing, boy?"

Cassius held his hands up, shook his chains.

At a nod from Galerius the guard placed the sandals on the ground and pulled Cassius's hands close and unlocked the shackles. In the torchlight of the hallway, Cassius could see his hands were swollen, discolored. He rubbed his left wrist, tested that hand's range of motion delicately. Then he donned the fresh tunic and kneeled and strapped the sandals to his feet.

Galerius headed down the hallway, and the bearded guard motioned for Cassius to follow, which Cassius did, the bearded guard at his back.

"Where are you taking me?" Cassius asked.

"The general wants to see you," Galerius said without turning.

It was dark outside, the sky moonless and clear. Cassius had arrived at the fort at sunrise, which meant he had been imprisoned no less than a day. Maybe two. It felt like two. He had never spent time in a jail cell, though, and maybe the passage of time there felt different.

They were inside the fort, waiting by the squat stone jail. The general arrived with an armed escort, a legionnaire on either side of him and one behind him wielding a crossbow.

He was a small man and solidly built. His hair was gray and close-cropped, almost shaved, as though he were some raw recruit newly arrived at his first post. He wore a rich, short cloak the same red as his tunic and trimmed in yellow. He wore it draped over one shoulder, covering half his body, a display fashionable amongst spellcasters who fought in the arena circuits, so that crowds and opponents could recognize them by their standard. His bore the image of an eagle with spread wings, one talon gripping a spear, the other a bolt of lightning He kept his arms tucked inside his loose-fitting tunic, and no gauntlets hung from his belt.

He spoke briefly with Galerius, the bearded guard bowing low at his approach, then he stood before Cassius. He had a long nose, a heavily lined brow. His eyes were deep-set, dark.

"I'm General Quintus." His voice was firm, weary.

"I know who you are," Cassius said. He thought his voice might waver, but it did not.

"You look like you've just seen a ghost."

"I don't believe in ghosts."

"Walk the jungle at night. You'll believe then." Quintus's face was grave, as though warning a traveler of danger on the road ahead.

"I'm game if you are."

"Right now?" Quintus's brows arched.

"Make a believer out of me."

Moving behind Quintus, he could see the outer wall of the fort above the nearby buildings, most of which were shapes of black against a black sky, so that he could not tell which was a barracks house, nor which a granary or administrative building. He had studied the legion's standard for fort construction, though, and had visited this place in his mind many times.

They passed through the gates, and here Quintus waved away his escort. One of the men protested, but Quintus stood firm.

"Never ghost hunt in a pack," he said offhandedly, as though this were common knowledge.

They descended a road that was not the one Cassius had ridden to the fort. It was unpaved, narrow for a highway. Overgrowth loomed on either side, and tree limbs stretched across its expanse, roofing it, so that it appeared more like a tunnel than a road, and a tunnel near to collapse.

"Where does this lead?" Cassius asked.

"North." Quintus gestured forward.

"And what's north?"

"Jungle. Jungle all the way to the ocean."

"It just leads into the jungle?"

"It leads through the jungle. The only way into the jungle is to step off the road."

Quintus was in the overgrowth now. He seemed to move through it with little difficulty. He tossed the short cloak over one shoulder and slid his arms out of his tunic. He was unarmed.

Cassius kept directly behind him but still had trouble navigating the brush. Low-hanging branches scratched at his face. His feet caught in fallen vines.

Quintus kneeled, motioned for Cassius to do the same.

"Now we wait," Quintus whispered.

"For ghosts?"

"To make a believer out of you."

The smell of the jungle was wet and lush. They had stepped only yards off the road, but it was hotter here, and already Cassius was sweating. Mosquitoes buzzed the scabs on his forearms.

"Why did you bring me here?" Cassius asked.

"You wanted to come."

"I mean why summon me from my cell?"

"Would you rather go back?" Quintus asked.

"Is that a threat?"

"I don't make threats, Cassius."

The sound of his name sent a chill up his spine.

"And to answer your question," Quintus said, "I brought you here because my son is not well. And I would have some questions answered."

"And you want to hear the answers? Not Galerius?"

"I don't need Galerius to tell me when a man is lying."

"Does that mean your runners to the city have returned?"

Quintus was silent.

"That's what I figure," Cassius continued. "The runners returned and they confirmed what I told Galerius and now you need me to describe the situation in the city. Did your men have trouble getting into Hightown? Is that what this is about?"

"Keep your voice down."

"Cinna won't talk, will he? Or if he is talking, he's not making sense. And, of course, he won't let the runners pass through the Market to Lowtown. Then you'd have Piso's perspective and maybe could piece together your own version of events. So you're stuck with me, last man out of Scipio."

"There. Do you see it?"

Cassius squinted into the distance. He could see only jungle at first, then he glimpsed movement. Through the brush emerged three figures bathed in light the color of rum. Tall and lithe, they moved with a fussy, catlike grace. They were nude and painted smoke white, and their long hair, dark and straight, bounced at their backs. As they drew closer, he could see they were women. The one in the lead carried a large candle with both hands and she had a belt of shells around her waist that made noise as she walked. The other two held what looked like parcels suspended from braided tethers.

"Lost your heart?" Quintus whispered.

"Who are they?" Cassius looked up. The tops of the black trees were limned like teeth against a shelf of white stars, as though he were staring out from inside a mouth about to close.

"Native emissaries."

The three halted. They were facing the fort now. The one in the lead raised her candle high and kneeled and stood again. She loosed a long wailing cry, almost singing.

"What are they doing?"

"Making offerings."

The two began to spin their parcels overhead in wide circles.

"Of what?" Cassius asked.

"Skulls."

"Human skulls?"

"Anything less would be an insult."

The two released the skulls, which sailed crashing through the jungle.

"They're trying to ransom back someone they lost," Quintus said.

"From who?"

"From me. From Death himself as far as they're concerned."

The lead woman blew out her candle and threw it. The three figures turned abruptly and began to walk back into the jungle from which they came. They moved stiffly at first but after a dozen steps they all three broke into a panicked run, charging like hunted boars. The brush seemed to swallow them.

"You're a smart man, Cassius."

Quintus sat before a small hearth in his apartments, watching the flames lick at a kettle that hung in the fire, the kettle steaming and whistling.

"I don't know about that." Cassius sat cross-legged on a pile of strange skins and furs. The room was heavy with a warm, wet smell. The wood of the walls seemed waterlogged, and the steady dripping noise on the ceiling meant that a light rain was falling outside.

"The way you guessed my position earlier. I'd call that smart."

"I'd call it observant. There's a difference." Cassius rubbed his eyes. He was exhausted after his stay in the cell, his body sore and weary. His head throbbed.

The room was large but cluttered. A round table dominated the center, big enough to support a massive feast but littered with scrolls and maps instead, dice, bones that might have been human or animal. A diviner's deck of ivory tiles was played out across half its surface.

"Observant?" Quintus said. "You were locked in a jail cell for a day. What was there to observe? No, the skill you employed was projection. You were able to see outside yourself. To judge my options and to know which I'd pick and why. Ever consider a life in the legion, boy? You'd make a hell of a tactician."

"Are you willing to hire me?"

Quintus smiled, the first smile Cassius had seen from him. "There are rumors about you."

"Should I be worried?"

"You worked for Cinna, is that true?"

"It is," Cassius said.

"And then double-crossed him for Piso."

"Also true. Although I'd take exception with the term double-cross. He meant to have me killed. I was a mercenary. I owed him nothing."

"And you'd work for me if I paid you?" Quintus asked.

"I would."

"At what price?"

"I'm sure you'll offer compensation to match my skill."

"So your loyalty is to the highest bidder?"

"I fought to save your son," Cassius said. He fixed Quintus with his gaze. The general's eyes were deep and black, like two holes bored into his skull. "And in doing that, I ruined every contact I had in this city. I'm unemployable now. I'd hate to seem crass, but yes, it's true, if you don't hire me, I won't find work on this island. I will serve you well for your money, though."

"There's talk that you had a hand in the troubles at the Market."

"Talk from who?"

Quintus shrugged. "There's always someone willing to talk in Scipio."

"Can you trust these talkers? Half of them would sell their children for the right price."

"Did you have a hand in the troubles?"

Cassius sat up straight. He could feel Quintus watching him, measuring each reaction. The thought made his heart quicken, and his weariness ebbed. He could remain calm in the face of monsters and storms of fire, but the general's stare unsettled him.

"I fought at the Market," he said. "So did half the killers employed by both bosses. Should I be chastised both for disloyalty and for doing the job I was paid to do?"

"There's talk you helped instigate it."

"The bad blood in that city was there before I ever set foot on this island."

The kettle continued to whistle. Quintus lifted it from the fire, his hand wrapped in a thick rag. He carried the kettle to a small desk, where two glazed ceramic cups were set, the cups decorated each with the image of a crane in flight.

"Porcelain," Quintus said. "From the Eastern kingdom of Xin." He poured each cup half-full of steaming water and placed the kettle on top of the hearth. He searched the desk drawers until he found a small wooden box and a spoon. He opened the box and spooned out two portions of a brown powder into each cup, then stirred the cups and carried both across the room, offering one to Cassius.

"What is this?" Cassius asked.

"Something to help you sleep."

"What makes you think I need help sleeping?"

"Must everything be a confrontation? I'm extending some hospitality. Accept the gesture in the spirit it was offered. I'm not trying to poison you." And then, as though to drive home the point, Quintus drank.

Cassius held the cup close to his face and inhaled, trying not to appear as though he were scenting it for toxins. He took a small sip, then, as Quintus watched, a bigger one.

"And if I were trying to kill you, I'd have soaked your cup in scorpion venom long before you ever set eyes on it." Quintus laughed. A barking, unpleasant sound.

"You're funnier than I thought you'd be."

"Did you give much thought to my sense of humor?"

"Some." Cassius set down the cup.

"Well, I'm full of surprises."

"Why don't you wear your gauntlets?"

"Why would I wear them?" Quintus asked. "For protection?"

"A spellcaster always wears his gauntlets. I've not felt myself all day without mine."

"Is that your way of asking for them back?"

"I figured they'd have been split up and the spells sold off already."

"Do you think so little of me, Cassius."

"Will you answer my question?"

Quintus held his hand in midair. He did not speak, but only looked at the hand, and seeing where his attention was focused, Cassius watched as well. The hand trembled.

It was a slight motion, but it continued without pause until finally Quintus clenched the hand into a fist and folded his arms across his chest, tucking his hands one under each armpit.

"Answer enough?" Quintus asked.

"That's not an uncommon ailment."

"It's a sign."

"Sign that you should give up your spells?" Cassius asked.

"My body can't handle the energies I wielded. I was hurting myself."

"You're touched."

Quintus was silent.

"I am, too," Cassius said.

"Well, that makes sense. A man as young as you, fighting as well as you do. You would have to be either gifted or well trained."

"I'm well trained, too."

"Where did you study?" Quintus asked.

"The Isle of Twelve."

"You don't have to lie to impress me."

"I'm not lying."

"You don't lie?"

"I do," Cassius said.

"But not now?"

"Not to you."

"Why?"

"I want you to know who I really am."

Quintus sat on the edge of his large table. He prodded a pile of trinkets with his index finger, a piece of jade, a silver necklace, some whittled ivory ruined by a bad craftsman.

"So you trained in the best spellcaster school in all the world?"

"I don't know if it's the best," Cassius said. "But they train the touched exclusively."

"Are the rumors true? Do they make you sleep on rocks? Feed you once a week? Beat you daily?"

"It was a hard life there."

"Why endure that?"

"To make myself strong."

"Shouldn't you still be there? They train students for decades."

"I ran away."

"Had enough of that rot?"

"I wanted to work."

"In Scipio?"

Cassius nodded.

"Strange choice," Quintus said.

"I felt it calling me."

"Maybe that was just a voice in your head."

Cassius looked to Quintus. "Have you ever felt that?"

"A voice in my head?"

"Yes."

"They say I'm mad, don't they?" Quintus asked. "Too much spell-casting, right? Or else it's in my blood?"

"Your father was a spellcaster, wasn't he?"

"Touched. Like me. And his father before him and his father before him."

"It skipped Vorenicus though," Cassius said.

"I held out hope for years. When you're touched, the ability comes late. I was fourteen before it happened to me."

"I was a little younger than that."

"But it never came to Vorenicus. It upset me for a while, that we wouldn't share this. But now I think it's for the best."

"How is he?"

Quintus shook his head. "Not well."

"I'm sorry to hear that."

"I have healers working on him now. It's a slow process when dealing with a head injury. Or so they say. They're terrified of his waking up without the ability to speak or some such thing."

"You don't trust their talents?"

"Would you? You're a killer. How do you feel about healers?"

"They're hacks. Or else too scared to put their abilities to a true test."

"A true test?"

Cassius raised his hands as though to cast a spell.

Quintus smiled again. "Be careful, boy. Wave your hands like that at me, and I might take you up on the challenge."

"I don't have my gauntlets."

"And if I gave them back? Would you accept?"

Cassius was silent.

Quintus laughed. "A wise answer."

A light, airy feeling filled Cassius's chest now. The pain in his arms dulled. He felt straighter, as though the tension in his shoulders had been massaged away.

"What's in that tea?" Cassius asked.

"Why did you save my son's life?"

"Answer mine, and I'll answer yours."

"It's an old Native concoction. In strong enough doses, those animals use it to perform surgery. They could cut your foot off, and you wouldn't know it was missing for half a day. Or care for that matter." Quintus downed the rest of his drink, setting the cup on the table afterward like proof of the deed.

"I admire Vorenicus," Cassius said.

"You must take me for a fool. Feed me a line like that. Has the tea gone to your head already, boy? I thought we were being honest here."

"I meant what I said."

"Admire him for what?" Quintus asked.

"For the same reason the people in that city laughed at him. He believed in something. Had the conviction to work for it."

"That's my fault probably. I loved him too much."

Cassius looked away.

"I raised him soft," Quintus said. "Might have done him some good to see a bit of hardship."

"Oftentimes, that's the crime of a mother."

"His mother died in childbirth. He never knew her. If there's blame to be laid, it rests with me."

"What will be your response to Piso and Cinna?" Cassius asked.

"I haven't decided yet."

"It doesn't seem like such a tough choice to me. They slaughtered fifty of your men. And nearly killed your son. They have to be held accountable for their actions."

"So I should march the legion down there this very night? Wake the whole lot of those bastards with a rain of arrows and fire and the like?"

"They'll think you weak otherwise."

Quintus's eyes grew sharp, focused. "They're not stupid enough or blind enough to think me weak."

"So why not show them your might?"

"Because if what you say is true, if they're fighting amongst themselves, then they're doing my work for me. If I show up at the gates with three thousand men, then those two whoresons will stop killing each other and join forces to fight me. And that's a headache I don't need right now. So let them fight till their exhausted. And then I'll smack their hands like the naughty children they are."

"What of your men?" Cassius asked. "Won't they be mad, you leaving the deaths of their brothers unpunished?"

"You think there's a man in this fort who hasn't seen a brother killed in action?"

"And if Vorenicus dies? What then?"

Quintus turned to the hearth. He considered the fire.

"I think that's enough talk for tonight."

THE ONLY DEFEAT IS DEATH

O n the Isle of Twelve, they called him Spider, but in the world between, the voice called him by his true name. A boy of fourteen, he had been training for six months when an errant spell during a sparring match sent him tumbling into a ravine. The spell had loosed a concentrated shock wave meant to disorient him, but Spider had been fighting recklessly. Overconfident, he had lowered his guard while pressing an attack, and the shock wave, a spell he otherwise would have recognized and avoided, struck him with full force.

He had angled his sparring partner, a boy two years his senior, to the edge of a cliff, hoping to force him to yield. The boy, named Walrus, was doughy and slow but had a patient disposition and had timed his strike perfectly. Spider was unconscious before he hit the ground.

His momentum as he fell carried him off the edge of the cliff. He fell for twenty feet and landed on his back, lying motionless in the ravine for hours. Walrus took his time in getting help. He walked back to the initiate barracks slowly, spent time searching for a senior initiate instead of alerting the first person he saw, and then, as the sun set, had difficulty locating the cliff where the boys had sparred.

All the while, Spider lay dying, his mind adrift in the void and a faint voice from behind him calling his true name.

The Masters did not expect him to live.

"Dead by morning," Master Tarek declared, standing over the boy in the dank confines of the infirmary. The light of dozens of candles played across Spider's broken body. His chest and belly purpled with deep bruises, his ribs mashed, back broken.

In the void, Spider never heard this pronouncement. He floated in the dark, listening to a lullaby about rain and a river.

The next morning found Spider still alive in the infirmary, his blood soaking into the stone table. He breathed in shallow, ragged gasps, muttered incomprehensibly. Master Tarek was impressed by the boy's resolve.

"It seems he wishes to live." Tarek stood over Spider's body, probing with indelicate hands. He pressed on ribs, felt them crunch and shift under his finger. He palpated the bruised belly, watched as Spider writhed and moaned in response. "Very well then. Summon the underclassmen. We'll let them practice their healing spells."

The initiates spent all afternoon casting healing spells on Spider's body. Inexperienced and with little concern for Spider's life, they eschewed the reserved approach of most healers. They knit bones in hours that a practiced hand might take days to mend. All the while, Spider bucked and sweated on the stone table, his hands and feet lashed to keep him from resisting.

In the place between, Spider felt himself floating through endless fire, his world reduced to searing pain. In the distance, he heard a familiar voice calling to him. The voice was faint, barely discernible. *"Stay your path,"* the voice said. *"Nothing will stop you."*

The initiates finished their practice by sundown, and Spider passed a tortured night in the infirmary. He drifted between waking and dreaming, sometimes listening to the sound of the voice, sometimes hearing his own screams. All the while, his body hummed with remembered pain.

When he woke the next morning, he found Master Tarek standing over him.

Master Tarek was a short man, bronze-skinned, with a long, thin mustache and curly hair. He wore a purple robe with a high collar trimmed in gold thread. A long scar snaked up the side of his neck and the back of his head, ending just behind his right ear.

"I did not expect to see you breathing this morning." Master Tarek eyed Spider curiously.

Spider made to respond, but his mouth was dry, his throat raw, and he could muster only a croak.

"Easy now." Master Tarek patted Spider's arm. His hand was cold and his touch made Spider's skin crawl. "Don't strain yourself, you've been through enough already. The initiates worked on you for the better part of a day."

Spider could barely recall drifting in darkness, but the agony that had nearly overwhelmed him in the place between was still fresh in his memory. Anger built inside him, and he made to sit up, eager to choke the smug smirk from Master Tarek's face. But as he reached, leather restraints dug into his wrists, bound him to the table.

"You forget yourself, my little Spider." Master Tarek squeezed Spider's forearm, his fingernails digging thin half-moons into flesh. "It's death to touch a Master. Would you endure all that suffering, clinging defiantly to a flicker of life, only to see yourself snuffed for such a transgression?"

Spider breathed deep and lay back on the cool stone. He shut his eyes, unable to bear the sight of Master Tarek.

"You think I've done you harm, but you're wrong." Master Tarek's voice sounded harsh and piercing, like a mistuned lyre. "I've taught you a great lesson these last days, and if you wish to become something more than you are, you'll heed it."

Spider licked his cracked lips. If his mouth were not so dry, he would have spat.

"You heard a voice in your head. Did you not?"

Spider remained still.

"Answer or don't, it matters little. I know you've heard it because I've heard it as well. All the great Masters have. It's the voice of madness, worming through the dark of your mind. It will eat you if you let it."

A voice. Spider had the faintest memory of a voice. He could not recall what it said, but it was there, just beneath the memory of pain.

"Look at me, boy."

Spider felt cold fingers grip his face. He opened his eyes.

"It speaks to all of us who have endured pain, who have slipped through Death's grasp." Master Tarek's face twisted with rage. His skin flushed red, the long scar on his neck shining white. "It is the voice of madness, but also the voice of greatness. It will eat you if you let it, but only if you let it. If you survive it, if you listen, there is much to learn. Do you understand me?"

Spider closed his eyes. Master Tarek released his face.

"You hate me now, boy. And maybe you're right to hate me. But there aren't many people in this world willing to teach you such a lesson." Spider heard the Master's sandaled feet scrape across the stone floor. His voice grew distant. "Get some rest. And when you wake, you're welcome to come to my chambers. You may thank me or try to kill me, the choice is yours. That is our way."

16

They made a place for him in the barracks. There were forty men in the room and forty cots. Cassius was offered a pile of blankets near the door. It was late, and all were asleep.

In the time between sleeping and waking, he thought he heard a voice calling to him. Sometimes he could understand its speech and sometimes it was like listening to an unfamiliar tongue. It was addressing him, though, that much was clear.

He left just before dawn, the legionnaires still asleep except for the few who departed to man early posts. Flies had gathered over his wounded arms and he shook these off now and rose and folded his bedroll and wandered out into the fort. He watched the mist retreat from the jungle under the approaching light of the sun.

He wondered how he had arrived here. He had pictured himself in this place many times, but now he was here although the odds against that were staggering. He could trace his steps back, but following his trip, point to point, was only a partial answer. He was aware of the disparity between what he was now and what he had been, and his transformation from one to the other was closer to what he sought although still incomplete.

Growth was the wrong word for it. It was more akin to a diminution. He had shed something of himself many times along the way and what was left was here because there was no place else it could be.

Looking back, he wondered where lay the line past which he could not return. Had he even noticed when crossing it and what had he forfeited there?

A handful of legionnaires were about, but no one asked his business. Camp attendants scurried from building to building, emptying chamber pots, feeding dying hearth fires, carrying laundry. Most of these were Native women or young Native girls. They spoke their own tongue and he listened to it in the quiet of the morning and his stomach knotted to hear it.

He moved deeper into the complex. There was a small clearing to the side of the general's quarters and here stood a large stone statue of a spellcaster in full legion battle dress, segmented steel cuirass, greaves, widebrimmed helmet, short cloak, gauntleted hands raised to the sky, a swirl of sculpted fire at his feet. He was advancing, head upturned, as though prepared to climb over the outer wall and march into the jungle.

Someone called his name, and he turned to see Galerius walking with a man who held a ledger.

"Early to rise I see," Galerius said. "In another life, you could have made a good legionnaire."

"Maybe in this life," Cassius said.

"Admiring the statue."

"It's quite a piece of work."

"It's of the general's father, in his younger days."

"Is the resemblance any good?"

"It captures his spirit at least."

Galerius produced an oilskin bundle from the pouch on his hip and handed the parcel to Cassius without naming it although Cassius knew its contents by the way his fingers warmed to touch it.

"These are a gift from the general."

"Does the general often make a habit of gifting people with their own property?" Cassius unwrapped the gauntlets and hitched them to a thin chain on his belt, the jewels rainbowing in the dawnlight.

"I was referring to your right to carry them in the fort."

"I'm grateful. I had a coin purse, too."

Galerius seemed surprised by this. He opened his hip pouch and rooted inside and produced a few silver coins, offering them to Cassius.

"I had more than that when I was taken," Cassius said.

"It's all I can spare."

Cassius accepted the coins and slipped them into a small pocket in his tunic.

"How was your talk with the general last night?" Galerius asked.

"Informative." Cassius scratched at his bandaged arms. "We spoke of the city."

"I'm sure you did."

"What are his intentions?"

"Only the general knows his thoughts."

"And yours? Do you plan to stay idle while Piso and Cinna sit unpunished?" Cassius voice was edged with challenge.

Galerius stiffened. He had the reserve of a well-trained soldier, his anger hidden behind a stoic face.

"I won't discuss that with you," he said.

It was clear Galerius was not a man accustomed to insolent tones. Still he had not dressed down Cassius, a subtle sign but an important one. Cassius held no rank here, wore neither the legion colors nor the mark of either boss, yet Galerius, a man of considerable authority, did not speak freely to him. Power was in flux here, flowing, shifting. It was a familiar feeling to a spellcaster, one Cassius relished.

"Any word from the bosses?" Cassius asked.

"That's none of your concern."

"And how is Vorenicus?"

"Progress has been slow."

"I'd like to pay a call on the general this morning."

"I'll see about that. He hasn't been feeling well today." Galerius nodded stiffly and began to walk off, the man with the ledger at his heels. "There's a physician's tent by the eastern granary. See that those arms are tended to before they rot off."

At the physician's tent, he stripped naked and washed himself with buckets of cold water. The physician was a young Native man with a long, sharp face. He had an old woman for an assistant, and they spoke the Khimir tongue openly while he bathed, mocking him.

They called him skinny and sickly and they made an informal wager as to how long before one of his wounds infected and killed him.

"Are you sure you won't see a healer?" The physician's Antiochi was impeccable.

"No healers," Cassius said.

"Some of these wounds are beyond me."

"Do what you can."

The physician smeared the wounds on Cassius's arms with a cool salve, then held Cassius's arms while his assistant wrapped them in fresh bandages.

"How much will this cost?" Cassius asked.

"Three silvers," the physician said.

"That's a bit steep."

"The general wants you in fighting shape, so he's picking up the tab."

"Can you give me something to ease the pain?"

"Kaota leaves. Chew them for a few hours. Don't swallow them, though, or you'll get sick."

"I'd like something else as well," Cassius said. "If you have it to sell."

"What exactly?"

"Garza root."

The physician dropped a pair of bloody scissors into an earthenware bowl. He wiped his hands with excess bandages.

"When's the last time you slept?" he asked.

"I slept last night," Cassius said.

"It doesn't look like you did."

"Are you saying I'm lying?"

"I'm saying you look like a man who hasn't slept in a month. And the last thing someone like that needs is Garza root."

"What do you care, I'm a dead man anyway." Cassius heard the words as though they had been spoken by someone else. He was unsure if he had said them aloud, or if they had even come from him, but the physician's look was proof enough.

"I don't think that's something the general will pay for."

"I'll cover it, then."

"It will cost you."

"It always does."

. . .

He watched a thousand legionnaires drill in the early afternoon. Separated into three squads, they marched from one end of the fort to the other. They presented their arms. They formed themselves into a wedge, then re-formed into an inverse wedge, a diamond. They made themselves into a tortoise, a circular formation in which each man held up his shield and the men in the middle ranks lifted their shields overhead and spears bristled from all angles. Above them, disks of whirling fire spun and shed sparks.

When they fell back to marching formation, they filed out of the fort. They passed the barricades and moved out into the clearing before the jungle and there split into smaller groups, to skirmish with wooden weapons. The sound of their boots in lockstep made him uneasy.

"It's a beautiful thing."

He turned and found the general two paces behind him. He looked ill. He stood with his shoulders stooped, head lowered. His wide brows were furrowed and sweaty. He was wearing the same tunic as yesterday although he had shed the short cloak. His clothes seemed too big for him, as if his body had shrunk beneath their folds.

"What is?" Cassius spat a wad of bitter Kaota leaves and wiped his mouth.

"War."

"Do you believe that?"

"It's not a popular thing to say. But it's true. And if you speak to someone who talks truthfully about war, they'll tell you as much."

"What about spilled entrails?" Cassius asked. "That's a part I've always found unpleasant."

"It's not only beautiful. It's other things as well. It's horrific and frightening, mean, cruel. But if you talk about it completely, then you have to be thorough as well as honest. And if you are both these things, you will admit it is beautiful. Troop formations. Glistening weapons, armor. The effects of spells. The martial beat of the drums. Flags and standards. There's nothing like it."

"I never thought of it that way."

The general reached into a pocket and brought out a wide green leaf, rolled and wrapped with twine. He untied it and peeled open the leaf carefully. It was filled with a brown powder like the kind he had poured into the tea. He tilted the leaf's contents into his mouth, swallowed, then licked the leaf, crumpled it, and tucked it into his cheek.

Cassius looked away. "Are you okay, sir?"

"What do you mean?"

"You don't look well."

"I'm fine." The general's cheek bulged from his chewed leaf. "Forgive me for mistaking you for a man cultured enough to hold a conversation."

"I didn't mean to offend you."

"When a man talks with you, it's a violation of his trust to dismiss what he's saying."

"I'm sorry," Cassius said.

"You harden your heart to a man when you won't listen to him."

"Forgive me. I've forgotten my manners after my time here. I've found cities will do that to a man."

The general licked his dry lips. "I haven't left this island in years. The mainland is just a memory now. And I've never been to the capital. I fear I'll never make it now."

"Why?"

"My father died on this island. His last command. Same for my grandfather in the Jutlander wastes. My great-grandfather in the Fathalan borderlands."

"You're not dead yet."

"Last night, I dreamed you killed me."

"Sir?"

"You were a spider." The general's eyes were locked in a faraway stare. "You wore your web for a mask, and you crawled through my window while I slept."

"That was just a dream."

"I knew you'd say that."

"Sir, please."

"The Natives believe the dream world is as real as this one. More real in some senses."

"Do you believe that?" Cassius asked.

"Maybe."

"And if it is true, what does it mean? That I'm a spider? That doesn't make any sense."

"I don't know. But there's someone I can ask."

They had been traveling north for an hour when the sun set. They were six men in total. The general and Cassius, four guards. The road, which leading from the fort had seemed crowded by jungle life, had ceased to be a road, devolving into a footworn path through brush. The feeling Cassius had experienced on his first trip into the brush, of being pressed in on all sides, was gone now. They had passed into the tangle completely.

The overgrowth seemed to writhe as Cassius moved through it, everything wet and dripping. Bushes shook and buzzed. Strange cries echoed overhead. Twice he thought he heard drumming in the near distance, but each time that he stopped to listen, it faded.

The general muttered to himself as he walked, angry whispers the guards pretended not to hear. He fought his way forward, shaking vines, snapping branches, yet seemed surefooted and comfortable in his movements.

They came across a young Native boy, but before they could speak he fled, slinking away in a crash of jungle noises, birdcalls, monkey howls, the rustle of leaves. Later, a wild boar crossed their path and a guard hurled his spear at it but missed and lost the spear.

When they reached the clearing, Cassius saw the huts first, then saw the body. A wide opening in a wall of pricker shrubs led to a clearing, and here stood the body. It hung impaled through the chest, head down, arms tied behind its back. It looked shriveled, little more than a skeleton wrapped in skin, blackened and dried. Its hair swayed stiffly in a breeze.

"What is that?" he asked.

No one answered. They continued walking, diverting around the gruesome marker, and now he saw two more bodies impaled behind and to either side of the first. One of these, a body so small it might have been a child's, was missing its head. The stench seemed a physical presence.

The general shouted that he was come to see the wise grandfather, shouted this in the Native tongue. There were three mud huts in the clearing, each roofed with jungle leaves. From the two closest huts emerged four legionnaires, their faces painted red. They had long hair and wore mantles of bright feathers and bone. At first, Cassius thought them Natives dressed in the colors of the legion but he could see that they were Antiochi when he looked closely.

They saluted the general in the manner of the legion, tapping a fist to their heart. He acknowledged them with a nod, then two of the men entered the hut farthest from the opening. They returned moments later, dragging an old Native man between them.

"Good day to you, grandfather," the general said, still speaking in the Khimir tongue.

The guards forced the Native man to his knees before the general, forced him to bow his head till it touched the ground. They released him, and he rose slowly and with great effort.

"Why have you called on me?" The Native man was short and fat. He had slender arms and a distended belly, wide hips leading down to wide, stubby legs. His hairline had receded to the middle of his head, and his gray hair hung to his shoulders, straight and thin. He was shirtless, his soft chest painted with swirls of red and black, and he wore long shorts and was barefoot.

"I need your eyes to see what I cannot."

"What troubles you?" The Native man was missing most of his bottom teeth and all but two of his upper teeth, which were black, separated by a wide space.

"I died in my dreams last night. Murdered by this man."

The Native man looked to Cassius. His eyes were small and thick-lidded, with hardly any white. He had big pupils that shone with the last bit of sunlight, a sharp, hard luster like the gleam on obsidian.

"Who is this man to you?"

"No one," Quintus said. "A mercenary. He claims to have saved my son's life, but I cannot be sure. He confounds me."

"He has the metal hands and carries the secret of fire in his blood as you do."

"He does."

"Have him tell me his name."

The general turned to Cassius. "He wants to know your name."

"I'm called Cassius." He spoke slowly and overloud.

"Have you tried to kill him?" the Native man asked. "If you fear him so much, why not be rid of him?"

"I think he might be valuable," Quintus said. "If he is not lying to me, if he is what he claims to be, he can be an asset."

"He has seen much hardship. It is a wonder he is not dead already. Maybe it is for the best that you do not try to kill him. He might be cursed."

"Cursed how?"

"Cursed to be unkillable."

"Can you see into his heart?" Quintus asked.

"I will try. Let me prepare while the sun fades. I will be ready shortly."

The Native man retired to his hut. The legionnaires lit torches and staked them into long poles outside each hut and on either side of the entrance to the clearing. The general sat with his back pressed against one of the huts and ate another leaf packed with brown powder.

"Who is that man?" Cassius asked.

"A former chief of the Natives," Quintus said.

"What's he doing here?"

"He's my prisoner. Has been for years now."

"The ghosts offering ransom last night. They were trying to buy him back from you?"

The general nodded.

"Why did you take him?" Cassius asked.

"He was an instigator. I had to stop his troublemaking."

"Why not kill him?"

"He'd become a martyr. And while he's alive, custom dictates the tribes can't officially recognize a new chieftain. So a number of factions are jockeying for interim power."

"And none can gain the support he had?"

"Precisely."

"Couldn't they come capture him back? He's so far from the fort. Guarded by just a handful of men."

"If they took him against my will, they know I'd retaliate. To hear him tell it, they think me some vengeful god come to punish them for straying from the old ways. It's not easy to encourage men to fight what they think is beyond them. Easier to prove their bravery killing each other. At least that's an enemy they understand."

By the opposite huts, the guards were sharing a few thin cigars. They were two distinct groups, the soldiers from the fort forming one unit, the others, in their outlandish dress, a separate set.

Cassius nodded toward them. "Why do they wear those costumes?"

"It heartens them," Quintus said. "They think it lends them some of the power of the jungle. Not all, of course. Some disdain it. But the ones stationed at forward posts always adopt it. Given enough time."

"Doesn't it hurt discipline?"

"The uniform code is relaxed when a legion is in the field during wartime."

"Has the senate declared this a war?"

The general rubbed the underside of his chin, scratching at the fresh stubble there.

"I know what a war looks like. I don't need the senate's help with that."

The Native man appeared in the doorway of his hut. He held a clutch of what looked like yellow-green sprouts, the sprouts afire and spreading thick white smoke. He dusted the entranceway with the smoke and stepped outside and did the same to the roof and then entered the hut again.

"What's he doing?" Cassius asked. Although an accomplished practitioner of Rune magic, his arcane knowledge did not extend to older magics, ancient sorceries and enchantments. They produced in him the same unease that the sight of his gauntlets produced in others.

"I don't understand his methods," Quintus said.

"Are those bodies his handiwork?"

"No, they're his family."

"Your handiwork then?"

"Yes."

"To humiliate him?"

"To remind him, in his moments of quiet introspection, that just maybe I am that god of vengeance he fears so much."

They sat in a circle, the three of them. The door to the hut had been closed with a flap of cloth, and the guards waited outside. Two bushels of the yellow-green sprouts burned on either end of the hut, and the smoke had settled to the floor. Cassius's eyes stung, and breathing left his chest raw.

The Native man held a clay bowl in his lap, a thin pool of black liquid in the bowl. He lifted the bowl to his lips and sipped from it. He tilted back his head and exhaled through pursed lips, spraying the liquid into a cloud that quickly dissipated in the smoke. He sipped from the bowl again, swallowing this time, and passed it to the general.

"Drink," the Native man said.

The general drank and grimaced.

"Now to him." The Native man motioned to Cassius.

The general passed the bowl to Cassius and Cassius drank, the liquid burning his tongue and throat. The Native man took the bowl from Cassius and set it aside. He reached into the smoke and retrieved a pouch decorated with a snake's skull and fished out four odd-shaped bones, then shook the bones and cast them to the floor.

He looked on the bones, then looked to Cassius.

"Ask him if his mother is still alive," the Native man said.

"He wants to know if your mother is still alive," Quintus said.

"What does that matter?"

"Answer him."

"I don't know," Cassius said. "I haven't seen her since I was a child. We were separated. She might be dead or—"

"Or what?"

"I don't know."

"He is not sure of his mother," Quintus said. "She might be dead or she might be alive."

The Native man nodded absently. "Ask about his father."

"He wants to know if your father is alive."

"Yes," Cassius said.

"Yes."

"Is he sure?" the Native man asked.

"Are you sure?"

"I believe it. Yes."

The general nodded to the Native man.

Cassius felt light-headed now, detached from his body. His aches remained, but he experienced this pain at a remove. He lifted his hand and lowered it slowly. There seemed a delay between his intention and the action. The smoke no longer hurt his lungs.

"How did he kill you in the dream?" the Native man asked.

"He came to me as a spider and bit me," Quintus said.

"And you died?"

"Yes."

"You did not wake up before you died?"

"No, I was dead."

They passed the bowl again. The Native man produced a thin, curved knife and slit his own palm. He spat on the palm and poured onto it a small measure of the black liquid and slapped Cassius's face hard, smearing his cheek.

Cassius saw the approach of the blow but felt powerless to dodge it. He composed himself, and the Native man slapped him on his other cheek. Cassius lowered his head. The Native man sprang forward and snatched Cassius by his hair, tilting back his head so that he could stare into his face.

"Look," he said in guttural Antiochi. And Cassius looked to him, gazing up into those sullen eyes. The Native man released him and licked his own palm.

"You said he saved your son's life." The Native man was yelling as though struggling to be heard above some loud noise, a storm maybe or the sound of waves crashing on a beach, but the room was quiet.

"So he claims," the general said.

"Is your son alive?"

"Yes, but he is hurt."

"If your son dies, you must take this man as your son. It is the only way to save yourself from him."

"Is he trying to kill me then?"

"I do not know. I do not think even he knows. He burns inside. It keeps him alive, but it scares him as well. He knows it is the only thing that can kill him, even if he does not know it exactly." And then, as an afterthought, "He belongs to the jungle."

"How?"

"I am not sure." The Native man seemed troubled by this, but it was unclear if he was troubled by the fact itself or his inability to reach an answer.

"But you are certain?"

"I can see it to look at him. He has its resiliency. Its cruelty and secrets."

"I have no fear of the jungle."

"Then you should not fear him. But respect him as you would the jungle itself."

The cloth covering the front door lifted and a legionnaire poked his head into the smoke.

"Sorry to interrupt, sir." The legionnaire was panting and sweated. "I'm a runner sent from the fort. Commander Vorenicus is awake."

The walk back to the fort seemed endless. Cassius's feet were leaden, sluggish. He knew the direction he wished to move but could not will his body to proceed there, as though he were buried in the tomb of his own flesh, forced to watch its exploits passively. He stumbled often. He felt no pain from his falls, sometimes not realizing he had tripped until he hit the floor.

His mouth was dry, filled with a terrible taste. He heard drums again. Steady now but still distant, faster even than the beat of marching boots. He called to the others to see if they heard the drums as well, but he received no answers.

When he fell behind, the legionnaires continued without him. He watched their torches move farther into the distance, and a horrible dread settled over him, as though all the light was passing from the world and leaving him alone in this wet, hot void, ruled by that dark rhythm he could not place.

He was kneeling before the statue when Galerius found him. He was staring up into the stone face, trying to glimpse its eyes.

"Cassius."

He heard the voice in the dark; and then Galerius's hands were on his shoulders.

"Cassius, come with me. We'll get you off to bed."

Galerius helped him to his feet.

"Did he ever speak with you, Galerius?" Cassius staggered forward, steadying himself with a hand against the smooth stone of the statue.

"General Sabacus? No, he died six months after I joined the legion."

"And after he was dead. Did he speak with you then?" Cassius tripped and landed on his side. He rolled to his back and stared up, the stars overhead seeming to whirl in concentric circles of diamond-colored light.

"No. Now please sit up."

"There is a voice in my head. I would know whose it is."

"We'll find out in the morning."

Galerius draped an arm around Cassius's back and lifted him to his feet and began to herd him toward the barracks.

"Is Vorenicus well?" Cassius asked.

"He is much improved."

"Will I see him in the morning?"

"I think he wants very much to speak with you."

17

He woke with a terrible headache, the light against his closed eyes a discomfort. He opened his eyes slowly and took in the sight of his surroundings. He lay on a cot in the barracks, the other beds in the room empty. His mouth was dry and bitter. He rolled to his side and spat on the floor.

He was fully dressed, his gauntlets still hitched to his belt, boots on his feet. He could hear rain on the roof. He rose and staggered to the entrance and stared out into the gray haze of a downpour. Two guards stood post at the door.

"We've orders to take you to Commander Galerius when you woke." The legionnaires' cloaks were drenched with rainwater, the striking crimson now a shade closer to dried blood. Great streams of water poured from their wide-brimmed helmets, from their shirts of polished mail, and the great bowed shields strapped to their backs.

"I'd hate to keep him waiting," Cassius said.

They crossed the fort to the officers' quarters. The legionnaires escorting him walked briskly, as though on parade. He admired their discipline. They had not seen war in years. Had long been denied the succor of triumph, of spoils and pillage. Cut off from the Republic, with no hope of returning home and the faces of those they had sworn to protect long since faded. Still they remained vigilant, even in the face of chaos itself, the jungle.

Its tree line stretched higher than the walls of the fort, ever reaching, ever hungry, eager to erase this man-made scar carved upon its face. It was the worst kind of enemy, one assured of victory.

"Feeling better?" Galerius sat at lunch, his table set with bread and grapes, slices of cold beef. He did not offer Cassius a seat.

"Better than what?" Cassius asked.

"Last night?"

"Last night I felt wonderful."

"So you said. Many times."

"Is Vorenicus receiving visitors?"

"He is, and he's expecting you."

Vorenicus's quarters were warmed by a large hearth fire. At a corner table sat two healers. They were conversing softly over cups of tea. A book lay between them, open to a page showing cross-section figures of the human head.

Vorenicus lay in bed. He was pale, his hair unkempt. He smiled when Galerius announced Cassius.

"Good to see you again." Vorenicus made to rise to greet Cassius but Cassius motioned for him to stay reclined.

"Are you feeling better?" Cassius sat on the edge of the bed.

"A bit of a headache, but otherwise all right."

"That's good to hear."

Vorenicus stared silently for a while. "Thank you," he said solemnly.

"It was nothing."

"Not to me. It was something very important to me. I wish I knew what to say."

"No need to say any more."

The healers stopped speaking, and the room grew quiet.

"What happened to me?" Vorenicus's gaze was sharp and searching, as though the answers he sought could be found in this room if only he looked hard enough.

"Didn't they tell you?"

"They did. But they weren't there. You were there. I want to hear it from you."

"What do you remember?" Cassius asked.

"Next to nothing. I can see pieces of a battle. Not much."

"A fight erupted in the Market."

"Over what?"

"Who can say? There's been so much fighting the last few weeks. You and your men were there, probably trying to stop it from escalating. I don't know how the fight went for you. You were only about fifteen strong when I saw you."

"A retreat?" Vorenicus asked, the shame on his face plain.

Cassius looked away. "I couldn't say."

"You can tell me."

"It looked like a retreat. The men were injured."

At the mention of his men, Vorenicus lowered his eyes. "And what were you doing there?"

"Trying not to get killed in the chaos. I was ambushed, along with you and your men. I played dead and subdued our attackers while they were looting the bodies."

"Subdued them?"

"Killed them," Cassius said flatly.

"I see."

"The rest of the men were dead."

"How did you know I wasn't?"

"I felt your hand twitch."

"You were holding my hand?"

"I was pressing a coin into your palm."

One of the healers set down his cup. The room was so heavy with stillness that even this small noise seemed a great disturbance.

"For the ferryman?" Vorenicus said. "Because you thought I was dead. Because I was dead."

"It was a grim scene."

"And later?"

"I hid us in a storefront," Cassius said. "Then bribed a coachman to drive us to the fort."

"How resourceful you are, Cassius." Vorenicus flashed a pained smile. "If I'm ever near death again, I hope I have the good fortune to have you close by."

. . .

The general was not well enough to see visitors in the afternoon, and that night, Vorenicus and Galerius and Cassius met in the general's quarters. They had expected him to be alone, but he was with a serving girl. Young. Native.

She excused herself, and no one mentioned her presence. Galerius cleared a place at the large table for a map.

"Are you here to teach me the shape of the world, Galerius? Like I'm some schoolboy." The general smiled languidly.

He looked weak. He sat hunched in his chair. There were two cups on the table next to him and two on the floor, empty but for brown residue.

"I have no such intentions, sir," Galerius said. "This is a map of the city."

"The city my father built? Would you presume to educate me as to its structure?" Quintus laughed. "I know it as I know my own body. It is my body. Come now, Galerius. Bring me a map of my foot. Let us sit and debate its contours and the advantages to be gained by positioning ourselves—"

"Father, please." Vorenicus set a hand on Quintus's shoulder.

Sitting together, Cassius was struck by how alike they looked. The shape of their faces was similar, the nose, the brow, the hair. But their eyes were identical. Same color, possessed of the same deep-set, frenzied energy, even ailing as they both were.

"Galerius, ever prepared," Quintus said. "You'd bring a coffin to your funeral. I kid you, of course."

"It's no bother, sir."

The general turned his attention to Cassius. "Have you joined my inner circle now? You whom I've known two days."

"He has news from the city," Vorenicus said. "He worked with both Piso and Cinna and can offer insight into their motives. We'll need all the information we can gather before deciding our course of action."

"The only motive either of those bastards ever had was the desire to see the other fail. Offer them a loaf of bread, and they'd fight over it until both were dead. Motives." Quintus spat on the floor. "There are your motives."

Vorenicus produced a handkerchief and handed it to Quintus. He whispered to the general, and Quintus nodded bitterly and wiped his mouth and leaned back in his chair.

"Out with it," the general snapped. "One of you talk."

"How do you want to proceed against the bosses?" Vorenicus asked.

"I don't. Let them fight. What do I care?"

"Should we reclaim the council hall?" Galerius asked.

"In time. I care more about their men slaughtering each other than I do for that eyesore of a building."

"And what about the safety of the city?" Vorenicus rubbed his temples. "If we let the bosses' fighting go unchecked, casualties will be high."

"I should hope so. That's the point of our not sticking our noses in this till it's goddamn ripe. Let them weaken each other, so that later, when our forces reappear, it's clear we're superior. They'll have no will to fight us, and we'll take back what's ours. Plus force them to pay restitution. The tight bastards won't like that."

"And what of the cost of innocent life?"

The general smiled at Vorenicus. "My son. My beautiful sweet boy. There is no innocent life in Scipio. There will be deaths, of course. But the city will endure. It always does."

"May I speak?" Cassius asked.

"Please do. I've been waiting anxiously." Quintus picked up a glass and made to sip it but saw that it was empty. He stood and crossed the room to his desk.

"I don't know what the skirmishes of the past were like," Cassius said. "But this one feels serious to me. Cinna lost his second a few weeks ago."

"Nicola is dead?" Quintus produced his box of powder, sprinkled two spoonfuls into a glass. "That rat-faced bastard. I hope there's a demon having his way with him as we speak."

"And Piso lost his nephew. They're angry at each other. They want blood. If we go in now, they won't join forces against us."

"Us?" Quintus filled his glass from a kettle. "Have you been conscripted, Cassius?"

"The legion. They won't join forces against the legion. If you ever wanted to take the city back from them, now is the time."

"Wait a minute." Vorenicus held up a hand. "We shouldn't—"

"Take the city back from them? What in the hell would I want with that pisshole?" The general was shouting. "Let them keep it for all I care. And more to the point, it doesn't belong to them anyway. It belongs to me. They tithe to me. I am ruler here. Let them play at being bosses in the filth, day and night. When it comes time to collect, they know who holds their markers."

"I respect your candor, Cassius," Vorenicus said. "But I don't think more violence is the answer. If we arrive with a sizeable, but not an intimidating force, the bosses won't risk a second attack. They'll know they're stretched too thin as it is, and to attack again would risk counterattack. We can then set about containing the violence and opening up peace negotiations."

"Peace negotiations." Quintus stirred his cup. He licked the spoon and set it on the desk. "There can be no peace in a city divided like that."

"Something has to be done," Vorenicus said.

"Yes, yes. So you've said. What are your thoughts, Galerius? Show us a chart that we might understand you better."

"I think action is necessary. I'd prefer a plan of direct confrontation. But if we don't go that road, then we must at least return a force of men to the city to exert our authority."

"And wouldn't our authority be better exerted in a month's time?" Quintus asked. "When the best men of both bosses are dead? Then, when we arrive, we can round up any number of offenders and punish them as you see fit. Flog them, hang them. Anything you like. And the bosses and the people will beg us for mercy and we will grant it and they will know us the deciders of their fate."

"Won't the delay in delivering the message mute its meaning?" Galerius asked.

"Not if the message is made clear through action."

"I see."

"Do you, Galerius?"

"I do, sir."

"When the Uprising ended, there were people in that city scared to speak my name aloud for fear it would summon me like some vengeful spirit. That is authority."

"Those days are done, Father. No one wants to go back to that time."

Quintus drained his cup and set it on the desk. He paused as though in thought. His hand began to shake, just a slight tremor, noticeable only because the rest of him was so still, then he swept his arm over the desk, sending everything clattering to the floor.

"Get out. Get the hell out, all of you." Quintus had sustained a cut to the side of his hand and he wiped at the blood now and licked his fingers. "And send that whore back in here to clean this up."

"I didn't mean to undermine you in there."

Cassius and Vorenicus were walking toward the officers' quarters. The rain had calmed to a misting drizzle. Galerius had abandoned them to drink in the mess.

"I understand," Vorenicus said.

"I thought we were there to present the general with all sides of the problem. And that was my side. But if your plan is to win back the peace, I'll help in any way I can."

"Will you?"

"If you let me."

"I appreciate that." Vorenicus shut his eyes and grimaced. He pinched the bridge of his nose.

"Are you all right?"

"Another headache."

"Maybe you should lie down," Cassius said.

"I think I should."

"And in the meantime, do we wait to hear from the general?"

"Yes."

"And if he chooses to let the bosses' war continue?"

Vorenicus stood silent, measuring his next words. "Then we wait until it's over."

"Even if that means people will die?"

"You didn't seem too concerned for loss of life a minute ago."

"If we took the city by force," Cassius said, "I believe it would have saved lives ultimately."

"We may never know."

"There's got to be something we can do."

"You heard the man." Vorenicus lowered his head. In the moonlight, his face looked gaunt and pained. "This island operates under his authority. Act accordingly or face the consequences."

"You can do something."

"I won't cross my father." Vorenicus pointed a finger at Cassius. Moonlight pooled in the dark of his pupils.

"Even if it's the right thing to do?"

"To brotherhood."

Galerius held his glass high, the whiskey inside the color of olive oil. He smiled at Cassius and waited smiling until Cassius raised his own glass, then both men tapped glasses and drank.

"To brotherhood," Cassius said.

The whiskey was greasy and as close to sweet as any whiskey Cassius had ever drank. He washed the taste from his mouth with a dry wine.

"I'm sorry you had to see the old man like that tonight. But I guess it's best you get used to it now." Galerius refilled Cassius's glass with another measure of whiskey.

The mess hall was filled with a hundred men. There were massive dice games occupying all four corners of the room. Two men were wrestling in the center of the hall, and a crowd had formed. At the tables, men drank and ate and rolled cigarettes. There was no bar, but each man brought his own provisions, and the haggling over the cost of a cup of wine or a pinch of tobacco was fierce enough to rival the merchants in the Grand Market.

"Is he always like that?" Cassius asked.

"Always. As fierce and opinionated a man as I've ever met. When he thinks a course of action is right, there's no swaying him. Not by reason anyway. Although the crack about the map was uncalled for."

"You were just trying to be helpful."

"If it had come to talk of an invasion, he would have wanted the map. If it had come to that, and no one in the room had brought a map, he would have been furious."

"Did you think he would support an invasion?"

"I didn't know." Galerius sweated in the heat of the room. He wiped his face on the sleeve of his tunic. "I never do. Every time I think I have his mind figured, he does something I'd never expect."

"Must be hard to work for a man like that."

"He's brilliant. I know that to be true. And he's a great leader. But he can be hard to please." Galerius drained his mug and refilled it.

"And do you think he's right about this?"

"It's the right move for what he intends."

"Meaning to keep the bosses divided," Cassius said.

A cheer went up from the crowd near the wrestling pit. Galerius stood on his chair to see over the heads of the men to the action.

"Portius has never been beaten."

"Sit down before you fall." Cassius set his hand on Galerius's side to steady him.

Galerius whistled and clapped. He climbed down from his chair and took a swig from the bottle of whiskey.

"What were you saying?" Cassius asked. "Quintus picked the right move for what he intends. Meaning this plan only works because his goal is to keep the bosses divided?"

"That's right."

"But if he wanted something else, he should act differently."

"What else would he want?" Galerius asked.

"I don't know. It just seems strange to me that he's kept up this arrangement as long as he has. The bosses controlling the city and tithing up to him. He could take that city if he wanted."

"He hasn't yet. Isn't that proof enough of his feelings on the matter?"

"And why hasn't he?" Cassius asked. "Not from fear of the bosses. Is he scared of the senate's reaction?"

"I told you already, I don't know his mind. And he certainly won't tell me what he's thinking. Not unless it's important that I know it."

"Does he not trust you? You're a capable commander."

"Twenty years in his service." Galerius lifted his head and squared his shoulders as though being called to attention. "His service. Not anyone else's."

"The men respect you. You know the island."

"I see it in my dreams."

"I bet you could run that city better than either Piso or Cinna." Cassius's voice was a whisper, his words spoken swift and quiet, like a snake coursing through underbrush.

Galerius snorted. He snatched up the whiskey bottle and brought it to his lips and paused, his eyes locked in a faraway stare.

"That would never happen," he said.

"Never?"

Galerius drank. He shook his head.

"Not so long as the bosses are in power," Cassius said. "But they won't be alive forever."

"Those two bastards will live to be a hundred. And die throttling each other."

"Maybe one of them won't survive this war."

"They've survived dozens of these things. Part of me thinks they like fighting each other. If one was killed, the other would die from loneliness."

Cassius brought out his box of Garza-root powder. "But if we had gone with your plan. With legion intervention."

"Then what?"

"Then maybe the odds of the bosses making it out of this alive would be much slimmer." He pinched a bit of powder and snorted it, then offered the box to Galerius, who accepted, snuffing from the back of his hand.

"Maybe. But Quintus would never go for it. Nor Vorenicus, for that matter."

"You're right," Cassius said. "Vorenicus is too interested in peace."

"Always has been."

"Strange for a soldier to be that way."

"I suppose."

Cassius drained his mug. Galerius poured two more swigs of whiskey, and they drank, toasting this time to peace.

Cassius knew he was not supposed to accept succor from an enemy. He had a code. This was different, though. This was not a drink imbibed for pleasure. This was a drink to water the mind and the tongue of an opponent. He could endure the slight to his personal honor if it meant furthering his goals. He had endured worse.

"But what if Vorenicus were more practical?" Cassius asked. "If he knew that peace between the bosses was foolish and backed your plan."

"That's unlikely to happen."

"But if it did happen, do you think the two of you combined could sway the general?"

"Maybe," Galerius said. "He does trust that boy more that anyone. But Vorenicus is for peace."

"Only because he doesn't know that peace is impossible."

"Do you plan to lecture him on the error of his ways?"

"What if he saw for himself?"

"Maybe if the bosses killed him. If the kid said something stupid enough that one of those bastards slit his throat for him, then Quintus would act."

Cassius did not like even the hint of violence against Vorenicus. The man was honest and true, with an idealistic streak that left him vulnerable in so corrupt a place. He had lived with rats like Galerius all his life yet still managed to avoid fleas.

"Don't say that." Cassius sat forward, his voice even and final.

"I didn't mean it."

"It's wrong to say that."

"Don't get sensitive now. We were just talking here."

Galerius poured another round of whiskey. They drank without toasting.

. . .

Lying on the floor, Cassius watched the ceiling spin. When he breathed, he tasted whiskey. He could not sleep for the whispering in his head. The whispers came and went, so low that he could not discern the words being spoken nor if the voice was the same he had heard these past days.

His heart was racing. His jaw ached and his throat was numb from Garza root. He rose and stumbled to the door and did not make it around the side of the barracks before relieving himself on the wall. He finished and wiped his hands on his tunic.

The moon overhead was silver, so low he could see the craters on its surface. He raised his hands, held them up against the glare, and by that light marked the bruises and cuts and discolorations. He recalled the old woman's words.

There is blood on your hands, boy. No bath can wash that off.

He heard the clink of metal on metal and turned to see the general reeling in the dark. He called to him, and Quintus did not respond but continued walking. Cassius could see that he wore his gauntlets on his belt and held a bottle in his hand.

He called again and followed after him, but the general did not stop until he had reached the clearing near his quarters. Once there, he kneeled before the statue of his father and kissed his own hand and touched it to the stone. He sprinkled some of what was in the bottle on the ground.

Cassius approached.

"I wanted to say a prayer," Quintus said. "But I don't know any. And by the time I realized, I was already on my knees."

"If he's watching, he'll know you meant well."

"He isn't watching a damn thing. You need eyes to watch. And he has none."

Quintus stood and dusted his knees. He sipped from the bottle and offered it to Cassius. It was a rich wine, fruity and bold.

"Did he believe in the afterlife?" Cassius asked.

"No. I learned my disbelief from him. The same with prayers. He knew none and he taught me none and so I have none to offer at his monument."

"What else did he teach you?"

"He taught me most every spell I ever learned. He taught me not to trust anyone. He taught me to be a soldier and how to roll dice."

"Do you miss him?"

"No," he said. "Is that strange?"

"I don't know."

"You lost your mother."

"Yes," Cassius said softly.

"Do you miss her?"

"In a way."

"In what way?"

"I missed her very much for a long time. And then, when I learned I was touched, I decided to make myself a spellcaster. I dreamed of using my abilities to find her because I thought then she was still alive. As I grew older, I realized I would never find her. Would never know even if she had died. This almost killed me although at the time, I didn't know that this was what was killing me. And by the time I did, I had decided to come here."

"And now?" Quintus asked.

"Now I think of her every day. Except it isn't really her I think about. I can barely remember her face, her voice. So who is this person I see in my head?"

"I don't know."

"Neither do I."

"And your father?"

"What about him?" Cassius asked.

"How did he take the loss?"

"He didn't notice."

"How did he not notice?"

"That was the nature of their relationship."

Quintus sighed. "You are a strange one, Cassius."

A pair of sentries passed. They were talking amongst themselves and did not recognize the general in the light of the moon and did not salute him.

"Why are you wearing your gauntlets tonight?" Cassius asked.

"For protection."

"I thought you didn't need protection."

"Then because I like the way it feels to be near them."

"When was the last time you put them on?"

"Maybe last year, briefly." The general stared off. "Maybe before then."

"Do you miss it?"

"Don't be sentimental. Should we stand here all night and talk of things we miss and things we don't miss?"

"I'd miss them."

"You say that now. Live to be my age, and you might feel different."

Cassius did not respond. They stood in silence but for the sounds of the jungle.

"I was too hard on Vorenicus today," Quintus said after a time. "Did he mention it to you?"

"He didn't say he was upset by your words."

"He's a good soldier. I should trust his instincts more."

"Do you believe his view has merit?" Cassius asked.

"Not on this occasion. I know the bosses more than he does. I made them. He's wrong on this, but he's usually right." Quintus paused. And then, "I love him very much."

"I know he feels the same." Cassius's voice was low.

"I hope one day he has kinder words to say about me at my grave."

"Now who's being sentimental?"

"Forgive me," Quintus said. "I'm drunk."

"So am I."

"Trouble sleeping?"

"Yes."

"I can make you some tea if you'd like."

"No, thank you."

"What were you thinking about?" Quintus asked. "What was keeping you awake?"

"How do you know I was thinking about anything? I could be awake because I'm drunk."

"Maybe."

"Or because my heart is racing. And that I don't like sleeping in unfamiliar places."

"Why won't you tell me?"

"I'm thinking about people I've killed," Cassius said.

"That passes."

Cassius looked to the stars. "And people who died because of me. Not by my hand, but because I failed them."

"I see," Quintus said. "No sleep for you, then."

"Have you lost people that way?"

"Many."

"Does that pass?"

"Mostly."

"But some stay?"

"Some do stay," Quintus said.

"And what do you tell yourself to put them from your mind?"

"I tell myself that I am an agent of forces beyond the scope of man. And that I am not bound by the morality of man."

"Do you believe it?" Cassius asked.

"With all my heart."

"And in the face of that, death is nothing?"

"Death is like me. An agent of great forces. And when he comes for me, we will meet as equals and as old acquaintances."

"A nice thought," Cassius said.

"There are men who die with clean hands and spend every day from their first to their last in fear of death. They sleep unwell, too."

"I see."

"Do you believe it?"

"I want to," Cassius said.

18

⁓•⁓

The sun crested the jungle tree line, its light stabbing down through a scattered cloud cover to beat on Cassius's brow. He wiped sweat from his eyes, averted his gaze like some sinner unable to look upon the face of a disapproving god. He had been summoned from the barracks by Vorenicus. The runner said it was an urgent summons, said this twice, then told Cassius to leave the fort by the front gate and to walk. He did not say when to stop walking.

Now Cassius was on the slope leading down from the fort, the overgrowth here cleared by slash fires so that intruders would have no coverage from spearmen and from ballistae when approaching the walls. It had rained in the morning, and the puddles underfoot trapped the shimmering sunlight. In each small pool, Cassius could see insects and small vermin, worms, toads, the ever-present mosquitoes. The raw life of the jungle seemed to manifest everywhere, as oppressive as the heat itself.

He was ten leagues past the fort when he spotted Vorenicus near the side of the road. At a glance, he could pass for a common officer. He was garbed in the legion uniform but wore light mail instead of his muscle cuirass, which had been abandoned in the Market. He wore a new helm dressed with new eagle feathers, each as tall and straight as the original pair.

"What are you doing out here?" Cassius asked.

"Sometimes the fort, like the city, has too many listening ears. Hard to find a place to have a word in private."

"Meaning you don't want your father to hear."

"Why would you assume that?"

"He's the only man in the fort whose judgment you'd have to fear."

"I fear more for your sake than for mine."

"Me?"

"It came this morning." Vorenicus held a scroll in one hand and shook it in the air. "Word from the city."

He had been drilling when the letter arrived, testing his strength in the shield line, measuring his sword arm against veteran centurions. He looked tired and pale, sagging under the weight of his armor.

"Addressed to you?" Cassius asked.

"My father. For all I know, the bosses think me dead."

Vorenicus made his way toward the jungle, his boots loud on the pavement. Cassius fell in behind him. Overhead, a large bird wheeled against the sky, curling left.

"From Piso or Cinna?" Cassius asked.

"Cinna, although he said Piso would agree with the points he raised."

"And what were those?"

Ahead of them in the overgrowth, a squad of scouts-in-training consulted a map. Six men in legion garb and light leather armor, some kneeling, some standing. All wore jungle charms, snake teeth, tusks, dabs of paint, feathers.

"That hostilities are high," Vorenicus said, "but he's confident all parties can reach an accord."

"He's calling for a truce?"

"With conditions."

"What conditions?"

"Your head."

The scouts rose and walked off and as Cassius watched them move, in the full light of the sun, they vanished. Not a spell. They were there, then they were gone, swallowed it seemed, and a breeze picked up and the jungle shook, like a great intake of breath.

"Guess I left an impression on the man," Cassius said.

"Why do you think that is?"

Cassius shrugged. "I quit him for Piso. He's still sore."

"In the letter, he mentioned that Piso would want your head, too. That killing you, or turning you over to them, would cement the peace."

"I left Piso, too. To come here. To save you."

Vorenicus removed his wide-brimmed helmet. He drew his arm across his sweating brow.

"He says you caused all this recent trouble."

"Where is his proof?"

"This is Scipio, Cassius. No courts. No need for proof."

A distant howl carried through the jungle. It was answered by low grunts, a crash of branches, then silence.

"What are you saying, Vorenicus?"

"You have to appreciate the position I'm in."

"Will you hand me over to them, knowing they'll kill me? And for what? The trouble in the city? How could one man cause all that? They'd have me play their scapegoat."

"The night before the fight in the Market, I had convinced Piso and Cinna to lay down their arms. Nothing was finalized yet, but we were nearly there. And then that fight broke out."

Vorenicus clutched his head, as though the act of remembering pained him.

"What does the general want to do?" Cassius asked.

"Ignore the letter. He has no interest in peace."

"And you?"

Vorenicus set his hand on Cassius's shoulder. "You saved my life. I won't sanction your death by turning you over to the bosses."

"And yet?"

"And yet they would talk peace. I must hear them."

"As sure as I'm standing here, I know how that talk ends."

Vorenicus clenched his hand into a fist and held it over his heart.

"I give you my word, as a legionnaire and as a friend, that I will not buy this peace with your life."

Cassius was silent. They stood on the edge of road, straddling the pavement and the jungle both.

"Do you believe me?" Vorenicus asked.

"I believe you're the last honest man in Scipio," Cassius said. "If anyone can get to the truth, it's you."

The bandages on Cassius's forearms tore as he crept through over-growth. Thorns scratched his legs. He stayed alert for whipping branches but he was without a torch and could see little in the dark. Twice he scraped his face on low-hanging tree limbs and thorned vines, the second scrape deep enough to draw blood.

"Can we trust these men to be there?" he called into the dark ahead.

Vorenicus's back was a black shape moving against a drab canopy. "They'll be there."

"And they won't spread word of this when they return to fort? Regardless of how it ends? Your father might not take kindly to news that you're negotiating peace behind his back."

"These men are friends," Vorenicus said. "I trust them with my life. And I'm not here to negotiate peace. I'm simply starting a dia-logue. Talking is better than killing."

"Depends on who's doing the talking and who's doing the killing."

"Hammer," came a call from the dark.

Cassius froze.

"Anvil," Vorenicus replied.

Cassius heard branches parting, delicate steps as feet padded through the tangle.

"Are you well, Commander, sir?"

Cassius was surprised by the closeness of their voices. He still could see no figure in the dark apart from Vorenicus.

"I'm fine." Vorenicus said. "Are you prepared to leave?"

Cassius felt a thrumming in his chest and reached for his gauntlets reflexively. A dull pop sounded, and a small spire of shaky green light, as tall as a wine bottle appeared in midair, balanced on the gauntleted hand of a grim legionnaire. There were four men to either side of him, all dressed in segmented steel armor, with shields and spears strapped to their backs.

"Will we be keeping to the jungle for the entire trip?" the lead scout asked.

"Only until we're out of sight of the fort," Vorenicus said.

"And then?"

"And then we'll take the road. We're to be met at the city gates."

"Begging your pardon, Commander. But wouldn't it be wise to bring more men?"

"The number of guards was set before the meeting was agreed upon."

"Let's hope the other parties are as upright as you, sir."

The pavilion stood in a clearing near the city walls. A massive table was set under the tent, fixed with food and drink, and men milled about, most dressed in armor but a few of the bosses' advisors and hangers-on dressed more civilly, in the kind of gauche clothing that could only exist in Scipio, where trade was plentiful but culture nonexistent. Gold-stitched tunics, cloaks of ermine, jeweled mantles, sealskin boots. The entire scene had a solemn air, like a religious ceremony in which a necessary but unpleasant ritual was to take place, a sacrifice or a letting.

It smelled of ash near the tent. A slow breeze carried northward from the city. It was too dark to see smoke against the sky, but at his approach, Cassius had noticed a strange glow past the walls, deep in the sprawl of the city, most likely a fire.

Cinna sat at one end of the table. He had a plate of food before him, slices of mutton and green apples, which he picked at with his fingers. A bearded man was seated to his right, and behind him were five more men, all with weapons on display, long, curved knives, greatswords, even a man with gauntlets hanging from his belt.

He greeted Vorenicus distractedly.

"Welcome." Cinna rose from his chair. "Help yourself to anything you like."

"I'm not hungry. Thank you, though."

They shook hands, Cinna's fat, limp hand enveloping Vorenicus's small strong one, then Cinna took his seat again. He looked to Cassius and sucked his teeth, his doughy face an exaggerated sneer.

Piso stood talking in a circle of his guards. He seemed not to notice Vorenicus's presence until someone announced him, then Piso detached himself from the group, greeted Vorenicus with a hug. In the light of the torches, his scars were the color of ham. He approached the table with an arm around Vorenicus's waist and took his seat, all without glancing to Cassius. Five armed men were clustered behind him, and seated at his elbow, serving as his second, was a spellcaster Cassius had never met before, a pale, gray-eyed Murondian with long dark hair. He acknowledged Cassius with a nod.

There were two chairs set on one side of the table, midway between both bosses, and Vorenicus sat in one of these chairs and motioned for Cassius to join him.

"I didn't think he'd have the balls to show," Cinna said.

"Is that a problem?" Vorenicus asked.

"That man is devious. And his sitting at your right hand, instead of chained at your feet, doesn't speak well of your intentions."

Vorenicus raised his hands. "Let's not start the proceedings with insults."

"You insult us by letting him sit at our table." Piso pounded his fist on the ashwood board.

"I think we have more important matters to discuss than my choice of seconds."

"Just get on with it, then," Cinna said.

"This most recent bout of violence has reached the attention of the general."

"Only because that pig can't keep his goddamned cutthroats in line," Piso said.

Cinna gestured obscenely. "I wouldn't trade one of mine for ten of yours."

"Ten solid men for one child toucher, is that the going rate now?"

A groan went up from the knot of men standing behind Cinna.

"Savages," Cinna shouted. "The whole lot of you. Raping and stealing and killing without a thought for the consequences."

"Lies, lies, lies. The only thing that ever comes out of your mouth. What goes in your mouth, that's a much longer list. But the commander here has only so much time—"

"You're drooling again, Piso. Wipe that excuse for a face before you make me sick."

"Gentleman, please," Vorenicus leapt up shouting. "Acting like children gets us nowhere. Our city is falling apart."

All grew quiet.

"Now if you want to force the general's hand to action, then continue operating the way you have. But if you want to see this resolved, then let's discuss terms."

"Terms?" Cinna said. "Terms start with your friend there." He pointed to Cassius.

"We'll discuss his role in this in due time," Vorenicus said. "For now, I want to make sure both sides are willing to set aside their arms."

"Are his men going to help me rebuild the docks now that half of them have burned? And the huge crater in Scab Row from the spellfight last night? Who pays for that?"

"You started this fight," Cinna said. "You should pay."

"Me?" Piso waved a hand dismissively. "I didn't start a thing."

"You killed Nicola," Cinna yelled, bits of mutton spraying from his lips. "And tried to steal my money."

"You attacked my safe house."

"I did no such thing."

"I have bodies as evidence, burned to a crisp. Corpses don't just fall out of the sky."

"Well, it wasn't on orders from me." Cinna snatched up a mug of wine, downed its contents.

"Your man already confessed to me," Piso said. "There's no use denying the truth."

"Who told you such things?"

"That maniac." Piso nodded across the table. "Cassius."

"He's a lying dog." Cinna jumped up, slapped his plate from the table. The men behind him tensed. A few reached for their weapons. From the other side of the tent, Piso's men shouted for hands to stay in the air.

"Cinna," Vorenicus said calmly. "Take your seat please."

"I won't have lies thrown in my face." Cinna stabbed a plump finger onto the tabletop.

"I understand that," Vorenicus said.

"I'll cut the other half of his face off before I let him lie to me."

"There's no need for that."

Cinna sat. He shouted over his shoulder, and one of his guards fetched him a fresh mug. He drank, then belched. The guard leaned forward and whispered in Cinna's ear. They conferred briefly and squinted across the table.

Vorenicus looked to Cassius, and Cassius stared back, trying to appear calm. He thought about the old woman from the bath, about his goals, then pushed this thought from his mind. He was aware of every twitch in his face now, the pace of his breathing, the set of his mouth. He wanted a mask.

"Last time you had me lay down my arms," Piso said. "He attacked me, the sneaky pig."

"I attacked you?" Cinna snorted. "What a sense of history you have. Everyone knows you sent this madman across the Market at me, even after Vorenicus had us both agree to keep our forces out of there. Lunatic picked a fight with forty men."

"Is that why your men attacked our good commander here?"

"Those men were tricked."

"Is that true?" Vorenicus whispered to Cassius.

"What?" Cassius could not match Vorenicus's gaze.

"Were you in the Market before the fighting started?"

"Vorenicus, you have to listen—"

"Tricked into attacking a phalanx? Do you really expect us to believe that?" Piso threw up his hands.

"Do you deny that you sent Cassius after me?" Cinna shouted.

"Yes, I deny it. And point that sausage finger at me again, and I'll bite it the hell off."

"Did it happen that way?" Vorenicus asked.

"What do you mean?" Cassius said.

The tent fell silent, tense. Everyone seemed to wait for Cassius's answer.

"Were you in the Market despite the injunction?"

"Explain yourself, you bastard," Cinna shouted.

"Shut up."

The Murondian leaned close to Piso, and Piso nodded and whispered in his ear.

"These cowards are trying to pin this on me." Cassius's tone was measured, but he could feel his heart racing. He tried to focus, to find the calm that allowed him to walk through fire. But he was too tired now, too beaten down, his mind clouded. And although he felt his control steadily ebb, his rage only grew.

"Answer the question," Vorenicus said. "Were you in the Market?"

"You think one man could do all that?" Cassius asked. He could not look to Vorenicus. It was no great feat to lie to Piso or Cinna, both expert liars themselves. He was only using their own weapons against them. But Vorenicus was different. "Open your eyes. They want you to mistrust me so that you won't believe what I know about them."

The men standing just outside the light of the tent grumbled. He heard the legionnaires whispering behind him.

"Why can't you answer me?" Vorenicus asked.

"Tell him, whoreson," Cinna shouted.

"Watch your pig mouth."

"Cassius?"

"I should have known about you." Cinna grinned. "Any man who won't screw a whore is no man to trust."

Piso slapped the tabletop, roared with laughter.

"Would you trust their word over mine, Vorenicus?"

"Piss on his word. I have witnesses," Cinna said. "Citizens. Not my own men. People who saw that he attacked the guards at the Hightown barricades. That was the spark that triggered the entire fight. Was there bad blood beforehand? Were our men on edge? Of course. But that doesn't change the fact that he started this. Do you agree, Piso?"

"My men responded to the violence already taking place in the Market. If you say he attacked you, I believe it. But he wasn't acting on orders from me. I never even gave the boy my brand. I knew he wasn't to be trusted."

"See," Cinna said. "When have you ever known us two to agree on anything? You have a snake underfoot, Vorenicus. Step on it before it bites you, too."

"Your men attacked me," Cassius shouted.

"My men were ordered to stand down," Cinna said. "As our good commander here knows."

"Vorenicus, you were there," Piso said. "What did you see?"

"I was injured. My memory is fuzzy."

"Injured by who?" Piso asked.

Vorenicus considered the question. "A spellcaster."

"Like our friend here?"

"No," Cassius said. "That's not what happened. I saved you."

"And what of your men, Vorenicus?" Cinna asked.

"They all died."

"Convenient."

"They're twisting this," Cassius said. "They're lying."

"First he burns the piglet," Piso said, counting off Cassius's crimes on his fingers. "Then he starts the fight in the Market. Then he escapes with you before having to stand my wrath. Now that's one devious cunt."

"Cassius?" Vorenicus said.

Cassius stared into the middle distance, warm torchlight playing across half his face, the other hidden in shadow.

"We'd laid down our arms already," Piso said. "Why would we start a fight one day after agreeing to do that unless provoked?"

"Explain yourself, Cassius."

Cassius stood from the table. "I don't have to explain myself to any of you."

"Sit down," Vorenicus said. "That's an order."

"Liars." Cassius was yelling now. "Thieves and murderers. You would take their word over mine?"

"If you don't sit down, I'll have you shackled." Vorenicus leveled his gaze on Cassius.

Cassius closed his eyes. The sound of his heartbeat in his ears was a drum, strong and fast.

"Shackle me, Vorenicus?" He opened his eyes. "Like a criminal? The only criminal in a land with no laws. Who would be my judge? Piso? Cinna?" He spat the names.

"Those weren't my words," Vorenicus said. "I never called you a criminal."

"Who else wears shackles? Only criminals," Cassius said. "And slaves."

Vorenicus started at the word, as though struck a blow. "Slaves?"

"You heard me," Cassius shouted. "It wouldn't be the first time these bastards clapped irons onto their enemies, sold them off in the dead of night."

Vorenicus looked away, then looked back to Cassius, as though seeing him for the first time.

"These are peace talks," Vorenicus said. "And you're under my banner of truce. My father's banner of truce. Act accordingly."

"Control your man, Vorenicus," Cinna said. "He's making me nervous."

"I should, you fat-faced murderer."

The Murondian roared and leapt to his feet. Cassius felt a thrumming in his chest. He ducked and reached for his gauntlets, his fingers barely inside as he drew the fire-ward rune in his mind's eye. A sound like a great rip rent the air, and a tongue of white flame flashed before him.

His gauntlets were on his hands as he hit the ground. He smelled smoke, heard a terrible scream. He rolled and hopped to his feet, circling wide to gain some distance from the tent. A legionnaire was afire. The man lay turtled on his shield while Vorenicus beat the flames with bare hands.

Cassius glimpsed a flash of light in midair, a hand ax. It sailed inches to the side of the Murondian and stuck in the chest of one of Piso's guards. The man coughed blood and fell on his ass, bouncing comically, then loosed a strangled cry. The legionnaire who had hurled the ax charged Piso.

Piso toppled in his chair and rolled into the dark. His men drew their weapons and advanced. A cone of fire spiraled across the table, hurled by a legionnaire. The Murondian stepped into the flame, and it died on his chest, but not before the tent had caught fire.

Cassius raised his hands to cast but was struck with a counterspell. Sparks shot from his fingertips.

Cinna backed into the dark as his men leapt across the table.

Cassius felt again the stirring in his chest. The Murondian jutted the heel of his palm at Cassius, and a jet of steam rose from the ground. The steam smelled sharp, like lye, and seconds later a crocodile emerged from the cloud and crawled forward on all fours. It was six feet long, with a thick tail that hung stiff above the ground. It licked its muzzle with a thin gray tongue and hissed deep in its throat.

Cassius clapped twice at the lizard, and a sand eddy dusted the road and cascaded to the floor, and where the sand fell, a fearsome dire wolf now stood. The wolf nosed the air and growled.

The crocodile crawled forward and, at its approach, the wolf angled downward and snapped at its front paw. The crocodile bent double, and its long tail whipped over its body and caught the wolf a blow on the shoulder. The wolf's shoulder broke, and the wolf dropped to its face and lay whining. The crocodile ambled forward.

Cassius took a few measured steps backward, drawing on the rune energy.

The Murondian conjured next a funnel of cold wind, flecked with snow. When it collapsed, a large white bear lurched into the light of the flaming tent. It reared, gazing around at the chaos. The Murondian raised his hands to his temples, and the bear hoisted itself onto two legs and swatted at a legionnaire.

The Murondian cursed, and the bear settled onto all fours. It paused as though lost in thought, then trotted in a slow circle and wheeled on Cassius.

Cassius dropped to his knees and placed a hand on the ground. He splayed his fingers and slapped the floor and from the dark above the bear came a sound like a wave breaking. A stream of what looked like incandescent honey poured from the sky, enveloping the bear and splashing nearby fighters.

The bear released a tortured scream. The lava had already melted huge sections of its body as it toppled to the ground. Its flesh spilled along the pavement, under a cloud of hissing steam.

One of the pavilion's poles snapped and a sheet of sparks drifted out into the jungle and, by the light of these embers, Cassius could see men hacking at each other in the tangle.

The Murondian, limned in firelight, moved toward him.

Cassius cupped his hands and raised them and tufts of yellow smoke rose from the ground. In the smoke, a mass took shape.

A misdirection spell burst near his face, a harmless display of pyrotechnics. There was a shower of sparks and a loud report, but he was undeterred, and the yellow smoke rose and grew thinner. From inside the smoke, two dawn-red eyes formed and took sight of the world.

Cassius felt weak. A light-headed sensation overcame him. He kneeled, and although his eyes were closed, he could see the world through a new set of eyes.

A breeze cleared the smoke. The Murondian gasped.

The scorpion was eight feet long and stood as tall as a rhinoceros. Its shell was smooth, colored sand brown and rust orange and marked with streaks of jet along its legs and its back and up the length of its tail.

Cassius urged it forward, but it did not move. Images of the Murondian, broken and bloodied, flashed from his mind to the mind of the creature, a wordless command to kill. But still it stood motionless.

Cassius felt his nose dripping blood. He screamed, eyes wet with tears.

The beast stirred. It stepped sideways, each spindly leg striking earth with a sound like a pick biting into stone.

The lizard halted at the sight of this new beast and hissed.

Startled, the scorpion hunched down and shot its tail forward and stung the lizard, which stiffened, then lay still. The scorpion withdrew its stinger with a sound like sucking mud. It edged closer to the Murondian, the jaw parts beneath its head shell twitching. Its pincers opened slowly, with a wet noise like the peeling of an eggshell.

The Murondian held his hand out, palm open, and a circle of fire appeared on the floor. It spread quickly, ringed the scorpion. The creature reared in the flame, its tail dragging through fire. It arched upward, and the flames rose.

The scorpion bucked, pincers snapping air. Its tail shot upward and hooked the cloth of the flaming pavilion. It lurched and yanked its tail free, and another section of the tent collapsed. A pole ripped from the ground, spinning end over end, and struck the Murondian in the back.

He staggered. The flames encircling the scorpion died and, as they did, the scorpion sprang forward and speared its stinger through the Murondian's chest. The sting jutted from his back and he twisted, swatted awkwardly at it. He cast a weak flare that imploded with an audible pop, and the scorpion retreated, dragged its stinger out of his body, and the Murondian collapsed forward with a long exhale.

In the dark, Cassius could see no one and could hear only the sounds of the fire and the wind. He felt no thrumming in his chest. He dismissed the scorpion with a wave, the creature vanishing in a puff of yellow smoke.

He reeled, clutched his head. The breeze carried a scent like a snuffed candle. His scalp was hot, itchy. He walked to the Murondian, and beneath the sound of his footsteps, he heard a faint voice calling him by name.

He kneeled to retrieve the Murondian's gauntlets, and the blow struck him at the base of his skull. He felt a heavy, numb pressure in his head. And then he was falling into darkness.

He woke in the jungle, to the sound of his own crying. The pain in his head was so strong, he wondered if his skull had not split open. His cheeks were filmed with dry tears, and the world around him was black and smelled of rich mud.

He tried to sit up, but the world spun. He pressed his forehead to the damp earth and groaned and heaved. Footsteps approached.

"—ie down. Lie facedown righ—"

The voice came from faraway, like a scream heard underwater. It drifted in and out of focus while, in the distance, the sound of heavy drums rose.

He felt a boot on his back. He collapsed, his mouth filling with wet loose dirt.

"—ve and I'm going to kill you. Do you hear wha—" The point of a blade pressed against the base of his skull.

Something struck his spine. The boot again, he thought. The blade lifted off his neck. He closed his eyes.

He felt hands grip his shoulders, small hands but strong. They worked down his arms. One gauntlet, then the other slid from his hands, the warm pinpricks fading. He knew he was unarmed now, knew he should be afraid, but he was not afraid. There was an air of the inevitable about this, he thought. Or maybe he was just glad to see it finished.

Arms wrapped his waist and lifted him and laid him with his back against a tree. He sat for a time before opening his eyes. When finally he did, he saw a blackness so complete, he thought himself blinded. Then he glimpsed light in the jungle, a fire in the middle distance, and by this light he saw the legionnaire take shape.

He saw the silhouette of the long tunic, the silvery mail glinting with firelight, like a sunrise moving over the surface of the ocean. He saw the shape of the short, stabbing blades, one in each hand, and saw also the wide-brimmed helmet.

How many times had this figure appeared in his dreams, chasing him through jungles.

He thought the fear would return then, the child's blind panic that he had trained for years to subdue. But when he saw the white of the eagle feathers, he knew this was not the monster from his dreams come to claim its prey after long years of pursuit.

"Are you hurt?" Vorenicus stood staring down at him, his face obscured by darkness.

"I don't think so," Cassius said. His voice did not sound his own, did not seem to come from him at all, although he was aware of his mouth moving.

"What do you have to say for yourself?"

"Is this a court of law? Must I enter a plea?"

"What they said back there, the way things have played out these last few days, it's all true, isn't it?"

"Are we here to talk of truth?"

"Yes, goddamn it," Vorenicus said. "The truth for once. Or so help me, I will bury this blade in your chest."

Cassius dug his hands into the warm earth, worked the loose rich soil between his fingers. It seemed charged, electric, like the heaviness in the air before a lightning strike. To be sure, there were magic users who pulled their power from the earth, stormcallers and firedancers and shamans who spoke the language of the Primal Ones. But he was no such mage, and the charge he felt in the jungle was not a magical one. It was unlike anything he had felt before, and he knew from that first touch he had no way to control it.

"There's no need for threats," he said. "They cheapen us. You for speaking them and me for responding. And besides, I would not think you the type to threaten a man who saved your life."

"Saved my life? You instigated that entire fight in the Market. You got my men killed. And nearly got me killed as well."

"I did those things, and I also saved your life. You were on the brink of death, with the ferryman's coin in your hand. And I could have left you there, but I didn't."

Vorenicus rubbed his palm as though he could still feel the coin. "Why?"

"Why didn't I leave you?"

"Why any of it?"

Cassius looked up. "You're not the only one who worships justice."

"Justice." Vorenicus exhaled the word. "You think this is just?"

"Is it just to let the guilty walk free?" Cassius rubbed his temples. A dull pain throbbed deep in his skull, pressing against the backs of his eyes. "Men with blood on their hands? Men who committed unspeakable crimes?"

"Unspeakable? Is that why you kept your intentions hidden?"

"I am one man, and my enemies are legion," Cassius said. "The only way to see my work completed was to gain their trust, turn them against one another."

"You lied to me," Vorenicus said.

The disappointment in his voice was plain and the sound of it shamed Cassius and Cassius looked away.

"I was as honest with you as I could be," he said. "I had to be careful with my words or risk exposing myself to my enemies."

"And who are your enemies?"

Cassius gritted his teeth as the throbbing in his head grew stronger. The pain spread down his neck, into his shoulders.

"Don't play the fool, Vorenicus."

"I would hear you say it."

"What do you remember of the Uprising?"

Vorenicus did not answer. The sound of the fire was distant, and the word seemed to hang in the jungle air, humming, like the ring of steel on steel.

"Not much," Vorenicus said. "I was just a boy."

"I was just a boy as well. And I remember much."

Vorenicus sheathed his blades, the swords hissing as he drove them home, as though wary of the man sitting against the tree. He kneeled until he was eye level with Cassius although in the dark, neither man could see the other's face.

"You're from here," Vorenicus said. "You're Scipian."

"Half," Cassius said. "Born of a Khimir mother and an Antiochi father. Born in the legion fort, under the legion eagle, but surrounded by the jungle."

"Your father was a legionnaire."

Cassius nodded.

"What was his name?" Vorenicus asked.

"Even now, I don't think I can bring myself to say it aloud."

"And your mother?"

"A servant." Cassius tried to recall her face, but he could not. He pictured a Khimir woman, short and thin, with dark hair and a bright blue dress. But her face was gone and had been for some time.

"And what happened to them during the Uprising?" Vorenicus's voice was searching, tinged with something harsh.

"After the attempt on the general's life, there was a purge of the Khimir at the fort. Do you remember that?"

"No."

Guilt. That was the harsh note in Vorenicus's voice. Whether it was guilt for the act itself or guilt for not remembering, Cassius could not say. But he was familiar enough with the feeling to know it by sound alone.

"Sometimes I still dream of that night. Running through the woods while legionnaires gave chase. The barking of war hounds." Cassius paused. "Many died in the jungle. We were lucky to make it to the city, or so we thought."

"The legion had pulled its men from the city by then," Vorenicus said.

"That's right. Cinna and Piso controlled the city. Their army pillaged and looted, killed hundreds. They claimed to be targeting legion loyalists, but they were only grabbing for power, settling old scores. I was too young to understand the struggle or discern a rebel from a loyalist. But not too young to witness the bloodshed."

"It must have been terrible."

"It was nothing compared to the violence when the legion arrived."

Thunder crashed in the distance. Cassius realized his heart was pounding. He wiped his forehead.

"Nothing to say about that?" Cassius asked. "No lecture on the nature of justice?"

"I would never defend the legion's actions during the Uprising. It was a horrific time."

"Or so you've heard."

"That's not fair."

"Not fair?" Cassius asked. "Not fair is watching your mother beg for food. Listening as she cries herself to sleep at night. Not fair is hiding under floorboards in a run-down bar while legionnaires sweep for Natives. Men, women, children. Knowing that breathing too loud, or leaning on a creaky board will get you killed. No, I suppose

I haven't been very fair to you, Vorenicus. But then life is not fair. Scipio taught me that."

"You escaped, though."

"With help. I was smuggled aboard a cargo ship bound for the mainland. My mother was not so lucky."

"Killed by the legion," Vorenicus asked, his voice just above a whisper.

"Sold by the legion. To Fathalan slave traders. She was caught while we were in hiding. And her silence bought my freedom and my life." Cassius rubbed the bite mark on his palm. "A debt I intend to repay."

No one spoke for a time. A strong breeze picked up, and the trees overhead shook and swayed and finally parted to reveal a dark sky flecked with cold, uncaring stars.

"I don't know what to say, Cassius. 'I'm sorry' seems an insult. 'I understand' would be a lie."

"You don't have to say a thing," Cassius said. "Your listening has been enough."

"I don't know where we go from here."

"I'm not finished yet. Too many guilty still alive. Too much blood still calling to me."

"And yet you spared me," Vorenicus said. "A man who wears legion colors. A boy who sat safe and well fed in the fort during the Uprising."

"You never did me harm."

"I don't believe that. You've hurt too many. You've let no one get in your way. If you wanted my father to attack the bosses, you could have killed me in the Market."

"I couldn't do a thing like that."

"You've killed dozens," Vorenicus said. "Hundreds."

"But not a brother."

Silence. Even the jungle, which only minutes before had seemed a living creature, breathing and shaking and buzzing, now fell still.

"I don't believe that," Vorenicus said.

"You don't have to."

"Everything you say is a lie."

"You don't have to believe my words," Cassius said. "I'm a killer. And touched. The proof of that is clear."

"That doesn't prove a thing."

"There have been others. There must have been. The general's taste for Natives is well-known."

"I've never seen—"

"Then you've heard," Cassius shouted. "Or else played blind and deaf."

Vorenicus shook his head. "Why would I believe this?"

"Why would I save your life?"

Vorenicus stood. He turned his back to Cassius. The fire in the distance had spread. Thick smoke rolled through the trees, like a shadow come to life. And Vorenicus, in his flame-lit armor, seemed the fabled hero come to vanquish it.

"My plan was to destroy this city," Cassius said. "To burn it to ash and watch the jungle swallow it up. But I realize now there's another way."

"And what happened to change your mind?"

"I met you." Cassius's throat tightened. He swallowed, fought to keep his voice from cracking. "Together, we can save this city."

"Do you think me so vain?" Vorenicus asked. "Or are you so desperate you've turned to naked flattery to sway me?"

"I'm not trying to sway you. I know your nature. You'll do what's right. You always do. After I carve out the rot, when the bosses are dead and the general is dead and their armies broken, you will take power. And you will guide this city toward a just future."

"Do you think I'll let you kill my father?"

"I don't need you to let me."

Vorenicus drew his sword and spun, leveling the blade at Cassius.

"You're alone and unarmed. There's nothing to stop me from killing you where you sit."

"Nothing except that I am alone and unarmed," Cassius said. "Have you killed such a man before? It's not an easy task, not even for the ruthless. For you, it would be impossible."

"Would you bet your life on that?"

Cassius opened wide his arms. "I already have."

Vorenicus lowered his blade. "I won't kill an unarmed man. But I am still a commander in the legion of Antioch, and I am placing you under arrest. For treason and sedition and crimes against the Republic. Stand up."

"I'll do no such thing."

"I have the authority to take you by force if I must."

"You must."

Cassius did not see the blade in the dark, but he heard it whistle as it cut air. A killing stroke, except that Vorenicus tilted his wrist at the last. The flat of the blade struck Cassius on his temple. In that instant, the smoke that had gathered in the clearing became a mouth that opened wide and devoured everything, the trees and the fire and Vorenicus, swallowed even the terrible secret that had given it life.

And again Cassius was falling.

The rain woke him. He did not feel the rain but heard it rustling the underbrush instead. He felt the hard weight of the rock in his hand, slick and warm. He opened his eyes and found the world still dark. The pain in his head was gone, replaced by a sensation like hot pinpricks working across his scalp.

He crawled to his knees, his arms limp and his face upturned to the rain. The weight of the rock in his hand felt good. It would keep him tethered to this world and stop the falling.

The scream was like the wail of a kettle but loud enough to shake mountains. He saw a flash of red and something gleaming. The monster's face was all mouth and teeth, a mouth open wide like a toad's, with knitting-needle teeth, white like the white of exposed bone. When he saw it, his pain vanished, and all the world seemed to shrink to a small point, as it sometimes does in dreams. There was no past and no future, no falling either, and the voice was gone and the drums and there was nothing to fear but the monster.

Unlike in his dreams, he could will himself to move now and he leapt at the monster and it seemed taken aback by this and when he fell onto it, the rock seemed to move his hand, moving it down and down and down until he felt something give, a caving in, and then the rock slipped free. A flash of lightning lit the sky, so close he could taste it on his tongue, a taste like warm copper or blood, and then he was falling backward.

"*I am proud of you.*"
    The voice was sharp, a knife in his brain.
    He was adrift in a void and the only direction was the direction of the voice, behind him, always behind him.
    "*You stumbled but you never fell. And lesser men have fallen before. But not you. And now here you are, so close to finishing your work.*"
    "I am dead now," he said.
    And he heard the voice laugh, a sound that made the void rumble.
    "*That is not what you meant to say.*"
    "What did I mean to say?" he asked.
    "*Why must you make me say it for you?*"
    "I am dying now. Is that what I meant to say?"
    "*You were closer the first time.*"
    "Closer to what?"
    "*To what you have been searching for.*"
    "And what is that?" he asked.
    "*The truth.*"
    "But not dead?"
    "*No.*"
    "Do not lie to me."
    "*Open your eyes.*"
    And he opened his eyes, and the jungle was a roof above him. The rain had stopped, and the sky was the gray of near dawn.
    "*Do you think yourself dead now?*" the voice asked.
    "I cannot feel my body."
    "*Then sit up.*"
    And his back arched, and he sat up. He felt the misting warmth of the jungle at first, then the familiar aches returned. His ravaged arms, his frayed nerves, the throbbing in his skull. His hands were bloodied, and he began to cry.

"Why are you crying?" the voice asked.

"I hurt."

"You should wear this pain like epaulets. Badges of honor. It is brilliant this hurt you have done yourself, crafted piece by piece like some splendid armor."

"You mock me."

"Never. Not I."

"Who are you?" he asked.

"I am a black star in your head."

"What is your name?"

"I am the sunless dawn."

"Why are you here?"

"You birthed me."

"No more riddles," he said.

"Of course," the voice said.

"I would know you totally."

"You already do."

"I would set eyes on you."

"Then look."

And he turned to see the jungle behind him and sitting stiffly, with its back to a tree, was a man's body. Its red tunic was trimmed with gold. Its hands were small but strong. Its head was tilted at an impossible angle, and where its face should have been was a hole. Maggots writhed in the hole and giant roaches, and set deep in that blackness was a spider with red glowing eyes like a cluster of stars.

He blinked, and the body was gone. The world seemed hazy and imperfect. He could see well enough but could not focus his eyes completely and on his periphery was a halo of white, like frost on the edges of a window.

He rose to his feet, his body stiff and unresponsive. He felt as though something had broken inside him. He could not name it, and there was no pain from it but the rhythms of his body seemed off, like an elaborate clockwork with a loose spring.

Something sparkled ahead of him and he moved toward it, clomping loose-kneed through the tangle until he had come upon a gauntlet. He checked his waist and saw that neither of his gauntlets hung there, and he picked up this gauntlet and examined it and finding that it was his, hitched it to his belt. He continued on a little ways and found another gauntlet, then continued on a bit farther and saw the body.

It lay on its back, arms pinwheeled, legs spread. He stood staring at the ruin of its face for some time. If not for the one good eye, he would never have recognized it for Vorenicus.

Next to its shoulder lay broken teeth, some knocked out whole, roots intact, and also a bloodied rock. He lifted the rock with one hand, felt its heft. He wondered if he should not be feeling something else and, wondering this, hurled the rock into the jungle.

19

―⟞⟨⟩⟝―

He wandered in the light of this new day. He sought the road but knew not where it lay, nor his direction. He did not worry over this but continued moving and trusted in the jungle to guide him. When the path he walked became impenetrable, with a thicket of trees packed too densely or a pit of quicksand he could not circle, he changed course and continued moving. Sometimes when he closed his eyes, he heard the jungle rearranging itself, and when he opened his eyes, a wall of brush would stand before him where no wall stood before, or a puddle that seemed impassable, and he would move on, walking where resistance was lightest and the land seemed to slope downward.

When he reached the road, he did not stop to consider in which direction lay the city and which the fort. Knowing his destination, but not knowing his course, he chose to walk. He came upon the city as the sun neared its zenith. A vision overcame him then.

He saw the city deserted, its buildings crumbling husks, great webs of vines spread over the council hall, and the docks carpeted with moss. He saw the Grand Market flattened and its pavement cracked and broken by the roots of great trees. The ground was a tangle of plant life, where nested insects and small vermin so plentiful the floor seemed always to writhe. Above it all the statue of the mute jungle goddess watched with downturned eyes.

When the vision cleared, he found himself kneeling, and he stood and turned for the fort.

. . .

The soldiers at the gate had marked his approach, and by the time he reached the fort proper, the men had gathered as though to greet him like a conqueror in triumph. They were shouting to him, but he could not understand their words. He walked steadily. He had been moving for hours, but there was no pain in his legs—he was beyond pain.

He passed through the legionnaires soundlessly. They parted before him, granting him a wide berth, as though his wounds were communicable. And then Galerius appeared and clutched him tight about the shoulders and he collapsed and Galerius eased him to the floor.

Galerius was speaking, the words a tremor against the side of his head.

"Vorenicus is dead," Cassius said.

And the tremor against his head stopped, and the silence that followed was the quiet of an ocean after a storm.

He lay unsleeping in Vorenicus's bed. Attendants stripped him and sponged him clean. Two healers arrived and considered his naked body as they would a chessboard they had come upon with a game already in progress and one side in a difficult position.

A young Native girl wrapped his arms in fresh bandages, wrapping them tight, her smooth hands working deftly. A tray of food lay on the floor next to the bed, and he could smell burned bacon and oatmeal sweetened with honey and fresh bread, but he did not eat.

They dressed him in a legion tunic, red trimmed with gold.

When Galerius arrived, he cleared the room. He sat on the edge of the bed and did not speak for a time, made no eye contact with Cassius until Cassius sat up.

"Can you hear me?" Galerius asked.

"I can," Cassius said.

"The healers say you're mostly unresponsive."

"I don't want to be healed by spell."

"Have you slept?"

"No."

"You should get some rest?"

"I'm not tired." Cassius's voice was flat and lifeless, as though he were reading aloud a forced confession. He stared off into the middle distance. His face was pained, but he did not appear to be hurt, like a man who has long lived with a deep discomfort and resigned himself to it.

"What about eating?" Galerius grabbed a piece of bacon from Cassius's plate and folded it and ate it, licking the grease from his fingers. "That will give you back some of your strength."

"I feel strong enough," Cassius said. "Have you spoken with the general?"

"I have."

"When does he want to see me?"

"He hasn't asked to see you."

Cassius looked to Galerius. "I'd like to see him. I have things to tell him."

"Yes, you've said that," Galerius snapped. "Again and again. And besides that, you mostly said nonsense. The peace talks fell apart and Vorenicus is dead. He knows that. There's no reason for you to ramble at him right now."

"There are things he must hear. About the bosses. About the city."

"That wouldn't be such a smart thing for you to do right now," Galerius said.

"You're scared."

"Scared of what?"

"You wished Vorenicus dead, then it happened."

"I did no such thing."

"Don't talk to me as though I'm simple. I was there. I remember."

Galerius patted his arm. "Just get some rest for now. You did a good job."

The drums played all afternoon and into the night. Marching rhythms. Clacking snares and deep bass, and beneath even the bass, the sound of boots as soldiers moved in formation. He heard trumpets, too, the slow grind of massive wheels, the whine of worked pulleys. A great orchestration just beyond the walls of his room. He wondered if this were the sound of the world ending.

He emerged from the officers' quarters and, in the pale light of the moon, saw rows of legionnaires assembled, the light glinting from their helmets and spears like the streetlamps of a distant city. Centurions stalked alongside the squares of men, some wielding two swords, shouting, exhorting the soldiers to form up or to move or to present their arms and some shouting for the thrill of it.

War machines lumbered about the clearing, catapults, siege towers, wheeled battering rams pushed by dozens of men who, from a distance, looked like centipede legs.

Standards flew above the ranks. He spotted lions and horses and boars, numbers wrought from gold, bizarre beasts with names older than any language he knew, dog-faced men, apes with snakes for arms. And above all this parade of grotesqueries soared the Antioch flag, an eagle with spread wings, gold against crimson.

The scale of the procession stunned him and, looking on with his strange new vision, he knew the terrible beauty in it.

The general sat before the hearth, shuffling two handfuls of ivory tiles. The tiles were part of a diviner's set. Thin as wafers and each one painted with a different figure, they were popular in the far east as a tool to predict a man's future. The general did not turn as Cassius entered.

The room was ravaged, the massive table overturned and the floor scattered with scrolls and parchments. A kettle hung in the fire. Curls of white-blue smoke drifted through the air. The smoke smelled of tobacco and something Cassius could not identify. He stood watching the general for a time, just inside the door.

"Announce yourself," the general shouted.

"It's me," Cassius said. "Do you have time to talk?"

The general continued shuffling.

"I've time." The general spoke slowly, his voice far away and low. "All the time in the world."

Cassius stepped into the room and righted a chair and sat. He saw now that Quintus's gauntlets lay in his lap. The box of brown powder was set at his side, and the box was open and powder spilled around it.

"Would you have news of Vorenicus?" Cassius asked.

"Do you think me so slow as to not hear of my own son's death? The news has reached me, boy."

"I'm sorry for your loss."

"Sorry that I bear it or sorry that you couldn't prevent it?" The general finished shuffling and set the tiles on the floor facedown. He turned the top tile slowly and placed it on the ground.

"I'm sorry it happened at all."

"Because you admired him?" The general looked up now, his eyes glazed and the pupils very small.

"Yes."

"But did you believe in him?"

"Believe in him how?"

"Did you believe his vision was right?" Quintus asked. "You claimed he was mocked in the city and that you didn't mock him. But did you keep faith in what he believed?

"No, I did not." An image flashed through Cassius's mind. *A monster with gleaming teeth.* He shut his eyes.

"I see."

"I could claim another opinion if you'd prefer."

"I didn't ask you to do that."

"I thought you'd appreciate my honesty."

"Did I chide you for it?" Quintus revealed a second tile and a third. "At least you admit to it. As opposed to others, who would feign sadness and profess their respect. And all the while think this a matter of a foolish boy meeting his end foolishly."

"I wouldn't do that."

"Too honest for that sort of thing?"

Cassius inspected the tiles. They were arranged in a mirror spread, and the top tile bore the figure of the King of Wands. He wore a red robe and sat upon a lion's throne and at his feet crawled a salamander. Two tiles were set below this, one to either side. The first was the Five of Wands, and on this tile, five men with five sticks were fighting. The second tile, directly opposite the five, was Justice, and it depicted a seated women, crowned and with an upraised sword.

"What happened out there?" Quintus asked.

"The talks didn't go well."

"Why am I not surprised?"

"An argument erupted, and one of Piso's men attacked me. A melee followed." Cassius saw the flaming pavilion, smelled the thick smoke in the air. He heard the crash of erupting spells, the clang of steel on steel. He balled his fists and held his breath and the vision faded. He returned to the general's quarters.

"And what of my boy, Cassius?" Quintus placed two more tiles directly below the previous two. The Tower, burning, crumbling, and the Hanged Man.

"I don't know."

"Goddamn you." Quintus sprang to his feet. His face glistened in the light of the hearth fire. The look from his pointed eyes pinned Cassius through the chest. "Come to me with news of my son's death? And then feign ignorance? I've killed men for less."

"A fit overtook me."

Smoke had gathered around the general, and he seemed to draw up into it and grow taller, like some fearsome djinn from Fathalan myth.

"What did you see then?" Quintus asked. "Do you remember?"

"I do."

"Tell me."

"A terrible monster." Cassius felt the weight of the rock in his hand, felt its slick, hard surface. He checked his hand, but his hand was empty. "All teeth and mouth."

"And then?"

"Then there was a voice in my head."

"A voice?" Quintus's tone softened. "What did it sound like?"

"Like no other voice in the world."

The general stared off, lost in thought. He began to mutter, so softly Cassius could not hear his words.

The kettle whistled and startled Quintus awake. Cursing, he

reached into the fire and grabbed the steaming kettle and hurled it across the room.

He shook his hand and cupped it, brought it close to his chest. The skin had already begun to blister. He seemed awake now, more alive in the eyes than he had been when Cassius arrived. He tucked his hand behind his back, as though embarrassed by it, and then returned to his spread.

He revealed two more tiles.

"You ordered the army mobilized?" Cassius asked. "Are they marching for the city?"

"They'd march to the gates beyond the veil if I so ordered. Storm the kingdom of Death himself."

"And do you mean to take back the city tonight?"

"I mean to rip the gods from their thrones. Crumble mountains. Boil oceans." Quintus gripped the front of his tunic with both hands. And the anguish on his face, the menace in his voice, made Cassius believe he could do the things he said, if only tonight.

"Can I accompany the troops?"

"Why would you do that?"

"For vengeance."

Quintus did not respond.

Cassius approached the diviner's spread. Over the general's shoulder, he could see the two new tiles. The Queen of Cups, the Ace of Wands.

"Did you hear me?" Cassius asked. "I said I'd go to see vengeance done."

"What do you know of vengeance, boy?"

"I know that in the old days, in the age of heroes, the death of a son demanded two deaths in turn."

The general played the last tile, placing it below and between the previous two, in line with the first tile played. It was the Ten of Swords and it depicted a prone man, pierced with ten blades and bleeding.

"Go," he whispered finally. "And if somehow you survive this night, never return here."

20

~~~

assius marched in the middle ranks of the procession, hundreds of wide-brimmed helmets arrayed before him in the night and each one lit by torchlight, so that the entire column seemed a river of fire flowing toward the city. Nearby, a circle of retainers orbited Galerius, holding maps and scrolls, flags for signaling, reports from centurions.

The beat of marching boots matched the beat of Cassius's heart.

He wore legion armor, a segmented steel cuirass, greaves on his shins, a wide-brimmed helmet, a short, stabbing sword at his hip. When the wind picked up, he heard a high reeling sound in the dark, on either side of the road, and he wondered if the jungle were laughing at him.

He had not yet donned his gauntlets as he came in sight of the city walls. The front ranks had already joined in battle, hurling volleys of spears and arrows as they struggled to raise siege towers.

The front gates were barred, but he could see they would not hold, the wood warped and ancient. As a battering ram drove home its first blow, a sound like thunder rang, and the gates splintered.

Sheets of white-and-blue flame rained down from the guard towers and counterspells rose to meet this inferno, three or four for every offensive spell cast. Sparks erupted as spells fizzled and died, and the colorful effects of the counters themselves made the air throb and pulse with ethereal light.

Down below, men caught under an unblocked spell broke formation and fled into the jungle, some drenched in flame, casting light out into the night like wraiths.

A catapult loosed a flaming boulder that struck a guard tower with a deafening crack. The tower pitched drunkenly, then hung suspended in midair, resisting the fall. Men spilled from inside the tower; and then, finally succumbing, it collapsed and broke open a section of wall.

"Breach! Breach!"

The cry went up from the front of the column to the rear, carried by every legionnaire. Men stampeded forward. Cassius tripped and nearly fell underfoot but managed to right himself before he was trampled. He charged ahead, shouldering into the wall of soldiers before him, eager to be part of the violent scrum.

Above the din, he heard the clear, strong voices of the centurions calling their men to hold ranks, to not break lines.

As he drew nearer the wall, he felt a thrumming in his chest. He donned his gauntlets, and his hands burned.

Embers drifted above the streets of Hightown. Flames had swallowed entire blocks, and smoke hung thick in the air.

Cassius's eyes stung. His throat felt raw, and his chest burned with each sooty breath.

The massive column of legionnaires that had poured down out of the jungle like some mythical plague, like some cursed red tide come to wash over benighted lands, had broken into smaller formations once past the city gates.

His own company was two hundred strong, the avenues not wide enough to accommodate larger units. From nearby lanes and alleys, he heard the sound of other companies moving through the city, the cries of their centurions audible above the din of battle and some men singing soldier's chanteys as they moved, songs of martial glory and the triumph of Antioch.

The men in front of him marched in lockstep, shields held high, stabbing swords at the ready. Centurions shouted for the men to tighten their lines, while Galerius urged them on with cries of "For Vorenicus."

A mob had gathered in one of the main thoroughfares leading

from the city gates, a few hundred strong, mostly men but with some small boys and even women. They hurled rocks at the legionnaires, taunted them, shook their weapons in the air, swords and spears and makeshift weapons as well, chair legs for cudgels, woodcutter's axes, torches.

A centurion called the line to halt and, as one, the line halted. Cassius had never before witnessed such precision. He felt himself a part of some terrible beast, with steel for skin and swords for teeth.

"Arm!" a centurion called.

The legionnaires hoisted their spears.

"Loose!"

Cassius did not see the first spear thrown, but he saw the first to land. It sailed in a graceful arc, then curved and fell from the sky to plunge through a man's thigh. More spears followed in quick order. Bodies collapsed in a spray of blood.

Still, the mob would not scatter. They drew together, defenseless as they were, not a shield amongst them, and retreated up the lane, leaving their wounded to lie bleeding on the ground they had abandoned.

The legionnaires continued forward. They approached an intersection, and the centurions slowed their pace.

Cassius felt the familiar tug in his chest, the feeling hollow and discomforting. A blinding flash lit the sky, and when it cleared, three purple-pink flares hung suspended in air.

"Take cover," Cassius called.

But he was no centurion. He knew not the words to move the beast, to make it speed up or attack or defend itself.

The flares hung motionless for a second; and then, one by one, they fell, ripping through the legionnaires, shattering shields, punching through armor.

When the last spear had fallen, the legionnaires lay kneeling with their shields raised to the sky or lay prostrate. The centurion called for the men to regroup and most of the men rose to their feet, but some did not.

From an adjacent street, two men approached, one bald and with a long beard and the other with a plumed helmet but otherwise unarmored. The houses behind these men were afire, and the men moved through the flames unscathed. In their wake lay a dozen bodies, some bent at impossible angles, some smoking and charred.

"Spellcasters! Left flank!"

The bearded spellcaster raised a hand over his head. A high-pitched whistle sounded, and the roof of a hut across the lane exploded in a geyser of steam and boiling water. The house crumpled, wood and thatch and boiling water raining down on the legionnaires. He had time enough to cast this single spell before a spear struck him in his ribs. He pitched backward, sparks exploding from his fingertips as he fell.

The spellcaster with the plumed helmet moved to aid him. With a quick gesture, a wall of fire erupted from the ground, blocking the lane.

Cassius felt a throbbing, strong now, like a second heartbeat. A great trumpeting sounded, not from the ranks of the soldiers but from down the lane.

The flame wall parted, and from behind it emerged what seemed, at first glance, a giant gray bat, with wide wings that beat the air as it moved. And then it lifted its head and Cassius caught sight of its tusks and its large trunk. The rest of its body crashed through the wall, and it did not seem to run so much as to fall forward and catch itself with each massive step. The ground shook. One soldier, then another dropped his shield and fled.

As the legionnaires turned to face this new threat, the centurion shouted for them to hold fast.

Cassius heard Galerius curse.

He closed his eyes, and the shape he pictured was a maze of sharp angles. The heat at the base of his skull made him shiver. He opened his eyes and held out his hand and sighted to the middle of the lane.

There was a sound like thunder, and the ground trembled. The elephant wobbled, then regained its footing, momentum carrying it forward. A narrow crack split the lane; and then the crack opened wider and stretched until the chasm was ten yards across, and the elephant, moving at a run, tried to halt but could not, and toppled over into the pit with a great cry.

The flame wall broke again, and a fireball rocketed down the lane. It struck the ground and bounced forward, trailing fire and smoke. It arced over the pit and sailed above the intersection, and the centurion shouted to raise shields, but his cry was lost to the explosion.

The blast knocked Cassius to his knees. Bits of flaming rock showered down on him, and from over his shoulder, he glimpsed smoke rising from scores of shields. But he was not burned, was unharmed completely, aside from a ringing in his ears.

Around him, legionnaires lay crumpled like discarded playthings.

"Forward," Galerius yelled.

And some of the men were rising to their feet, but most were not.

"We've cornered him, sir." The legionnaire had lost his helmet. The hair on the left side of his head was singed and patches of scalp visible there. "It's a dead-end street, so there's no retreat."

"Is the building surrounded?" Cassius asked. He was a step behind the legionnaire and Galerius as they hurried through the lane.

"It's covered on all sides."

"Good," Galerius said. "Any resistance?"

They rounded the corner, and in the street, they found a squad of fifty legionnaires shield to shield with an equal number of Cinna's men.

"Some."

There was a spellcaster on the balcony of the Purse. He leaned out over the balustrade, hands raised high. A golden glow throbbed steadily in the lane below, and when it vanished, a giant appeared.

The giant stood nearly as tall as the Purse, naked and one-eyed. It wielded a tree trunk with two hands, its skin glistening with a wet gold film. It roared and swung its tree trunk overhead and strode up behind Cinna's lines to join the fray.

"What the hell is that?" Galerius shouted.

The legionnaires panicked at the sight of the giant, holes opening in their ranks as men deserted, casting aside their shields and wide-brimmed helmets.

A soldier loosed his spear, and the spear arced upward at the creature and passed through its chest, out its back. The creature never slowed, nor did any wound appear.

From the middle ranks of the formation, spellcasters raised their gauntleted hands into the air and loosed geysers of fire, a cone of ice shards sharp as razors, an acid mist. But the giant, by some unknown enchantment, marched through this arcane volley unscathed. Seeing this, the ranks of the legionnaires buckled and finally broke. All while the centurions cursed them as craven and fought to drive them forward.

"It's an illusion," Cassius said.

"They don't know that," Galerius shouted. "Do something, or they'll be routed."

Cassius clenched his fists and shut his eyes. Warmth spread through his belly and up into his throat, growing hotter as it moved. He trapped this heat in his mouth, let it build until his face burned and tears streamed down his cheeks. When finally he opened his mouth, an unearthly howl rent the night air. Men fell screaming, clutched their bleeding ears. Cassius fixed the spellcaster on the balcony with his gaze and as the demonic yell struck him, the spellcaster staggered, then toppled gracelessly over the balustrade, falling to his death.

The giant vanished in a flash of gold.

A cheer went up from the remaining legionnaires. The centurions urged them to tighten their lines, and the men regrouped and started forward, advancing with renewed strength. The Purse guards faltered.

Cinna appeared on the balcony. He was dressed in ill-fitting armor, a cuirass too small to fit over his gut, leather greaves bulging from the girth of his legs, an unbuckled helmet. He looked like a pudgy boy playing war.

He held a wine bottle in one hand and he took a long pull of this and surveyed the skirmish. He cursed his men, shouted for them to defend their flank.

He looked up the lane and spotted Cassius. Their eyes met.

"You filthy traitor," he yelled. He spat toward Cassius, hurled the wine bottle.

In the lane below, the legionnaires had outflanked the Purse guards, broken their lines, and Cinna's men fled while soldiers ran them down, speared them in their backs.

"Cinna," Galerius shouted. "It's not too late to surrender."

Cinna gestured obscenely and retreated into his chambers. He was inside for a few minutes. When he reappeared, he climbed up onto the balustrade, climbing nimbly, like some fat, spry monkey. A rope dangled from his neck, knotted at the back of his head and leading up into the other room.

"Be sure to give the old man a message for me," he shouted. "I'll be waiting for him beyond the veil."

He leapt and, to Cassius's surprise, the rope held.

The Market was an inferno. Great pools of flame covered most of the square and storefronts burned uncontrollably. Standing on the northern side and facing south, Cassius scanned for movement. He could see no figures amidst the ravaged stalls, nor any standards. Strange beasts bayed in agony, and occasionally, a spell lit the sky.

A burning building on the edge of the Market collapsed and spilled flame across the pavement. For a brief moment, Cassius glimpsed a massive rider charging through this fire. He wore a cloak the color of poppies. His face was bloodstained, and he had long red hair pulled back in a braid. He wielded a forward-curving blade, twirling it above his head, and from his saddle, severed heads dangled from straps.

"More," he cried. "More."

The rider turned his head and locked eyes with Cassius. He smiled. His teeth flashed gold in the light of the fires.

And then, as suddenly as he appeared, he vanished, like an apparition in the flames.

Cassius turned back to the command tent. It had been assembled hastily, and for all the slaughter of the night, a table could not be recovered in the ruins. Galerius and a lieutenant kneeled on the pavement, maps spread between them, and a circle of legionnaires stood guard over this makeshift war council. Cassius squatted and listened.

"We've pushed the mob back to these three choke points." The officer tapped the map three times, smudging it with soot. He wore his helmet pushed back on his head, his thin face smeared with grime and blood.

"I don't care about the mob," Galerius said. "I care about Cinna's forces. Are they still fighting now that he's dead?"

"There's no difference between the mob and Cinna's men at this point, sir. We're fighting all sides."

"Can you finish them in these places?" Galerius asked.

"It'll take time."

"We don't have time, soldier. I need to cross this Market and get to Lowtown before Piso can fortify his defenses."

"The Market can't be crossed, sir."

"I don't want to hear that."

"What I mean, sir, is we can't march across it," the legionnaire said. "There are spellcasters hidden around the perimeter. Dozens of them."

"Piso's?"

"Most of them, I'd assume. But probably some of Cinna's leftovers as well. They're waiting in ambush for anyone who steps into the Market. There's not enough cover to protect the men in there. They'd be caught in a cross fire."

"Where are our killers to run interference?" Galerius shouted.

An explosion sounded in the distance.

"We tried that with Third Company, sir. With nearly twenty of our killers backing their play. It was a massacre."

"We'll go around the Market then."

"That'll take time. The wide avenues let us use size and numbers to our advantage, sir. Lanes and alleys won't. It'll be slow work."

"Listen to the words I am speaking: We don't have time."

"The advanced guard has already reached the docks, sir," another legionnaire reported. "A half dozen spellcasters. They've burned nearly all of it. There's no retreat for the Lowtown forces."

"Some good news for once." A drab pouch lay by Galerius's side, and he patted this reflexively. "I want a total sweep tonight. Execute anyone even suspected of belonging to Piso or Cinna. Tell the men to accept no surrender."

"That's a bit ambitious, sir. Our hands are full containing the Hightown mob."

Galerius fixed the legionnaire with a cold stare. "Is that how they taught you to speak to a commanding officer, legionnaire?"

The legionnaire tapped his heart with a fist, bowed his head. "Forgive me, sir. I spoke too freely."

"You spoke like a coward. Do you mean to tell me we can't put down this rabble?" Galerius swept out a hand, indicting the entire city.

The bold legionnaire did not respond.

"Speak, damn you," Galerius shouted.

"We're fighting well, sir. But the mob won't quit. It's proving hard to break them. We're reporting casualties of nearly one-fifth our forces. And we're already outnumbered as it is. Extending our lines into Lowtown would stretch us thin."

"What if we pushed them into the Market?" Cassius asked.

The legionnaire stared silently, unsure if he should acknowledge the comment.

"What do you mean?" Galerius asked.

"Why not funnel the mob down into the Market?" Cassius said. "Concentrate our forces in one place. That way, we wouldn't spread ourselves too thin. And we'd have enough people to survive the crossing."

"We'd still lose a lot of men," the legionnaire said.

"Would we make it to the other side with a force capable of fighting Piso?" Galerius asked.

"Sir, the losses would be—"

"Answer the question."

"We would, sir."

"We could march down the main avenue," Cassius said. "We'd be at Piso's front door in an hour."

"Do we need to feed our men into a meat grinder when there are other options available to us?" The legionnaire glared at Cassius. He would not be so bold with a ranking officer, but he felt no need to hold his tongue when addressing a mercenary.

"Mind your tone, legionnaire," Galerius said. "This plan seems to be the only one that takes account of time. Can you assure me Piso's reinforcements won't arrive by ship in the morning? Or that the general won't call us back to fort? Can you?"

"No, sir."

"Then all this would be for nothing. And Piso would still be standing."

"Even with most of our spellcasters in one place," the legionnaire said, "the opportunities for ambush are tremendous. And what about the mob?"

"The mob will get caught in the Market cross fire as well," Galerius said. "But without the protection of our spells. They'll help shield our men, and we'll finally break them. Two birds with one stone, as they say."

"Sir, this will end in a massacre."

"It won't be the first massacre this Market has seen."

White sheets hung from the windows of Piso's hall and from the windows of the barracks. The horde of fighters they had expected to find in the plaza were absent. The streets were mostly empty, and only a handful of men stood guard outside the entrance to the hall. These men were unarmored, and their weapons lay at their feet.

"This might be a trap," Cassius said.

"I wouldn't put it past the bastard." Galerius motioned for two legionnaires to follow him inside. A heavy drab pouch dangled from his belt. "But he has to know that if something goes wrong, the legion will burn this place to the ground."

They found Piso seated at the long table in the center of the room, a feast set before him, a single guard at his side. The guard was young, probably sixteen or so, and unarmed, like the men out front. He made a show of raising his bare hands as the legionnaires entered.

"Forgive us." Galerius bowed mockingly. "If you're busy, it's no trouble for us to come back later."

"Sit." Piso was gnawing the last scraps of meat from a chicken bone. "Eat if you want."

There were plates of roasted chicken, thick stew, rice, pigs' feet in oil, cheese, and wine.

"Were you expecting Cinna?" Galerius sat across from Piso.

Cassius remained standing.

"No," Piso said. "I figured it would be Vorenicus."

"Vorenicus is dead."

Piso stiffened, as though struck a physical blow. "In the melee at the truce talks?"

"That's what I'm told," Galerius said.

"I had no idea."

"Of course."

"You think I'm lying, you dolt. If I had known, maybe I would have been more prepared for your attack. Cinna, too." A long, curved knife was dug into the table. Piso plucked the knife from the wood and cut away a small bit of chicken and ate it directly off the knife. He tossed the bone aside.

"How Vorenicus died is irrelevant. What matters is that the general has had enough of the old system. Your time is up, Master Piso."

"I see." Piso nodded. He sipped from a mug of wine and leaned back in his chair. "I see it all now. It's brilliant really."

"I don't know what you mean."

Piso turned to address his guard. Cassius could see only the scarred half of his face.

"It seems Galerius here convinced that lunatic to kill Vorenicus," Piso said to the guard, as though the boy cared at all for the intrigue that had led to this moment. "With Quintus's son out of the way, Galerius becomes the general's second-in-command and his avenger."

"I'm here to discuss terms for your surrender," Galerius said. "If you'd rather not, I have—"

"When the general learns the boy's dead," Piso continued, still addressing the guard, "he seeks to punish me and Cinna for it. So he sends our hero Galerius to town with the entire legion. And when this is all finished, the commander here can swoop in and run the city while the good general mourns."

"Shut up," Galerius yelled.

"You rat-hearted bastard. How long have you had your daggers at Vorenicus's back?"

"I won't take that from you."

"I could understand the maniac here." Piso motioned to Cassius. "He just likes to cause trouble. But you, Galerius. You took an oath. The deepest pit in the great hells is reserved for oathbreakers."

Galerius stood from his seat. "Enough of this."

"Sit down, Galerius," Piso said calmly.

"I don't take orders from you."

"No, but you'll want to hear what I have to say. You too, lunatic." Piso nodded gravely.

"Speak then," Galerius said.

"That was a good move you pulled on the docks. Burning my means of escape and the like. And before I even realized war was at my goddamn gates."

"Maybe if you and Cinna were on friendlier terms, he would have warned you."

"Oh, the pervert told me the legion was on its way. Figured it best we combine our forces. But by the time he spotted your formation, you bastards were halfway down the damn road. Even a man as talented as me is at the mercy of time."

"You were beaten by a superior force." Galerius smiled. "There's no shame in that."

"Well, let's not go ordering a triumph just yet." Piso laughed, a slow, humorless sound. "See, I'm not the type to surrender. Just don't have it in me. Old legion blood in my veins. Did you know that, Galerius?"

"I did."

"Had an uncle served as an officer under Aentilius. Died fighting the Widsith in the Black Forest. Beautiful funeral ceremony. State funded and everything. You think they'll give that to you when you die, Galerius? How many years in the service for you?"

"Twenty."

"Twenty. That is commendable. I swear before the gods, there's nothing I respect so much as a man who serves the public good." Piso raised a mug in toast. He drank, then slammed the mug down. He belched. "Of course, the state does frown on rebellion."

"Rebellion?"

"Yes, that's what you're doing, Galerius. You and your army out there are taking an Antiochi city by force. And since our good general and his army aren't actually recognized by the senate, I wonder how they'll take the news that the crazy bugger is no longer content to rot in his jungle and extort his neighbors. Instead, he wants to sack cities and install governments. I can't imagine they'll be pleased."

"What are you talking about?"

"Do you have family on the mainland, Galerius?"

Galerius did not respond.

"How about you, maniac?"

"No," Cassius said.

"Friends then?" Piso asked.

"None."

"No family or friends. All alone are you?"

"I have a father living yet," said Cassius.

"Good for you. But I'll bet old Galerius here has a lot more relations than that. And do you know what the senate does to the families of rebels?" Piso licked his burned lips. "They take their lands. They take their money. They strip them of citizenship and strike their names from public records. They turn them into exiles, lower even than foreigners or slaves. And any honest citizen who wants to rob them or kill them, well that's just between them and the gods. Because the law doesn't protect exiles, does it, Galerius?"

"Is there a point to this, Piso?"

"The point is, you can have this island if you like. But out in the real world, you're going to be doing yourself a world of hurt."

"Are you coming with us or not?" Galerius stood.

"I wouldn't trust the general not to torture me to death if I did surrender. So no, I'm not going with you, Galerius."

"Fine, then." Galerius headed for the door. "We'll settle this a different way."

"You didn't encounter much resistance getting here, did you? Not once you passed the Market. Did you expect to find my men in full armor and formation, trading blows like you found in Hightown?"

"I expected a fight at least, you coward."

"Know why you didn't see any of my men in the streets?" Piso called. "Because they're not in the streets."

Galerius stopped.

"They're hiding. Ferreted deep in the slums. And when your army begins to march back north, they're going to spring up and attack and slink away again. No standing fight. No protracted spell battles. Just one hit and one kill, then they're gone again. Imagine that repeated every three blocks. And if you want to stop it, your men will have to go house to house to flush them out."

"You gutless bastard. I turned Hightown to ash, I'll do the same here."

"I heard you suffered quite a few casualties in the Market. Do you really think you have a force big enough to sweep half this city?" Piso grinned. "I don't. Lowtown is a killing field now. Enjoy your trip home, you sons of bitches."

"You don't think you'll make it out of this, do you?" Galerius shouted.

"Of course not. But at least I got to enjoy one last meal before I went to hell." Piso turned to his guard. "Do it. And make sure I don't feel a thing."

The guard raised his hands and Cassius felt a thrumming in his chest. He reached for his gauntlets and dove. The blast sent the table spinning end over end. A cloud of fire sped outward from the center of the room, washing over Cassius.

When the smoke cleared, he found Piso lying facedown, unmoving, the back of his tunic afire. Galerius's arm protruded from under the table and when Cassius lifted the edge of the table, he found the body sprawled like a broken marionette, its face charred.

At the door, the blast had knocked the two legionnaires on their backs, but the fire had not reached them. They rose now, moving slowly, checking themselves for wounds.

"What in the hell happened?" one asked.

"Did you do this?" the other shouted at Cassius.

"Not me." Cassius retrieved the drab pouch that Galerius had carried out of the Purse, looping it around his belt and knotting it on the hip opposite his gauntlets.

Piso's guard was kneeling just past his boss's corpse. His right arm hung limp, the thumb and index finger of his right hand burned to bone, and the small pocket of flesh between the two, where he had held the jewel in secret, a mass of seared gristle. He was trembling.

Cassius approached him. The boy did not look up.

"My hand," the boy said. "My hand."

From outside, Cassius heard the soldiers of Galerius's personal guard fighting with Piso's unarmed men. The two legionnaires ran for the door. Cassius headed for the stairway to the upper floors.

"He told me it would only hurt a little," the boy muttered. "I can't feel my arm."

Cassius found the rooms on the second floor ransacked. Beds stripped bare and footlockers overturned.

He kicked through piles of clothes until he found a tunic large enough to fit over his legion uniform, the tunic olive green. He searched the rest of the rooms but found nothing worth taking.

On the fourth floor, he found a cloak with a hood to obscure his face and found also a box embossed with a death's-head skull, the kind sometimes carved into Antiochi gravestones. He opened the box and what he found inside made his heartbeat quicken.

The only defeat was death. That's what the Masters taught. Anything less was a setback, an inconvenience. But what of a man such as he? A man who had cheated death, who refused to die.

The Masters had no such lessons to guide him. But there were other words that he recalled, the general's words.

He was an agent of great forces, the general had said, beyond the ken of normal man. He was the equal of Death, and they would meet as such in the end.

Cassius ran his fingertips across the embossed skull of the box. Equals.

He gathered the box, the tunic, and the cloak, and then returned downstairs.

The spellcaster with the wounded hand was gone, as was Galerius's body. Piso's body still lay facedown. He found the large knife on the floor, next to the overturned table. He snatched it up and approached the body, his free hand working to undo the knot in the drab pouch.

When he finished, he exited through the front door and discovered that the legionnaires had killed Piso's guards. They had dragged Galerius's dead body out of the front room, using one of the white truce flags to lift it, and had laid it in the plaza. They stood ringed around the body, looked down at it as though it were a sleeping Galerius and the men afraid to wake him.

He passed them and headed for the mouth of an alley.

"Hey," one of the men called. "Hey, what happened in there?"

Cassius did not acknowledge the question. As he walked, he threw the large cloak over his armor.

"To hell with him," another man said. "Never trusted that one at my back anyway."

The cloak smelled of urine and of a sharp body odor. The hood obscured Cassius's vision, but the streets were mostly quiet, and he kept to the shadows. There were few streetlamps in these lanes, and when he crept into alleyways, there were none at all. He passed scores of bodies, most dead but some calling out to him for aid or for release.

He was a block outside of Hightown, back in legion-occupied territory, when he shed the cloak and the green tunic to reveal the legion uniform and armor underneath.

He returned to the Market and scanned it in the dark. Where tents and merchant stalls had once stood, now lay the remains of legionnaires and civilians, Antiochi and Khimir, men and beasts. The entire square was slick with blood, and above it all floated a cloud of oily smoke.

The Market moved. Shapes thrashed in the light of the fires, and the cries of the wounded were loud. Small skirmishes still raged, spells flashing and the air shaking with explosions. Creatures stalked through the carnage, wolves and lithe jungle cats and apes with ponderous brows.

The council hall was in flames, two of its pillars smashed and one corner of the roof collapsed. Bodies lay prone on the steps, locked in grotesque poses, reaching or hunched forward or with arms spread cruciform, like some grim painting.

Cassius could see the goddess erect above it all, so white she seemed to shine. He knew there were pools of blood at her feet, and he waited for her to awake, to sweep those blank eyes over this terrible scene and acknowledge a sacrifice unrivaled in all the history of the world.

But instead, she stood and stared.

Cassius found the bar undamaged. Farther up the street, a crowd had formed to fight a house fire, but otherwise, the lane was deserted and the houses mostly untouched by flame or violence. The entrance through the stables was unlocked.

In the dark, Cassius scanned the bar until he found a candle. He lit the candle with the smokeless spell fire, and by the cornflower-blue light, he checked each of the rooms and saw that they were empty.

He found a shaving mirror in the drawer of Lucian's nightstand and found also a small bar of soap, a straight razor, and a scissor. He took these to the guest room.

He set the box on the bed and the items from the drawer as well.

He walked downstairs and wet his hair with water from an earthenware pitcher and filled a small bowl with water and returned with it to the room. He shuttered the window and locked the door.

Cassius stripped naked, discarding the armor, setting aside the drab pouch, and then opened the box. He removed three large clay jars, each one stopped with a massive cork, and lined them on the floor. He pulled out the white tunic and placed this on the bed, still folded, then removed the white short cloak and the white belt.

He sat on the floor. Using the scissors, he cut the bandages off his arms. He wet his face and lathered up a handful of soap and dabbed it along his cheeks and neck and shaved in the light of the candle.

He cut his hair with the scissors. Then he lathered up more soap and worked it through the remaining stubble on his head and shaved himself bald. He shaved his eyebrows and the fine hair of his arms, doing his best to avoid the scabbed wounds there. He shaved his armpits, his pubic hair, his legs.

After this, he inspected himself in the mirror. The face, while different, was still recognizable. The bent nose. The deep-set, bruised eyes, heavy with discolored bags.

He opened the first jar. It contained a matte white paste. He spread the paste along his legs, to the tops of his thighs, covering each leg in white completely, then spread more along his feet and the bottoms of his feet. He opened a second jar and painted his arms and shoulders, his chest to his sternum. He covered his neck and the back of his neck, then covered his face totally, front to back, his eyelids and inside his ears. He left his lips uncolored and his hands.

The third jar contained a blackberry dye. He poured this into his mouth and swished it over his teeth for a time and spat it out. He dipped two fingers into the dye and smeared the dye over his lips. He wiped his fingers dry on the bedsheet.

He donned the white tunic and the white short cloak. He tied the white belt around his waist and hitched his gauntlets to it. Finally, he painted both hands.

He picked up the hand mirror and gazed into it and there, for the first time, he saw his true face.

He was sitting at the table in the far corner when Lucian returned. He sat with his back to the wall, his hands under the table. The drab-colored pouch lay before him on the tabletop and next to it stood the candle lit by the blue flame.

Lucian entered through the front door. He crossed the room slowly, dragging his feet in the dust of the floor. He saw the figure in white, and he stopped. He stared. His face was like the face of a man looking on some small animal wounded beyond his abilities for repair.

"I was out helping with a fire," he said, as though offering an excuse for arriving late.

"It's good to see you, Lucian."

"Yeah, well, it's . . . it's good to see you, too. Are you hungry? Can I get you a drink?"

He shook his head.

"All right, then. I'm going to get a drink. For me. A big one." Lucian walked behind the bar. He moved slowly, deliberately, like a man might move before the face of a reared snake. He checked under the counter and came up with a brown-glass bottle and poured himself a measure of something from this and mixed in water from a nearby pitcher. He drank the mixture in a single gulp, then took a swig from the bottle. He returned to the table.

"Can I sit?" Lucian asked.

"I'd like that."

"All right." Lucian pulled up a chair. He sat. "I was worried I wasn't ever going to see you again. And then all this tonight."

"I've brought you a gift."

He reached for the pouch, and Lucian rocked back. When Lucian accepted the pouch, their hands touched briefly, a bit of white rubbing off on Lucian's fingers.

Lucian peered inside the pouch, then dropped it.

"By the gods, are those—"

"Yes."

"Oh hell." Lucian nudged the pouch away with his foot. "Goddamn it."

"You don't seem pleased."

"Of course I'm not pleased. Why would you bring that to me?"

"I came to thank you."

"With that?"

"Have you been to the jungle, Lucian? Have you moved through it?"

"I don't know. Maybe when I first got here."

"You'd remember."

"Then no. All my time here, I lived in the city."

"It's a different world."

"I'd imagine." Lucian wiped his hand on the underside of the table.

"I still meant what I said."

"And what's that?" Lucian asked.

"Thank you."

"For what?"

"For everything."

A look of discomfort came over Lucian. "Don't say it like that. Not everything."

The room fell silent. "I should be going."

"Going where?" Lucian asked.

"Home."

"And where is that exactly?"

"You know."

"Do I?"

"Besides me, you're the only one who knows."

Lucian nodded. "Of course."

He stood from the table, and Lucian stood with him. He gathered up the drab pouch and headed for the door. He stopped before stepping out into the street, his back still turned.

"Do you regret it?"

"Regret what?" Lucian asked.

"What you did for me?"

"Don't ask me that."

"Would you take it back if you could?"

"I can't." Lucian waved his hand.

"But if you could."

"I had to do it then, given the circumstances. What kind of person would I be if I didn't do it?"

He was silent.

"I didn't know what would follow," Lucian said.

"And if you could take it back? Could undo all that has happened these last weeks?"

"How?" Lucian asked. "By denying shelter to a scared, helpless boy all those years ago? I wouldn't."

He considered this. "Thank you."

"Cassius?"

He did not respond but continued out into the night.

It was near to sunrise before Lucian realized that the room upstairs was afire with blue flame, and by then, too late to stop it, time enough only to flee.

21

〜〜〜

The road was dark, and to light his way, Cassius set fire to the jungle. He hurled fireballs into the overgrowth, summoned clouds of glowing embers and great streams of liquid flame. Swarms of jungle birds took flight from the assault, and sometimes he caught glimpses of ghostlike people in the sudden flashes.

There were five guards posted at the entrance to the fort. When the figure in white appeared, they shouted for him to halt, leveled spears at his face.

"What are you?" a legionnaire asked.

"I'm here to see Quintus. He's expecting me." The figure in white offered the drab pouch to the nearest guard. "This is for him."

The guard looked to the bag. "What is it?"

"It's for the general."

The guard sniffed and grimaced. "Smells awful."

"Just take the damn thing," another man shouted.

The guard set his spear to rest upright in the cradle of his shoulder. He took the pouch and opened it.

"Can't see a damn thing in the dark."

"What is it?"

The guard turned so that he was standing in the light of the moon. "I can't believe this."

The guard passed the bag to another of the legionnaires, and the second man recoiled at the sight inside.

"Someone has to see these," he said.

"The general," the figure in white said. "That's why I'm here."

"Who sent you?"

"The general."

"I didn't ask who sent for you," the guard yelled. "I asked who made you come here."

"The general."

"Listen to me, you loopy bastard—"

He tossed aside his short cloak and shook his gauntleted fist at the guards. There was a sound like air squeezing from a bellows. A cloud of yellow smoke rose from the ground. The figure in white lifted his short cloak to cover his mouth and to cover his nose and stepped back.

The guards froze. They clutched their throats, and one man loosed a slow, rattling gurgle, and then they toppled.

He summoned a gust of wind that blew the cloud clear. He retrieved the drab pouch and continued through the front gate.

The fort was quieter than he remembered. The men who normally patrolled at night were now in the city, some probably looting in Hightown or fighting in Lowtown, and some with their guts spilled over the Market calling to gods for mercy. The mess hall was deserted and all the barracks.

He passed under the gray likeness of General Sabacus, the statue with its eyes focused on the jungle.

The door to the general's quarters was locked. He shattered it with a concentrated shock wave, the door bowing inward under a hail of splinters.

He heard a high-pitched scream, then heard fumbling. He stepped into the room and found the general with his servant girl.

"Get out."

The girl stood and covered herself and slipped past him out the door, her head lowered.

The general reclined nude in his chair. He rubbed his paunch, scratched at his ribs. His eyes were half-closed, and he was sweating in the light of the hearth, his hair soaked and his face very pale.

"So it has come to this." The general wiped at his mouth. He closed his eyes.

"I bring gifts from the city."

The general opened his eyes slowly. He looked around the room as though seeing it for the first time. He motioned for him to bring the bag.

The figure in white crossed the room and presented the general with the drab pouch.

"A gift for me?" Quintus asked.

"That's right."

"I can't remember the last time someone brought me a gift."

"You'll remember this time."

Quintus opened the pouch. He stared inside for some time. It was clear that he recognized the contents, but he seemed to be considering an appropriate response. His face was calm, almost sleepy.

"Beautiful," he said flatly. And then the general closed the pouch and set it on the floor very near to his feet, next to his gauntlets.

"What do you think?" the figure in white asked.

"I think that's the end of that," the general said. "I also think I told you not to come back here. Didn't I say that? What were my words to you?"

"I don't recall."

"This is no safe place for you. You don't belong here."

"This is the one place I belong."

"Why is that?"

"Because my work is not done," the figure in white said.

Quintus looked down. "Who sent you? I'd have thought it was Cinna or Piso, but we know now that can't be so."

"No one sent me."

"You came on your own."

"As you see."

"To do what exactly?"

"Will you step outside with me?"

"No." Quintus pushed himself out of his chair with great effort. He spat into the hearth. He shuffled to the back of the room and began to pick through baubles arranged on a bookcase.

"Dress yourself," the figure in white said. "Come outside."

"This is what killed my father. This small thing." Quintus held up an obsidian arrowhead, pointed with it across the room. He raised up his little finger next to the arrowhead for comparison. "You see? Nothing. Just some small thing."

"I see it."

"It pierced through his throat. Lodged in the bones of his neck." Quintus crossed to the figure in white, the arrowhead in his open hand and the hand held before him like an offering. "Do you want to hold it?"

The figure in white took the arrowhead and held it by the pointed tips of its base. Quintus stood close to him.

"Was it painful?"

"Oh, I'd imagine so," Quintus said. "He was a long time dying. And once he died, the healers wanted to leave it in him. Just cut off the shaft of the arrow so he could be buried."

"But you wanted it."

Quintus nodded. "Made them cut him open. You should have seen the cowards. Grown men, witnesses to every death in existence, weeping while at their work. They loved him."

"Did you?"

"No." Quintus laughed to himself.

"Why?"

"Different reasons. Father and son things. I remember once he beat me so hard, he couldn't close his hand the next day." Quintus smiled. "It swelled up, thick and stiff. I was almost proud of myself for that."

"A hard man, then."

"Of the sort they no longer make. A hard man and crazy. Built for this place."

"What does that mean?" the figure in white asked.

"He told me the secret to the savages once. I wasn't much older than you at the time."

"He ruled here then?"

"He did. There had been legion commanders here before him, but it wasn't a popular assignment. They cycled through a lot of generals.

But when he arrived, old Sabacus knew this was it. Right man, right place. I wouldn't use the term destiny, but you get the gist."

A sharpness had come into Quintus's eyes.

"He used to take seizures on occasion," the general continued. "Occupational hazard amongst our people, as you well know. When he came to, he liked to walk. Sometimes just a lap or two around the fort, or down to the docks and then back up to the gates in Hightown if he was in the city."

"Alone?"

"Always alone."

"I've felt that way sometimes," the figure in white said.

"Once he wandered out into the jungle and didn't come back. He was missing a full day. We found him in the ruins of a small village. Something like ten or twelve huts. He had burned it to ash, the villagers all killed." Quintus paused. "He had decapitated the dead. A handful of people, some children. And when we came upon him, he was sitting in the dirt, making spears sharpened on both ends."

"To post the heads around the village."

Quintus nodded, his eyes cast to the side. "When I asked him why he had done it, he said he knew why he would succeed where the other legion commanders had failed. He knew the secret to ruling the savages."

"And what was that?"

"They prefer their leaders mad." Quintus rubbed his hands as though washing them. "They're like the Antiochi in that way."

"What's the point of that story?"

"The point is," the general said, "do you think you're the scariest man that ever asked me to step outside?"

The figure in white did not respond.

"Come in here, dressed that way." The general began pacing. "Talking of your work. You got a job to do? You got work still unfinished? Then do it. Be about your business."

"We can discuss this outside."

"Is that how you pictured this? You and I both with our gauntlets. Right here in the fort. Maybe even a ring, some circle dug into the ground. I bow to you. You bow to me. We salt the ring. A hard fight but fair, and the best man is the one left standing. Is that how you thought this would go?"

The figure in white stood silent.

"Wake up," Quintus shouted. "This isn't some goddamned fairy tale. In the real world, when you come to kill a man, sometimes he's getting blown by a maid. And you have to look at him naked, realize he's an old man. And sometimes he refuses to fight you."

"I have—"

"What do you do then? Do you still try to kill him? Or do you jaw at him for hours, try to get him to put clothes on and step outside. And to what end anyway? To preserve your honor? Because you don't want to kill someone unarmed, as though you haven't done that before?"

No one spoke, and the sound of the fire was loud.

"Did I do something to you?" Quintus asked.

"You don't know?"

"A man of my age and my inclinations, the list of people who want you dead gets so long, there's no use keeping a list."

The figure in white crossed the room to the chair where he had found the general. He slid the gauntlets across the floor with his foot. By the fire he could see the diviner's set Quintus had played at the beginning of the night still ranged along the ground.

"Pick them up," the figure in white said. "And defend yourself with them."

"Or what?"

"Or I will kill you where you stand."

"I don't think you will." Quintus leaned back. His head passed into shadow. "These are treacherous moral waters you find yourself in, boy. Especially a man who lives by the code you do. No guides out here. You're all alone. Except for me." Quintus's teeth shone in the firelight.

"I don't need advice from you."

"Yes, you do. Out where we play, you and I, there's no one around for miles. You're scrambling right now. But let me make this easy for you. Lift your hand and burn me to ash. Do it right now, as I am. Or would you prefer to have this conversation when Galerius and the legion return?"

"The legion won't be coming back."

Quintus stiffened. "What does that mean?"

"Piso killed Galerius."

"And about the legion?"

"Galerius marched the legion through a spellcaster cross fire in the Market. The part left standing is trapped in Lowtown, under siege by Piso's men."

"No," Quintus whispered. "No, you lie, boy."

"Not to you."

Quintus moved to the desk. He opened a drawer and fished out the box of brown powder. He was mumbling to himself.

"That's something Vorenicus would never have done," the figure in white said, "getting your army killed off for you."

"Vorenicus is dead," Quintus roared. He hurled the box of powder, and it shattered against the wall.

"Just you and me left now. All alone."

Quintus's eyes dipped to where his gauntlets lay on the floor.

"Go on. Pick them up."

"Who am I to you?" the general asked.

"You don't know?"

"No. And that upsets you for some reason."

"I'll be outside."

The figure in white stepped over the broken door and out into the small clearing beside the general's quarters. The sun was beginning to rise, the sky still black, but with a strip of warm gold visible very low on the horizon. He did not wait long.

The general emerged from his quarters without his gauntlets. He was still naked and did not acknowledge the figure in white but instead moved past him, moving toward the northern gate.

"Where are you going?"

"To the jungle," the general shouted over his shoulder. "To die in peace."

The figure in white lifted his hand and aimed. A dark cloud formed overhead, and a smell like sulfur descended. The fireball shot from the sky with a great gust of wind and struck the statue.

He closed his eyes against the shower of dust, and when he opened them again, he saw the statue broken to the knees. Chunks of stone lay smoking at the base, and small fires had sprung up on the grass.

The general stopped. He turned and looked to the ruined statue. He crossed to the edge of the blast and continued on, walking barefoot through the rubble. He kneeled, pressing his hand to the base, then withdrawing it from the hot stone with a yelp of pain. He sank into himself, and his shoulders began to shake. He covered his face.

In the distance, a mastiff barked.

The figure in white looked away, not wanting to see Quintus that way, and the rock struck him on the side of his head. He reeled and nearly fell. He touched his hand to the spot above his right eye, and when he pulled it away, his gauntlet was streaked with blood.

He heard another rock sail by his ear. He looked and saw Quintus on his knees, arm cocked and with both hands full of stones. His face was red, eyes wet.

A rock struck his mouth. Blood spurted from his lip. He felt something solid on his tongue and spat a black tooth. Then he was running.

He tackled the general, and they fell together awkwardly. He landed on top, the general beneath him wiry and tough to pin. He felt as though he were wrestling a cat, as in control and as dignified.

"All those years spent on the Isle of Twelve, is this how you thought it would end?" Quintus stabbed a finger up into the cut above his eye.

The figure in white slammed his knee into the general's ribs, and the general exhaled sharply. He mounted the general's waist and gripped his throat with both hands. He squeezed, digging his thumbs into the soft flesh on the underside of the general's jaw.

Quintus's face was a violent red-purple. A blue vein throbbed in the middle of his forehead. He grabbed at the gauntleted hands throttling him, his fingers spread across the rainbow of jewels.

"I—I know," Quintus gasped, his eyes beginning to close.

The figure in white eased his grip. He could feel Quintus's throat spasm as it gulped for air.

"I know who you are now," the general whispered.

"Say it."

"You are—"

"Say it," the figure in white shouted.

"You are Death, my deliverer."

He squeezed tighter.

Quintus smiled faintly. "And Death, my avenger."

He felt a thrumming in his chest. And then he felt nothing.

The figure in white lay trembling in the grass, the sound of his breathing ragged. The explosion had bowled him over backward and he was looking up at a dawning sky now. His eyes hurt when he blinked, a pain like ground glass sprinkled into the folds of his eyelids. He was numb through the rest of his body though, and he thought his back broken. Soon the numbness faded to a feeling of pinpricks and then to sharp cold pain.

He sat up. The general's quarters were afire. Wisps of small flame had sprung up in the field, and a thin haze hung overhead. His tunic was shredded, soaked through with blood, his own and Quintus's. Ribbons of burned skin dangled from his arms. He stood and walked to the general, each step shambling and painful.

The corpse lay with its hands on its chest, like a body composed for a viewing. Both hands were burned to the bone and the bones blackened, the fingers so near to dust that a stiff wind could have scattered them.

He nudged the corpse in the ribs with his foot. He felt something give.

He had pictured this moment many times before, but now he was here, and he was not sure what he should do next. He felt that maybe he should say something, but what was the point in that? There was no one to hear it, and he did not know what to say besides.

He stood staring for a little while longer, then he turned from that sight and headed toward the southern gate.

The sun was risen when he reached the city. There were no guards posted at the shattered gates, and huge fires still burned in the heart of Hightown. The streets were mostly empty. When he did pass people, they gave him a wide berth.

He made his way through the Market slowly. Cutpurses were moving about the bodies. Most anything of obvious value had been taken, but there were still gold teeth to be plucked and other small trinkets the night looters had missed in the dark. He caught sight of these people staring, watching him as vultures atop carrion might watch some wounded beast.

He collapsed against the base of the statue. He kissed the warm stone there, its surface stained with blood that had been wet only hours before. He closed his eyes and listened to the quiet of the Market. He fell asleep, and he did not dream.

He woke to find Sulla standing over him. She was nudging his foot with her own and staring down at him, horrified. She had two daggers tucked into her belt. Her hands were bloodied, and he wondered if this was his blood.

"I thought it was you," she said. "Are you all right?"

"No," he said.

"How long have you been here?"

"I was going to ask you the same."

She looked around the square, glancing with furtive eyes.

"We've got to get you to a healer," she said.

"Find the Yoruban."

"Who the hell is the Yoruban?"

"In the east end. Charnel Row. He'll come."

"All right, then. It might take time. Everyone is scattered and hiding. I'm going to leave and come right back. Okay?"

"Okay."

"Okay," she said. "Give me your gauntlets."

"Why?"

"Because if you fall asleep again, someone is going to take them."

He tried to pull his left gauntlet off, but he was too weak. He held his hands up to her, and she slid off each gauntlet and cradled them.

"Why the hell are you dressed like this?" she asked.

"I am Death," he said.

"What?"

"Death the deliverer. Death the avenger."

"Don't talk like that."

He closed his eyes.

"Cassius?" she asked.

He shook his head.

She touched his face gently, her fingertips smeared with white paste and blood. He opened his eyes, and she looked at him, her gaze soft. She stared for a time. She smiled sadly.

"I'm sorry," she said.

"I left you no choice."

"I didn't want them to hurt you or Lucian. I didn't want anyone to get hurt."

"You did the right thing."

"And what happens now?"

He did not respond.

"I'll find you a healer," she said. "I'll find the Yoruban."

"Sulla."

"Yes?"

"We're free now, you and I and all the others," he said. "The guilt. The pain. It's all been made right now. It's all finished."

"Finished because of you?"

"Yes."

"And was it worth it?"

He took a slow breath and opened his mouth to speak when a man with a club stepped from around the side of the statue and turned to face the prone figure, his back to Sulla. At this distance, she could see now that he was no man but a boy and big for his age, thick, and with a head covered in black stubble.

He lifted the club high. "For Junius," he said. The boy swung the club, but before his strike hit, a spray of blood splashed Sulla's face.

She shouted, wiped at her eyes. When her vision cleared, she saw the boy with the club slumped forward, a ragged wound in his back. A tall man stood astride the boy, his long red hair bound with gold rings and a jeweled kopis gripped tight in his massive, bloody hands.

The red-haired man shook the blood from his blade and sheathed it. He stepped forward and gathered the figure in white into his arms, hefted him over one large shoulder.

Sulla made to shout, and the red-haired man turned to face her. She stared into his eyes, and a queer sensation overcame her. She felt dizzy, unsteady on her feet.

The red-haired man smiled, his teeth glinting gold. "This man has a debt to me," he said, as though an explanation were needed, as though law or custom applied here.

Sulla tried to speak but found herself voiceless. The red-haired man lifted the gauntlets out of her arms, one and then the other. He stared at her, as though waiting for some final protest, but she did not move. Nor did she say anything, so stunned was she.

The red-haired man turned calmly and walked off, gauntlets in one hand, the figure in white over his shoulder. He approached a wall of flame and, without slowing, stepped into it. Then he was gone, swallowed by smoke and fire.

After working in publishing and as an editor for Marvel Comics, **Will Panzo** found his true calling as a physician assistant for an emergency department. *The Burning Isle* is his first novel. He lives and works in New York City.